THE SALVATION ARMY TALES

A NOVEL ABOUT
AMERICAN WAR RESISTERS IN CANADA
DURING THE VIETNAM WAR

by

Nancy Naglin

9/6/17

Doug.
Hope you enjoy!
Many [?]

To all my exiled compatriots...
But especially for Larry, two Michaels, Dave and
another Larry.

TABLE OF CONTENTS

PREFACE 2017

Interest in the Vietnam War era is ongoing and when members of the war resister community in Vancouver, in conjunction with their archival efforts, contacted me about resurrecting **The Salvation Army Tales**, one of the few personal and fictional accounts of the AMEX (Americans In Exile) experience, I thought, "Don't look back." That's what one of my war resister characters said—and it's a good enough mantra to live by when you're starting out—but I did, with trepidation and then excitement, at a forty-five-year-old manuscript—and discovered anew in a coming-of-age tale inspired by a needless war and its many regrets, the joy, discovery and ordeal of youth. It was pleasant to spend time again in The Salvation Army with characters who grasped then and, growing up, came to understand with certainty the meaning of "You Can't Go Home Again." I hope this book will find both a new and old audience, for **The Salvation Army Tales** celebrates the hopefulness, effervescence, wonder and yearning of young people and that experience—always fleeting and frequently fraught—is eternal.

Heartfelt thanks again go to Larry Martin, who belived in this book over the decades and encouraged me to bring it back to life. Thanks also to Joseph

Jones (contact: http://www.vcn.bc.ca/~jjones/), who produces the web site Vietnam War Resisters in Canada, hosted by Vancouver Community Network (http://www.vcn.bc.ca/~jjones/amcan.html).

I'd like to thank Tom Barnes and, in particular, *VideoScope* art director Kevin Hein for help in digitizing a typed manuscript. Appreciation goes to Cultmachine (cultmachine.com) founder John Huff for his enthusiasm and interest in this project. I can't give enough thanks to Cultmachine co-founder and editor Andreas Kossak. This book would simply not exist in its present form without his generosity, commitment, technological expertise, and unflagging dedication to detail and design. And, of course, for a lifetime of encouragement and support, thanks to Joe Kane.

PREFACE 1972

This book grew out of my experiences with a very close group of friends who happened to be war resisters in Vancouver. Although some of the tales are based on semi-real experiences and have as their basis real people and events, they are really an assortment of scraps and shreds of reality that I hope convey some message of what it is like for some people who have left the United States and have had their lives altered by the war in Indochina.

Some of these tales may treat the condition of exile lightly and sometimes the characters themselves may seem to discredit the authenticity of their dissent, but the situation is real. The more I wrote about Faggot and Mother and Salamander and Mushmouth's exile from the States, the more I knew I was writing about a larger exile that often interferes with politics. With these characters, semi-fictional-semi-real, I try to epitomize the most hopeless and frustrating aspects of exile that all resisters encounter, although thankfully many are far more successful and happy in their new lives than my fictional devices suggest.

The situation fictionalized here is my private view, personally distorted and selective and not meant to be representative of the exiled community in Canada.

Regardless of differences in background, education and political sophistication--the exiled community here has resisted the war. Regardless of varying intensities of political motivation, or commitment or soul-searching--they have chosen to leave their home rather than fight an unjust war--and for that there can never be any amnesty.

There is very little additional thanks I can say to Larry Martin for his support and encouragement.

I hope these tales will entertain some and delight the few who know me and shared my life in Vancouver.

Toronto, 1972.

THE SALVATION ARMY TALES

A NOVEL ABOUT
AMERICAN WAR RESISTERS IN CANADA
DURING THE VIETNAM WAR

APRIL 15

It was raining for the fifth consecutive day. George told Breeze it was the beginning of the monsoon season. He didn't really know what that meant but he'd seen it in a book once and he heard somebody else say it yesterday.

"Yeah, I bet you it is," said Breeze who was standing over a broken-down armchair in the middle of the churchyard. That old armchair had been sitting in the front lawn through five monsoon seasons and now it was completely soaked through and through. Breeze, who didn't know any better, thought it was turning into a giant sponge.

"Hey, go look at the giant sponge in the front yard," Breeze shouted through the vestry door.

There were some old mattresses and broken cups and a few hand-me-down shoes out there on the grass beside the armchair. Everything--cigarettes, old stockings, plastic bags, chicken bones, kleenex-- flopped around the yard waiting for something to happen. Across the street were the seventy-year-old houses where the thousands of Chinese people lived. They sat in their doorways on small stools or on rickety porches in the rain with nothing better to do than watch the church where the litter collected day

3

by day.

"Boy, oh boy, what a sponge that is," Breeze said.

The door to the vestry was half-open. There were some people wandering around on the bottom floor who couldn't seem to make up their minds about the door. Sometimes they wanted the drizzle to come in and wash away the cooking odors and sometimes they decided they could stand the stuffiness and cigarette smoke for one minute more.

On the ground floor there was a couch, a bulletin board, a kitchen and a long table that was unsteady. There was a picture of Chairman Mao where the monstrance used to be. Upstairs there were beds and a toilet without a seat.

George was hanging over the armchair with his pitchfork. He was wearing a red bandana around his neck. His undershirt was somewhere in Nevada. His shirt was upstairs on the bed he had to share with Breeze who often slept in his sleeping bag when he wasn't there. George didn't like to wear his shirt when he played in the front lawn.

"Hey, what's happening, man? What's happening with the pitchfork?"

"I'm getting it together with the pitchfork," George said.

He stabbed the armchair in the back and it vomited out its life in dirty spurts of foam rubber stuffing.

"Man, you sure can hit that sponge," Breeze said nodding his head up and down.

"Yep, just like a bayonet." George waited until he was sure Breeze was watching and then he stabbed the armchair again and again until there was a nice neat pile of yellow armchair stuffing flowing all over the lawn. Some of the stuff from deep inside where it had been hidden for at least a quarter of a century looked brand-new.

"Man, you sure got that old sponge changing colors for you." Breeze took his eyes off the dead chair and watched George plunge into a pile of sodden clothes and curtains and old milk cartons. He had that stuff ripped to shreds in no time.

"Boy, you're some devil with that thing."

George twisted the pitchfork into the ground and rested one foot on top of it. He smiled at Breeze who was standing on top of the armchair's vital parts trying to undo a leather knot at his belt.

"I think I'll play you a little tune," Breeze said. He straightened up with an harmonica pressed in his hands, glued to his mouth. He tapped his foot against the armchair and found his rhythm. He bent over at the waist, shook his head back and forth and bobbed up and down. Three notes came out. He played his three notes for about five minutes while his foot tapped faster and faster and his head bobbed up and down in more and more frenzied rhythms. When he was done, he shook the saliva off his instrument and put it back in the leather pouch at his side.

"I've been playing for four years," he said.

George turned around and jumped up on the old armchair bottom. He raised his pitchfork in the air as soon as he saw a beat-up Buick pull onto the lawn. He waved his pitchfork in wide semicircles, first to the left and then to the right. Breeze watched the end of the pitchfork move back and forth until he looked like a cross-eyed pendulum.

"That's how we do it in the navy," George said.

Faggot, Motherfucker, Salamander and Mushmouth got out of the car.

Breeze watched Faggot cut across the lawn. He was standing in his puddle of sponge trying to undo the leather knot as fast as he could. He wanted to play a tune for their homecoming but Faggot was on top of him before he could get his harmonica out.

"Did you see the giant sponge George killed with the pitchfork?"

"Lord," Faggot said. "It's time to rent a house."

THE HOUSE

The house Faggot rented was a gray weather-beaten two-story frame house with no heat and no utilities. The landlady was a single woman who lived with her miniature barking dog somewhere in the Oak Ridge Development. She never asked any questions as long as she received one hundred and twenty-five dollars every month in a wrinkled brown envelope.

Faggot would personally drive to the landlady's place in the first, but usually the second week of the month. He slapped his hair into shape, pulled up his pants and walked across the badminton grounds to the side door where the lady waited behind a crepe curtain. She opened the door as far as the inside lock and chain would allow. Then she slipped her hand through the crack and took the envelope without a word.

Faggot got the address of the landlady from the Committee. She never asked if she was renting to fugitives of the law. If she knew, she said nothing, for the badminton set and the clipped hedges and the pickaninny on the front lawn were twenty-five minutes by car, forty-five minutes by Faggot's car, from a house that could never be called a bargain.

A broken wire fence set the house off from the sidewalk. Inside were the remains of a garden that survived on the scraps of love and care that some unknown gardener lavished on his home years ago. Flowers accustomed to years of regular care were beginning to straggle out of set patterns and borders. They were wild and abundant and, unasked for and unattended, they grew carelessly for whoever stopped to look.

Now nobody who lives in that house knows the names of any of those flowers. There are beer caps lodged between the roots of tiger lilies and dandelions. Cigarette butts and flower petals lie side by side. In the summertime the grass is knee-high and the sun shines on broken glass.

The house was old. Mild climate and gentle neglect combined to let it weather naturally. Good fortune and benign indifference on the part of all the former tenants were responsible for holding it together. The water ran and the windows shut. With occasional manual adjustments to the inner workings, the toilet flushed. The garbage collection was free-- whenever someone remembered to put it out.

Lilacs leaned against the house and drooped onto the porch. They began to die in the steady heat of summer and filled the early mornings of Vancouver's year-long spring with the sweet, rich smell of decay. In the evenings the smell of dying lilacs filtered through open windows and settled in radiators that would never work in the wintertime.

There were four cabinets in the kitchen. An old-fashioned sink, a pantry and a rickety green table came with the house. They attached a string from a bakery box to the insides of the toilet while they talked about the real repair. They bought a stove and watched its four replacements fall apart one after another. The refrigerator came from a friendly junk man. They never remembered to put the garbage out.

The front porch and the view from the bathroom window were the nicest features. There was never a curtain or a window shade in the bathroom. Just the open window with the breeze curling around the remnant of plastic shower curtain. In the backyard a huge tree with quivering leaves leaned against the house and there, in the bathroom window, was nearly close enough to touch.

From the bathroom window it was possible to see the whole city. You could stand beside the sink and see mountains in the distance. Below you was the glistening steel and glass and concrete of Vancouver. The bridge was to your left and farther away on the edge of the city where the land meets the water were the pleasure boats. Hidden away in different pockets of the sea were the scraps and shreds of timber. Everywhere were wood telephone poles, totems of another era.

The railroad ran directly behind the house. Signals, tracks and a bell. The train that comes and goes with its load of lumber or produce or machinery and sends up its whistle in the early morning and the afternoon...and in the nighttime when it reaches you across the pillows and slides momentarily between the bed sheets.

There they saw the early morning for the first

time in Vancouver. From the first bathroom window in *Canadia* they viewed the exile beginning--with the ash cans and railroad ties and telephone wires and Voice of China radio station that make up the backyard of Vancouver.

Faggot rented this house in his name with the money he collected from his friends and from borrowing and from pawning his tape recorder three weeks out of every four. Faggot lived in the front room. Mother lived in the living room. Salamander and Mushmouth lived upstairs. For the short time Tex was there he lived somewhere on the floor.

There were no jobs. There was no money and nobody was landed. War had come to the States. They refused to go or had refused to go on anymore after they had already refused and had come north to This City. Here the Committee sorted, consoled and advised. In hopeless confusion and lack of funds and make-believe solidarity, they did what they could, then left them to manage on their own.

Occasionally people were discovered and deported. Oftentimes people took on false names and identities, scouring the library files of birthdates and names and years to assume a new personality. Frequently people returned home to the States in a frenzy of disbelief and homesickness that was madness and many were never heard from again. Mostly people stayed and lived off of one another and off of hearsay and rumor and canned meat and peanut butter, imagining in wild drug fantasies that the President of the United States had ended the War and called home all the boys from *Canadia.*

But they awoke to find newer arrivals until weathering one month, then two, then six, seven, eight different hostels, they knew they were veterans of sorts. Finally there was some bitter-sweet pride in that, too.

Some got landed on the merits of college educations that their parents unsuspectingly purchased two, four, five, six years ago and which were never fully appreciated or valued before. Others went to the Plains to find work. A few hitchhiked east to get landed. A lucky few married Canadian girls, were saved and left one army for another. Some, the most misguided, wandered to Montreal, only to join up with Easterners who slowly grew to realization through the long winter nights that they would never survive and function in the too-French, too-European background with their New Hampshire educations and Boston activism. Many never got landed.

Some foot-loose New Yorkers got off the 401 at Toronto. Others, traveling now with dope dealers, deserters and McGill students, now with fourteen year-old virgins in search of the impossible lay, cowboys and small-town teenagers out to make a cool million, camped out for days and stole fruit from the A&P while the Plains' winds snuffed out their Eastern prejudices and attacked their Brooklyn accents and made Westerners of them. Later, they would live on the communes off the coast of Vancouver Island and wonder how they ever lived in and loved New York City. They would spend five years forgetting while they religiously stood in line for thirty-five minutes to buy tickets for the one and only International Film Festival in Vancouver.

Perhaps one in a thousand found the Edmonton real estate financier, an exiled resister of the Korean War, who fed and clothed and occasionally employed the younger image of himself. The majority, however, silently melted into Kitsilano. There they wore away at indifference until an angry mayor in a fit of rage that was lunacy of another sort lashed out at the hippie convergence on The City.

All day they sneak around the streets wondering at the mess in their minds and how it got there. Afraid to cross the street against the light for fear they will be picked up and prosecuted and sent home to stand trial and to see their mothers and fathers and aunts and uncles lined up with handkerchiefs at their eyes and their faces frozen into agonizing looks of anger and reproach and love, all framing the unanswerable question: WHY? WHY YOU MY SON WHO IS THE FLESH AND BLOOD OF OUR BODIES AND FOR WHOM WE HAVE WORKED AND SAVED AND SLAVED SO THAT YOU MAY DO BETTER THAN US? WHY YOU MY SON WHOM YOUR MOTHER AND I LOVE MORE THAN WE LOVE OUR OWN LIVES?

For fear of that question and some in utter hopelessness because there exists no one for them and no girl-woman-child who will raise the sincerity and faith and trust in so young a man to ask that question, thousands wait aimlessly on the corner for the lights to change. There are endless excursions to Murchie's Import Coffee Shop, the post office, the library, the parks and the Committee while some small mechanism in the mind stumbles toward resolution or limps into some new rationale. But always the crazy flea brain in their heads buzzing round and round and...

THE ALUMINUM CRAB

It was early evening. About 6:00 o'clock. Too
early for the BOWMAC sign to go on and too late to go
to the beach. It was one of those bright clear days
Vancouver has in the spring--you would never believe
that it rains all the time in the winter and that the day
after tomorrow can be damp and miserable. When it's
sunny in Vancouver you've got no problems, but when
it rains you ache.

I was thinking of eating at The Black Cat, at the
corner of Broadway and Granville but I only liked that
place in the dark when the cat tail swings on the
broken-down neon fixture outside. I walked by the
Ararat Rug Store and turned the corner. On the other
side of the street was an architectural firm, a gasoline
station that gives away filtered oil and a B.C. Hydro
stop.

The houses are mostly ramshackle wood cottages
scattered helter-skelter up and down the street. Each
house has a garden and a chimney. Every other house
has a porch or an upstairs window or a make-believe
garage. Every house looks different but with the
chimneys and upstairs window and back porches
rearranged, they're all the same house. At the end of

the street is an elevated green ramp, a skinny overpass that leads to the Burrard Bridge. The shady area underneath looks like the ideal place for rats to live. There are two stores under there. A variety store and a cafe next door. I could see some palm trees on the sign and in a few steps more I could read the name, "The Trade Winds Cafe."

Halfway down the block, on my side, I saw a burnt-out lot. The place was vacant and there were lots of wild flowers growing. I couldn't get over that. A plot of wild flowers in the moldering inner city belt of a city that styles itself the metropolis of the West. I wandered over and picked a bouquet. Just like that.

It was weird picking flowers from a garden that didn't belong to me in a place where I couldn't keep them and with no one in particular in mind. I guess I thought I would carry them around for a while and get rid of them before they melted in the sun. "Jesus," I thought, "you must be crazy walking down the middle of the street with a bouquet of buttercups and dandelions and little purple ones that you don't know but that you really like. You're going to look absolutely crazy."

I came out of the lot and tried to brush away the weeds that were stuck to my shoes. I was standing in the middle of the street with a bouquet of wild flowers that most people would call a mangy bunch of weeds, looking at my feet and brushing shoe against shoe to make the burrs go away. When I looked up there were eight eyes watching me. That's four sets belonging to four different people.

One guy was wearing a cowboy hat with a leopard

hatband. He had a long piece of grass in his mouth and he was leaning forward in his chair with his arms hanging over the porch railing watching me. The other three guys were standing in a half-circle behind The Leopard Man in the chair. They looked like a mock-up photo of prospectors from a gold mine.

I picked off the last burr and dropped it in the air. Leopard Man was nodding and smiling. The other three weren't moving. Leopard Man was watching everything I did. I tested him. I looked down the street to The Trade Winds and he looked down the street. I looked up the street to the architects' and he looked there, too. I looked straight at him and he looked straight back at me.

I picked up the bouquet and walked across the street. There was a gate to the house that I opened and very carefully re-latched. When the three guys in the semi-circle saw me coming through the gate, they seemed to retreat against the wall. It was as if they all took a big breath in and held it. Leopard Man's eyes got big. "Howdy" he said.

I stood at the foot of the porch and looked at Leopard Man. I waved. He smiled. I watched the piece of grass bobbing up and down in his mouth. He bobbed and tipped his hat.

"Do you always sit out here smiling and bobbing at people or are you making fun of me?"

Leopard Man looked vacant. The three against the wall looked like they were undergoing compression. I expected them to squeeze off the sides of the porch and disappear. Leopard Man nodded again and looked like he was thinking. I waited politely for the answer.

"Dunno," he finally said. I leaned forward. Leopard Man was missing a front tooth. "Guess I jes sit here and nod my head jes natural-like." He seemed satisfied and the piece of grass bobbed up and down again. He looked like he just swallowed a grasshopper. He turned his head backwards and looked at the three against the wall of the house. They confirmed what he said. "Yeah, he always sits there and he does that," said one of them who was wearing pants that stopped somewheres above his ankles and a shirt that showed his belly button. "He's harmless, though," he added. Leopard Man nodded, "Yes."

"Oh."

"Lemme out of here," shrieked the one who was the farthest from the door. At the same time he began crawling over the feet of the others who didn't move to let him by. He waved his hands in front of him like a pinwheel and the others bent out of his way. "You are a bunch of fuck-ups," he said.

The one who spoke before came out of his spot behind Leopard Man's chair. He didn't have shoes on. His feet were filthy. He pursed his lips and said, "Feh," to the one who ran into the house. "Why don't you come up here and sit down for a minute?" he asked. He picked up the back of Leopard Man's chair and the Leopard Man began sliding downhill towards me. I stepped backwards but Leopard Man recovered and moved sideways. Then the barefoot boy patted the empty chair and smiled encouragingly. "That's right," Barefoot Boy said. "Give Jones a chair."

"They're for you," I said offering the flowers to

Barefoot Boy.

He sniffed them and held them to his breast. Then he said, "Thanks," and handed them to the Quiet One who hadn't said anything. "Put these in a vase," Barefoot Boy said. He pronounced "vase" in the slow English way with a broad "a"—"*va-ase*."

"A what?" asked the Quiet One.

Barefoot Boy leaned over me and said in a loud whisper, "These lackeys have to be told everything. A bottle," he said.

"Sure, Boss, sure thing," said the Quiet One, taking the flowers and scampering away.

"What do you do?" I asked Barefoot Boy.

"I live here," he answered.

"Oh," I said. "I see."

I sat in the chair for a while looking at the wild garden across the street. The sun was getting ready to set and everything was in that hushed pre-dusk state. Stillness and quiet. There were birds singing.

"You have a very pleasant place here," I said.

"Yes, we like it," said Barefoot Boy. "It's close to the sea. What do you do?" he asked me.

I waved my hand through the air. Now it was his turn to say, "Oh."

Leopard Man was making a cigarette. Barefoot Boy looked sideways. I looked sideways and saw a string bean person hiding in the doorway. He didn't seem to know whether he wanted to stay in or come out. He looked the situation over and seemed disgusted. When Leopard Man finished making the cigarette, String Bean Person came out of the doorway and swiped it out of his hands. Then he disappeared again.

I looked at Barefoot Boy for explanation. "Make another one," he ordered. Nobody talked while Leopard Man made a second cigarette. This time Barefoot Boy took it. "Thanks," he said flashing a smile. He held it and froze. It was a still. He snapped his teeth twice and his face relaxed.

I moved to get up.

"Where are you going?" asked Leopard Man. He looked sorry to see me move.

I laughed and waved my hand.

Barefoot Boy said in a small, hurt voice, "Hey, wait. Don't go yet."

"But I..."

"Have you seen the Aluminum Crab?" he asked.

"No I...The what?"

"Aluminum Crab," he repeated trying to stick his hands into his pockets but only making his pants sag under his stomach. "If you haven't seen the Crab, we'll take you with us. If you really have to leave, you shouldn't go without seeing the Aluminum Crab."

"That's right," broke in the Quiet One. "The Aluminum Crab. The A-lu-mi-num Crab. It's fantastic. You have to see the Aluminum Crab." Then he started to talk so fast he began spitting. Barefoot Boy looked at the Quiet One and he pulled out a handkerchief and began to mop up his drool. "It's stupendous heavy shit. It's the most marvelous thing there is and you have to see it. Everybody should see it. There'd be no more wars if..." The Barefoot Boy stared at him and he put the handkerchief in his mouth and shut up.

The Leopard Man said the Aluminum Crab was really far-out. He said they went to see it almost every night and no matter how many times they saw it, it was always different.

I said, "Yes, I'll go see the Aluminum Crab."

"Whoopie," shouted the Quiet One. "She's gonna see the Crab. She's gonna see the Crab," he sing-songed into the house through a cracked window that looked out to the porch.

The Barefoot Boy leaned over me again. "The kids make a lot of noise," he said.

Then the skinny one who'd disappeared when I first sat down came out. The String Bean Person came back to stand in the doorway. He tilted his head on an angle and looked at the Barefoot Boy as if he was about to ask something.

The Quiet One jumped over the porch railing and did a somersault in the front yard. "We're off to the Crab. The Aluminum Crab. Hooray. Whoopie." He lay on his back and pulled tufts of grass out of the ground and threw them in the air. When they fell back on him, he picked them up and threw them at Barefoot Boy and at the skinny-stick one.

"Okay, that's enough of that," said the Barefoot Boy.

"Are you coming?" Barefoot Boy asked the String Bean Person. The String Bean Person slunk into his doorway and disappeared.

"He's a fuck-up," the skinny Stick said.

21

"Don't listen to him," said the Quiet One. "He doesn't mean it."

"He doesn't mean anything," added Barefoot Boy.

The Stick took a boxing stance and stood in front of the Barefoot Boy. He pretended to hit him but his hands went back and forth like pistons two inches in front of his face. Barefoot Boy took a deep breath and blew at him. Then he took a drag on his cigarette and blew smoke in his face.

"Let's go. Let's go," the Quiet One was screaming all over the street.

"You ready, Jones?" asked Barefoot Boy.

"I guess so," I said.

"Okay, we're going," the Barefoot Boy announced in a low baritone through the window. He waited for a few minutes but the String Bean Person didn't come to the doorway again. Barefoot Boy looked upset for a second. He caught my eye and jerked his thumb in the direction of the window and made a face.

Meanwhile the Leopard Man was shaking the Quiet One upside-down by the ankles. The Quiet One was screaming like a wounded Tarzan.

"For chrissake," said Barefoot Boy and Leopard Man dropped the Quiet One. Then Leopard Man threw his hat in the air and caught it. He banged it against his jeans and dust blew out of it.

"He's a cowboy," said the Quiet One from the ground.

"Shut up," the Leopard Man said as he put his cowboy boot on the Quiet One's chest.

We walked down the street towards the ramp that leads to the Burrard Bridge. When we were in the shadows I could see that there were no rats living there but maybe there were rats in the variety store that was called "Leonard's Handy Store." We walked by The Trade Winds and I looked in and saw all the pictures of hamburgers on buns spread-eagled against the wall.

In the middle of the next block the Quiet One caught up with us and handed everybody two pieces of licorice--one red and one black.

"I don't like red," said the Stick as he grabbed a black one away from the Leopard Man. Then Barefoot Boy pulled the Quiet One's fingers out of Leopard Man's hand. When they were finished the licorice had traded hands half a dozen times. Two pieces fell to the ground and the Leopard Man put his boot on top of the Quiet One's hand. The Quiet One howled. Barefoot Boy squeezed a quarter out of one of Leopard's pockets, twisting his arms back and forth so he managed to bring his pants back over his stomach at the same time. He gave the quarter to the Quiet One to go back and buy some more.

We kept walking. I hadn't the slightest idea where the Aluminum Crab was. I asked if we were getting close but the Quiet One said, "When you see it, you'll know it."

"Okay."

We walked by rows and rows of dilapidated houses full of people. Sometimes they were old people on porches in swinging chairs like New Hampshire and sometimes they were ordinary people working in their gardens. And because it was still suppertime, we smelled a lot of different things coming from the kitchens of all the different houses we passed.

On one street we saw a police car. There was an officer talking to a young man with shoulder-length hair. The man was pointing to the doorway of his house where his wife in a long dress stood with a baby in her arms. There were three or four other people on the porch and the officer was taking down everything the man with the long hair said in a hand-sized notebook. He kept turning pages and the man kept talking and the woman in the doorway kept looking at the man with the long hair beside the police car.

When we got there, we shut up and kept walking. The Quiet One moved next to Barefoot Boy and the Leopard Man kept taking the cigarette in and out of his mouth. I looked back over my shoulder at the man and at the police car and at the lady in the doorway with the baby. Nobody had moved.

When we were three houses away, Barefoot Boy turned around and offered the people on the porch an out-stretched peace sign in the form of a Nazi salute. The corner man on the far side of the porch caught the sign and touched two fingers to his forehead lightly. Everybody, except the man talking to the police, gave a slight nod.

"Poor bastard," Barefoot Boy said.

"What do you think he did?" asked the Quiet One.

"I don't want to know," said the Stick. "It's always the same."

After that we were quiet for most of the way. We were walking down all the tree-lined streets and front lawns that smell like orchids while I figured we were moving towards the water. That made sense since this thing was a crab anyway.

We kept walking in the direction of the beach--in the opposite direction from W. 4th and Cypress Street where all the hippies hang out across the street from the Winnipeg Cleaners. Then we cut along the pathways and in between Vancouver couples with their dogs and wives on the leash and around the big Indian totem pole that is supposed to be a tribute to the Native Peoples of the Northwest but looks like a Woolworth's imitation and through the picnic tables. Finally we came to the back of a big building and the Quiet One shouted, "There it is. The home of the Aluminum Crab."

I didn't see any Crab or anything. All I saw was the back of a building that looked like the back of a municipal building.

It was the Science Museum.

"I want a Coke," said the Barefoot Boy.

"Me, too," said the Quiet One.

"How about her?" The Stick pointed at me. "Does she want a Coke? You ask her if she does."

"Jones, do you want a Coke?" Barefoot Boy asked.

"Okay," I said.

"Who's buying?" the Stick wanted to know.

"You are," answered Barefoot Boy.

"Shit. Like hell I am," the Stick said.

There was a cafeteria inside the Science Museum. We took a table near the window.

"Icky," said Barefoot Boy as he swept some dirty paper cups and napkins off the table with his forearm. "Sticky."

The Stick made "tch tch" noises and picked up all

the stuff and moved it to the wastepaper basket. There was a blond girl behind the counter in a starched pink dress with matching pink cheeks who was looking at us funny. Leopard Man was smiling at her.

"Well, boys and girls, what are we gonna get?" asked Barefoot Boy in a voice that was two tones louder than it should have been. He placed both hands together with the fingers touching and half-clapped, half-pressed his hands together. "Hostel meeting, hostel meeting" he lisped.

"Shut up, you fuck-up," said the Stick. "What do you think she'll think?" he asked, jerking his thumb at me. I shrugged and watched the pink lady behind the counter.

Barefoot Boy stuck out his tongue at Stick and then he showed it to everybody at the table. The Quiet One stuck his tongue out at Barefoot Boy and Stick stuck him in the ribs with his elbow.

"Who's buying?" the Stick asked again.

Barefoot Boy pushed back the table and stood up. He dug up a handful of coins from the bottom of his pockets. When he leaned sideways to get into his pocket, his shirt rode up his chest. It looked like one of those kiddie T-shirts. Then he swaggered across the room to the Pink Lady, shaking his ass. In spite of himself Stick folded over and giggled.

Barefoot Boy came back with five paper cups of Coke. He said they were a quarter each. But the Stick said twenty-five cents was robbery because you could buy a six-pack of Coke for less money than shitty Coke that came in paper cups from a Pink Lady who didn't smile.

Then everybody started to figure out how much money they were losing by buying Cokes in a shitty place like the restaurant of the Science Museum and Barefoot Boy and the Leopard Man rattled a few chairs and threw a couple of paper napkins around. The Quiet One and the Stick started to drink every Coke in sight while Barefoot Boy and Leopard Man were busy pretending to trash the place.

"Hey gimme that back." Barefoot Boy stuck out his lower lip. Then he took the Coke out of Stick's fingers by bending Stick's hand back until the cup popped out. Before he had time to drink it, Leopard man snatched it away. Leopard Man only had a third of the cup when the Quiet One grabbed it from his hand and would have finished it if Stick hadn't twisted it away from him and drained it all except for the last swallow that barely tinted the bottom of the cup brown.

Stick smacked the cup down in front of Barefoot Boy. "Here you are, Faggot. It's all yours."

"Gee, thanks," Barefoot Boy smiled. He got up and came back with four more Cokes. This time everybody started snatching everybody else's Coke before Barefoot Boy had his hands off them. The Stick, who got ripped off as much as Barefoot Boy, encouraged the Quiet One and Leopard Man to keep the cup out of Barefoot Boy's reach. They passed the cups around and around and when there was a single sip left, they gave it to the Barefoot Boy.

"Hostel meeting," said Barefoot Boy after we all had about three Cokes each except for Barefoot Boy who'd had twice as much as everybody else because he drank out of every cup he brought to the table. He said it was his due because he was supplying a service by bringing it to the table and he deserved to be paid.

"Let's go to the Crab."

We walked through the main lobby and out the front entrance of the museum. In a courtyard in front of a parking lot was a jet spray hosing down a shiny sculpture.

"That's the..."

"That's right." The Quiet One nodded enthusiastically. "That's The Aluminum Crab." He smiled and leaned backwards to see it fully. "Isn't it marvelous?"

The Aluminum Crab is a stylized metal sculpture of a Pacific Imperial Crab. It is the offspring of a cubist painting and a car wash. The knees looked like shiny hub caps. They caught the last rays of the sun and threw them back at the sky. If you stood in front of the knees and stared at the Crab, you would be blind.

"That's stupendous. It's heavy shit," the Quiet One said.

The eyeballs were truly magnificent. They hung suspended on thin aluminum wires four inches from the sockets.

We were standing on a sun deck surrounding the museum and overlooking the Crab. We were walking back and forth bumping into each other to get a better view of the thing and to change perspective. "That way," said the Stick, "it never looks the same twice."

He said that was why it was such heavy shit. Because it never stayed still but never went anywhere, either.

Barefoot Boy checked his pockets for change. He pulled out the linings of each pocket. We watched change and keys and lint bounce off the floor. He bent down to pick all that stuff up and when he looked up, he pushed back his glasses with a jab of his thumb. His cigarette drooped out the corner of his mouth. He dragged heavily and exhaled through his nose. His pockets stuck out at his sides and his pants were tight across his hips.

"You know, Faggot, you're a fuck-up," the Stick said.

"Gee, I know," said Barefoot Boy. "But I can't help it."

He gave me three pennies to throw at the Crab. He said they were not to wish on or anything but just to throw away. I held two in my hand while I aimed at the knee. I missed and Barefoot Boy, the one they called the Faggot, laughed and said, "Try again."

I threw a second penny and I missed again.

"You get one more throw," the Stick said directly to me.

I threw the third penny and it disappeared into the jet spray squirting the Crab. "I almost hit it," I said.

"That's all right," said Barefoot Boy. "No expectations." He threw two pennies at the Crab and hit each time. The pennies made a little "ping" and fell backwards into the water.

Everybody was throwing pennies at the Crab and nearly everybody was hitting. When the Quiet One had used up all the money he had in his pockets, he looked to the Barefoot Boy and the Barefoot Boy held out five pennies on his outstretched palm.

I looked into the water and wondered how much money was in the fountain. I said something to Barefoot Boy about coming back in the night and picking up all the loose coins. I told him how a boy lived for an entire summer at the New York World's Fair doing that and showing a profit as well, but he wasn't listening to me. He'd emptied all the money from his pockets and was throwing dimes and quarters at the Crab. The Stick clutched a handful of change in his fist and threw five coins before shoving all his money back into his pocket. Leopard Man threw a couple of times, short fast hits that whacked the Crab in the stomach and in the groin and was broke.

Barefoot Boy almost threw his keys away but he caught himself in time. When he'd thrown all his money away he left the sun deck and stood by the Crab with his pockets pulled out at his sides and one hand on his hip. His head was tilted back and he was laughing. The kneecap came alive and sent a square patch of sunlight into his face. He squeezed his eyes shut. His hand dropped to his side as the sunlight from the Crab poured over him, mixing with the red-yellow of his features and flushing him golden. He leaned back with the light and when he had gone too far, losing the sun, he looked surprised. Then sorry and confused.

He ran his fingers through his hair and tucked in his shirt. "Pretty," he said as he did an imitation model pivot.

I clapped. "Very nice."

"Thanks, do you want to live with us, Jones?"

"Don't ask her that, you fuck-up," Stick hissed. His eyes looked like the Crab's for a second. "Boy, you're really a fuck-up, aren't you?"

"My name is not Jones."

"Yes, it is," Barefoot Boy said. "When are you coming to live with us?"

The Stick was talking to himself. I wondered what was wrong with him that he was mumbling to himself. He kept saying "shit" over and over like a kind of litany. "Shit. Shit. Shit."

"Hostel meeting," Barefoot Boy announced. "Who wants to go to the beach now?"

"I do. I do," said the Quiet One who always wanted to do everything and always seemed to enjoy everything, too.

So we went to the beach. We cut around the Science Museum and walked a few feet towards an embankment. We stood on top of it looking at the ocean.

"If you could see directly across you'd be in Japan," I said. Just then a rock hit the water and I looked behind to see Leopard Man bending over a pile of stones.

Stick and the Quiet One went out to a breakwater and were busy dropping rocks directly into the water. I thought it was a pretty weird thing to do but I guess they liked to see them go straight down because the water was very clear and very cold. They said you could almost see where the rocks went when you hung over the edge of the waves.

31

Barefoot Boy plowed down the bank and waded into the water. He stood there with his hands beside his pulled-out pockets smoking. He became strangely still. It was as if he wasn't there anymore.

I stood by the water's edge and looked at the other two on the breakwater. A splash hit Barefoot Boy in the face and I saw Leopard Man behind me with another rock in his hand. He was laughing.

Barefoot Boy lit another cigarette and walked farther into the sea. The waves circled above his knees. His pants were stained a darker color where they were getting wet. He was immobile.

Leopard Man gathered a few more stones and positioned himself behind the breakwater. When nobody was looking he started to throw rocks. A few fell short of the Quiet One and the Stick but they looked up in time to see the splash. Finally one hit Stick on the hand. "Hey, fuck-up, what the hell do you think you're doing?" he yelled. He stood up and shook a fist. Leopard Man laughed and handled a few more stones. Barefoot Boy stared out to sea. The Quiet One started yelling and waving his arms around as more rocks started to hit the breakwater. Then the two of them quit dumping rocks into the water. Stick threw a few stones that fell short of Leopard Man and headed for the shore. Leopard Man cut it out and moved away. He hid behind me. He was looking at the Barefoot Boy with a rock in his hand but then Barefoot Boy turned around with a silly grin on his face and Leopard Man dropped his rock.

"Naughty, naughty," Barefoot Boy said pointing first at the rocks on the ground and then to Leopard

Man and then to the two coming towards us. "Who wants to go swimming?" he asked.

Everybody laughed. Stick was swearing at the Leopard Man but nobody was listening to him.

Leopard Man waded into the water towards Barefoot Boy who was holding his hands out to him. "Here I come," said the Leopard Man.

Stick snickered.

Barefoot Boy retreated farther and farther into the waves. He was up to his thighs. Stick was running along the water's edge shouting, "You're a fuck-up. Boy, you're really a fuck-up."

Finally Barefoot Boy was in about as far as he could go without saying he hadn't been swimming. The Stick and the Quiet One darted in and out of the water as far as their rolled-up pants let them without getting wet. Leopard Man threatened Barefoot Boy with a nudge and Barefoot Boy, in avoiding him, went down. In a few minutes he came to the shore and they pulled him out. He was dripping water on us from a pair of formfitting pants he said came from the Salvation Army and cost fifty cents and were the best fitting pair of pants he had ever owned. When he said that everybody told him what a fuck-up he was and he laughed. But he said his pants needed to be washed anyway.

"Well, Jones, have you made up your mind?" he asked.

"Are you serious," interrupted the Stick. "Do you think she'd live with a bunch of fuck-ups like you after what she just saw?"

"Ask her," said Barefoot Boy.

"Oh shit," said the Stick shaking his head. "Oh shit."

We climbed up the bank and stood in the sunlight. It was watery now like lemon Kool-Aid cut twice. Barefoot Boy was soaking wet. He kept trying to wring himself out but as soon as he wrung out the bottoms of his pants, all the water from his shirt and hair would have dripped down to his legs and he would be right back where he started from. "Fuck," he said in a small boy voice. "It's cold." He spoke to the water in hurt reproach. "Cold. Cold."

"Fuck-up," said Stick.

Barefoot Boy flashed another frozen smile and we began to walk away from the beach, back to Broadway.

Barefoot Boy was walking like a robot. He held his hands in rigid pantomime slow-motion monster walk. He went after the Stick but he got away.

We cut through the picnic table area. There were trees in there and it was cold. There were no more people anywhere. Everybody had gone home.

Barefoot Boy must have been freezing. The Quiet One swung on a tree branch. He was singing, "Everything's gonna be fine in *Canadia*. I'm so glad I'm here in *Canadia*."

"What are you doing in Canada?" I asked.

"We're draft dodgers," he said. "I'm a deserter."

"YOU FUCK-UP, MUSHMOUTH," the skinny one screamed. He screamed so loudly he nearly choked himself. Barefoot Boy waved his hand in the air. He was shivering.

"You fuck-up, you had to go and tell her we're a

bunch of draft dodgers. You think she wants to live with a bunch of fucked-up dodgers. You think she wants to live with a bunch of fucked-up draft dodgers like you. Do you?"

"Shut up, Salamander," said Barefoot Boy.

I looked at the skinny Salamander and at Barefoot Boy. "Who's who?" I asked.

"You're Jones," Barefoot Boy said.

"I know. But who's he? And him and that one over there, the one with the leopard hat?"

"He's the fuck-up," the skinny one, the Salamander said.

Barefoot Boy whistled through his fingers and called, "Hostel meeting. Hostel meeting." Leopard Man came over to the trees to see what was going on.

"Hostel meeting," Barefoot Boy repeated. "Important business. Jones says she wants to live with a bunch of fuck-ups like you," said Barefoot Boy looking at Leopard Man.

"Oh shit," said Salamander like he was going to be sick. "Oh shit."

"I didn't say anything," I said but Barefoot Boy called for silence by holding his right hand in front of him in a peace sign. When Salamander wouldn't shut up, he raised and lowered the peace sign into his face, creeping closer and closer to his eyes every time. Salamander shut up.

"Business," Barefoot Boy said. He grabbed the Leopard Man's cigarette and clapped it into his mouth. He was motionless for a few seconds as he exhaled through his nose. Then he smiled one of his still smiles and the rest of the smoke slipped out between his teeth. Before Salamander had a chance to escape he began speaking.

"First, Jones is living with us. Salamander, you're moving into Mushmouth's room. Tex is leaving." He smiled again and patted everybody on the head with his peace sign while he rubbed his own head with his left hand. Salamander squirmed away when Barefoot Boy's hand descended on him. "Don't touch me, you fuck-up," he shrieked. Barefoot Boy said, "You're right. I should make you pay for touching my body."

"Who is who?" I demanded.

Barefoot Boy held up the peace sign again. "Introductions," he said clapping his hands together twice. You're Jones," he said.

"I know."

"She's Jones," he repeated for the benefit of everybody else.

"Jones," he said pointing at me. "Salamander," he said pointing at the Stick.

"Why Salamander?"

"Jones, Mushmouth." He pointed to the one who was always saying how great it was to be in *Canadia*.

"Tex," he said pointing to Leopard Man who I thought was better as Leopard Man.

"Who are you?" I asked.

He crumpled into silly laughter. "I don't know," he said semi-seriously.

"He's Faggot," Salamander said. "He's also fucked in the head."

"Who's the other one? The one who stayed behind. The String Bean Person?"

Faggot laughed. "He's the Motherfucker."

"Oh."

"When are you coming to the house?" asked Tex.

"Tomorrow," I said.

"You know that nobody ever comes back tomorrow. They jes say that but they don't ever come back."

"Jones'll be back," Faggot said.

Tex didn't have anything to say to that.

Faggot clapped his hands twice. "Hostel meeting over," he said. He flashed a peace sign in the form of the Nazi salute and stuffed his hands into his pockets. "Cold," he said. "Home."

I started to walk fast. My feet were freezing. Faggot was walking behind everyone squeaking at every step. He was pale.

Tex caught up with me. "Jones, you in a hurry to go someplace or something?" he asked.

I waved my hands. "It's cold."

"Well, we're in no hurry," he said. "There's nothing to hurry for."

THE CHURCH

Tex had been waiting for the past half hour for Faggot's car to drive up on the lawn. At first he thought they'd gone in Salamander's car but when he looked out the vestry window he saw Salamander's car was sitting on the lawn behind the church, so he knew that Salamander was still unable to borrow five dollars to get the fan belt fixed.

That meant they'd gone in Faggot's car. Tex nodded his head and the leopard hatband twitched. Well, that was one more thing he knew now. But the most important thing was how they managed to go without him. He'd stayed pretty close to Faggot for the last week, so he didn't know how the Faggot had been able to plan this and take off today without his knowing about it.

Greater than the possibility that he might be excluded from whatever Faggot was planning, was his fear that his touch was slipping. But that was impossible. He was professional and they, even the best of them, were amateurs at this. Why he'd spent a whole lifetime at this kind of thing and as far as he could tell, except for a handful, most of them were college kids or Easterners who didn't have the slightest idea. They knew a lot more about drugs, that was all. And that kind of knowledge wasn't any kind of edge when that was all they knew. All that could be learned in a week or two of keeping your eyes open and walking around the streets and already he knew that, too.

He rolled himself another cigarette and propped his chair against the wall. He balanced himself with his long thin legs and went all over it one more time.

First Faggot didn't have the money to rent a house. He just fucking didn't have the bread to pay the first month's rent. Mushmouth was the only person with any money. Some said he had five hundred dollars in cash when he first came up here but he couldn't possibly have that much now. Nobody could. And that leaves only Salamander. Nobody knows how much he's got. He lives like he's got no money but he acts like he can get landed. So he'll probably be able to get a job as well. But I have a better chance of getting landed than either Mushmouth or Motherfucker--so why the fuck is he taking Motherfucker instead of me?

The chair slipped forward and Tex's feet slammed the floor. Motherfucker is useless.

His eyes got shrewd. He folded his hands across his tight belly and considered the situation again. He exhaled and flicked a tiny piece of stray tobacco from his lip. He smiled through his eyes. He would manage.

He wet his top lip and his tongue automatically slipped into the vacant spot where his front tooth used to be. He waited calmly in the kitchen.

Tex heard Faggot's car pull up on the lawn but he didn't move from his spot against the wall. He waited until he heard Salamander go upstairs. He knew that Motherfucker would lie down. Mushmouth didn't count. He might have the money but because he was young, Faggot took care of the decisions.

He waited. He heard Breeze playing his three notes in the vestry. There were people in the vestry so he waited a little longer yet for the others to question Faggot first. He wanted to give Breeze time to annoy Faggot before he went in there. He would just bide his time and when it came to patience, well, he had all the time in the world.

"What's your hurry?" he'd asked Salamander who seemed all in a tizzy to get landed and get a girlfriend and get laid. "What's your hurry, boy?"

He chuckled to himself. "There's plenty of time to get drunk on and get laid in and for things to change." That's what Salamander had to learn just yet. A little patience. "It's best to bide your time and hold your peace 'cause when you're dead, you're dead a long time."

Tex heard Faggot lie down on the couch. Soon it would be time to go in there. Breeze put his harmonica away.

He heard a voice ask, "Where you been, Faggot? If you been grocery shopping, how come you didn't bring no ice cream home for us?"

Faggot said he wasn't shopping.

"How long do you plan on staying in the hostel? How soon until you'll be landed?"

Tex rolled himself another cigarette while the questioning went on in the other room.

"Have you been out looking for a house to rent?"

"No. I plan to live here a thousand years."

"This guy Medusala he lived for a thousand years," said Breeze.

"Then he must have been eligible for about a hundred wars. He could have died in any one of them," Faggot said.

"You mean like the sponge George killed this afternoon? It was a-creeping and a-crawling out there with big antlers and a huge red tongue that was licking up all the cigarette butts out there on the lawn like a vacuum cleaner. It would have been sick if George hadn't killed it."

"Breeze, you want to go float away a little. Go over there and play your harmonica a bit." Faggot waved his hand toward the stairs.

In the kitchen Tex nodded his head up and down. Behind Faggot's back George did a fairy imitation of Faggot's wave that Faggot couldn't see.

"Faggot, you want to hear this new tune? I've been practicing a new song I wrote."

Tex waited for Breeze to untie his harmonica. He waited while Breeze played a faster three minute rendition of his tired three notes. When it was quiet in the other room, Tex got up and walked through the vestry doors.

"Faggot. You gonna let me live in your house with you, Faggot?"

"No."

Tex didn't expect success the first time. He tried again. "Faggot..."

"No."

Unruffled, he persisted in a pleasant, patient

drawl. "Faggot, you're gonna let me live in your house with you and help you wash the dishes and scrub the floors, ain't you, Faggot?"

"No."

"Now wait a minute, Faggot. Give a man time to talk, will you. Who else is gonna keep that big old house clean all day while you're off to work?" Tex wet his lips. "Who else is gonna get to live in that house and keep it clean and help you pay the rent and all?"

"A nigger maid."

"Hold on a minute." Tex began to make a cigarette. "Who've you got for the wintertime when you gotta get coal to keep warm on? Bet you haven't thought of that, have you? I know for a fact that you ain't got none of your ex-wives or some old girlfriend from sunny California who's gonna want to come all the way up here just to sit by your coal furnace and mind the fire and warm your toes. I know..."

"No."

Tex was his ingratiating best. He looked over his shoulder and he paused.

"Who says that Faggot went out and rented a house?" a voice asked from the stairs.

"Tex. Tex says that Faggot's rented a house and is moving out on the first."

A few people crept in from the yard. Someone rested on the steps on his way upstairs. In the vestry you could hear the bathroom faucet dripping as clearly as it drips in the night. Now the living room demanded an explanation. This was what Tex had waited half a day for.

"Faggot. Tex says you've rented a house. Faggot.

43

Faggot?"

Faggot said, "Wow! Like heavy shit, man." He twirled his finger in a lame spiral of congratulations. "Bloop," he said.

"Never mind heavy shit. Shit or no shit, did you? Did you rent a house or what?"

Faggot got up from the couch where he'd been stretched out with his feet hanging over a cracked chair that had no back. In getting up, he kicked the crippled chair over. An empty wine bottle fell to the floor. Faggot's hand swept out to catch it, but he was seconds too late and it rolled harmlessly to the door.

When he stood up he was taller than Tex, but not healthier looking, although he was stronger and heavier-built. He was taller than any other person in the room except Motherfucker. They were the same size. His face was pale--the color of sunburned orange fading in the winter. Underneath his skin were the shadows of tiny blood vessels that come to the surface when you first smoke and drink too much and stay awake without falling back into sleep or rest or joy.

From force of habit Faggot scratched the center of his shirt where a tie would have been. Once he owned a purple satin shirt. His hands were large and strong. He had stubby, thick fingers and wide palms. The first time he wrestled with Motherfucker he said, "Watch out you little motherfucker because I can kill you." On the employment questionnaire the Committee asked him to fill in for their work file and for their sponsors in the States, he'd written in a nearly illegible scrawl, "Former music teacher, unemployed musician." He had strong wrists because he played the drums.

"Well, Faggot, did you or didn't you rent a house?"

"Yes, that's right." Faggot spoke slowly, pronouncing every syllable in his slow even radio voice. It was a put-on. When he did it super slowly, people thought he was retarded. "Yes. I want to rent a house. Yes, I want to live in some relative peace and quiet again. Yes, I rented a house."

"Where'd you get the money for it? You don't have a job and you're not landed."

Faggot drew a large envelope from his back pocket that was folded down the center and again into halves. He waved it slowly back and forth in front of them like a fan. Their eyes moved from left to right and back again.

"Now give me a cigarette," he ordered.

Tex offered him the freshly rolled cigarette from his own lips. He lit it for him with the match hidden in his hand. Faggot just said everything Tex had waited to hear.

Faggot inhaled deeply. "The Canadian Government Department of Manpower and Immigration wrote and told me I am an officially landed immigrant. I will be a legal tax paying resident of *Canadia* in two weeks."

Tex smiled faintly through his eyes, his lips pressed tightly together, a thin drawn line.

The person on the steps turned his back and continued upstairs.

There were two more weeks remaining in the

month. Salamander had repacked the smaller of his two suitcases. The other suitcase he had never unpacked because he thought somebody would steal his clothes.

The week before the big move Salamander spent all his time with his fish. He had brought his aquarium all the way from the bookcase of his mother's living room with each fish wrapped in an individual plastic baggie and he would be damned if his fish were going to die now. He was preparing them for the move to the new house just like he had prepared them for the big move from Portland to Vancouver.

Motherfucker said Salamander was crazy and talked all the time about flushing his fish down the toilet, like kittens or babies. But when Salamander told him how he had smuggled his tadpoles into *Canadia* right under the noses of the Immigration people, Motherfucker shut up.

Salamander never expected all his fish to survive but they did. The first week when Salamander showed up with the aquarium and started to age water in Faggot's empty beer bottles, Faggot said, "Lord." Then he said, "Fuck, shit, piss" and Salamander said, "Boy, you're a fuck-up." Right away Faggot named Salamander "Fucked-Up Fish Boy" but switched to Salamander when he discovered a tadpole swimming around in a wine bottle. Later that same week Faggot gagged on some of the water he drank out of a beer bottle he thought was real. Salamander nearly killed himself laughing. He doubled over and cackled to himself. After that they got to be pretty good friends.

46

In the last week before they moved, one of the four tadpoles died. Salamander buried it in the churchyard under a tomato soup can. In between packing and talking about how great it was getting out of that shit-hole of a hostel, Salamander was busy figuring the survival ratios of his three remaining tadpoles. He liked the fish all right but he was crazy about his tadpoles. Mushmouth, who didn't know what they were until Salamander told him how they would turn into frogs one day, got interested in watching Salamander take care of them. Mushmouth named them Ho, Chi and Minh. He thought Chi was a girl and when he asked how you could tell the difference in tadpoles, he and Salamander became real friends.

Faggot spent all his time fixing up the details for his house. There were some papers to sign and he was trying to get a job at the same time. He spent as little time at the hostel as he could manage because he said that most of the people there gave him a headache. Salamander said he was born with a headache but Faggot shook a peace sign at him and called him a syphilitic hippie.

Breeze always kept an eye open for Faggot and whenever he caught sight of him he asked, "When you move into your new house, can I come by and take a bath now and then?" And Faggot kept telling him, "Sure. Sure, Breeze, anything. I'll check it with my lawyer."

On Monday they said good-bye to the hostel forever. Salamander took his suitcases, including the one that nobody had ever seen, and lugged them out

47

to his car in the churchyard. Then he went back upstairs for a carton of records and another carton of books that he had kept under his bed and never opened for fear that someone who knew how to read in that place would rip off all his cartoons and comics. Then he made a third trip for his aquarium with the three surviving tadpoles and came out with two suits on a hanger and a record player that nobody knew he owned. All this time he made Mushmouth stand by his car that looked like another piece of hostel junk except that it had wheels, Oregon plates and a registration sticker. Mushmouth was supposed to watch for anybody who might sneak out of the church to steal stuff when Salamander went in and out of the hostel for his things.

"Don't worry," Mushmouth said leaning up against the car snapping a piece of Bazooka Joe bubble gum. "If anybody comes, I'll stomp his balls." He flashed Salamander a peace sign and then they traded places.

Salamander locked all the doors to the car except the driver's side where he stood ready to get in and drive off if anybody came near his stuff. After about fifteen minutes Mushmouth came out dragging his one big suitcase along the ground. There were ragged edges of clothing sticking out the sides. It looked like a plump tuna on rye with a border of lettuce hanging over the bread.

"That took you so long?" Salamander asked.

"It's heavy," Mushmouth complained kicking it the last few feet. "Besides, I couldn't find my other underwear. I have three pairs."

"Shit," said Salamander and they left the hostel forever.

Breeze followed Faggot around like a puppy dog playing a harmonica. Faggot kept blowing smoke in his face but it didn't make any difference. Breeze wanted to be with him until the last. Finally he played a parting tune as Faggot, Motherfucker and Tex simply got into Faggot's car on the other side of the churchyard and drove off. Faggot wore everything he owned, Motherfucker took his shaving kit and Tex had his sleeping bag and his duffel bag.

When Faggot pulled off the lawn, Motherfucker rolled down the window. "Don't take any shit," he yelled at the church. Faggot threw a peace sign and blew Breeze a kiss. Then he flipped his butt out the window and shifted into gear. They were gone.

Breeze stood in the middle of a garbage pile in the front of a church in the middle of the poorest Chinese district in Vancouver and played his three notes. It had occurred to him as he saw the two cars leave that he would soon be responsible for making some decision about the state of his life. He would have to practice more if he wanted to become a famous harmonica player.

He scuffed and fluffed out the remains of the old armchair with his toe and thought sadly about George who had been picked up by the police for possession of an illegal drug and now faced the possibility of extradition. The old armchair sagged in self-pity and looked in bewilderment at the entrails of itself everywhere.

Somehow he had to get it together.

HOUSEKEEPING

Salamander got down the huge black cast iron fry pan from the hook above the stove. He stood in front of the stove in shirtsleeves with his scrawny arms bent at the elbows, contemplating the shiny black bottom of the fry pan. He turned the pan over and saw the thick lines of rust or dirt or caked-on grease from breakfasts of bacon and eggs that had been cooked months ago.

"Where does Faggot get all this stuff?" he asked himself.

He balanced the fry pan in one hand and gave a nervous shake of his shoulders. He was not very tall but he seemed taller than he was because he was so skinny. Without a shirt his ribs showed through his skin. Faggot said Salamander was an animated fish bone.

Upstairs in one of the two suitcases he hadn't yet unpacked, Salamander kept a large jar of nutriment. Every morning at breakfast he drank two heaping tablespoonfuls in a large glass of milk. The nutriment came in three flavors, chocolate, strawberry and vanilla, but Salamander always drank chocolate.

"What's the difference what it tastes like?" he wanted to know. "The important thing is what it does for you. There's no point in eating food that doesn't do anything for you. What's the point of eating after all?" he asked. And he answered himself right away before anybody could tell him how food can be tasty and give real pleasure like a cigarette with coffee in the morning. But since he didn't smoke, either, it was hopeless.

"The point of eating is to eat food that counts. Only dumbasses put food into their mouths that isn't food. Like potato chips and shit cereals that aren't food, that have no nutritional value, that do nothing for you but pollute you with non-food."

Salamander held the fry pan up to his nose, then placed it on the burner and turned on the stove. He scraped the inside of the pan with his fingernail and was satisfied. He went to the refrigerator and brought out a package of meat wrapped in a brown bag. There was blood on the outside of the bag.

"When is that meal going to be ready?" a voice called from the porch. The front door was open and from the stove there was a clear view to the street beyond. There was a patch of blue sky visible above the mound of earth in the vacant lot directly across the street.

"When it's done," Salamander shouted back.

"Well, when is that going to be?" the voice wanted to know.

"When I decide it is. That's when it will be done."

"Salamander, I sure as hell hope you know how to cook those steaks."

There was laughter from the porch and sounds of a scuffle and then everything was quiet again.

Blue smoke rose in a haze from the fry pan where the steaks were beginning to relax on the stove. The smoke hung about the stove in lazy circles like weird cigarette rings from the lips of an invisible smoker.

The fry pan was larger than the burner and hung over the sides of the red coils. In the center of the pan the steaks were sizzling. Salamander poked a few with a fork and they bled. He turned his back on a joke of a stove that was a four burner enlargement of a hot plate. He opened the refrigerator and stared inside.

At this time now his mother would be cooking dinner. His father would have been home from work for at least a half hour. He would be eating earlier because he would be going out. Besides, he would prefer not to eat with his father anyway and his mother always gave him his dinner early on the nights he wanted to go out. He never realized that his mother was an excellent cook. He could not remember a single time he felt his mother cooked a good meal when she used to make lunches for him when he went half days to the University of Portland and worked half days in a Federal Reserve Bank. He never questioned if he loved his mother or if she loved him. It never crossed his mind. It was her job to make his meals and to serve them to him whenever he wanted to eat them. It was that simple.

He shut the refrigerator door. In his hands he held two large onions. Awkwardly Salamander brought them to the sink and prepared to cut them. He began to slice the first onion. He remembered he hadn't had any decent cookies or cake since he left home.

In the first hostel there had been a cook. He and his girlfriend used to cook for everybody in the hostel. Mark's meals weren't too great but at least he didn't have to cook for himself every day. Everybody gave three dollars a week and Mark and his girlfriend shopped and made lunches and suppers. Motherfucker said that they used too much cheese and everything they made tasted like cheese. He thought it was all right because it was better than he could do for himself.

Faggot said that Mark and his girlfriend would probably get married and then get divorced. Salamander never thought they would get married. Faggot thought they would get divorced because he had been married twice and thought that all marriages end in children, then divorce. But then Salamander couldn't see how any girl could stay married to Faggot. Mark didn't know how lucky he was. He would find out, though, if that girl left him in the wintertime.

The onions were in a small pile on the sink. Salamander brushed his eyes with the back of his hand. Then he scooped the onions into his palms and brought them to the stove where the steaks were smoking. The steaks in the middle of the pan were burning and the steaks on the outer edges of the pan where the heat never reached them were raw. He shifted the positions of the steaks and poured the onions around the edges of the pan. The onions steamed and smoked.

Salamander's eyes darted here and there inside the pan. He made periodic jabs at the meat with a fork. His face was expressionless.

The mixture of steam and smoke rose from the pan and curled around his head and his brown hair, cut short in order to get landed on his job offer from the Canadian Imperial Bank of Commerce. He seemed to belong more to the rigid self-righteousness and reserved frigidity of Protestant New England than to the lush Pacific undergrowth and the Oregon strawberry fields where he had worked summertimes as a boy. Non-smoking, non-swearing, non-coffee drinking Midwesterners could claim him more securely than the crisp, efficient FBI agent who would appear unannounced some day at his mother's house in Portland. But his people were pioneers--the original settlers immigrant Jewish boys read about and believe in three thousand miles eastward in New York City. His grandparents came from Ohio to settle in the mountains and forests of Oregon. The wild fecundity of the land overwhelmed them and they clung desperately to their prairie innocence and insulation.

Salamander made his discovery in the reading room of the University of Portland Library. There the young librarian mindlessly filed away the subversive reporting of another world, all the while thinking of her boyfriend and her wardrobe and the campus social calendar.

For a year Salamander read each new edition of *Ramparts* and *The New Republic*. He stopped going to his accounting class. When a small group of activists at the commuter school began to hold noon vigils for the Vietnam War dead, he held a candle for fifteen minutes a day. He grew his hair long and read underground literature. He doubted what the school taught him and what the President said on television. He laughed at the finger-pointing Oregon road signs of Uncle Sam asking the American public why the United States trades with communist countries. He spoke less. He sneered more at the campus coeds who simultaneously attracted and repulsed him. He dropped out of school for one quarter and read the history of Vietnam in the school library and worked in the Federal Reserve Bank. He carried his draft card in his wallet beneath his license.

Salamander stepped away from the stove because the smoke was bothering his eyes. From the cabinet above the kitchen sink he pulled out a dirty plate. When he'd rinsed it, he used it for the two steaks that were burnt.

"It'll be ready soon," he yelled out to the porch.

"You've probably ruined them by now. That's our fault for ever letting some dumbshit like you try to cook them."

Salamander recognized Tex's voice. He smiled. "If you wanted it any other way, you should have cooked them yourself. I wasn't stopping you. I never said I was the great chef."

"Fuck you, boy."

Salamander laughed. His lips curled upwards and his eyes came alive. He reached for the pan. Another steak was burning. Immediately his lips compressed away the warmth. He wasn't aware he had changed.

He was endlessly amazed when he found out how most people came to Canada. Faggot flew from San

Diego with the FBI hot on his trail when the plane fueled and took off. Breeze blew in. Tex just got here somehow...

But he had been much more careful. Now Vancouver seemed much different than that day in April when he had driven up. He knew the day his mother handed him the sealed induction notice. He never had any intention of showing up because he knew that there was no way to avoid being drafted--he had that much respect still for the United States Government. He could not fake homosexuality or bedwetting or being crazy. The deceptions the people from New York and California attempted seemed outrageous. He refused to allow them to let him debase himself like that. He retained that much of a public school education and had acquired that much new righteousness.

He had never been outside of Oregon in his life, yet he managed the border perfectly. He located the Committee and the hostels where draft dodgers could stay. He received legal advice about getting landed. For the first time in his life he spoke to someone from Chicago, Philadelphia and St. Louis. He made an appointment with a representative from the Canadian Imperial Bank of Commerce and received a job offer as a Bank Manager Trainee. He had every intention of holding that job.

Today was a Friday. On Monday he would be at the Bank at 8:00 o'clock in the morning. It was money.

Salamander put the rest of the steaks on the plate. He threw the fork down on the stove and wiped his fingers on his pants. Then he took another plate from the cabinet and without wiping it off, took two steaks from the pile on the stove and potatoes from another pot on a back burner.

"Okay, it's done. Come and eat."

Four people came in from the porch.

"You could smell those steaks all over the street. From here to Texas. You must have burned them away to nothing, boy." Tex held one up on the end of a fork and dangled it over a plate for everybody to see. "Look how small they are."

A boy with bell bottom jeans and a leather vest held a plate underneath Tex's steak. He looked like a high school kid who was dressed up to take a girl to the Fillmore.

"C'mon, Tex. Put it in. Just drop it in the plate. Don't look at it. Just put it in the plate." He shook the plate up and down while Tex slowly let the steak down. A dirty white handkerchief flopped out of his back pocket. He wore wire rimmed glasses that looked expensive. He laughed and made jokes. He and Salamander stood together and watched the potatoes.

Tex joined Mushmouth and Salamander at the stove.

"Hey, Mother. Quit staring. Get something to eat before it's all gone," Faggot said.

"Yeah, everybody eat fast and eat as much as you can so Faggot won't get anything to eat," said Salamander.

Mother laughed. "Sure." He strolled into the kitchen and began looking for a plate and a fork. He picked out a fork from a cardboard box on the floor.

"It's dirty," he complained. He looked for a knife but he couldn't find one. "Who has a knife I can use?" Mushmouth slid a knife across the table and Mother picked it up and wiped it carefully on his jeans. Salamander stayed by the stove eating with rabbit-quick bites. He never ate much in a single bite. His hand and fork made a series of semicircles in a path from the plate to his mouth and back again.

"Did you cook these potatoes, Salamander?"

Salamander watched Motherfucker push potatoes around in the pot. "There's still skins on some of them. Why there's dirt in there, you little bastard. Don't you know how to cook potatoes? You take the dirt off them."

Salamander turned his back. He balanced his plate on the edge of the stove and opened the refrigerator. "Next time you cook them." He poured himself a glass of milk.

"Hey, Salamander, can I have some milk?" Tex was wearing his cowboy hat made out of some kind of fur with the imitation leopard skin hatband. "C'mon, man, give us some milk." He was rolling a cigarette. He raised it to his lips to glue it together. Expertly his tongue ran along the gummed edge. At the end of the paper, he flicked in his tongue lizard-like. All the time his eyes never left Salamander's face.

Salamander was thinking about the chocolate nutriment upstairs in his suitcase. He should start drinking that stuff again but with all these people around it was impossible to buy any food and have any left for himself. He thought if he left the nutriment lying around, Tex would learn to roll it and smoke it. That way it would be cheaper than tobacco.

"No. Buy your own milk."

Mushmouth wiped his mouth with the handkerchief he pulled out of his pocket. He blew his nose and put his plate in the sink. Faggot stood by the table eating in big mouthfuls. He went to the cabinet and took out a loaf of bread. He cut off a huge slice, then a slightly smaller one that he pushed across the table to Mother. Mother didn't say anything to Faggot. Instead he turned to Salamander. "Get out the butter, little creep."

Salamander brought the butter to the table. The others cut off bread for themselves.

Faggot left his plate on the table. He belched. "You boys decide who's going to clean up the kitchen. I want this place spotless. Somebody wash the dishes."

Nobody listened to him.

"Sure," Mother said. "We're gonna clean up the kitchen. Tex, you're gonna wash the dishes for Faggot, aren't you?"

"Okay," Tex said. "Okay." But nobody believed him. He cut the end of his ash off with his fingernail.

"Who's got a cigarette?" Faggot asked. "Mother, you want to roll me a cigarette?"

"Won't you ever learn, Faggot?" Mother bitched. "When are you gonna learn to roll your own cigarettes? You're a big boy now."

"Never. I'm going to get a job that pays me five hundred dollars a week and I'll buy cigarettes to throw out."

Faggot kicked the box of silverware on the floor. "I

think I can get more stuff from where I got this. They have more dishes and some pots."

Mother lit a cigarette from the stove and left the kitchen. Mushmouth and Salamander walked around the silverware box and followed him to the porch.

"You there, boy," Faggot pointed to Tex. "Do a nice job on the dishes, you hear? A nice clean kitchen."

Tex leaned up against the stove and laughed. "Sure, Boss. Sure thing. I'm gonna...."

"What are you gonna do, Tex?"

"Well, now. I don't exactly know." Tex crossed one foot over the other. "Maybe I'll stay here a while and maybe I won't. Maybe I'll start east and get landed." He whistled through the hole that belonged to his missing front tooth. "Regina maybe. But there ain't nothing left of today, so there ain't much point in deciding anything, is there?"

Faggot laughed. "Sure. Sure thing." He stood in front of Tex. Half-gently, half-roughly, he shook him by the shoulder. "You tell 'em in Regina."

It is evening. That special Northwestern spring evening when everything is slightly fresh and slightly damp and the whole world has bathed and awaits a lover. The night noises come on very quietly, mouse-like in the dark. The lights blink on one by one but you never remember seeing them come alive. Instead you sit in the shadow grays of the early evening and watch day-lit orange slip over the edge of the sky.

You look across at the night lights of Vancouver. The flashing blue BOWMAC sign, the street lamps spread out in spider web design, the Black Cat restaurant flashing its blue and yellow tail.

You think of all the places you have ever been and all the places you can never go and you try to recognize them in the street lights of the Burrard Bridge. You hear the other noises of the other spring evenings that are beyond you...there is the bridge and the Black Cat and BOWMAC and...

At night the city is a huge metropolis, by a trick of lighting seemingly as large and as complex and as mysterious as New York. But Tex had never seen New York. Just Houston.

And the spring evening in Vancouver is only about different people on different porches who inhale the lilac's breath and rest from the day.

FAGGOT

In half an hour Faggot came back with a brown bag under his arm. He flung the front door of the car shut and hustled up the path so that his ass rolled just ever so slightly. He used the same backhand gesture to throw the gate shut. The latch made a decisive click in the dark. It rang for a few seconds and then everything was still.

Faggot sat down in the yellow wicker chair in the corner near the steps. The chair had a retractable foot rest hidden under the seat. Automatically he kicked out this foot rest while he reached inside the brown bag and brought out a bottle. The cap came off easily in his fingers because he had already started to drink in the car on the way home. He tilted the bottle back and drank from it for a long time. After every drink he put the cap back on. Then he cradled it in his large hand on his lap while he leaned back and lit a cigarette from a package he kept in the pocket of his shirt.

"The night is coming on very nicely," he thought. There were the shadows of the street and the large gray house jutting up to the sky. The air was cool but fresh. The street was deserted. Occasionally someone would walk by but in the night they seemed to walk softly.

The house was quiet and he was all alone in it. Faggot thought of the hostel and unscrewed the cap from the bottle. A very slow smile spread across his features. He raised the bottle to his lips while afterthoughts of his former lives and wives and girlfriends fluttered across his mind. He replaced the bottle cap and his lips tightened and pursed. Already his upper lip was getting stiff.

"Well, well, well," a voice came through the shadows. It was a voice without a body. Soft and gentle. It was a voice suited to the shadows and the nighttime.

"Just take a look, will you, at what the little boy's gone and bought. Now you're going to invite me over and share some of that fine liquor, ain't you? Now, now. Don't go on shaking your head back and forth. After all, you know, you're going to be rid of me in a few days. Mmm. Mmm. That's right. You just take a minute or two to make up your mind while I roll me a cigarette and take in the night airs."

Faggot leaned his head into the woven nest of straw. "Jesus," he thought. "This chair must be at least thirty-five years old. It's older than me. It's as old as my second oldest bitchiest sister. It's as old as my mother was when my father died. It is..."

"Time you've decided, huh?"

"Sure. Sure, Tex," Faggot said. He looked down at the bottle and examined it in the dark. He turned it over and over in his hands while the words rolled around in his mind. "I hate your guts, Tex, and I want

64

you out of my house. But I'd give you a drink. I'd give anybody a drink if they really needed it." He laughed. "And you need it, all right."

He leaned back in his chair laughing into the shadows. Generously he held out the bottle and watched the space in front of it fill up. He was waiting for the arm to materialize out of the dark and take away the bottle. He wanted to see the arm connect to the body and go into Tex's mouth.

Tex's hand stretched out and effortlessly pried the bottle loose from Faggot's grip. "Now that's a mighty fine thing you've done, Faggot. I mean I can really appreciate that."

"It's nothing, Tex. I mean I'd do it for you anytime."

In the dark Tex's eyes darted into Faggot's face. Like a cat in the dark, Tex groomed himself secretly.

Tex brought the bottle back to Faggot's hand but instead of going away into the shadows, Tex stayed by the wicker chair. For a matter of minutes he watched Faggot drink from the bottle. Without hesitating he dragged his kitchen chair out of the shadows and brought it up alongside Faggot's.

"It's not bad wine," he said.

"No, it isn't. It's $1.05 a bottle. The wines are better in *Califor-ni-ay*. There's more variety in that price range and you don't have to go the B. C. Liquor Control Board. Everything's better in *Califor-ni-ay*. Especially the climate."

Tex didn't know if Faggot was serious or if he was kidding. He couldn't tell with Faggot because Faggot joked about everything.

"Hey, do you think you could drink a whole bottle without coming up once? You know, with one swallow?"

Faggot laughed. "Sure. Sure I could do that."

"Let me see you do it then. I'll finish this one and you take the other one like that, okay?"

Faggot handed the bottle over to Tex. Tex looked Faggot straight in the eye and tilted the bottle back. He drank steadily. He never took his eyes away from Faggot's face. The Adam's apple in his neck bobbed up and down. Faggot watched him chug half a bottle.

Faggot opened up the other bottle and leaned back in his chair. He closed his eyes. His hand bent backwards at the wrist. His wrist, his arm and his mouth were in perfect coordination. They moved in one motion, never getting ahead or behind one another. He really could have been a fine athlete.

"God." He took a deep breath. "Jesus, I haven't done that in a long time. God." He rested his head against the back of the wicker chair. In other days there was probably a cushion there. He squeezed his eyes tight. "I wish it was scotch."

Tex laughed. It was an animal laugh in the dark. "D'you finish? D'you take it all? Lemme see."

Faggot opened his eyes and held the bottle up to the light that came from a street lamp. There was about an inch of liquid left. Tex's hand shot out and Faggot handed it over to him. "Go ahead, boy, drink your face off." He laughed.

They were silent then.

"You know," Faggot said, "I feel like I used to when I played in the clubs. We used to play half the night and I'd be drunk all the time. I played good, then, too." Faggot lit a cigarette. He breathed it in and out rhythmically.

"Faggot, would you ever play again?"

"Naw, you get tired. The money's good but you can't keep it up long. Unless you really make it, it wears you out. It eats you up."

"No, I mean wouldn't you like to play? You know, for kicks? Just like that? 'Cause if I knew how to play an instrument that good I'd want to play for myself. Now take this cat I lived with in Houston. He was learning how to play guitar."

Faggot clamped his first two fingers around his cigarette and waved it through the air in an extravagant semicircle. He exhaled slowly through his nose without moving his face or opening his mouth. The insides of his nostrils were singed from the thousands of cigarettes he'd smoked that way. Now he was actually listening to Tex.

"You know, I realized I wasn't gonna go into no army when I listened to that cat practice guitar every day. I grew my hair and smoked up a lot of weed. I was just a kid, though. I really thought I had it all figured out."

"I'd like to get a flute. I'd like to learn how to play flute."

"I have to get it all together again. I have to find the nice things. I mean I know what's right and all. It's just that I have to go about it a little at a time and put everything back in its place again. First I have to get landed. Faggot, is your mother alive?"

"My mother? Oh yeah, she's alive. She took over

my father's insurance stuff when he died. She does real estate, too."

"My aunt, Faggot, was the bitchiest woman who ever lived. She hated my mother and she hated me."

"Why?"

"Because my mother got pregnant. And then because she had me."

"She probably hated you because of the way you are. You probably drove her insane all the time."

"Nope. She was crazy to begin with. But I didn't figure all that out until I lived with this cat in Houston. Like I was really close to him. We talked about a lot of things. Then I had to leave because..."

"You know, Tex, I'm not interested in your aunt and I don't want to talk about this stuff and I hate your guts. You're really a fine person except nobody can trust you. A person would have to be pathological to trust you."

Tex smiled. He nodded his head up and down while Faggot talked. He understood everything Faggot was trying to tell him. "I think I'm drunk," he said. "You know what, Faggot? You're right. You're one hundred percent right." He put his hand on Faggot's shoulder and leaned into his face. "And I really like you, Faggot. I wish you didn't dislike me so much."

"I don't dislike you. I like you very much. Only I wish you wouldn't whine and wheedle all the time."

"I'm glad, Faggot. I'm really glad. I mean there's no reason why we should dislike each other. I mean if you have to live in the same house together, there's no reason why you can't learn to get along with one another and love each other. That's what's wrong with the world now. There's no love and no understanding. People want what everybody else has instead of being satisfied with what they've got. But like...Well, Faggot, you've been really good to me. Letting me stay in the house and all."

"It's nothing, Tex. Like don't worry about it, Tex. You just take your time and leave whenever you're ready."

"Yeah, but I want to tell you. I want you to understand, Faggot, that I really dig you. That..."

"Tex, like I said. I don't hate you. I LIKE you."

"Faggot, Faggot," Tex called in his little boy voice. "Faggot, are you really a faggot?"

"No."

"Then how come they call you Faggot? When I came to the hostel they all called you Faggot."

"It was a joke. Anybody could be Faggot there. Anybody could be anybody they wanted to be there. Now you take Breeze. He could be crazy and he was crazy there."

"Why'd you call him Breeze?" Tex sounded as if he was almost crying.

"Because," Faggot waved his hand in the air, "because he has nothing up here." He waved in the general direction of his head. "There's a breeze in there. You know that."

They were quiet. Maybe Tex dozed off. Maybe Faggot thought so. But maybe Tex merely drooped his eyelids and looked out through his watery eyes at The Faggot stretched out in relaxation six inches away.

Maybe it was an hour. Maybe it was two. It didn't matter. Faggot got up to go inside. He leaned over and saw Tex curled up like a child fast asleep in his chair.

"If only he wasn't such a bastard," he thought. He lit a cigarette and fumbled for the inside of the door frame in the dark. The door was open. In fact, the back of the door was pushed against the wall. "It will wear away the wall there," Faggot said.

Inside Faggot took off his pants and his watch and his shirt. He lay down on the collapsible bed in the living room. Tex had to go. He was a parasite.

He closed his eyes. He went into a fitful sleep. He was with his wife. This time it was with his first wife. The one he thought he loved. The one who was divorced but yet endlessly divorcing after three-and-one-half years of marriage, after one girl child whom he still loved and dearly missed, after two years of mutual and vindictive adultery with all their best friends. He married her when he was eighteen because he had got her pregnant and he thought it was the right thing to do then. He was playing in all the clubs and making more money than he would probably see at one time for the rest of his life.

She wrote him a letter in which she said she was going to have another baby with her second husband. The man she had married after they were divorced. He remembered what he had said when she found out what was going on between him and her best girlfriend, Carolyn. He had said, "No." "No," he lied. Maybe if he had said, "Yes," then things would have been able to be saved. No, he didn't think that was true.

"No, I won't do that for you," Faggot said aloud. "No. I won't do that for you. I may be drunk out of my mind but I won't do that for you, either. Whatever your name is. Miss Oklahoma? Nebraska? Fargo? Tulsa? You want to, don't you? Well, it doesn't matter. I may remember in a little while. You keep asking me and I may remember. Whatever your name is. Whoever you are."

Motherfucker was a tall, lean bastard. He never smiled or sang or said "Howdy" in public unless it was absolutely necessary and then he would think of some way to get out of it. He hung out in all the doorways of the house but especially the living room and kitchen doors. If company came or if there was some sort of fracas, he stayed put in his doorway until it was safe to sneak across the room into another one.

He was about six-foot-one. Crouched up in the door frame with his hands slouched into his pockets, he looked a little shorter. His long, lank frame contracted into his shifty eyeballs that were centered above his belt buckle. Some people said that if he were a couple of inches taller and lighter, the army wouldn't have been after him. He never said anything about that one way or the other.

The only time he spoke to anybody first was when he was out of tobacco or if he thought he could rustle up a store-made smoke. "Give me fifty cents for tobacco," he would say. Motherfucker never whimpered for anything. That was because he was the Motherfucker. He never apologized or said, "Thank you." He was silent and moody and very proud.

Nobody knew how the Motherfucker got his name. But whatever he did to become the Motherfucker must have been beyond comparison because nobody, not even Breeze or George, would mention it. But then again, it might have been nothing. Nobody would say.

One thing was certain. Motherfucker was proud of his name. Anybody who called him "Mom," even for fun, was looking for serious trouble. Mushmouth called Motherfucker Mom on a day when the Motherfucker was out of sorts. Mother dangled Mushmouth over the hall banister. Faggot ran in from the front porch and collected all the money that fell out of Mushmouth's pockets. "Hey, don't drop that boy," he yelled up at Motherfucker who nodded and said, "Sure thing, Boss," and kept Mushmouth dangling. Salamander said that holding people upside-down was the way to give a person an embolism of the brain. Motherfucker said he'd remember that. Mother was just fine but Motherfucker was better and The Motherfucker was just about the best.

Mother had no ass and really no hips, either. He was a long hairy chest that disappeared into his groin. That was all. A huge chest connected to his legs by the zipper of his jeans. At night when he lay on his bed finishing off the day's butts, his red flannel shirt would open to the bottom button. Faggot would come in with his bottle of Tanqueray Gin and yell, "Mother-fucker, your pubic hairs are showing."

"Give me a drink of that before you drink it all,

you stupid-ass drunk," Mother answered.

And Faggot would collapse into a tizzy of silly drunken laughter thinking about Mother's hairy chest. Mother stretched his long graceful arm and pried the bottle from Faggot's grasp and took long greedy gulps. In the morning he would wake up about noon and be back in the kitchen door looking for something to eat.

He had beautiful hands. Piano hands. The fingers were very slim and wiry and strong. Maybe he could have been a really fine ladies' man, if he tried, but he didn't seem to care very much one way or the other. No Mother will turn his back on a good lay but Mother never strained himself. Instead he waited in doorways and watched for what came his way.

He slept in a big twenty dollar bed in the front room. He never had a twenty dollar lay in that bed but he would get up each morning looking like he had been up all night. Next to his bed there was a neat pile of his things--jeans stiffened into stilts that slowly relaxed through the long nights of his sleep and a notebook and an envelope and parts of a shaving kit.

In the afternoon he played guitar and looked down at his shaving kit and smiled. The smile was mean and sad and angry and despairing all at the same time. Then he would sit on his bed and listen to Bob Dylan records on Salamander's record player. Whenever he spoke it was an accident. He talked with eyes and with deliberate half-gestures of his arms and hands that were long and loose. He painted pictures with his hands in the air and was upset when nobody understood the things he tried to leak through his face.

It seemed that in the beginning he set out for Alberta with a friend. He wanted to get landed somewhere in Alberta and then come back to Vancouver. His friend stopped for gas and Mother got out of the car to buy a candy bar. His friend drove away with all his luggage and money and the shaving kit. After a while Mother saved up some money and the first thing he bought, before the brass bed even, was a new second-hand shaving kit.

In the mornings he smoked cigarettes he made from day-old butts. Then he went upstairs and shaved with his razor that Faggot used every morning before he left for work or for job-hunting or whatever he did. He would stay in the little bathroom that looks out to the whole city over a worm-eaten apple tree and the neighbor's wash. He stood in front of the open window and a slight breeze would come in off the sea and liven up the whole room. There was no curtain on the window and he could see clear across to the construction workers who were building a warehouse that summer next to the Voice of China broadcasting station. Then his feet would come slinky-like down the steps and he would fill the whole doorway with his arms and shoulders and early morning grin. "That faggot's been using my razor again."

Mother searched the whole house for leftover things when nobody was home. He cleaned all the ashtrays filled with four different brands of butts that he carefully salvaged and re-smoked. He licked Salamander's peanut butter knives and watched to see what went in and came out of his special cabinet. He knew more about Salamander than Salamander knew himself. Mother knew all the secret hiding places where Salamander hid his food. Like the tin of homemade toll house cookies Salamander's mother sent with the news that the FBI had come to the house asking questions. Salamander never opened those cookies and hid them so well he had forgotten all about the FBI until Mother scavenged up the news inside a cookie tin he found hidden under a pile of old leaves and gunny sacks next to a pot of moldering potatoes in the pantry. And Motherfucker wasn't even looking for cookies. He wanted jelly.

Mother held onto himself and counted time. He knew that soon there must be some release, that things could not continue as they were forever. In the meantime it sufficed for him to be in the same room, the same house with the others. Maybe he ruminated on the justice of this world where a man is punished for wanting a ten-cent candy bar. It was difficult to know because the second time he lost everything he owned, he grew quiet and added that loss to the list of all the other things he had lost and would not talk about.

BREAKFAST

In the morning Faggot lay across his bed asleep on his back. One arm was flung to the side, outstretched on the mattress of his collapsible frame bed. He always draped a dirty yellow blanket over his body and in the morning it settled in dusty folds along the floor. Sometimes he twitched in his sleep but Motherfucker, who shared the next room, was oblivious to anything he did. Tex was in his sleeping bag near the threshold of the kitchen door. He slept in the hall outside the kitchen, a sort of living room when everyone wasn't in Faggot or Motherfucker's bedroom.

There was an old man who lived in the room opposite the bathroom. When Faggot took over the lease he made an agreement with the landlady. Jimmy was supposed to move out in two weeks but nobody ever saw him. Maybe Jimmy moved around in the middle of the morning when everybody was supposed to be at work. In that case, Motherfucker never believed in his existence at all because he slept every day until noon, curled up on his side in his big brass bed in the front room with the blanket neatly pulled across his shoulders and his thin legs and slender waist in tidy silhouette. And he never moved in his sleep.

Every day Faggot was the first one to get up. He would lean over the side of his bed and fumble for a cigarette between his broken alarm clock and his watch. In the next few minutes he tried to locate a match while his body drifted in and out of sleep. But once he lit his cigarette, he stayed awake.

Faggot was the first to get up because he drank the most and had to go to the bathroom first.

On the way to the bathroom he woke Tex who slept fitfully like a child, all rolled up in a ball. Faggot always expected to see him with his thumb in his mouth. When he came into the hall, Tex opened his eyes. He turned over on his back and looked up at the Faggot pleasantly. "Mornin'." Tex smiled and pushed back his sleeping bag with his long tanned arms. He stretched his bare limbs leisurely beneath his flannel coverings.

"Hmph." Faggot looked down at Tex. His lips congealed. He took a deep drag on his cigarette and exhaled partly through his nose and partly through his open mouth. It looked as if it hurt him to smoke so early in the morning.

Faggot's feet made heavy banging noises as he walked up the stairs and tramped across the upstairs hall to the bathroom.

Tex lay back and smiled. He sat up and began to make a cigarette from the tobacco pouch and paper wrappers at his side. He heard Faggot moving around in the bathroom and he stopped with his tongue hanging over the paper. Absent-mindedly his tongue fell backwards into the hole under his top lip where his front tooth used to be. Then he remembered the cigarette in his hands. "Yep," he said. "I'm gonna get me a new tooth, too. That's one of the first things I'm gonna do. Of course, after I have breakfast, that is."

He lay back on the floor and listened to the other noises that came from Faggot through the grate. In a little while Faggot came down the stairs and re-crossed the hall floor, gingerly skirting Tex's bed. He put on a blue perma-press shirt and a brown hand-woven tie. Then he got down on his hands and knees and picked up all the things that had fallen from his pockets the night before when he had taken his pants off. Then he put all these things into the pockets of a suit that hung from a hanger above his bed. Last he put on his glasses and immediately became more coordinated. He patted his hair in place and ran his hand across his tie. Then he carried his shoes in his hand and dropped them on the floor next to Tex's head.

Tex looked up to see Faggot's feet descending into his huge shoes. Faggot leaned over to fasten one of the buckles. He leered into Tex's face and said, "I hope that one of these days I'm going to get up and you're going to be gone."

Tex smiled. "Sure, Boss. Sure thing. Why I might even go tomorrow, I feel so good today."

"Fine." Faggot straightened up and checked the change in his hip pocket. "Have a good day," he said as he walked out of the hall.

Tex waited for the door to close. When he heard the door fit itself back into the frame, he inhaled the last of his cigarette. He rolled over on his side and in a few minutes he fell asleep again.

The next time he woke up he was sweating. The flannel padding of his sleeping bag was sticking to his body. The sun was coming directly through the window in the front room where Motherfucker was still silently asleep on his side.

Tex pushed back the bag and lay on his back. In a few minutes, right before stupor overcame him, he slid out of the bag altogether. He lay on top of his sleeping bag nude for a while and then he got up and put on his jeans. Stealthily, without making any noise, he left the room and went upstairs.

When he came down, Mother was sitting up on the edge of his bed. He was rubbing his hand back and forth across his mouth. "Give me a cigarette," he said.

"Why should I?"

"Shut up, Tex. Just give me a cigarette. Don't give me a lecture."

Tex threw a rolled cigarette across the room to Mother. It landed on the bed.

"Faggot's gone, huh?"

Tex stepped into his cowboy boots.

"TEX."

"Yep."

"When did he go?"

"I don't know. I think it must have been about 8:00 o'clock."

"It should have been 8:00 o'clock," Mother said to himself.

"Maybe later. He woke me up."

"But he's always late." Mother put his elbow on his thigh and turned away from Tex.

80

"Where'd he go, Motherfucker?"

"That's none of your business." Mother lit the cigarette and inhaled delicately. His eyes shifted over his shoulder. They were half-closed. "When are you goin'?"

"That's none of your goddamn business, Motherfucker." Tex wriggled back and forth in front of Mother's doorway. "My, my aren't you touchy this morning, you poor baby. You sleep up there in your big brass bed and you get touchy when you wake up at noontime and don't know what the fuck from four hours ago."

"Tex, you were upstairs already, weren't you?"

"Yeah, so what? So was Faggot and Salamander and Mushmouth." Tex stopped wriggling his ass around. "Why? You afraid I'm gonna steal your razor or something?"

Mother slid off the bed and stared at Tex from the undersides of his eyelids. "I hadn't thought about it," he said, "but now I will." He turned his back and lifted his shirt off the bedpost. He walked deliberately in front of Tex. Barefoot he walked up the stairs smoking his cigarette and carrying his shirt over his arm.

"Mother. Hey, Mother," Tex called.

Mother didn't turn around. Tex heard him open the bathroom door.

"Hey, Motherfucker," Tex yelled. "Fuck you."

Upstairs Mushmouth turned over in his mattress on the floor. He hated to get up because today he promised Salamander he would go to the Vancouver Library and start looking up suitable aliases for himself. He needed a new name if he wanted to get some kind of temporary work. He groaned in his bed. He had so few points towards getting landed.

Through the grate in the hall Tex heard the sound of running water. "Jesus, that Motherfucker's going to take a bath." He went into the kitchen and poked around the cabinets. There was some rice and a loaf of stale bread. Somebody had left the bag open and the first few slices were hard.

He opened the refrigerator and brought out a brown bag. It was a half pound of sliced salami that belonged to Salamander. The bag said, "Fuck off. Keep your fucking hands off my food. Fuck you." Tex peeled off three slices and put the first one in his mouth. He went to the window and pushed the plastic drapes aside. Outside he could see the Voice of China Radio station. "Funny," he thought. "You never see any Chinese go in or out of there." Tex dropped the curtain and looked at the fry pan in the sink. He wanted bacon and eggs for breakfast. With toast. Who was the dumbass who left the fry pan in the sink? He went to the sink and ran water over it. He ate another slice of salami and congratulated Salamander on buying that brand. It wasn't bad stuff.

He shut the water off because he felt somebody was watching him. Mother was staring at him from the doorway. Tex could feel the last slice of salami sweating into his hand. They said nothing to one another.

Tex turned back to the fry pan and Mother watched him clean it off and wipe it with the corner of a dirty dish towel.

"You know that Faggot used my razor this

morning," Mother said.

Tex kept wiping away at the inside of the pan with the dirty dish towel.

"I can't stand to have anybody use my razor."

Tex walked to the stove and put the pan on the largest burner. It was the only one that worked. When Faggot first got the stove, it was possible to have either burner on high or on low, but never both at the same time. Now only the left-hand burner worked.

"And if he has to use my razor why can't he clean it off? Why does he have to be such a slob? I can't stand a dirty razor. Especially before I eat breakfast. It ruins my whole day."

"Maybe you shouldn't shave then. Maybe you should grow a beard," Tex suggested.

"I've done it before," Mother snarled. "And I didn't like it." Motherfucker was glum again. "Did you eat anything?"

Tex closed his fist over the salami slice. "Nope."

"Is there anything to eat?"

"Nope."

"Did you look?" Mother's voice drilled a hole into the kitchen wall.

"Nope."

"Well, there's bread in the cabinet."

"I didn't know that," Tex said.

"Sure." Mother nodded at the cabinets. On the bottom door someone had written, "Fuck off. Leave my fucking food alone. Fuck you," in red letters an inch high. "There's bread left over from last night. We can have toast. And then when Mushmouth gets up, we'll see if he has any money on him. We'll have eggs."

83

"Mushmouth doesn't have any money," Tex said. "He gave the rest of it to Faggot last night."

"How do you know?" Mother had his hands on the sides of the doorway and leaned forward like he was going to take the doorway with him.

"'Cause I was there. I saw Mushmouth give over the last. He doesn't have any more. Where did Faggot go so early this morning?"

Mother shifted himself around in the doorway. He was the only person in the world who could be more comfortable in a doorway than in a chair. "He went to see an employment agent who can get him a good job. No more part-time shit like the record store he got landed on. I hope he took all his recommendations with him. You know what, Tex?" Mother drove his eyes into him. "You're going to buy breakfast today. I'd help you," he shrugged, "but I bought it yesterday and I don't have any money." His eyes tightened. "I don't even have cigarette money."

Tex looked back at him in the doorway. "All right," he said. "That's fair. I can understand that. But Faggot'll buy supper."

Mother took his eyes off Tex for a second and Tex slipped the salami into his mouth. His face didn't move. He took out his cigarette papers and started another cigarette. He watched Mother watching him from the doorway. He smiled and threw the cigarette to Mother who caught it easily in one hand. "It comes with breakfast," Tex said.

Mother looked Tex in the eye and nodded. He stepped out of the doorway to let Tex through, then followed him to the front porch and watched him go down the three steps and through the gate. "Where you going to buy it?" he wanted to know.

"Leonard's," Tex said as he turned out the gate and started down the street.

"Tex. Hey, Texas. Buy cheese." Mother wanted to be sure Tex heard. He grunted in disgust. Tex wasn't in a rush for anything. That was his problem. He would never turn around and ask, "What do you want cheese for?" or "What kind of cheese do you want?"

"The trouble with people like Tex," Motherfucker thought as he shook out a chair and sat down on the porch, "is that they have no imagination. They have to be told everything." If he'd been Tex he would have asked, "What kind of an omelet are you going to make?"

When Motherfucker and Tex were finishing their morning cigarette routine, Mushmouth had come downstairs. He was wearing his vest and his pinstripe shirt. "Hi, Mother," he said barging through the front door. Because he didn't smoke he had less to do with Motherfucker than anybody else in that house except Salamander who told Motherfucker to his face that he wasn't exactly crazy about him. "Where's he going?" Mushmouth asked, waving one hand up the street after Tex and fumbling around with his glasses with the other.

"To buy eggs."

"Hey, Mother, did Faggot go this morning?" Mushmouth was polishing his glasses with his handkerchief and leaning over the porch railing at the same time.

"Yeah."

85

"Goodie. Boy, I was afraid he'd oversleep or something." Carefully Mushmouth placed his glasses on his nose. He checked to make sure the wire frames fitted securely behind his ears. "It's a nice morning, isn't it?" he said shaking the lilac bush.

Motherfucker didn't answer. Mushmouth picked some dead lilac blossoms off the front of his shirt. He turned around. Motherfucker was gone. He'd probably been gone since he said hello to him.

"Boy, I wish Doreen was here," Mushmouth said aloud. He broke off a lilac branch and beat the railing. He scuffed around the porch in a pair of boots that looked expensive once. He fished around in the side pocket of his bell bottom jeans. He pulled twenty-five cents out of his pocket. Two nickels, a dime and five pennies. He threw the lilac branch over the railing.

"What took you so long?" Motherfucker demanded to know when Tex came through the kitchen door with a bag of groceries. "I know. I know. The old man is dying every minute--but he usually takes quicker than this to find everything."

"Well, today he was having trouble adding it all up on his little machine," Tex said.

"That's because he's got a little brain, littler than yours. Did you get the cheese?"

Tex took it out of the bag and waved it back and forth. He threw it on the table and started to roll his sleeves up. "Now, you want to leave me alone while I make breakfast or do you want to make breakfast while I leave you alone?"

Mother melted into the living room. Tex broke a dozen eggs into a large mixing bowl. He shook the silverware box on the floor, noted a few pieces he particularly liked, and picked out the lightest fork. Mother could have cut the cheese or made toast but Tex didn't want to be watched. Even when he worked as a short-order cook, he didn't like anybody standing over him and watching. He put each of the broken egg shells back in the egg carton. He cracked nine of the twelve eggs perfectly. It made him nervous to have Mother in the same room with him.

He dropped a chunk of butter in the pan and waited for it to bubble. In a few minutes he knew that Mother would be in the doorway smelling the eggs. He bent his wrist and the eggs slid into the pan. "He's waiting for me to fuck up." Tex waited with the fork in his hand.

The sound of the eggs muted other noises. Tex turned around and saw Mother take plates from the cabinets above the sink.

"Mushmouth is eating?"

"Yep."

"Is there anything to drink, Tex?"

"I bought milk."

"That was nice of you." Mother took three cups from the cupboard. Tex turned around to see Mother's face but his back was turned to him.

Tex scraped the sides of the pan. He watched the egg fall into holes behind the fork. He lanced the eggs again and again and when they had scarred and re-healed, he spooned them into the three plates. "If you want to be useful," Tex said, "you can tell Mushmouth that breakfast's ready."

Mushmouth came in eating a Mars bar. Mother

looked up expectantly but Mushmouth ate the last bite out of the paper. He tossed the wrapper into the egg carton and dumped the whole business on top of the rest of the garbage beside the stove.

Single-file they followed each other to the porch. Tex sat down in the wicker chair where Faggot always sat. Mother sat in Tex's kitchen chair. Mushmouth leaned against the wall of the house, holding his plate under his chin and shoveling eggs in with a spoon. He didn't like forks.

Tex leaned back in his chair and looked up at the sky. "It's a mighty pretty day," he said.

Mushmouth balanced his plate on the railing and got out his handkerchief. "Those eggs were good," he said. "Why don't you do all the cooking around here?"

Tex laughed. He was rolling two cigarettes. Automatically he handed one to Mother whose hand was already outstretched for it. "Because I have to get it all together again and all," Tex said. "I have to start doing the right things again."

"When are you going to go?" Mushmouth asked.

"I don't know. Maybe tomorrow. Maybe the next day." Tex gave a side glance at Mother who was getting up to bring his plate to the kitchen. "Before my money's gone."

"Do you think you can get landed in Regina?"

Tex laughed. "Boy, there's one thing I know. I can't get landed here."

Mushmouth broke off another lilac branch and began hitting the wall with it.

"Boy, just look at what you're doing to that lilac bush. You've chewed up half of it already. Now that's no way to treat nature."

Mushmouth stared at the lilac bush.

Motherfucker came back with the Warren Report. He pulled his chair to the other side of the porch and began to read.

"Shit. I don't know," Mushmouth said. He threw the branch over the railing and went inside.

Tex went into the garden and hunted around until he found the perfect blade of grass. He was just breaking it in when Mushmouth came back outside. He was wearing his camera. He told Tex he was going to the library to look up birth records and take a few pictures. Tex nodded and watched the end of his grass wag up and down. "Have a good time, boy," he said. "Write if you get work." Motherfucker didn't look up from his book.

Mushmouth bounced down the three steps and stopped in the middle of the walk. He turned around and ran back to the porch. "Gee whiz," he said. "Oh shit." He handed Tex and Motherfucker a penny piece of licorice each. "It's for the afternoon."

Tex nodded to him as he went down the steps. Mushmouth opened the gate and said, "Bye. See you guys later."

Motherfucker put the book down. "Wait."

Mushmouth froze with one hand on the top of the gate. He looked behind him without moving the rest of his body.

"Did Salamander go to work this morning?"

"Yup," Mushmouth said shaking his head so fast his hair fell over his face. "Yeah, it was his first day. That's why he went to bed early last night. He had to

be at the Canadian Imperial Bank for 8:00 o'clock."
Mushmouth waited with one hand on the gate but
Motherfucker didn't have anything else to say. He
picked up his book and said, "Hmph," to himself. Tex
waved good-bye from the porch and Mushmouth let
the gate fall shut.

When Mushmouth went to the library he usually
made a whole day of it. Nobody really knew what he
did in there, except maybe Salamander who believed
in keeping his mouth shut about other people's
business. Especially when he lived with what he called
a bunch of half-assed rip-off dipshits. He said he
didn't know how anybody could be interested in what
a half-assed dipshit did with his day unless it was
another half-assed dipshit who was asking.

Salamander was working at the Bank and Faggot
was working at finding a job and Mushmouth was
busy keeping busy until Doreen came. Tex was busy
doing nothing and Motherfucker could keep himself
happy all day minding the house and not talking to
anybody. He liked that.

So during the afternoon Tex and Mother did very
little except make each other nervous. Tex chewed up
three or four pieces of grass. After a while he let
Mother smoke as many of his cigarettes he wanted as
long as he made them. Tex looked up and down the
street "looking for things" he said while Motherfucker
tried his best to ignore him.

Motherfucker said he was tired of Tex and went
inside in the afternoon. In the late afternoon he got
hungry and then tired. He tried playing some of
Salamander's records for a while but it didn't take

away his hunger. Then he played guitar on his bed and wound up taking a nap.

Tex spent the whole afternoon sitting in the kitchen chair watching people from the porch. He had a rush of activity around 12:30-1:00 o'clock when people on their lunch hour came down from Broadway to buy soft drinks in Leonard's or use the phone in The Trade Winds. He was busy for the full hour with all the comings and goings on the street.

After lunch hour Tex inspected all the cars on the street and decided which ones he would or would not steal. At one point he was advanced enough in his thinking about an MG Midget that he was driving through Banff along the Trans-Canada. Right around this time Mother got hungry again and woke up. He wanted cigarettes all the time. Tex said he was the most difficult person to be with in all of Canada. He said it made him glad he hadn't stolen the MG because he couldn't bear the thought of having to be cooped up in the same jail with Motherfucker. "Boy, you just have to learn to control that restlessness," he told Motherfucker but Mother didn't take any notice.

Later on Tex got involved with the people who came back from work and got in their cars and drove off. He watched for the owner of the MG but he went to the bathroom sometime around 5:00 o'clock and missed whoever came for it. Sometimes he thought a man owned it and sometimes he thought it might be a woman with patent leather boots and tiny kid gloves. For a while he thought about the man and for a while he thought about the woman. But he couldn't get anywhere thinking about either one because

Motherfucker started waiting for Faggot.

But Mushmouth came home first. "That figures," Tex said, "because he doesn't have a job and if he comes home too late, he might miss Faggot and Salamander who do." Motherfucker said Salamander and Mushmouth didn't count. Only Faggot counted. Tex disagreed and said, "You can never tell who counts."

Mushmouth jumped up the steps and shouted, "Hi," as he went through the house and upstairs. Tex opened his mouth to say something but Mushmouth was gone. He listened and heard the toilet flush. Then Mushmouth came bouncing down the stairs like Peter Cottontail and burst through the porch door. Mother recoiled in his corner. "Boy, what a day I had! I was watching this girl with blond hair and her girlfriend all afternoon. And I looked up about a hundred names and I had three Mars bars. Boy, Canada's great."

"Are there a lot of girls in the library?" Tex asked.

"Are there a lot of girls? The place is loaded with girls. The place is loaded with Canadian girls."

Mother dropped the Warren Report into his lap.

"Look, I go in there, right, and I don't know where the birth records are or anything so I ask this girl. Well, this girl doesn't know so she asks her girlfriend. Then we all go and ask this librarian who sits behind this little desk and she takes us to the birth records. And then these two girls help me look up all the birthdays. And then we went into the Reading Room and then we went to this patio outside with tables and chairs. It was really nice there." Mushmouth pulled out his handkerchief and started to rub his nose. "One is a Pisces and one is a Gemini," he said from behind his handkerchief. "I talked to the blond one, the Pisces, for twenty-five minutes. She was really nice. You know, I didn't tell her I was a deserter or anything."

"Why not?" Tex asked. "You tell everybody else."

"Because I didn't want to scare her away or anything. She was just a young girl, you know."

"How young?" Motherfucker asked.

"Oh, I don't know." Mushmouth threw his hands up in the air. "About fifteen or sixteen."

Tex hissed through his one front tooth. "You should have told her how you ran away from the United States Navy and all. How you jumped ship and escaped with your life. Girls, they like that kind of thing. Especially when they're only fifteen and sixteen."

Motherfucker picked up his Warren Report. "Oh, c'mon, Tex. They're not stupid, you know. Just young."

Mushmouth broke off another lilac branch and let the bush swing free.

"LEAVE THAT BUSH ALONE," Motherfucker said.

Mushmouth dropped his branch. "Jesus," he said.

"What else happened in the library? Did you get a new name?"

"I have to go back to look up some more records." Mushmouth kept moving around to get a better view of the street. He was waiting for Salamander. "It's one helluva pain in the ass, you know that?" He looked at

Tex. "How's this for a name? Daniel C. Farbus. I tried it out for a couple of hours this afternoon but I don't think I could stand people calling me Dan or Danny. Then I found this one. Listen. Chadwick Bowering. Distinguished isn't it? Then there's this one. Mark. J. Whittaker. I like it because it's close to my real name but then I realized they'd ask me for my name and I'd blow it."

"You gotta pick a name you can feel comfortable with. It's gotta fit you," Tex suggested. "Like a glove."

"Yeah. So what do you do? Walk up and down the street saying over and over, 'My name is----.   I was born----. My mother's name is ----.' That could drive a person crazy." Motherfucker groaned. "Yeah, well, it could," Mushmouth told him. "After a couple of days of that I'd wonder just who the hell I was anyway. I'd get up in the morning and stand in front of the mirror and say, 'Okay, Mark, Simon, Paul, John, haul ass. George, Steven, David, Peter, Robert WHO ARE YOU?' I'd say, 'Answer me, WHO ARE YOU TODAY?'" He was waving his arms around and beginning to drool.

"Lord," Tex said. "Take it easy, boy."

"'Take it easy,' he says," Mushmouth repeated. "I gotta get a name if I want to stay here. I gotta..."

"Do you think that girl will be there tomorrow?" Motherfucker asked.

"Girls. You ask me about girls when I need a name." Mushmouth rolled his eyes to the sky. "Girls. There's a million girls in there."

"You don't want one of those girls," Tex said. "They're all part of the bourgeoiset."

"Don't tell me what I want." Motherfucker smacked the Warren Report against the side of his chair. "Don't tell anybody anything around here."

Tex shut up.

Mushmouth stayed on his side of the porch near the lilac bush. "She said she might come tomorrow but maybe her girlfriend won't want to. If her girlfriend doesn't want to go, they'll probably stay home. Girls always do what their girlfriends want to do." He swallowed. "Hey, Tex, what do you think of this one? Leslie Ross." He said each letter slowly and spoke very clearly. "L-E-S-L-I-E-R-O-S-S."

"It sounds like a Jewish name to me," Tex said. "What the fuck do you want to be Jewish for?"

"Oh fuck you," Mushmouth exploded. "What do you know? And you..." He pointed at Motherfucker and ran into the house before Mother could get out of his chair.

Mushmouth went upstairs and lay down on his mattress in the room he shared with Salamander. He tried to sort through the various names he had discovered in the afternoon and he tried to remember exactly what the blond girl looked like and what she said and how he felt when he sat with her at the table in the courtyard at the back of the library. Then he took the picture of Doreen out of his wallet and counted off the days until she came on a pocket-size calendar from a Wells Fargo Bank.

Tex kept himself quiet on the porch. Motherfucker didn't talk to him. He'd had just about enough of Tex for one day. He was staring at the overpass at the corner of the street leading to the bridge that crosses the water to downtown Vancouver. Mother was thinking how Leonard must have had a heart attack when he first found out about their plans for the ramp. "Christ." Tex looked at him sideways but kept chewing. "A miniature expressway on the front lawn," Mother said.

Tex leaned sideways to get a good look and saw Salamander coming out of the shadows near The Trade Winds. He was wearing his black suit. His beard and moustache were gone. His hair was very short. The only outlandish thing about him was a skinny black ribbon tied around his neck that passed for a necktie. He looked like Maverick or a Doc Holliday anyway.

"Lord," Tex said as Salamander came through the gate. "Sweet Lord Jesus."

"Shut up. You're a fuck-up." Salamander said as he walked past Tex who was standing up to let him by.

"Did you see that" Tex asked Mother. His eyes were glued to the spot in the doorway where Salamander passed.

"Next Faggot comes and we can get this show on the road," Mother said.

Tex settled back in his chair and rolled two cigarettes.

In fifteen minutes Salamander came out on the porch in his yellow corduroys and a yellow T-shirt with pinprick holes in the sleeves. He didn't say anything to anybody but left the porch and walked directly down the stairs. Mushmouth came three seconds behind him, talking and waving his arms and calling to Salamander to wait.

"Where are they going?" Tex asked himself since Motherfucker stopped talking directly to him sometime in the afternoon.

Mushmouth followed Salamander to the empty lot across the street. Tex tried to keep track of them but the grass was so high he lost sight of them.

About 7:30 Faggot's car pulled up in front of the house. The motor stopped and the door opened. A few seconds later a Faggot came out carrying a portfolio under his arm. He walked up the path smoking a cigarette from a new pack sticking out of his shirt pocket.

Mother looked at him expectantly. Faggot waved to Tex and Tex got out of the chair. Faggot sat down and threw the cigarettes to Motherfucker. "I showed them my recommendations." He tapped the folder on his knee. Mother lit a Sportsman and put the cigarettes in his lap. "And I have a lot of experience from where I worked before. I spoke to this agent and he thinks it should just be a matter of time until I hear from them. Then he called up this guy who owns these stereo stores and we went down there and talked to him and then we went over to the store and it looks pretty good. It's salary and commission." Faggot was playing with the edges of his recommendations and shoving them in and out of the folder with his fingers. "This guy Stanley was all right. He plays flute so we had a lot to talk about." He took a drag off his cigarette and looked at the end. "I think I could really like it." He stopped talking and looked around. "Where are the kids?"

Mother pointed to the empty lot across the street.

"They're playing over there."

"Go get them and we'll eat." Faggot flipped the butt into the garden. "I'm starved." He went into the house and changed his clothes. He came out wearing his fifty-cent Salvation Army pants that he always said were the best fitting pair of pants he ever had. Faggot stood in the doorway all dressed up for supper and looked at Tex who was sitting down again in the wicker chair. "You're still here," he said. "I thought you might have left."

Motherfucker was standing over Tex's chair. He was animated for the first time all day. He was on his second Sportsman. He was leering at Tex while ashes dropped from his cigarette onto Tex's leopard hat.

Tex smiled at Motherfucker and at Faggot in the doorway. "Yep. Still here. Didn't go nowhere today."

Faggot threw him a store-bought cigarette but Tex shook his head and shut his eyes. "I like the ones I make myself," he said.

Faggot groaned and looked at Tex like he was truly retarded. Motherfucker broke out into one of his rare, brief grins.

Faggot whistled and Mushmouth and Salamander came out of the woods across the street. Mushmouth was straggling behind Salamander who was striding across the street. Motherfucker was already opening the car door. Tex and Faggot walked to the car slowly and then everybody got in. Mother sat with Faggot in the front seat and the kids and Tex were in back. Usually Faggot went through his routine of leaving someone or everybody behind and then picking them up at the corner but tonight he was too hungry and it was too late.

In the car Mother told Faggot about his day. Mushmouth asked Faggot if he should be Leslie Ross. Salamander asked Mother to put the window up and Tex didn't ask anybody anything.

Faggot had the last pay check from his last job. Also, he had holiday pay so he gave Mushmouth back some of the money he had borrowed the night before and took out a new loan for the next day. That way they traded nickels and dimes and never got around to the big debts.

Salamander didn't have any money yet. Tex hoarded his and Mother would never have any to speak of. That meant when they went to a Dairy Queen Faggot bought ice cream for himself and Motherfucker. Mushmouth, who only had enough money for the day but not the evening, relied on Faggot's credit. Tex hung around looking at everybody until Faggot gave him thirty-five cents for a strawberry sundae with vanilla ice cream. Salamander stood off to the side until he couldn't stand it anymore. Then he went to Faggot and shook his head back and forth and looked at the ground and scuffed his feet. Faggot gave him a dollar no questions asked and Salamander said, "Thanks, I'll pay you when..." And Faggot had already waved his hand in the air and turned his back.

That night they went to a Chicken Delight Take-out Diner. Salamander bitched the whole way there and the whole time in the take-out line because he said it was a waste of money to buy over-priced, rip-off mutilated chicken parts. Finally Faggot told him it wasn't his money and to either shut up or go outside.

Faggot and Motherfucker waited for the chicken in the pick-up line and then Faggot drove to Stanley Park for a picnic. Faggot said it was a feast because Tex would be leaving. In the middle of the meal Salamander got jumpy and took off. Mushmouth watched him go but couldn't figure it out. Faggot put Mother out of the car after reaching into the chicken basket and pulling out the largest piece and stuffing it in his mouth. It made Motherfucker think of his dirty razor again and he said, "You know, Faggot, you put me off my dinner." Faggot laughed and waved a chicken part at Mother. Motherfucker ate the rest of his chicken in silent rage and then removed himself to a separate tree to be free from the company.

At this time Faggot took the opportunity of telling Tex point-blank that he would drive him to the road any day next week.

Mushmouth was watching all the flowers growing out of the cracks in the sidewalk. He was shuffling his feet counting the concrete pavers on the way to Leonard's. He'd walked that way so many times he thought he should know how many square feet of cement it was. It would be a useful fact to throw at Motherfucker if he had to throw something at him. He kept to the inside track in case he met another pair of shoes coming up the path. Mushmouth didn't see how that was possible since nobody walked around this time of day. It was in between rush hours.

"Jesus Christ, look where you're goin', boy." Mushmouth looked into a pair of cowboy boots. They belonged to Tex. "What are you walking around like a mole in daylight for? Can't you see now?"

"You walked into me. What did you get at Leonard's?"

"Package of Export "A" papers."

"Do you know what the "A" is for?"

"Nope. Do you?"

"No." Mushmouth stuffed a flower back down its crack with his boot tip. "How is Leonard today, Tex?"

"Oh, the same as usual. You know, half-dead."

"Yeah. Tex, do you think he'll die before the summer's over?"

"Why? Are you fixing to buy the store when the old man croaks?" Tex brought out his cigarette makings and unsealed the brand-new package of Export "A" wrappers. "You know, you only get the twenty points for starting your own business. I don't know about taking over somebody else's business. But then again," Tex tilted his head and the leopard hat moved, "it seems a lot easier than starting a movie house with Faggot."

"Yeah," Mushmouth said. "But it'd cost a lot of money to buy a handy store."

Tex watched Mushmouth take out his handkerchief and wipe around his nose and mouth but he didn't say anything. Even Salamander remarked that he could be very polite.

"What are you gonna buy in there today?" Tex asked.

"Oh, a candy bar. Maybe a Mars bar. That's a dime. And five pieces of penny candy. Two of those five pieces will be licorice. I feel like black licorice today."

Tex whistled through the hole in his mouth. "Boy, your teeth are gonna rot. The way you eat candy every day."

"I know," Mushmouth said. He shut his eyes. "I know. But I can't help it. I'd rather eat candy than anything else and since I've come up here in April I've been too nervous to eat anything else. Besides, who could eat that shit at the hostel?"

Tex cupped his hand and lit his cigarette. "Well, it wasn't so bad when Mark cooked. He wasn't all that bad of a cook, you know. Anything was good as long as Breeze and George stayed away from it." Tex made the first move towards going back to his chair on the porch.

Mushmouth grabbed his sleeve. "Hey, wait a minute, Tex. Do you remember that guy who used to make meat loaf all the time? He was in the first hostel and he cooked for about two weeks. Really gruesome meat loaf and he put pepper all over everything. In the hostel before the church. Yeah, well, what was his name?"

"Bob?"

"No," that was his friend." Mushmouth was getting excited. He started to shake up and down. Tex expected him to shake his hands back and forth like rattles.

"Um. Um." Tex looked up at the sky. "You mean Jake?"

"Yeah. Jake." Mushmouth puffed out his cheeks and blew out. A thin spray of spit leaked out. Then he calmed down. "Yeah. What happened to Jake? Last night I was trying to go over in my mind all the people that were in the different hostels with me and I couldn't remember what happened to him."

"Oh, he had a really interesting thing happen to him." Tex took off his hat and scratched the top of his head. "It seems he took on somebody else's name and hitched to Regina to get landed. He was in Alberta, you know, when they picked him up. They asked him as nice as you please for his name and ID and all. And he gives 'em all his fake papers with his brand-new name he's picked out for himself." He started to chuckle. "Well, as things turn out his new name belongs to a guy who's wanted for murder. Killed his wife or somebody." Tex was laughing. "Boy, were those cops pleased as punch. We been looking a long time for you," they said.

"Then what happened?" Mushmouth leaned forward. He was chewing on his bottom lip. "Do you know what happened to him then?"

"Nope."

"Do you know what they did to him?"

"Nope."

"What would you have done, Tex. If you were him?"

"That's a tough question." Tex shook his head. "Boy, that's a ticklish one. Well, I don't know." He looked at Mushmouth. "I don't know what I would a done, boy. You'd need a lot of presence of mind." He squinted at the sky. "It's gonna be a real scorcher today."

Mushmouth tugged at Tex's sleeve again. Tex looked down at the hand on his body. "Tex, is it true you got a lot of money from your mother or somebody?"

"Who told you that?" Tex grabbed Mushmouth's arm. "Who told..."

"I heard it in the hostel. There was something about you getting some money or something. Did you?"

Tex shook Mushmouth's arm back and forth gently as if it was a roasted chicken leg he was testing instead of an arm. "Now maybe I did and maybe I didn't." He leered into Mushmouth's face. "But if I was you, boy, I wouldn't let on one way or the other. 'Cause, Mushmouth, there's many a man who came to grief on account of a big mouth."

"I know. I was just wondering if..."

"Well, you don't have to worry no more." Tex picked a piece of dirt off Mushmouth's shirt. "I got a check for three hundred dollars and a deed for five hundred acres of Texas bottom land." His fingers closed over Mushmouth's arm.

"I won't say nothing." Mushmouth held up his free hand and swore. "Cross my heart, hope to die."

CHEVRON ISLAND

This Tuesday the sun didn't shine into Mother's bedroom through the cracked window by Faggot's collapsible bed. Tex blinked at Salamander's tadpoles poking around in the bottom of their tank. He smiled when he remembered how Mother turned off the pump every night before he went to bed--except for the nights when he was too drunk to even undress himself.

He stared at the ceiling in the darkened hall with a cigarette between his lips. He rested his cheek on his arm and looked across at the Faggot fast asleep in his yellow baby blanket. Faggot said he couldn't wait to get him and Jimmy out so he could move his collapsible bed upstairs.

Tex rolled on his side and raised himself up on one elbow. At the same time he was trying to get away from his cigarette smoke, he reached beside him for his duffel bag. He wanted to be sure he had his favorite pieces of silverware. In the middle of the night he had gotten up and taken them from the kitchen cabinets. His fingers closed around the paring knife he had found lying in the sink. He figured it was 8:00 o'clock. Silently he lowered the bag to the floor.

He wanted an early start but then he relaxed. "No use rushing."

Tex looked across the room again at Faggot. His eyes followed the contours of Faggot's body, half-hidden under the yellow blanket caught around his feet. "Yep, Faggot'll get up soon and then there'll be breakfast and plenty of time." He brushed away the ashes on his chest. He stretched--just as his muscles were beginning to relax, he thought about the weather. He hoped it wouldn't rain.

Tex didn't fall back asleep that morning. For the next two hours he lay on his back and smoked the cigarettes he made for himself in the dark and sorted out his life. Once he heard Motherfucker groan in his sleep and somebody, maybe Salamander, piss in the toilet. When it got lighter, he watched the fish in the aquarium on the window sill nearest Motherfucker's brass bed. Then when Salamander came downstairs for his secret breakfast of Vita-B from his special cabinet, he pretended to sleep.

Around 10:30 Faggot woke himself up and headed straight for the bathroom. He waved a peace sign at Tex but Tex was still pretending to be asleep. Faggot woke up Mushmouth when Motherfucker's razor fell out of his hands. When Tex heard Mushmouth asking Faggot what the fuck was going on, he put on his jeans and started rolling up his sleeping bag.

The only one still asleep was Motherfucker. Faggot fixed that when he came downstairs. "C'mon, boy, haul ass, haul ass. Big Day. BIG DAY. Are you coming or what's the story?"

Tex watched Faggot jerk Motherfucker's blanket

out of his hand where it was clutched tightly under his chin. "Hey, what...?"

"Big Day, Motherfucker. Haul Ass."

"What the fuck," Mother said pulling the blanket out of Faggot's hands and sitting up in bed. "What the...?" He caught sight of Tex standing in the living room doorway and he slid out of bed. He stood in the middle of the room for a second rubbing his hand across his mouth.

"C'mon, boy," Faggot said.

Mother said, "Shit," and walked barefoot out of the room. Halfway up the stairs he yelled down to Faggot, "You know you could make a little less noise in the morning."

"Boo," Faggot said. "Tut. Tut."

Mother turned around and bumped into Mushmouth. Motherfucker's arms went out to grab him but Mushmouth escaped.

"Whew," Mushmouth said at the foot of the stairs looking from room to room to see where Faggot was.

"What's the matter with you so early in the morning?" Tex asked.

"Nothing. I just escaped from the meanest motherfucker of them all. I guess nobody's eaten yet, have they?"

"Well, if that Motherfucker nearly killed you for nothing, it means nobody's eaten, right?"

"I guess so," Mushmouth said.

Tex went into the kitchen to start breakfast. He wanted eggs and toast. Mushmouth, who was wearing the same clothes he had on yesterday, followed him to the stove.

Faggot was wandering all over the house looking for his shoe or his sock. He didn't know which. Sometimes he left his shoes or his socks or both of them on the front porch to air out. Now he couldn't find either thing.

"Has anybody seen my other sock?" Faggot asked in his third trip through the kitchen. He stopped at the table and stuck a slice of Wonder Bread in his mouth. "I can't find my other sock." He had one sock on and one shoe on his other bare foot. He was holding the other shoe in his hand. "I can't find my socks," he was saying.

Tex was measuring the eggs and adding salt and pepper. Mushmouth was two inches behind him and getting in his way. Tex liked to make breakfast. He said he made a better breakfast than anybody he knew, including Motherfucker.

"Mushmouth, go out and look for my other sock. Look behind the lilac bush. I can't find my sock," Faggot said.

"I want to stay here," Mushmouth said. "I'm talking to Tex."

"You're not talking to him. You're bugging his ass. Now go out to the lilac bush and find my other sock."

"Oh, gee whiz," Mushmouth said crumbling an egg shell in his hands and throwing it at the garbage pile.

"And if it's not behind the lilac bush," Faggot yelled. "Check in my car. What are you making for breakfast?"

"Eggs."

"Mmm," said Faggot sitting on a kitchen chair,

crossing his legs and holding his bare foot in his hands.

Mother came into the kitchen doorway with a full report on Mushmouth. "That kid's fiddling around with the car."

" I know," said Faggot. "I sent him."

Tex stood at the stove with his back to everyone. He was making the eggs and sampling them from time to time. When he put the fork in his mouth, Motherfucker burst out of the doorway. "TEX. Don't put that in your mouth. You'll get the food dirty."

"Oh, don't worry about it," Faggot said. "You can't get a venereal disease that way."

"I'm not worried about any venereal disease," Motherfucker said. "I just don't want my eggs ruined."

"But," Faggot said, "if Tex has syphilis, it's so far advanced into his brain it's not contagious."

Tex shut the stove off and put the fry pan on the table. Everyone helped himself. Faggot picked another slice of Wonder Bread out of the bag and scooped some eggs on top of it and ate them that way. Motherfucker rapped his knife across Tex's knuckles when Tex tried to eat from the pan before he'd chosen what he wanted on his new clean plate. Then Tex picked up the fry pan and started to eat what was left.

"I can't find your fucking sock in no lilac bush. Why can't you keep them in your shoes like everybody else?" Mushmouth shouted coming into the house. "Why do you have to drop them everywhere you go? Jesus Christ." Mushmouth barged into the kitchen holding a sock at arm's length. He threw it at Faggot. "It was in the glove compartment. It has rigor mortis and it smells." It landed on top of the Wonder Bread.

"Feh," said F'aggot pushing it off three exposed pieces of bread. He picked it up by the toe and held it over his nose. He sniffed very cautiously. His nose wrinkled up and he said, "It would have been better if it fell in the lilacs."

"Oh, Jesus Christ," said Mushmouth. "Hey, where's my breakfast? Did you fatasses eat up everything while I was outside digging up dead socks? Hey." He grabbed the fry pan out of Tex's hands. Tex let it go and watched Mushmouth nearly break his neck tripping backwards. Faggot caught him and held him on his lap for a second.

"Just take it easy for a minute, will you," Faggot said. He gave Mushmouth the three slices of bread that touched his sock and whipped the loaf of bread away. He swung it around his head a couple of times until the neck of the bag was twisted up tight and then he tossed it on the counter near Salamander's cabinet. He clapped his hands together twice and said, "Okay, boys and girls. Let's move."

Mushmouth picked at Faggot's leftover eggs with his spoon. Motherfucker was still eating quietly in his corner of the kitchen. Nobody could make him rush his breakfast.

"Do you know where you're going, Tex?" Mushmouth asked, his mouth full of eggs that were scrambling out the sides of his mouth.

"What? What d'you say, boy?" Tex looked at Faggot and moved his head. "For Chrissake, boy, I can't understand you when you've got nothing in your mouth, never mind when you got a mouthful."

"I said," said Mushmouth, "do you know where you're going?" He spoke as clearly as he could with half a slice of Wonder Bread stuffed in his mouth and another ragged half ready to stick in as soon as there was space.

Mother made a three-quarter turn in his corner and cut Mushmouth out of his field of vision.

Mushmouth pushed some egg pieces back in his mouth and looked at Tex while he chewed with his mouth open.

"No."

"You mean you're just going to go away? You're just gonna stick out your thumb and go wherever they take you?" Mushmouth asked.

"Yep."

Mushmouth turned to Faggot and said, "He says he doesn't know where he's going. He's just disappearing."

Mother got up and put his dish in the sink. When Salamander wasn't around Mother actually picked up after himself and washed things. Tex started to eat a half slice of toast that Mother left on the table.

"But, Tex, don't you have any idea about where you're going? You can't go nowhere. You don't just disappear. People don't do that. You must have some idea."

"Nope."

"You mean you're just going out to the road and...and..." Mushmouth waved his hands looking for some words to say what he meant.

"Yep."

Mushmouth looked away and then stood up in

front of Tex. "Do you know what you're doing?"

Faggot laughed.

Tex began to roll his after breakfast cigarette. "It doesn't matter," he said.

"How can you say it doesn't matter?" Mushmouth was jumping up and down in front of Tex who was pulling his arms closer to his body so he wouldn't spill any of his tobacco.

Mushmouth was angry and excited and genuinely upset that Tex was leaving. It upset the equilibrium. It challenged permanence and it said that people dissolve, that they can melt away into nothing. He didn't want to believe that. He didn't want to believe that even if it was only Tex who was dissolving.

Faggot bent down and put his sock on. "We'll leave in a few minutes, okay?" He went upstairs to the bathroom.

"Sure," said Tex.

"Sure." Faggot mimicked Tex in his Southern cracker drawl. "Sure, boy, we leave directly. You tell 'em in Regina." Then he left the room giggling to himself all the way upstairs. They could hear him laughing in the bathroom until the toilet flushed and blocked him out.

Mushmouth stayed by the table and looked at Tex. "You know, you must have some idea. Some idea about what you're going to do or where you're going to do it or how or...something?"

"Nope." Tex leaned against the stove. "How can I know what I'm going to do until it's time to do it? You know, you don't get to know what's gonna happen to you until it happens." He smiled and went into the other room for his duffel bag.

He came back into the kitchen wearing his crazy hat with the fake leopard skin hatband. Mushmouth was standing by the table looking troubled. He was kicking the table leg with his boot.

"You coming, boy?" Tex asked. "Are you coming for the ride?"

"Sure," Mushmouth said. He brightened up. "Sure."

Tex stood opposite the table shaking his head up and down with his crazy hat on his head. He was smiling at Mushmouth. "Sure," he said. "Sure you'll come." He put his arm around Mushmouth's shoulders and walked him to the kitchen door. "Sure you'll come." Then he laughed and Mushmouth laughed back at him.

Mother came into the kitchen then and saw Tex and Mushmouth laughing at one another. He said, "Holy shit," under his breath and left the room.

Faggot came down the stairs. "Who's ready to go?" he yelled. "Tex, are you ready now?"

Tex walked through the hall that used to be his bedroom and leaned up against the front door six inches away from Faggot. He was carrying his duffel bag in one hand and his sleeping bag was tucked under his other arm. He slipped his thumb under his belt buckle to get a firmer grip on his sleeping bag. "Man, you don't have to yell, you know," he said to Faggot who was standing on the bottom step of the stairs.

"Give me that bag, will you." Faggot snatched Tex's sleeping bag. "Motherfucker, are you coming or what?"

Motherfucker didn't answer but appeared from the living room and automatically went up to Tex and took his duffel bag. At first Tex held on to it but then he let go so Mother could carry it.

"Mushmouth..."

"He's coming," said Tex very quietly.

"Then let's get the fuck out of here," said Faggot.

Mushmouth ducked under Motherfucker's arm that was resting on the banister and raced ahead to open the front door and the car doors. Tex sat in back with Mushmouth. Motherfucker, of course, was up front with Faggot. Tex asked Mother to put the window up and he did it without any bitching.

Faggot made two stops. The first time he bought seventy-five cents worth of gas at the Chevron Island station where he usually took fifty cents worth. "I'm going on a long trip today," Faggot said to the attendant who was wearing a wreath of flowers around his neck.

"This is too much," said Tex.

"Yeah, it's far-out," said Motherfucker.

The station was decorated in imitation palm leaves. There were fake grass huts around the gas pumps and leis and flags flying around the "lubrication" sign. Big blue and red letters spelled out "Chevron Island."

"Do you always come here for gas?" Tex asked.

"What do you think?" Faggot answered. "I might win a free trip to Hawaii or five dancing girls or something."

"You couldn't take that trip even if you won it,"

Mushmouth said.

"Yeah, but he could take the five girls," Motherfucker said.

"Yeah, that's why I come here for gas. I want my fifty cents worth." Faggot rolled down his window and asked the attendant to check the oil. Motherfucker rolled his window down and asked the guy to check the left rear tire and wash the windshield.

Mushmouth asked Faggot for a quarter to buy an ice cream cone in a Peterson's Ice Cream Parlor across the street. Before he left he made Faggot promise he wouldn't leave without him. He said he'd never forgive Faggot if he did that and Faggot said, "Hurry up and get your ass out of here. Nobody's going anywhere." Mushmouth hurried across the street and came back with a double dip cone. Maple walnut on the bottom and chocolate chip brownie fudge on top. Motherfucker, who said he didn't know how anybody could eat ice cream so early in the morning and especially after a breakfast of eggs and toast, was the first one to grab the cone away from Mushmouth. He offered the maple walnut to Faggot. Faggot made a face. "Eech," he said. "I want a beer."

The attendant tried to get away without checking the air in the left rear tire but he thought twice about it when he looked through the windshield at the Mean Motherfucker in the front seat. He squeezed a blob of liquid cleaner over Motherfucker's face and began to scrub as hard as he could.

"Boy, there's a lot of weird things in this world," Tex said. "I don't know how anybody could think my hat is so weird."

"That's because you're wearing it," Motherfucker said through the rearview mirror.

"Now. Now," Faggot said slapping his hands against the steering wheel. "No fighting in the car, children." He looked around the station and moaned, "I want a beer. I want two beers and a new pair of socks."

"Give me a cigarette," Mother said to Tex.

Tex rolled Mother a cigarette at the same time Faggot rolled down his window and handed the attendant two quarters, four nickels and five pennies. He had to brace himself against the seat to get into his pocket for the nickels and the pennies. At first he only had three pennies but he smiled into the face of the attendant and arching his back triumphantly produced two pennies from his back pocket. He dropped the pennies into the attendant's greasy hand. "Thank you very much, Sir," he said in his best radio voice and rolled up the window.

The second time Faggot stopped he parked the car in front of a Chinese confectionary. Usually he made Mushmouth go into the store and buy what he wanted but this time he went in himself. They waited five minutes for him. Mushmouth got restless and wanted to get out to stretch his legs but Mother wouldn't let him. "Oh, let the kid go," Tex said but Motherfucker told him to mind his own business and worry about himself.

"I hope it doesn't rain," Mushmouth said pressing his nose against the window.

"Why don't you open the window, dumbass?" Mother asked.

"Oh, you. What do you know about looking out of windows?" Mushmouth shot back. "You're just a motherfucker. You think you know everything. Well, you don't. You don't know the first thing about whether or not it's going to rain."

Faggot got back in the car and broke open a new package of Matinees.

"That's the ladies' cigarette," said Motherfucker.

Faggot put down a brown paper bag on the seat beside him. After he inhaled a couple of times, he opened the bag with one hand and threw a package of Hostess Twinkies and two candy bars into the back seat. "Eat 'em later," he said. "That's when you get hungry."

"Thanks a lot, Boss," Tex said.

"I want a Mae West," Mushmouth said.

"You wouldn't know what to do with it," said Motherfucker.

They drove in silence for about fifteen minutes while they got away from the main traffic of the city and approached the highway. Tex smoked and looked easily out the window. Mushmouth sat beside him and wondered what Tex was doing. He stole glances at him whenever he thought nobody was looking. He looked at Tex's duffel bag sitting on the bump on the floor and he felt unbelievably depressed. He didn't understand it himself. He hated Tex.

Mother watched Faggot drive. He leaned forward in his seat and held onto the chrome around the small side window with his hand. He watched the road and the other cars, too.

They drove for another five minutes before they

made the turn onto the highway proper.

"I'll drive on a ways so you'll be sure to get a good lift," Faggot said.

"I appreciate it," said Tex.

"You holler whenever you see a good place."

"Sure."

Mushmouth looked out the window, watching for the good place, but his heart wasn't in it.

A couple of miles later, Tex said, "Over there. That's a good spot. There's a curve and some trees in case it rains."

Faggot slowed down and brought the car to a slow stop in the breakdown lane. He got out and opened the back door for Tex. He started to help with the bag but Tex already had it under control. Faggot followed Tex over to the side of the road anyway. About the same time Mother arrived with the sleeping bag and put it down on the ground.

Mushmouth didn't know what he wanted to do but he didn't want to stay alone in the car, either. In a very vague way he felt like crying but he knew he wouldn't feel any better if he did. He reminded himself he would feel ten times worse, especially for making an ass out of himself.

Faggot shook Tex's hand. He looked at him and said, "Write if you get work." Tex laughed and nodded. "Sure, Boss. I'll write you first thing."

Mother touched him ever so slightly on the shoulder and went back to the car. Faggot shook Tex's hand again but didn't have anything else to say. His whole body said, "I don't have anything else to say but for Chrissake take care of yourself, etc. etc." Tex looked up at him and nodded his head up and down. Mushmouth felt he was in a daze when he shook Tex's hand and said, "I hope things work out for you and peace and..." He trailed away shaking his shoulders.

Mushmouth followed Faggot back to the car. Faggot made a U-turn and blew the horn at Tex from the other side of the road. Faggot held a peace sign out his window and when they were almost out of earshot, Mother stuck his head out the window and yelled, "Don't look back." Tex raised his fist and shook it under a tree branch. Mushmouth looked out the back window as long as he could see Tex and then he hung over the front seat until Faggot told him to lean back because his breathing was bothering him.

Mushmouth sat alone in the back seat feeling miserable. It seemed to him that everybody was upset but he had no way of being sure. Motherfucker stared out of his side window and smoked a cigarette he held in his long, thin fingers. The smoke curled against the window and bounced back into the car.

Faggot stopped at an intersection. Carefully he looked to the right and to the left. Slowly he drove the car through the traffic. Slowly the first rain drops hit the windshield. Faggot put on the windshield wipers but only the left one worked.

"I'll have to get that fixed," he said. "Otherwise they'll take the car off the road."

"Tex doesn't have a good jacket," Mushmouth said.

"He'll be all right," Mother said.

There was neither reassurance nor regret in his

voice. It was simply a statement of fact.

"Yeah, but he..."

"Don't worry about him. He'll be all right," said Faggot.

The rest of the way they hardly spoke. Motherfucker told everybody how he hated the rain. Faggot said it was good for sea gulls. Before Faggot drove home he stopped at an Econo-Mart for hamburger and bread. Mother volunteered to make spaghetti for supper and Faggot began to think about him in the role of prospective cook.

When Faggot was parking in front of the house, Mother asked about borrowing the car sometimes to go the drive-in. Faggot said he'd see. Mother had to be satisfied with that.

Salamander's car wasn't parked across the street. He always parked in one place and Faggot in another. They never parked in the same area. Lately Salamander had been driving home for lunch. Either the fan belt split open again or maybe Salamander decided to walk to save money on gas.

Mushmouth was the first to get into the house. He didn't know what he was expecting but he hoped Salamander would be in the kitchen. Before Mushmouth ran upstairs he checked the aquarium in the living room, then the kitchen again. He found the dirty peanut butter knife Salamander left on the edge of the sink.

CHICKEN DELIGHT

It was suppertime and Mushmouth hadn't eaten all day. Oh, he'd had a couple of candy bars and a popsicle but nothing that classified as food. Most of the time it didn't bother him but now and then he got hungry and wanted something real. Salamander said everything they ate in that house was shitty and that was the only thing he and Faggot agreed on.

Nothing seemed to bother Mushmouth, though. There was very little that could keep him down. He said that Doreen was a good cook. He was always telling everybody what a great cook she was. One time Mother asked him how come if she was such a great cook, she'd stayed in S.F. and Mushmouth had come here. Faggot told him to leave the kid alone.

"Yeah, leave me alone," said Mushmouth. "You're always picking on me."

"Yeah, how come you're always picking on him?" asked Salamander. "Why don't you go pick on somebody your own size?"

"That's right, Mom, leave your kids alone," said Faggot.

"That's right," Mushmouth said picking it up. "Leave us kids alone." Laughing he said, "If you want to pick on somebody, go pick on Faggot."

"I don't pick on faggots," Mother said.

"Better not, boy." Faggot gave a little swagger with his ass near the fridge. He opened it and rummaged around in there for a beer. "Who's been drinking my beer?" he asked. He slammed the door shut. "Somebody's been drinking my beer." He looked at Mother.

"Well, you left it in there, didn't you?"

"What do I have to do?" Faggot glanced at Salamander and shook his head in his direction. "What do I have to do?" he repeated. "Go around sticking, 'Fuck off. Leave my fucking food alone. Fuck you,' on all my beer bottles."

"That's not all I'm gonna do," Salamander said. "I'm gonna get a padlock and keep you dipshits out of my food. I break my ass to pay for it and if I left it out in the open like you, you fool, I wouldn't have a slice of bread left by the time I got home. You're all a bunch of rip-off thieves."

Salamander looked around the room, flicking his eyes here and there looking for a rip-off thief. They settled on Mother who was hiding in the doorway and he slunk away.

"Hmph," said Salamander.

"Hmph," mimicked Faggot with a faggoty flourish of his hand and mouth. "Hmph."

"You fuck-up," Salamander said.

Mushmouth laughed.

Faggot waltzed out of the room. "Call me when supper's ready, children," he lisped over his shoulder.

"Call me when supper's ready, children,"

Salamander muttered under his breath. He made a face like he'd bitten into a bad banana.

"Well, what the fuck's to eat here?" Mushmouth asked throwing his arms up in the air and letting them collapse at his sides. He went to the fridge and rattled everything around with his hands. He beat an old celery against the door while he hung over the shelves. "There isn't much in here."

"Do you expect anything to last more than five minutes in here with that Faggot and all the other dumbshits who live here?" Salamander looked over Mushmouth's shoulder for his bottle of milk.

Mushmouth was twirling the celery in the air. He threw it down and turned around with a plateful of hamburger.

"Hey, Salamander, want some hamburger?"

"No."

"Why not? It's fresh. Really." Mushmouth held it to his nose and inhaled deeply. "It's fresh hamburger. I think it's only five days old. Go ahead. Don't believe me." He held out the container to Salamander and half-offered, half-pushed it into his face. "Smell it for yourself if you don't believe me."

"I believe you. Get it away from me." Salamander pulled back and made a series of "I'm-going-to-be-sick" faces.

Mushmouth held it up to his nose and sniffed. "Jesus, it doesn't smell that bad."

"Okay, so don't give him any. More for us," Faggot said from the doorway. He came into the kitchen and opened another bottle of beer.

"How come you don't want any?" Mushmouth

asked as he looked at it resting on the bottom of the fry pan. He poked the meat with his finger. "It looks okay to me."

Then he took out one of his hundreds of white soggy handkerchiefs and began to cough into it. He held the hamburger directly under his mouth and coughed on that, too. He wiped his mouth with the edge of the handkerchief and spit up some stray phlegm.

"It smells okay to me. How come you don't want any? What's the matter with you?"

Mushmouth wiped the corner of his eye under his rimless glasses and wrapped the handkerchief back up into a ball and stuffed it into his back pocket.

Salamander sat at the table with his arms crossed close to his chest. He looked grim. "Okay, I'll tell you. THE GREAT CHICKEN told me not to eat any more meat."

"THE WHO?"

"THE GREAT CHIICKEN," said Salamander.

Faggot whistled through his teeth and flipped a beer cap into a brown bag near the stove. He missed.

"Mushmouth, go ahead and make the hamburger. Just forget about him." He took the beer and left the room.

Mushmouth pulled out his handkerchief and rubbed the bottom of his nose. He looked at Salamander. He looked at the hamburger. He lost interest in doing anything more with his rag and shoved it back into his pocket.

"What are you talking about? C'mon, what are you gonna eat? Vita-B and peanut butter?"

Salamander propped his chair against the kitchen window and rocked himself back and forth with his feet. His eyes followed Mushmouth around the room.

"Remember that night we went to Chicken Delight for supper? You know we waited for Faggot to come home and he drove us down to this chicken place. Then we ate at Stanley Park?"

"Yeah, I do. I had a strawberry thick shake. Wasn't that the night you got a letter from home? You seemed really pleased. You were even friendly to Faggot for a little while."

"Yep, that's right." Salamander snapped his lips together. "Well, on the way home from work that night I took a tab of acid. That was the first time I've ever enjoyed a letter from home."

"You dropped acid?" Mushmouth's mouth was hanging open. "Why didn't you tell anybody?" He was standing by the stove throwing hamburger into the fry pan. "You could have told me." He flipped balls of clotted hamburger around. "Jesus," he said, "I wish Doreen was here."

"I don't know why I didn't tell anybody. Maybe I didn't want to. After all it was me who took the stuff nobody else. I guess I didn't want any of these dumbasses messing me up and interfering with my trip. It started to take effect just as we were in the chicken place. And that fat girl stuffing the chickens in the plastic bags and the chickens being too fat and falling all over her hands and the counter. Eeeck. It makes me sick just to talk about it. She was so greasy. She was like one of those chickens in the plastic bags."

"Yeah, I remember. You were obnoxious in there.

I mean of all the people here, you're probably my best friend but you were obnoxious in there."

"How's that?"

"Well, we were all in there deciding what to get. Faggot was trying to figure it out out with Mother. You know he doesn't have any money this week."

"He never does."

"I know but Christ he has to eat."

"No, he doesn't. Maybe if nobody fed him, he'd go away." Salamander leaned forward in his chair and pointed a finger at Mushmouth's chest. "You know what the problem is? I'll tell you what the problem is. He FUCKING expects it. I break my ass all day and he sits here eating my food." The chair collapsed under Salamander and he got up and rearranged it under himself without taking his finger away from Mushmouth's chest.

"So what do you think I do all day? I look for a job and I eat candy bars. I go to the beach and I go to Leonard's. I go to the library and I go to Leonard's. And I haven't looked for a job in the last three days and pretty soon I'm not gonna have any more candy money."

All the time Mushmouth was talking he was picking at the edges of the hamburgers with his fingers and sucking hamburger crumbs out of his fingernails.

"Yeah, but at least you don't sit on your ass all day feeling sorry for yourself and living off of everybody."

"Christ!" Mushmouth shouted. He sucked his finger. "Gimme that fork. I burned my finger."

Salamander threw a fork at the stove. It fell on the

floor and Mushmouth picked it up. He wiped it off against his pants and turned one or two hamburgers over. There was a pause where nobody said anything.

"So where were we?" Salamander asked.

"You'd just walked into the store and couldn't wait any longer. You ordered an individual plate and went outside to eat it."

"Yeah, I couldn't stand to wait around and watch Faggot and Mother go through the food routine. I had to get out so I went outside and sat down on the curb to eat." Salamander sucked in his breath. "That's the last piece of meat that's ever going to cross my lips."

"How come?" Mushmouth leaned against the stove picking apart the hamburgers in his impatience.

"When we got in the car Faggot had the carton of chicken next to him on the front seat. Right?"

"Yeah."

"And he was passing out some chicken parts while he was driving. Right?"

"Yeah, but..."

"Wait a minute. I'm getting there. He asked me, 'White or dark meat?' Do you remember that?"

"Well, sort of. Not exactly."

"Anyway, he asked me, 'White or dark meat,' and then he shoved this chicken leg at me."

"Yeah, okay. So what?"

"The chicken leg turned into a rooster."

"Uh-huh."

"This rooster was flapping its wings at me..."

"While it was in your hand?"

"It was going to peck out my eyes. It had its claws in my arm. It was the GREAT CHICKEN and it said..."

Salamander squeezed his eyes shut remembering. "It said, 'Don't eat any more of my children.'" Salamander leaned back in his chair grimacing. He clutched his arm and held his side.

"Far-out. Far fucking out. What do you think it means?"

"Obviously it means become a vegetarian," Salamander snapped. He relaxed. "Don't eat any more of my children. Become a human being."

"Did it say anything else?"

Salamander thought for a second or two. "Well, later at the Park when you guys were all sittting around eating chicken and Faggot was spitting skin at you, this bull came galloping up to me and it said, 'Heed the CHICKEN or we will devour you.'" He stopped and looked at Mushmouth. "It scared the shit out of me and if you think I'm dumbassed enough to eat any more meat, then you're crazy."

Mushmouth put the fork down and started to reach for his rag.

"That's some heavy shit," he said solemnly, "I sure hope the GREAT CHICKEN leaves you alone next time." Then he took the fry pan off the burner and brought it to the table.

"Hey, Salamander, do you think these are done now?"

SHOWDOWN

Motherfucker was in his usual spot on the front porch waiting for rush hour. He'd read parts of the Violence Commision Report and the first half of a book about hobos in the Depression that one of Faggot's old girlfriends had given him as a good-bye present. He'd gone for a short walk in the afternoon, played some guitar and taken a nap. Any day he expected a big envelope from his father with a check for $7.75. It had been only a mildly depressing day.

Salamander had been home for fifteen minutes. He wasn't driving anymore because he wanted to save money. Usually Salamander walked into the house without saying anything to Mother who was waiting on the front porch for Faggot. Then Salamander put on his Dylan records and went upstairs to change his clothes. Right after he came out of the bathroom, he went into the kitchen to eat. Midway through his porridge Salamander got up and turned all the Dylan records over. He always ate before any of the others came home, even if it meant eating fast. He liked to have his cabinet locked up before people were hanging around the kitchen door. He was still vegetarian.

Motherfucker was rolling a cigarette when

Salamander first came home. As usual Salamander didn't say hello or anything so Mother figured things were cool at the bank. Motherfucker was smoking and staring at the girl secretaries who were going home in rush hour. He had other more important things to think about but he vaguely realized that by now Salamander should have had the Dylan records on. In fact, Salamander should have been in the kitchen making his porridge. He took a deep drag and threw the cigarette into the garden.

He was thinking how he had to get his hands on some good shit because he was beginning to smoke cigarettes like dope. He heard a voice coming from upstairs. Mother got up from his chair to see what was going on but he could see fuck-all. He walked out into the street and he saw Salamander climbing out the bedroom window and standing on the porch roof.

"Sweet Jesus," Mother said. He stayed in the street with his hands jammed into his pockets somewhere around his groin. He was watching Salamander walk across the porch roof and stand midway between the two bedroom windows. A sly grin moved slowly across Mother's face and disappeared.

"Hey, what you doin' up there, boy?" he called. He was speaklng slow and easy like he didn't want to know. But he did. Like someone who'd leave his living room because he'd heard the corner house was on fire and he might have half a chance to catch the fifteen-year-old daughter in her nightgown. "C'mon, boy, what you doin' up there?"

Salamander didn't answer. He wasn't going to talk to Mother unless it was absolutely necessary and then only in a way that could pass as mild insult.

Motherfucker stayed glued to his spot in the middle of the street until Salamander raised his arms and held it up.

"Watch your step," Motherfucker called up.

"Is it even?" Salamander yelled down.

"A little more to the right. Yeah, that's it."

Salamander moved it over and right away tacked in two nails so it wouldn't slip or come off-balance. He didn't look down. When he was through he turned around and climbed back in through the open window.

"Sweet Lord," Mother said standing in the middle of the street swaying back and forth on his heels. He laughed to himself, a nice bitter, sardonic chuckle that was pretty good when he'd spent a whole day waiting for $7.75 and thinking about all his lost writing and songs. He laughed so much he began to cough. Then he walked back to the porch and threw himself into the chair. He had to wait for Faggot and then he could have supper.

A half hour later Faggot pulled up. He was wearing his brown tie and a green perma-press shirt. A cigarette stuck out the corner of his mouth at right angles to his nose. He looked exhausted. He opened the gate and started up the walk to the house. In the middle of the path he stopped short, took a double take and backed up. He walked into the gate, opened it with his hand behind his back and backed into the street. He wound up in about the same place Motherfucker had been. "Fuck," he said staring at the upstairs bedroom.

Faggot dropped the cigarette and charged the house. He stopped short of Motherfucker. "Who put that up there? Who put that fucking thing in that window?" He pointed skyward and his hand was trembling.

Mother looked puzzled. "The window? What's in the window?" He got out of his chair and followed Faggot out to the street. They stood in the same spot and looked up at Salamander's window.

"The son of a bitch," Mother said with respect. This time when he looked up at the window, he saw an American flag hanging upside-down as a curtain. Mother snorted and shook his head back and forth. "The little bastard," he said grudgingly.

Faggot left Mother standing in the middle of the street calling Salamander names. Mother heard him go upstairs looking for Salamander. "Christ," he said. "I wanted a cigarette, too."

Faggot found Salamander lying on his mattress on the floor. He hadn't changed his clothes yet and he hadn't played any Dylan records or eaten any supper. He was lying on his back with his arms folded behind his head. He was smiling at Faggot.

"What kind of a fuck-up are you, anyway?" Faggot demanded. "Do you want everybody to know who's living here?" he shouted. His face was getting red. It was almost as red as it gets after the first half bottle of wine.

"I don't care," Salamander said looking up at Faggot. "I don't give two shits. Nobody else does, either."

"Yeah, but I'm the landlord here." Faggot hit his

chest. "Take it down. It has to come down." Faggot loomed over Salamander. "Take it down."

Salamander sat up. He squeezed himself against the wall. "It stays."

"The fuck it does." The vein in the side of Faggot's neck was jumping. "The fuck it does," he said as he went to the window and ripped the flag down. He rolled the flag up in a ball and threw it at Salamander. "It goes," he yelled.

"It stays," Salamander yelled back, getting up and dragging the flag across the floor. "It fucking stays."

Faggot watched Salamander turn his back. He was flushed and he didn't know what he was going to do next.

"It stays," Salamander said again. "Just because the house is in your name you can't stop me from putting the things I like up in my room. It fucking stays," Salamander kept repeating as he tried to tie the flag back up and it kept slipping away from him and falling over his head. "I pay my rent," he shouted back at Faggot, stopping all the time to straighten out the flag and getting more and more frustrated by the second. "And that's more than some people do around here. And I don't owe you any money and that's more than the rest of the fuck-ups in this house." His voice hit a frenzied pitch. "And I think it looks good. Go ahead, you ask them. You ask them and they'll tell you they like it, too. THEY LIKE IT, ASK THEM. Don't give me that shit about it pointing out a whole house of draft dodgers. You're landed so what are you worried about? Mushmouth and Mother are the ones who have to worry and they don't care. THEY

FUCKING DON'T CARE."

Salamander turned around to face Faggot. "You'd better get used to it because it's not coming down," he shouted with his back against the wall. "You try to shove your weight around here, Faggot, but you're no landlord. It is not coming down."

"The house is in my name and I'm responsible. It comes down." Faggot couldn't catch his breath and his fists were clenched. "Take it down. I won't have it in my house. Take-that-god-damn-flag-down." He took two steps in Salamander's direction and Salamander squeezed his eyes together.

"It's not your house, Faggot," Salamander yelled. "I pay my rent and I can put anything I like up in the window. You're being an ass, Faggot. You know that. You're an ass, Faggot."

Faggot stood by the door. Salamander opened his eyes. For a split second he thought Faggot was going to cry but that was only the shape of the anger on Faggot's face.

Faggot stayed by the door biting his lips and saying nothing. Salamander lay down on his side and tried to ignore Faggot. He curled up on his side and pressed his arms into his stomach because he was trembling.

Faggot squinted at Salamander and did an abrupt about-face. He went into the bathroom and then he went downstairs and sulked in the kitchen for a while.

Later he went out to the porch and asked Mother what he thought about the flag. Mother said he liked it. He said he didn't care if it was there or not. He didn't think it mattered that they were fugitives of the law and had an American flag upside-down in an upstairs bedroom. Faggot began to say how he was the landlord and how it was a matter of principle that Salamander take the flag down. Mother looked at him and shook his head back and forth slowly.

"Man, you got a cigarette?" he asked.

Faggot looked Mother full in the face. He squinted at him like he'd squinted at Salamander. "No," he said. "No, boy, I don't have a cigarette for you today."

Faggot left the porch and walked towards the car. He opened the driver's side and rested his hand on the top of the door. He looked up at the window and leaned backwards.

Through the car window Mother saw Faggot's face change when he recognized what he'd missed the first time he looked at the upstairs window.

Nailed to the wooden siding of the house between Salamander's American flag and Mushmouth's paisley scarf, a cardboard, cut-out MICKEY MOUSE waved hello and good-bye to the whole of Broadway.

Saturday morning Salamander took Mushmouth to Queen Elizabeth Park. He said he needed some fresh air and a fuck-up like Mother wouldn't know how to appreciate the Park. Besides he said he saw Mother every night when he came home from work and he was tired of looking at him.

Mother stood on the porch and watched Salamander and Mushmouth get into Salamander's

1956 Chevie. The Chevie had Oregon plates and a rotten fan belt. The only thought running through Mother's mind was how one day Salamander would be driving aound and his fan belt would fall apart in the middle of nowhere. That would fix him.

Faggot slept until 11:00 o'clock. Mother thought he was dead but finally he woke up. He could tell because Faggot's corpse was smoking a cigarette.

"Hey, Faggot. Gimme the keys. Let me have the car if you're not going to use it."

"Go away. I'm asleep. Come back after breakfast."

"Faggot, what are you having for breakfast?"

"Bacon and eggs, toast, jelly and coffee." Faggot went directly to the refrigerator in the kitchen. He opened a bottle of Country Style and poured it into a frozen glass he found in the freezer behind a mound of petrified carrots.

"Who puts this shit in here?" he asked throwing a handful of loose peas on the floor.

"Faggot, can I have the keys? Huh?"

"Why? Where you going? The drive-in's not until 8:00 o'clock."

"I don't want to go to the drive-in. I just want to drive around."

"Why?"

"Because I'm goddamn tired of sitting around this house."

"Why don't you get it together and look for work?"

"Fuck off."

They glared at each other.

Mother was sullen. He went into the living room and played guitar for a few minutes on his bed. He listened to the pumps in Salamander's fish tank. Oh yes, the tadpoles were doing fine. Salamander didn't know yet that Mother pulled the plug on the pump because he said that he couldn't sleep with the racket the oxygen thing made. Motherfucker slept so much it was a wonder that the fish survived at all. They must have been a hardy breed.

Mother came out with the guitar in his hand. "C'mon, boy, give me a smoke."

Automatically Faggot tossed him an Export.

Mother took a drag and looked at the tip of the cigarette. "Why won't you give me the car?"

"Where the fuck do you want to go?"

Mother looked at his hands and said nothing.

"You want to go to the U. S. of A. or something?"

"I just want to get out of here," Mother said slowly.

Faggot made a chirping noise through his lips. He flicked the ashes on the floor. He made a fucking motion with his finger and said, "Blah."

"Cut it out," said Mother.

"Sure. Sure, boy." He did a faggoty pose and tripped out of the room. He went upstairs and called to Mother from the bathroom. "Write your congressman and ask him to let you in again. Tell your Uncle Sam you're sorry." He pissed in the toilet.

Mother smoked the cigarette right down to the butt. His last drag was three-quarters filter and one-quarter tobacco. Faggot didn't flush the toilet.

"I want my mail," said Mother. His voice was testy.

"Okay," said Faggot. He looked into Mother's face

and said, "Okay. Okay, we'll go down and pick up the mail."

"Okay," said Mother. He swallowed and ran his hands across his mouth. "Okay, Faggot."

Fagggot grabbed Mother by the shoulder and held him at arm's distance. "It's OKAY," he said. "Okay?"

"Okay."

They stopped at Leonard's for cigarettes. Mother wanted to make a phone call so he whipped into The Trade Winds Cafe next door. He wouldn't tell Faggot what the call was about. He just said it might mean money.

Faggot drove in the post-rush hour like traffic of a city that doesn't know what a traffic jam is. Mother chain-smoked and hung his arm out the window. He was looking for hitchhikers. Especially girl hitchhikers.

"Hey, Faggot, pick up that guy."

Faggot drove over the curb and a skinny boy with pimples and a dirty canvas bag got in the back seat. He looked like he hadn't eaten for the last three years of his adult life and was strung out on smack and speed and sunflower seeds.

Mother leaned over the back seat. The kid got nervous. "Where you going?"

"I don't know."

"Nobody knows," Faggot said.

"Where'd you come from?"

"I just got here. I just got to Vancouver today."

He showed Mother a crumpled scrap of paper with some address written on it. "I want to go to this address but I don't know any of the streets or anything. I just got here. I just got to Vancouver today."

"You know something, Mother?" Faggot said.

"What?"

"This kid just got here today. He just got to Vancouver today."

"Yeah, I just..."

"I know." Mother was staring at the kid. He turned to Faggot and said, "Let's take him to the Committee with us and then across town to the Drop-In Place." The kid was beginning to sweat.

"Sure."

Faggot parked the car in a no parking zone. It seemed that those were the only parking spots he could ever find. Mother stayed in the car with the kid while Faggot went in to check the mail.

Faggot came back in fifteen minutes. "Nothing for you," he said to Mother. He had three letters rolled up in his hand. "All for me. They love me so much at home."

The kid was sweating in the back seat. "You okay?" Faggot asked through the rearview mirror.

The kid nodded. He looked like he was going to be sick. They drove him to the corner of the street where they told him there was a place called Kool-Aid. He got out of the car and looked relieved.

Faggot waved his fingers around in a sick imitation of a peace sign. "Fucking hippies," he said. "They all ought to get jobs."

"You know what he told me?" Mother asked Faggot. "He told me he's a French Canadian. He used to live on this farm with his girlfriend down South. He

139

came to Vancouver to make some bread to go back to his girlfriend. She used to live on a farm in North Carolina. They wanted horses but they didn't have the bread to buy any. He wants to go back there and buy another farm. Next time they're gonna get horses. He said he thought North Carolina was the most beautiful place in the world next to Virginia. A French Canadian who can hardly speak English. Can you believe that?"

Faggot stared at Mother. It was the longest speech he'd heard Mother make. Longer than anything he'd ever said about FM radio.

"Far-out," he said.

"Yeah, far fucking out," Mother said to himself.

ORANGE JULIUS

Some Sunday mornings Faggot got himself up early and left the house in less than twenty-five minutes. Salamander couldn't figure out where he was going but then he didn't care to ask. Motherfucker never knew because Sunday for him was a day of rest. Mushmouth thought Faggot had a girlfriend somewhere but Salamander said that was the dumbest thing Mushmouth ever said. First where would a Faggot find a girlfriend and second what girl would be screwy enough to want to see a Faggot at 8:00 o'clock on a Sunday morning. Mushmouth shook his shoulders. "I don't know," he said. "Love's crazy."

Faggot wore his dirty perma-press shirt, the one he'd worn the day before to the Mighty Sound Center. He didn't bother with his socks at all. If he couldn't find them in less than five minutes on a Sunday morning, he went barefoot right up to the last minute on Monday morning when he had to step into his car and drive to work. All weekend he prayed that his car wouldn't break down because on a Monday morning he didn't have money enough for a B.C. Hydro token to take him to his job.

That's because Faggot spent his money on Sunday

morning in private, by himself, away from the rest of the people in that house who lived off of and through each other, but principally through the support of Faggot who knew he wasn't supporting anything.

Faggot went away in his beat-up Buick that he'd bought off a Chicago dodger who had left Vancouver for a logging camp in Alaska. Faggot paid for half the car in cash and the other half was waiting for Chicago whenever he made it back. Faggot was betting on never seeing Chicago again and Chicago was gloating because he'd overcharged on the first half anyway. Everybody was happy...

Except Faggot who had to work all week and worried every other minute that his car was falling apart by itself at the curbside in the nighttime. But on Sunday he gave up worrying and drove his car wherever he liked.

First he headed for Stanley Park. He took the inside road that cuts through the interior of the park and dumps you out in the middle of the tennis courts and croquet fields. Faggot parked his car next to all the posh vehicles and walked around the playing fields in his bare feet. Sometimes he sat down on the steps of the tennis buildings and watched couples play doubles or some of the more intense younger girls who still had hopes of becoming another Billie Jean.

He walked around the pedestrian paths and looked at the older people playing croquet with their gaily colored mallets. When a croquet ball left the playing green and rolled onto the pedestrian walk, Faggot, unthinking, put out his foot and stopped it from going off the grass. He looked up and saw a middle-aged man with whiskers who could have been a West Vancouver doctor or lawyer frowning at him. "I'm sorry," Faggot said. He shook his head. He couldn't imagine what was wrong.

He watched the couples strolling about in their freshly starched white outfits and he thought he was in a giant health club. At times it seemed to him that Vancouver was Sydney, Australia. He didn't know why he thought that because he'd never been anywhere outside of California until he came to Vancouver but so far British Columbia reminded him of all the travel shorts he'd seen on TV about Australia. The sun shining all the time, the sunny faces and all the people on the beaches or at tennis courts. "Sex and sports," he sighed as he sat down under a tree and hoped nobody would come and tell him to move away or sit someplace else.

He shut his eyes and listened for the footfalls of people on the paths. It seemed that all the people playing croquet were middle-aged but he knew in his soul he was older than they were. He reassured himself. Once he'd owned a ten-speed bicycle, too, and bicycled all over the place. Probably if he could have anything he wanted, he would ask for a ten-speed bicycle again. But who would he ask and he chuckled to himself under his tree in the middle of Stanley Park in the nicest municipal tennis courts in all of British Columbia. He decided it was the flags on all the bridges that made him think he was in Australia. The B.C. flag with its rising and setting sun on a backdrop of red flames waving at him from every bridge he went over. He crossed two bridges at least three times a day. No wonder he thought he was in Australia. Who else but expatriated British colonials would put a rising-setting sun on all their bridges?

Around 10 o'clock when all the couples broke for coffee Faggot stood up and brushed the neatly cropped grass off his back. The grass in Stanley Park is good grass and more likely to leave grass stains on his perma-press shirt. "Oh, well," he thought shaking his head. "It's just too much. All this is just too incredible."

He went into the Sportsman's Cafe, a luncheon spa on the edge of a chalet-like building that catered to the English appetites of all the tennis players. There were English muffins with jam and scones and dropped eggs. The waitress was a pretty high school girl who knew Faggot because he came every Sunday morning and ordered hot cakes and maple syrup. If Faggot still had some money left over from what he'd taken from Mushmouth the night before, he had a glass of milk, too. It was his concession to health. He figured a glass of milk once a week couldn't do him any harm. He hated coffee.

He enjoyed his breakfast in the Sportsman's Cafe once a week where he ate barefoot with the special consideration of the high school waitress who thought he was old-man crazy or eccentric, except too young for either one of those things. But he didn't care what anybody thought. He thought British Columbia was a nursing home for the British Commonwealth. Faggot liked eating his pancakes on a clean plate that he didn't have to wash with silverware that was brand-new and sparkling clean and that he didn't have to share with anybody. But most of all he liked the hot cakes that came in uniform size and thickness and were cooked all the way through and tasted like real pancakes. That was worth the outrageous prices that he didn't even think of unless Salamander was at his elbow reminding him all the time about the current rate of interest and the price of this and the price of that.

After breakfast he drove to the other side of the park and lay on a hillside where he could watch the sailing boats. He didn't particularly enjoy being sandwiched in between all the couples who should have stayed home in their beds instead of dragging themselves down to the beachfront to finish what they'd started three hours before. But the sun was nice, even if it shone through a filmy haze of clouds, and the weather was warm. He watched the children's sailing class and he wondered about his daughter. If he didn't keep up child support payments did that mean he couldn't be her father anymore?

He listened to the birds in the trees and he wondered what he was doing in *Canadia* British Columbia in the first place. Then he remembered how he had a BB gun when he was ten years-old. He was aiming at the birds on the telephone wire. He couldn't see fuck-all out of either one of his eyes and he pulled the trigger. He couldn't believe he'd hit anything but when the bird fell off the wire in a stiff dead heap, he knew he made a hit. He looked at the bird and he looked at the gun and he saw his reflection in the dead birdie eye. Then he knew it all made sense again.

Faggot stayed on the grass until the sun was

directly overhead. Even if it was covered with cotton-like gauze it was still brighter than the shadow ban CGE light bulb he saw advertised everywhere. He pulled himself off the grass and laughed. The "C" stood for "Canadian" General Electric.

It was noon and he drove along the social part of Stanley Park--the ribbon of road that follows the beachfront, squeezed between the edge of the city and the popcorn vendors sitting on folding chairs. "Even popcorn vendors don't have to hustle in this crazy place," Faggot said shaking his head and knowing he was too much American to be able to sell anything sitting down. "But I could learn," he said to himself. "I sure could learn."

Then he ate a hot dog for lunch that was really hot and drove across town for two Orange Julius from a franchise that just opened from the States. It made him sad to drink Orange Julius in Vancouver. He wished there was a Mexican place where he could drive in for tacos and enchaladas. In the back of his mind he played with the idea of opening a Mexican restaurant but he squelched it with a third Orange Julius.

Driving home he was thirsty again and stopped for a Coke. "Jesus," he said staring at the Coke in the bottom of his cup. "One addiction is enough." Then Faggot checked the gas gauge in his car before he could remind himself that it was broken. On the way home he stopped at Chevron Island and got fifty cents worth of gas and a free green lei. "Thanks," he said to the man who was always nice to him when Motherfucker wasn't in the front seat.

He pulled up in front of the house around 2:30 all set for a Sunday nap when Salamander ran out of the house and opened the front door of the Buick. "Oh shit," thought Faggot, "what's the crisis now?" He waited with his hands on the steering wheel and the green lei around his neck.

Salamander grabbed him by his lei. "Hey, Faggot Fatass, Mother's leaving. Do you hear? He's got a job."

"Oh shit," said Faggot laughing to himself and putting his head on the steering wheel.

"He's going out to the country. He's got a job building a log cabin for a professor. At least we won't have to see his ugly face creeping around here for twelve days. Maybe he'll like it in the country and never come back."

June 15

And a letter came today for Ed Parisien and I don't know who he is and nobody I know knows who he is. Jimmy lives upstairs locked up in his little room and I can never remember he lives here until the lock on the door reminds me. Sometimes it is locked and sometimes it isn't so sometimes he exists and sometimes he is dead for whole days.

This morning I heard some stirring behind the lock and I smelled the fumes of what must have been somebody's first cigarette of the day. I thought, "Jimmy is alive," but then I went into the bathroom and the stirring, like the noises a mouse makes going round and round in shredded newspapers, stopped. I flushed the toilet.

And so Jimmy is dead again. I haven't thought about him at all until I sat down here--here in this broken chair with the red cushion on the peculiar slant that makes me lean up against the green table opposite Regular Cream of Wheat and peanut butter and sugar and all the scraps and shreds of people's lives.

It is Saturday today. Salamander is still asleep. Mother is already playing his records but Salamander will never know until he wakes up. Faggot is passed out in the living room. He is waiting for Jimmy to leave so he can pass out in Jimmy's room in private.

Last night Faggot drank two bottles of wine. Salamander and Mushmouth shared a bottle and Mother drank a whole one himself. That makes four bottles. Faggot smoked a pack of cigarettes that are now lying in the bottom of a bottle of Medium Dry B.C. table wine. He says he likes Portuguese wines best. He says he is looking for a brand called Gumbo or Gimbza but he settles for Grao Vasco Dao.

I am waiting for my coffee to cool. Faggot does not drink coffee because he is an alcoholic. The bottles are waiting for Motherfucker because Motherfucker likes to clean each one out, cursing the Faggot for using them for ashtrays, and put them on the window sill. Already there are ten bottles there.

There are three more windows to fill up. The bottles are always waiting for Motherfucker but what is he waiting for? You shut your eyes. *You fall from the eternal hammock but you never get the relief of the final crash.* Tonight there will be four more bottles and that will make eighteen. What will happen when all the window sills are full?

I don't know. I really don't know anything at all. Perhaps when Salamander gets up we will go to the beach.

CALONA RUBY RED

With Tex gone the house settled into some kind of routine. Faggot said that everything was better now that Tex was out of the house and everybody could begin to live like a human being again. But Mother didn't say anything because he didn't have any money and Salamander had nothing to say because he didn't think Faggot or Mother were human beings.

There was money now that Faggot was selling stereo components at the Mighty Sound Center but Mother wondered how long he could keep it up. Salamander said it was just like Faggot to get a job through a Jew agent but everybody was relieved, especially Mushmouth and Mother.

Faggot went to work in his watch, twelve-dollar blue perma-press shirt and check suit. Nobody knew he didn't have any underwear. He had his black frame glasses and his radio voice and his blond styled hair going for him. He could have been an up and coming insurance salesman or a travel agent instead of a polite upper-middle class Faggot who wore his green permanent press shirt every other day and owned two ties and hung around the house in his business suit because he had no play clothes. "Boy, you're really a faggot," Salamander said when he realized he was living with a full-time insurance salesman.

But Mother didn't say anything about Faggot's clothes because he was too worried about Faggot getting up in time for work. Mother showed up at the Sound Center pretending to look for a record just to see the Faggot in action. He discovered that Faggot drank two beers for lunch or went to the Liquor Control Board and bought a bottle of wine that he kept in his car around the corner. When Mother found that out he bit off all the fingernails on his strumming hand and then bitched for a week because he said his sound was off. Salamander asked him what the fuck he was—a motherfucker or a kept woman.

And when Faggot came home, carrying the brown bag full of wine bottles under his arm, Mother was the first to ask him how his day was. "Have a good day, huh? Sell a lot, huh? Good. Sold a whole system to a Burnaby housewife? Shit. Two hundred twenty-five bucks. Sheet!" Then when Faggot had pulled off his tie and gone upstairs to piss, Mother talked to him through the bathroom door, "How much commission on two hundred twenty-five bucks?"

Every day Faggot woke up later and later and one day he never made it to work at all because his car broke down at 11 o'clock when he woke up. He didn't think it was worth going for the afternoon so he went back to sleep and got drunk that evening. He said it was one of the best days he'd spent in a long time.

Salamander's favorite day was Saturday because Faggot often had to work every day except Sunday.

During the week Salamander was too depressed to do anything except eat supper and go to the empty lot across the street for the few hours left in the day until it got dark. Faggot told Salamander they were going to build something there and he'd have to find another sandbox. Salamander called Faggot a fuck-up and said, "It figures," but Mother was angry, waiting for a developer the rest of the summer.

Salamander's favorite time of the day was the morning. When he'd worked part-time for the Federal Reserve Bank and studied the Vietnam War part-time at the University of Portland Library, he'd had all the time he needed to acquaint himself with the different parts of the day. After a year's observation he decided he liked the morning best because everyone is deprived of that particular experience because of work—but these thoughts usually brought him back to the subject of his job and he immediately became depressed again.

Salamander hated his job. He hated the dumbass quizzes he had to answer in order to become a bank manager, he hated all the girls who worked in the bank, including the few who hoped he would eat lunch with them, he hated the clothes he had to wear to work, and he hated having to be polite to a wide assortment of assholes, personnel and clients alike. Most of all Salamander hated having almost no money and having to come home to eat soup and peanut butter sandwiches for lunch. After the first three weeks he didn't hate that so much because he began to suspect that The Bank was plotting to steal his mind. He showed Mushmouth the loose-leaf notebook of situational exercises he had to memorize for his homework as a Bank Manager Trainee.

One night when he was drunk he showed Faggot the little notebook of bi-weekly tests he was subjected to and which, much against his will but in spite of himself, he excelled in. That week he had marred his near-perfect score by incorrectly answering the ridiculously humiliating question: "You are about to go on your lunch hour. Before you have officially announced that your window is closed by presenting the card, 'Next window, please,' a young lady approaches your window and expects your service. You should_____."

Faggot read the clear, mindless handwriting of the Assistant Manager who had penciled through Salamander's response and recopied the formula from page eighteen of the Manual for Bank Manager Trainees: "Smile politely, say, 'I am sorry to inconvenience you but I am about to go to lunch hour,' direct her to an open window and say, 'The person to my right (left) will be glad to help you,' and apologize for any inconvenience, remain pleasant, polite and helpful at all times, postpone your lunch several minutes if she is in need of further service."

On Saturdays Salamander began to cultivate his mind. He got up early, dressed as if he'd never heard of, never mind been in The Canadian Imperial Bank of Commerce, drove to different parts of The City, talked, read or walked. After several Saturdays the urgency to get out of and away from the house disappeared.

It was about this time, the end of June, that

Salamander began to paint. One Friday he brought a paint box home from work and was so excited he entirely forgot about supper. At first the motivation had been to elucidate the character and form of The Great Chicken for the benefit of the other people who lived in the house. In order to teach fuck-ups Salamander painted watercolor representations of The Great Chicken on hand-sized stones he brought home from the empty lot across the street. He said every picture, even the best ones, were mere approximations.

By accident when he'd been digging around for the stones, he discovered a lost cat. Salamander called the cat Cat and occasionally brought her little scraps of leftover food from the house. Mother didn't like to see any food leave the house, except for the time he brought a lost dog home and gave it ninety-nine cent hamburger. Mushmouth rather enjoyed feeding the cat but Cat wasn't always around and unless she was there Mushmouth lost interest in that same spot of deserted land. Faggot knew somebody might develop the land but now he was sorry he'd said anything, partly because he didn't want to destroy Salamander's tiny pleasures and partly because he didn't want to deprive himself of the entertainment Salamander provided.

After Salamander brought his collection of stones back to the house, he'd sit on the porch steps and mix his watercolors. Carefully, delicately, nearly metaphysically he'd describe and then execute the forms and shapes of his imagined beasts. Simultaneously entertained and entertaining, he presented various approximations of his Great Chicken to Faggot, Mushmouth and Mother with appropriate personal insults.

Although Salamander was religiously vegetarian, the fascination and terror inspired by The Great Chicken was rapidly slipping in his mind. He was watching Motherfucker fling his cigarette over the porch railing into the garden when he decided on his next project. He was going to beautify The Home. Now Salamander painted watercolor flowers on the stones and placed them in the garden. Faggot sat on the wicker chair offering Salamander a running commentary on his art work. Mother smiled and said a few words now and then. Occasionally Salamander looked up from his work and gave Mother flashy back-talk.

Mushmouth was always talking about Doreen. He didn't have a job yet and he still wasn't landed but somehow he thought things would get better when Doreen came. She'd sent her trunk of clothes Railroad Express and Mushmouth spent whole days figuring out who would sign for it when it came. Doreen had sent it ahead in her name and Mushmouth was eating himself up with worry in case it arrived before she did.

Early one morning Faggot confronted Jimmy on the steps and pleaded with him to leave the house before his time was up. He even offered him twenty-five dollars if he left by the end of the week. Faggot said that Jimmy made him nervous and that the house really wasn't his until Jimmy was gone. Nobody saw Jimmy move out but two weeks later he was living next door with the rose bush and the fat old man and his wife who rented out their upstairs bedroom.

Every night after supper the fat old man watered the rose bushes in his garden. He came as close to the house next door as propriety would allow and then casually, curiously, he would try to figure out what everybody was hiding in the tumble-down garden while the water from his hose flooded his rose bushes and ran out to the sidewalk.

In the daytime Mother picked up around the house and kept things tidy. Sometimes the disorder in the kitchen overwhelmed him and he'd wash the dishes and wipe the table. He kept his own corner of the living room meticulously neat. He couldn't stand disorder or dirt of any kind. Faggot's habitual uncleanliness triggered a smoldering resentment that Mother daily fought down.

The spring was rapidly fading into summer. Doreen was on her way. Salamander and Faggot were both landed, employed, and unbearably miserable in their horrible jobs. Motherfucker's depression was overpowering. Salamander told Mushmouth that nothing coud please Mother. Mushmouth was eating more and losing more weight. He said he'd lost almost twenty pounds since he'd arrived in Canada, The Promised Land. His pants were loose and he was obsessed with financial worries. He began to hope that Doreen was bringing lots of money with her.

Faggot talked all the time about opening an artsy movie house to show arty films to the University of British Columbia people and the Kitsilano population in general. He and Mushmouth had the money,

157

although it was temporarily tied up in Faggot's loans and credit. Salamander never had any faith in Faggot or in a Kitsilano Theatre. At first they tried to buy the theatre and when they realized they didn't have the bread for that they tried to rent it. While The Man was trying to make up his mind whether to knock the building down or put a car park on the corner of the street, they let the entertainment business ride. Salamander said they all had money troubles enough without trying to match municipal government for debt. But Mushmouth talked about a renovated Kits, fabulously successful, showing all the best flicks, employing Mother as Chief Usher, Doreen as Cashier, and he, Salamander and Faggot as Rotating Popcorn Salesmen.

Mother was more interested in getting a license to operate an underground FM station. Every time he was ripped out of his mind he talked about FM radio. Between pauses, gestures and sighs he could talk for an hour on the feasibility of bringing off a radio station. He even threw in words like budget and cost control and content...It was the one thing he wanted to do, it was the single thing he could not do. Not only would there never be enough money, there would never be any way of consolidating that kind of money for that kind of project. In silent frustration Mother ate his heart out on the front porch for the next week over a meager five hundred dollars that was un-attainable and unthinkable. He was smoking out his lungs and crying at the afternoon sun for a mere five hundred dollars.

Mushmouth spoke about painting the house and

making it really liveable. Salamander threw another chair out of the kitchen window because he said he was tired of fixing the broken legs. "We don't need any more cripples around here," he said staring at Mother lurking in the doorway. Faggot got infected with the homemaking trip and decided it was time for furniture and repairs. He took Mother with him to his favorite hockshop. They pawned the tape recorder next to "Joe's Tatoos, formerly of Scollay Square, Boston." Faggot went in and haggled with the guy while Mother went next door to examine the tattoo shop window display. Joe came out and asked Mother if he was interested in having some work done. Nobody knows what Mother said to Joe because he never told anybody. That was so much like The Motherfucker.

After Faggot got the cash they had Cokes and went to the Salvation Army and bought another batch of five-dollar kitchen chairs that would last two weeks in that house the way everybody insisted on leaning back in them. One of them came without a back and Faggot said it was a bargain because people could use it for a stool. Mother discovered an antique-type lamp under a pile of postcards and old ladies' underwear. He thought it would be good for the hall when it was fixed up as a living room.

Faggot looked lovingly at the double mattresses but he knew that it was simply out of the question. He got nostalgic about his former lives and was wondering what the fuck was happening to him when he saw IT stuffed in the corner with the stoves. He simply could not do without it. "M-O-T-H-E-R-F-U-C-

K-E-R," he said under his breath. "Mother, MOTHER."

Mother wandered over from across the room where he'd been poking under a basket of old irons, broken mandolins and electrical odds and ends. He didn't know what he was looking for but he had taste and style. That's why Faggot brought him.

"What?"

"Look at it. Just look at it, will you?" Faggot backed into the stove corner and turned around a 1930s three-and-a-half foot console radio. It had been around to broadcast the Fireside Chats and support three generations of African violets through the battle reports of the last war. Now it belonged to the Salvation Army.

"Does it work?"asked Mother. He rubbed his mouth and looked skeptical.

Faggot squatted in front of it and turned some of the dials. Mother leaned over him and turned other dials. It worked.

"I'm going to get it," said Faggot.

"It's probably expensive..."

" I'm getting it."

Faggot went up to the old lady cashier. She was busy tying up three pots in brown wrapping paper for an older man who probably lived alone in a room somewhere and got tired of having to wash out the same pot every time he decided to eat kidney beans instead of chicken soup. Faggot stood off to the side of the old man and waited for him to take away his three pots and disappear back into his room.

"Can I help you, Sir?" asked the little lady behind

the desk.

"I want it," said Faggot. He pointed to Mother who was standing beside the radio with his hands in his pockets and a vacant stare on his face. "I want that radio. How much is it?"

"$10.99. Will you be taking it with you or do you want it delivered?"

"I'll take it." He motioned to Mother who slunk up to the main desk. "$10.99," Faggot said .

Mother shook his head, "No."

Faggot looked helplessly at the little lady who was watching both of them. "I've looked a long time for something like this," Faggot said to the lady. "Once I had a lantern hanging over my bed." He swallowed.

Mother pulled his hand out of his pocket. He handed Faggot seventy-three cents.

"Thanks," said Faggot.

"$10.26," said the little lady. "Will you be taking it with your or do you want it delivered?"

Faggot searched his pockets. He put down $8.58 on the counter. Then he went through all his pockets again. The little lady adjusted her spectacles and leaned over the counter and watched Faggot's hands go through every one of his pockets again. Maybe she hoped Faggot would pull a white rabbit out of one of those pockets. Instead he found a B.C. Hydro Token. He put that down on the counter with the $9.31 in change and looked at the lady. She had never seen anything like this in all of her twenty-three years' experience working in Salvation Army stores and she'd seen many strange things in her career.

"It's even," she said. "Will you be taking it with

you or do you want it delivered?"

They put the radio in the small hall outside the kitchen. Faggot made Mushmouth straighten out the bookshelves and sweep the floor. Now it was a regular living room in there. The first thing Faggot did when he came home from work was turn on the radio. He could adjust it beautifully and properly tuned it began to pick up places like Chicago and Los Angeles and Salt Lake City. Mother kept it on all day for company, except when he was playing records on Salamander's record player. He told Faggot that he'd picked up Tokyo, Japan for two hours and thirty-five minutes. Faggot said it was possible but he'd believe it when he heard it.

Salamander was more put out than ever. Now that everybody was listening to the radio, he wasn't allowed to play his records when he came home from work. His only pleasure in the day had been to play all of his Dylan records while he went upstairs to change his clothes and try to forget that he was working at the Canadian Imperial Bank of Commerce. Now Motherfucker played his records all afternoon and Faggot played the radio all evening. Salamander was not impressed because it had once picked up Tokyo, Japan.

Now that Faggot had more money, they were eating better, except for Salamander who stayed with Vita-B, Nutriment, Red River Cereal, natural honey and peanut butter. He didn't worry if Faggot lost his job because Faggot didn't owe him any money. In the evenings Mother squeezed money out of Faggot for half-gallons of vanilla ice cream and strawberries.

162

Since Faggot was so wealthy, he also had more money to drink on. He started drinking as soon as he got home from work. At first beer but then he switched to the cheaper domestic wines, always making the B.C. Liquor Commission before it closed although he had such trouble making it to work on time.

"Things are improving all the time," thought Mushmouth. "There's more order now." Even Motherfucker seemed happier, less restive.

But Faggot knew better. When he was drunk he could see into his mind and he could say that he was going three steps backward for every four he advanced. He was going ten miles per hour. Backwards. But Mushmouth's eyesight wasn't too good. He wore glasses and rarely drank because he'd recently overdone it in high school when Doreen had temporarily left him and he'd drunk a quart of Red Mountain wine all by himself in the back seat of a car in a drive-in. He'd cried all through the movie and all the way home, although he never remembered doing that.

Mother didn't say anything. He didn't expect anything. Salamander watched the bottle pass between Motherfucker and Faggot and his hand darted out for his share whenever it went by. He drank in the evenings and painted his rocks and ate peanut butter sandwiches. In the dark he probably cried himself to sleep, too. When Faggot was drunk, he made jokes that everybody laughed at. He did improvisations and parodies and he was truly funny. But his face broke the same way when he was laughing as when he was crying.

Eventually the bottles lined the window sill behind the fish tank where the tadpoles were slowly turning into frogs. Every morning Mother emptied the ash trays and picked up the empty bottles from wherever they had fallen the night before. If anybody had put cigarette butts in the bottles, he carefully washed them out, too. He should have had an expensive apartment with gourmet foods and a canopy over his bed where he brought thousands of young girls oohing and ahing to be laid by The Motherfucker. But maybe he didn't want that, either. Maybe he didn't know what he wanted. That was what Salamander thought and that was what he told Mushmouth. But Salamander passed Faggot off as a degenerate and yet he drank his wine.

That way the spring evenings passed into summer, with Motherfucker suppressing expectation and desire and Faggot trying hard to forget whatever he'd ever known about those things. That way the bottles lined the sills all the way behind the fish tank and started to creep around the windows in the hall across from the radio. Bottles of all kinds. Bottles of Tanqueray Gin, Andres Medium Dry, Calona Ruby Red, 7-Up. Bottles of Ginger Ale, Andres Rose, Royal Vermouth, Calona Medium Dry. Bottles of Coke, J&B, Calona Ruby Red, Calona Medium Dry, Calona...

Mother was sitting on the front porch with his feet up on the wooden railing and a cigarette stuck in his mouth. It was a fine summer day and Mother was enjoying himself. Nobody was home.

He looked sideways at the yellow wicker chair on the other side of the porch and laughed. He got up and stood over it. He chuckled to himself in a way that was almost smirking except he didn't hold his hand over his mouth but laughed outright at the dead lilac bush and the dandelions gone to seed.

"Fuck," he said, kicking the chair and taking his cigarette out of his mouth so he could cough properly. "Jesus fuck."

Before Faggot broke it one night when he was drunk and sat down too hard, an antique dealer offered Mother twenty-five dollars for that same wicker chair.

Mother kicked it and the trundle foot rest let go of its final bamboo webbing. It skidded down the steps.

Maybe he was greedy or maybe he didn't want to give up something that was real, something that belonged to tradition, to the country porch in the summertime, but Mother wouldn't listen to no antique dealer. "No," he said. "NO." Maybe he thought if some dipshit antique dealer wanted twenty-five dollars for Faggot's favorite chair, he could find some other antique dealer who could be happy with thirty-five. But, no, the chair fell apart like everything else you try to hold on to or save or preserve without knowing why.

Still, Motherfucker could sit on the porch for hours at a time. Sometimes he waited for the mailman and wondered how long it would be until they were safe and a mailman could deliver letters to that house.

He ached to have his mail delivered like any other normal person. Sometimes he looked at the wicker chair and laughed himself silly. Other times he turned his chair away from Faggot's broken antique and stared at the overpass at the end of the street.

"Don't you ever get depressed?" Mushmouth asked him.

Mother shook his head and looked like he was going to jump out of his skin. "No, I never get depressed," he said. Then he went inside and listened to Arlo Guthrie sing "I Don't Want A Pickle I Just Want A Motorcycle." He sat with his head in his hands on the edge of the old beaten-up Chesterfield and was oblivious to Mushmouth standing at his side or noises from the kitchen or street sounds drifting in through the front door.

Afterwards in the afternoons he got up to talking a little bit at a time. He told Mushmouth things that explained so much of what it was like that summer between Salamander's toll house cookies and Faggot's gins and the vague hopeless rumors of getting landed so as to stay in *Canadia* and learn to forget everything that came to mind with every cigarette and the opening and closing of every refrigerator door.

"Please don't talk about those things," Mother said when Mushmouth was curious about his past and his high school and the acting he had done in the school theatre. "Please," he said. "Please."

But how to forget in the sunshine in *Canadia* with the FBI looking for you on two borders and the screen door slamming every time you go out to nowhere but just to cross the bridge downtown? How to forget when you stand on the Hudson's Bay corner and watch all the other people busy about their lives?

Mother waited. He measured time and counted days. He watched the sun travel from the bathroom window to the vacant lot across the street and finally, when he was lying exhausted on his bed, creep through the crack in his living room window. He wondered how much the sun gained or lost every day but there was no way of telling.

He waited for letters that never came. His father sent him a monthly allowance of $7.75. He waited for the mailman and for the weather report and for Faggot. He bought cigarettes and moccasins and root beer in cans. When the monthly checks didn't come anymore, he cursed his father and cried in the night. Salamander ignored him and Mushmouth stayed out of his way. But when no one was home, Mushmouth crept out to the porch and sweated out the afternoons with him. Mushmouth talked about getting landed and starting a movie house. He told Motherfucker about Doreen and the San Francisco he knew. He tried to cheer Mother up by listing all the street names he could remember from Berkeley. Motherfucker listened and ate Mushmouth's licorice.

When Motherfucker went to the woods, Mushmouth missed him. Although he never confessed anything to Salamander, it was lonely with Mother gone. Even a motherfucker was more company than tadpoles and alone all day the house gave him the creeps. Mushmouth told himself things would be better but he didn't know what to do with himself in the afternoons.

Motherfucker came back tanned and rested and nearly happy so maybe it was possible to forget with birds and grass and log cabins on your mind. Mushmouth said he was a changed person. He began to think how pleasant it would be to stay home with Mother. Salamander said rotten apples only get worse.

Motherfucker was different. He brought back some new restlessness from the woods. He couldn't bear to look at the ramp by Leonard's. He couldn't play guitar by himself and he couldn't listen to Arlo Guthrie for more than fifteen minutes at a time without getting up and walking from room to room.

"What's the matter with you?" Mushmouth finally asked after Mother made him change chairs three times in less than fifteen minutes. "Have you finished the Warren Report yet? Why don't you go sit down somewhere and finish it?"

"No."

"You want a popsicle? I have fifteen cents. If we get orange, I'll split it with you."

"No." Mother shook out his chair and threw himself into it. Pieces of paint chipped off the legs. It was the last one left from the Salvation Army.

"Jesus Christ. What's wrong with you today?" Mushmouth talked to the lilac bush. "You can't sit still. You can't go anywhere. You can't read. I mean, Jesus. You know, like one day I can't sit still but I can go places. Then the next day I can't go anywhere, I can't move. Then I..."

"'I'm in love," Mother said.

Mushmouth turned around. He didn't say anything for a few seconds. "Whew. I mean like that's. That's really heavy shit," he said.

"No it isn't. It's." Mother waved his hand in the air. The skin around his eyes tightened and flexed three or four times.

Mushmouth watched his hand and looked into his eyes.

"It's..."

Mushmouth nodded his head up and down. "'What is it?" he asked.

"A girl." Mother sighed. He faced Mushmouth. "She's a fourteen-year-old girl. Do you think that's ridiculous? I met her in the country."

Mushmouth didn't say anything.

"She's a really sweet girl. She's young and not spoiled. Just sweet. I don't know. I'm really in love with her. I know it sounds ridiculous."

THE BRIDE

It didn't take Mother long to figure out he was never going to get landed. There were those who could get landed on a Coke bottle and there were those who would never get landed. He was a Motherfucker and even *Canadia* won't take Motherfuckers. They'll take Faggots and Salamanders and the occasional Mushmouth but no Breezes, no Georges, no Motherfuckers. He didn't have to be a motherfucker on the day he got landed but Motherfucker was a motherfucker through and through and a motherfucker can't become a faggot or a smart-ass salamander even for one day.

A Motherfucker can't work in a record store or in a bank or take pictures for a third-rate photographer. A Motherfucker can't say "yes" when he means "no" and wear a tie and answer other people's dumb questions. You keep a Motherfucker around like a big pet dog to remind you what a motherfucker you are-- when you can pretend you don't have to say "yes sir" or "no sir" or go to the end of the line.

Motherfucker spent a lot of time thinking about FM radio. He wanted Faggot to stop that nonsense about a renovated Kitsilano Theatre and put some money into a radio station. Faggot looked at

Motherfucker and laughed. "You have to be kidding," he said.

Mother sulked in the mornings from the time he got up right through the day until he fell asleep drunk in his big double bed. Faggot never let him have the keys to the car because he'd heard that Chicago was back in town and he didn't want anybody to see his half of the Buick on West Pender or in Stanley Park or sitting in some drive-in.

Mother bitched that he'd only gotten the car once and that one time at the drive-in movie it rained. He made Mushmouth rent a car tarpaulin for fifty cents. Not only did Mother have to leave his brother's Long Beach license as collateral but the umbrella contraption wouldn't stay adjusted to the windshield. He had to drape the edges of the canvas over the tops of the car doors and shut them quick. Mushmouth's side was okay but his leaked. He fixed it three times and when it was finally right the speaker slipped off the window and fell to the ground. On the fifth try they had everything right with fifteen minutes good viewing until intermission. Then Mushmouth got hungry watching the cartoon figure eat his way through ten minutes of hot dogs, hot buttered popcorn, Coca-Cola, chocolate covereds and steaming apple pie. Mushmouth snapped when he saw an Aero Bar do a dance with a Sweet Marie. He jumped out his side and dashed off to the snack bar for his share of the hot dogs, candy bars and hot buttered popcorn.

"Sheet," said Motherfucker who snatched the tarpaulin off the windshield and threw it in the back seat. He followed Mushmouth over to the food carousel where he watched two twelve-year-old girls eat three giant hot buttered popcorns and counted thirteen children in sleeping suits. "Sheet," he said again. He leaned against the wall which was the closest thing to a doorway and made Mushmouth buy him a medium hot buttered popcorn all for himself, except he didn't want it buttered, he told the lady behind the counter, because he didn't like his fingers to get greasy.

"Get a load of this, Frank," she yelled. "This guy doesn't want it buttered because he's afraid his fingers'll get dirty. Cripes." She shoved a cardboard box across the counter and the top layer of popcorn slithered over the sides. Mother was about to say something when six of the under-eight set stormed the popcorn counter in little pajama outfits like snowsuits. Two of them climbed over Motherfucker's feet and he had to step aside. Their mother was a harried lady with a beer belly and a white shirt that stopped half an inch above the waistband of her olive perma-life stretch pants. She had blond hair with brown roots tied up in snap-on curlers. She had skinny arms and legs and a neck that Mother said was positively serpentine. She looked like a Japanese beetle in bed slippers.

"C'mon, sonny, are you through? Then get out of the way and quit hogging the counter." She jabbed Mother in the kidneys. "C'mon, move your butt."

Motherfucker faded to the relish tray. He leaned against the counter and counted his money. A fat man with a cardboard box full of hot dogs accidentally bumped into his unbuttered popcorn. Mother reached out to steady his box and noticed his hand was full of ketchup. There were little green things stuck to his palm that looked like dismembered parts of stale piccalilli.

Mother tried to locate Mushmouth and keep an eye on what was going on. He saw his lady friend belt one of the kids in the face. Almost at once half the people in snowsuits started to howl. Three girls about fourteen or fifteen were sipping Coca-Cola through straws. They were watching Motherfucker when he licked the ketchup off his hand. Two bikers were wolfing hamburgers while their girlfriends nibbled on potato chips with hands painted in Dracula colors. They looked Motherfucker up and down and turned back to their boyfriends.

Mother caught sight of Mushmouth on the other side of the hot food carousel. He was finishing a hot dog and had a bag of potato chips, two Mars bars and another Coke to go.

"Great, isn't it?" Mushmouth asked. "Jesus, I love the drive-in."

"Yeah, it's great," Motherfucker said. "Let's get out of here."

"Wait, I want to get..."

"Oh, shit," Motherfucker said. "I'll meet you in the car."

"You don't know how to enjoy yourself. That's your problem." Mushmouth shouted with half a Mars bar stuck to the roof of his mouth.

Mother couldn't hear him because the rest of the people under eight were shrieking and the loud speaker was announcing that the show was on.

Besides, Mother was already outside.

When Mushmouth got back to the car they fixed up the tarpaulin thing again. This time it only took them ten minutes but it still leaked on Mother's side. The feature was *The War Wagon* so Mother shut up and watched the screen while a puddle formed on the floor next to his foot. In the middle of the movie he had to start the car and put on the windshield wipers.

"Jesus, what if the battery goes?" Mushmouth asked in a half-whisper.

"Yeah, what if it does," Motherfucker said.

The windows steamed up and it was impossible to tell if the people next door were really making it or just going through the motions. Mushmouth said he thought they did it and Motherfucker said that was Mushmouth's problem. He believed everything he saw.

They got back about 2:00 in the morning. Mushmouth wanted to tell everybody how great the drive-in was but everybody was passed out. The next day he told Faggot how much he enjoyed it. Salamander said he couldn't see how anybody could enjoy anything with Motherfucker. Faggot wanted to know if they had such a good time how come somebody had to piss in the front seat.

Motherfucker didn't have anything to say about the drive-in. He was quiet for the next couple of days. Then he started pestering Faggot for the car again. Usually it took a week of negotiations for Faggot and Mother to work out a car agreement.

"Oh, c'mon, man, you're not driving it," Mother said to Faggot every time he met him in a doorway.

Faggot reminded him about Chicago and the bad battery and how he needed it for work.

"Oh, man, you're really making stuff up," Mother said.

But Mother had his lucky chance when Faggot ran out of gas an hour away from the house. Faggot made it home around 10:00 o'clock because he said he had to half walk and half hitchhike. He said he used to make better time between L.A. and S.F.

"You're full of shit," Salamander said.

"What are you going to do?" Mother asked.

"I'm not going to do nothing," Faggot said. He went to his collapsible bed and slept until noon.

Mother was hanging over him as soon as he was up, wanting to know where the car was. Faggot said he couldn't remember. Two days later he remembered.

"Mother, if you want the car," he said, "you go down and pick it up. You can take it anywhere you want as long as you pay for all the gas and bring it back here with enough gas to take me to work and back."

"Sheet," Motherfucker said and left the house.

That was the last time Mother got the car because a week later it broke down and nobody got to go anywhere. Faggot had to go to work every day by the B. C. Hydro. Now he had another thing he had to save his money for and meet payments on.

Mother went into a black despair. That had happened only once before when he couldn't find his razor, the third second-hand razor in three-and-a-half months, because Faggot dropped it behind the toilet.

Mother's despair lasted four days. Salamander

said Mother was impossible. He suggested that somebody ought to shoot him to put him out of his misery. Faggot turned a sick eyeball in his direction and Salamander said he was only kidding.

"Some joke," Mushmouth said.

Salamander refused to go into Mother's room unless it was absolutely necessary. Mushmouth asked him if he was afraid of Motherfucker and Salamander said only an asshole wouldn't be afraid of a lunatic. The only time Salamander would feed his fish was when he was absolutely certain Motherfucker wasn't there. And since Motherfucker wasn't going anywhere but the porch the fish were finally eating as well as the rest of the people in that house.

"What the fuck is this?" Salamander wanted to know. "A nursing home or a kindergarten?"

Faggot told him to calm himself down. Salamander said he wasn't going to keep his fish in the same room with Motherfucker. Since by now the tadpoles were nearly frogs anyway, Salamander said his fish couldn't be very happy living with frogs instead of tadpoles. On a Sunday afternoon Salamander and Mushmouth took the three near-frogs and a couple of goldfish down to Stanley Park and put them in the lagoon there. Salamander said he would rather visit them there than in Mother's room.

Mother was oblivious to Salamander. Faggot was too busy trying to stay drunk all the time. He was very quiet and sometimes never showed up for meals. Mushmouth hung around Salamander and Mother stayed in bed.

Around the middle of July Mother got a big

envelope from his father. Faggot brought it home and dropped it into his lap. "Somebody finally wrote you," he said.

"Yeah," said Mother.

Mother took it into his room and read it and re-read it. Nobbody could tell what else he was doing in there because he was curled up on his side with his back to the door and nobody wanted to go in there and find out. Salamander said he probably fell asleep reading it. Mother lay in bed and smoked a whole lot of cigarettes. When he came out he had a wicked grin on his face and he said, "Sheet."

But Salamander and Mushmouth weren't interested. Salamander because he didn't give a shit and Mushmouth because he was too messed in the head that week.

Faggot looked up, "Yeah, so what's happening?"

"He sent me twenty-five dollars."

Faggot stuck his finger in the air, "Bloop, Bloop, Blah."

Mother smiled. "I know," he said.

"You owe me a hundred and twenty-five dollars."

"I know that, too."

"Okay." Faggot threw him a kiss.

Mother kept smiling.

Mother was smiling for the whole week. But Salamander missed the sunshine because he stayed in his room pasting up statistics of dead Vietnamese and grotesque pictures of mutilated people. Faggot asked him how he could stand to sleep in there without getting nightmares. Salamander said he was glad Faggot asked because soon everybody would be asking the same question. "Then they will begin to understand the enormity of the Indochina War," he said. Salamander replastered the walls with war clippings and Amerikan advertisements and a couple of playgirl pin-ups. He said the ads and pin-ups were to remind him about capitalist-pig-amerika, but they were fun, too.

After a brief relapse of black despair Motherfucker pulled himself out of it for good. Nobody knew what brought it on and nobody knew what cured it. Nobody knew what Mother was up to except maybe the Motherfucker himself. In that case he wasn't telling anybody. But in the space of three days he changed his ways. First he cleaned his room and the area around his clothes-pile and shaving kit bag. Then he tidied up the whole house. Not just one of his regulars with a wipe-over of the rag but a real housecleaning. He washed out the kitchen sink and poured some Comet in the upstairs bathtub. He threw a bucket of water and Lestoil on the kitchen floor and another one down the toilet. Mushmouth was afraid he would ask for a rent reduction. He started to figure out how much he could get off his rent if he offered to make a deal with Faggot to wash the dishes once a day.

In the nighttimes Mother moved out of his room and sat at the kitchen table waiting. Just waiting. He was a professional waiter but this waiting had a new direction to it. It was waiting that was like static electricity. It made everybody nervous.

After the fifth day of waiting Mother left the house at noon and came back at suppertime.

"He wouldn't be stupid enough to go away without another free meal," Salamander said.

At quarter to six Mother came to the gate and let himself in. He went to the kitchen table and began his nighttime vigil.

"What are you doing?" Mushmouth asked.

"Waiting," Mother said.

"Yeah, but what for?"

"For the right moment," Motherfucker said.

"Huh?"

"What's going on?" Faggot asked from the kitchen door. "Oh, Jesus," he said looking at Motherfucker sitting at the kitchen table. "What's he doing?" he asked Mushmouth.

"He says he's waiting."

"Jesus Christ. Don't you look sharp, Motherfucker." Faggot walked around Motherfucker's chair and felt the material of his brand-new flannel shirt. "Real high-class flannel."

"Only the best," Mother said. He was smiling and showing both his top and bottom teeth. His two front teeth were set apart. The tops of his bottom teeth were still ragged from growth or maybe he'd just never chewed enough to file them down.

"He looks like a better dressed fuck-up, that's all," Salamander said. Nobody listened to him.

"I bought it today," Mother said. He leaned back in his chair and crossed his arms behind his neck. He looked partially happy. "It cost me $15.85."

"You couldn't get one from the Committee for free or for thirty-five cents and give us some of the money you owe?" Salamander spit his words at Motherfucker from the other side of the room where he was fiddling with the padlock of his food cabinet.

"Nope. I don't want to look like a fuck-up like you."

"Hmph."

Faggot raised his leg. "These are the best fitting pants I've ever had. They cost me fifty cents."

"I know. You're a real fuck-up," Salamander and Mother said together. They turned away from each other as soon as they heard the other's voice.

Faggot laughed.

"What's for dinner?" Mushmouth asked.

Faggot opened the refrigerator door and dumped a half loaf of Wonder Bread on the table. He took a slice out of the bag and stuffed the whole think in his mouth. "Supper," he said. "Good," he added rubbing his stomach with slow circular motions like Pinky Lee. "Very Good."

"Gimme that bread, you're fucked," Mother said laughing.

"Shit," said Salamander. He put the key to his padlock in his pocket. "I'll eat when you fuck-ups go away." He left the kitchen.

"Bye-bye," Faggot waved.

Meticulously Mother took a slice of bread out of the bag and began to butter it. He shaved the butter off in thin slices and laid them down one on top of the other. Faggot was on his third slice. Then Mother folded the bread into a half sandwich and ate it slowly. "I'm gaining weight on what I've been eating here," he said."

"Fuck," said Faggot as wet doughy drops of bread

fell out of his mouth. He sucked them back in and wiped them away with his hand at the same time. "Fuck, shit, piss."

Mother pushed the butter away and tucked the front of his shirt down his pants.

"Where are you going?" Faggot looked at him.

"I'm going courtin'," Mother said half-proudly, half-slyly with a big mean grin. "I'm gonna get me a Canadian wife."

Faggot whistled through his teeth. "What are you going to do with a bride?"

"I'm gonna marry her. That's what I'm going to do." A muscle twitched in Mother's cheek. "That's what brides are for."

"Uh-huh." Faggot looked across the bread and butter at Motherfucker. "Don't make me be your best man. I don't like weddings."

"Okay, Faggot. You're excused."

"Gee thanks. When's the big day?"

"Don't worry, Faggot, I'll tell you. We'll have a party."

"And we can all get drunk, right?"

"Right." Mother looked at Faggot from under his eyebrows. He raised his hand to his mouth and rubbed it back and forth against his lips. "And I'll be landed."

"Do you think you could live with her after?" Faggot asked. "You'll be married."

"I don't care. If she doesn't want to live with me that's cool. And if she wants to live with me that's all right, too."

"You have to stay married together for five years.

They send an investigator out to make sure you're living as man and wife in the same house."

Mother laughed. "Do they check the bedroom?"

Faggot shrugged. "I don't know. I never got married under those circumstances. I just got married by myself and each time I thought I knew the girl pretty well and it never lasted five years. It's a lot tougher than you think."

"Yeah, well, she's got a big farm somewhere in Ontario that's big enough for both of us to get lost in. If we stay friends I can sort of stay there often enough to make the investigator think we're together."

"What's in it for her?"

"Me." Motherfucker tapped his chest.

Faggot laughed.

"Why wouldn't she do it, Faggot? She's Canadian and it's nothing for her. Marriage is..."

"Nothing. I know," Faggot said.

"Man, you're just down on marriage because you've done it too often."

"That's not the problem around here."

Now it was Mother who laughed at Faggot's joke. He looked at his hand and smiled at Faggot through half-closed eyes but he was listening to him, too.

"Marriage is messy and it's expensive. All that legal shit. It's easier to get in than out."

"Yeah, but this is just a political marriage."

"They all are," Faggot said. He looked directly at Motherfucker and repeated himself knowingly. "Boy, they all are."

Motherfucker chuckled. "Man."

"Which fuck-up is getting married first?"

Salamander asked.

"He is." Faggot pointed to Mother. "I can't get married."

"Yeah, we know," Salamander said. "You're still married to Miss California."

"Salamander, you can be best man because Faggot doesn't want to be."

"I don't want to be nobody's best man, especially yours," Salamander said. He laughed to himself. "Boy, I'd like to see the lucky lady."

Faggot had a quick fit in his chair. "The lucky lady," he repeated to himself. "Jesus Christ. The lucky lady."

"They ought to make a law preventing you from getting married again, Faggot," Salamander said. "It would be for your own self-protection."

Motherfucker laughed his soft easy chuckle and stood up. He brushed a few crumbs off the front of his shirt. "Well, I'll see you guys later," he said. He started for the kitchen door.

Faggot escorted him to the porch. He stood inside the doorway and watched Motherfucker slink away up the street, tapping the top of the fences with his hand. When Motherfucker disappeared, Faggot stepped inside and slammed the door. "Poor bastard," he whispered.

Salamander and Mushmouth took bets on the wedding day. Mushmouth thought the first wedding in *Canadia* would mean something but he wasn't sure what. Salamander thought that if Mother really got married the wedding should take place in the church with Breeze as ring bearer.

Motherfucker was busy courtin' for a week and a half. It didn't leave him much time to get depressed because he was too busy consulting himself about the latest stage of development. Sometimes he came home happy and sometimes he was miserable but at least the Bride kept him out of another black despair. He got up at noon and waited through the afternoons for the time when he could see his Bride. Then he came home and got drunk with Faggot in the evening while he waited to see what would happen and what his Bride would do. Faggot said the negotiations between them were super heavy. He said that Bride was a pretty tough customer because she had the Motherfucker coming and going. It made Motherfucker's bargaining for car keys look like kid's stuff.

"How's it coming?" Faggot asked every other day.

"Sheet, man," Motherfucker said. Sometimes it was "fair" and sometimes it was "pretty good." Some days he didn't say anything. He still came home around nine or ten so Salamander said that if he was really courtin' the Bride didn't seem worth it.

Mother didn't say much about his Bride. Going into the second week of courtship, he said less about her than he'd said in the beginning which was next to nothing. Mushmouth asked him if she was pretty and he wouldn't say.

"Well, did she wear braces? You know, did she have orthodontia?" Mushmouth asked.

Mother went into his room and played guitar.

"Do we know her?" Faggot asked. "Did you know her before when we lived in the hostel?"

But Mother wouldn't say.

"The reason Mother has nothing to say," said Salamander, "is because Mother's going out with Breeze's sister."

Faggot laughed. Mushmouth ticked off all the women they all knew in *Canadia* and asked Mother if he was cold, luke-warm or hot.

The more questions they asked, the quieter Mother became. Faggot said the engagement was off. "You didn't buy a big enough diamond," he said.

"Yeah, like how big do I need?" Mother asked.

"The Hope Diamond would be a start." Faggot choked on a mouthful of Andres Rose and had to leave the room.

After another week of courtin' Salamander asked Mother if his Bride would haul a train. Everybody, except Mushmouth who was expecting Doreen any day, laughed.

"We'll see," Mother said. "We'll see."

DOREEN

The day Doreen came, Mushmouth wasn't home.
Nobody was home for that matter. Nobody except
Motherfucker who was always home.

Doreen was a nice, lower-middle-class girl from
San Francisco who had become a hippie instead of a
secretary. She was a little overweight and always wore
her shirt outside her pants or a long sweater, even on
a hot day. She wanted to have a lot of kids and wear
ankle-length gingham dresses and a bag made out of a
dungaree pocket. Mushmouth wanted to grow his hair
down to his ass. She fitted neatly into his shoulder
and his arm was the perfect size for her waist. They
looked like one of those commercial love posters
where the couple is locked in a fierce embrace on the
coastline of a deserted shore and the man looks off to
his destiny lurking on the other side of the horizon
and the woman nuzzles into his shoulder clinging and
clawing at the security and warmth that is supposedly
waiting for her there.

Motherfucker said Doreen came with a suitcase
and a shopping bag. Her trunk had been sent almost
two months before and was still on its way.
Mushmouth nearly developed an ulcer waiting for

that trunk every other day for two months and worrying about the customs men and signing for something inspected by the Canadian government on the front porch of Faggot's house.

Motherfucker said Mushmouth almost started to cry when he saw Doreen. He ran around for the entire afternoon saying, "Oh, man, this is it. This is really it." He could hardly wait for everybody to come home so he could introduce Doreen.

"It's gonna be all right now," Mushmouth shouted. "Things are gonna be just fine from now on."

Doreen stood in the middle of the hall, peering into Mother's room and afraid to go into the kitchen. She looked lost whenever Mushmouth went away to go out to the porch and wave his arms around some more and scream, "C-H-R-I-S-T. It's gonna be fine now."

When Mushmouth came back Doreen looked at him for direction and flashed a faded smile, hoping he would tell her what to do or where to put her shopping bag or who slept where and how they were going to live. But Mushmouth kept telling everybody who wasn't there how great it was going to be and how wonderful *Canadia* was. And when Mother finally got off his ass and moved into the living room that was his bedroom under the pretext of getting his cigarette papers, Doreen flashed him one of her faded smiles and pulled her sweater across her hips. Mother gave her the once-over in secret and looked at Mushmouth sideways out of his left eye with "what the hell is all this commotion about" and Mushmouth was quiet.

Somehow or other they got through the afternoon

because when Faggot came home they were all sitting quietly on the porch. Mushmouth introduced Doreen to Faggot and Faggot went into his girl-charmer routine. Doreen smiled at everyone and kept quiet. She was still tense but seemed less uptight about her sweater.

Salamander pretended she wasn't there. He kept his mouth shut through all the negotiations for a place for them to sleep. Mother kept his mouth shut, too, but he kept looking at everybody like a sea gull waiting for the scraps.

Mushmouth had the money coming to him that he had originally lent to Faggot to rent the house on and now with the extra money Doreen brought, they decided to get a small apartment. Doreen was set on the idea of getting an apartment and buying paisleyed imitation Indian fabrics for bedspreads and drapes. They wanted an apartment just like the apartment they would have had in San Francisco and they would be fine until they figured out that Vancouver wasn't San Francisco. It wasn't even Lima, Ohio. It was nowhere.

The first night Doreen was there, they slept in the room that used to be Mushmouth's and Salamander's. Salamander moved himself into the upstairs hall. The funny thing was he didn't make a big stink out of it. Everybody thought he would but he didn't. He liked to surprise people sometimes.

The next day they went apartment hunting. And the next and the next and the one after that, too. Things stayed pretty much as they were. Salamander in the hall and not bitching about it, Mushmouth and

189

Doreen in the upstairs bedroom and Doreen not liking it, Faggot getting ready to move into the room that used to belong to Jimmy. Mother always demanding pocket money, lying around in his big brass bed all day, leastways until noon on most days, and thinking about his Bride.

In the evenings Doreen cooked for her and Mushmouth while Mother mooched around the door. He was like a big stray dog who was happy with the leavings. It was hard not to let him in on the food, too. Salamander came in later and ate his health food crap and kept his mouth shut. He was getting quieter and skinnier all the time. Mushmouth came to the table when Doreen had the food cooked and he sat around afterwards while she cleaned off the table and put away the leftovers. She didn't eat much herself because she was working on losing weight and being able to tuck in her sweaters. She had a couple of Indian dresses that were very nice. She looked almost thin in those.

When Doreen had been there long enough to figure out the politics in the house, she sometimes tried to prime Mushmouth but he never caught on to her awkwardness or her embarrassment. And sometimes he embarrassed her himself. But if he had known what he was doing, he would never have forgiven himself.

Doreen baked bread. She said it was San Francisco sourdough bread. Whatever it was, it was delicious. Mother really dug that bread.

One day Mushmouth came home and said he had found an apartment and that he and Doreen were moving out. He asked Salamander to watch out for the trunk that still hadn't come and Salamander said, "Sure, I'll sign for it."

Like the time Tex left, Faggot went through the whole business of placing his arm on Mushmouth's shoulder and saying, "Write if you get work, boy," and all the rest of the crap that went with the good-bye speech. Faggot was pretty good at it by this time but somehow it didn't work anymore. Doreen packed all her extra long sweaters in her shopping bag and Faggot drove them to the new apartment house.

It was funny but everyone said Doreen was the neatest person who ever lived in that house. Not only neat but secretive. She lived in the house for nearly three weeks and you never saw anything that was hers lying around to tell you she was really there. She never left a comb on the table or a pair of underpants on the floor or on the clothesline or anywhere. Even Mother said it was eerie how a person could be so secretive and still be in the same house with you.

When Faggot brought all their things to the new apartment, Mushmouth looked at him like a little kid. "You'll come around, won't you, Faggot? You'll come and visit us, won't you?"

Faggot really dug good-byes. Maybe he liked to feel he had some power when he offered support that wasn't really support to people who were temporarily more confused than he was because they held bags in their hand or were waiting for a life or for the thing around the corner that hasn't come yet and isn't visible. It's hard to say. Especially when everybody goes away and comes back again half a dozen times except for the people who go away and can never come back.

Faggot put his arms around Mushmouth, a great big bear of a man hugging a little boy with a little boy body as he stood next to his girlfriend-wife and hoped for the best. "Sure, boy, we'll come and visit you all the time. You come and visit us, too."

"Maybe you and Salamander and Mother can come for dinner sometimes," Mushmouth said and looked at Doreen next to him. Doreen smiled and nodded encouragement with her hands tugging at her sweater, "Yes, we'd like that. In a couple of weeks after we get everything set up here."

"Sure. Sure. No hurry," Faggot said. And this time it was Doreen who looked jubilant and Mushmouth who was fading.

In the next couple of weeks things straightened themselves out at the house. At first it was strange for everybody to come home and find Mushmouth gone. It got to be a very close-knit community with Faggot and Salamander and Mother living in the house together and going their separate ways. It was tough on Mother to be all alone all day with too much time to think about a bride. To sit out every afternoon and to live in a month of Sundays...

Mushmouth told his landlady that he was a freelance photographer and that his wife was...Well, she was his wife. In the mornings he tried to look for work and in the afternoons he had tea from Murchie's Import Coffee Shop with Doreen. Sometimes they went for walks together and tried to discover Vancouver and recreate the life they had lived in S.F.

But there isn't all that much to discover in Vancouver and when all your friends are gone, it's hard to remember who you used to be.

Sometimes in the afternoons Mushmouth came to the house to talk to Mother and look around for Salamander. Since Doreen came, Mushmouth and Salamander suddenly had a lot to say to one another. Nobody knew what they talked about because they always went away and when they came back Salamander was his sullen old self.

Now wherever Mushouth went he carried his camera around his neck. It got to be a pain in the ass being a freelance photographer and having to wear his camera like a chain around his neck to remind himself all the time that the only pictures he was taking were for fun and even then he couldn't develop them himself. But he took quite a lot of pictures in those days. When he took days off from job-hunting (which was more often than he liked to admit or than Doreen liked to mention), he could spend the whole morning taking pictures and believing he was a freelance photographer while he practiced at getting good. That way he was almost what he thought he was until there were groceries to buy or Doreen wanted more Indian paisley things. And, of course, the landlady was always suspicious.

But they had lots of good times, too. They must have had. Everybody does when they sit still long enough to remember them. Like the day Mushmouth and Doreen took a picnic basket to the little park that was near their apartment house. Mushmouth took pictures of Doreen sitting on the grass and looking very hip and slender and attractive and Doreen chased Mushmouth around and for a minute or two they both forgot they were living on Doreen's money and when that was gone there were going to be hard times.

A couple of times when Mushmouth was looking for work, Doreen dropped by the house and left behind some of her fantastic sourdough bread. It wasn't hard to figure that she was probably getting to be as lonely as anybody else in Vancouver and probably more so because she didn't have any hate or fight or political thing to keep her going. The politics of the movement were pretty far away from her. She knew she had a Catholic father who she had just about killed by coming to live in Vancouver with a boy he thought qualified as the dipshit of the year.

The whole situation was getting to be like an egg-timer. The salt was running out and things were getting ready to explode but nobody knew what was going to cave in first. Luckily it was the floorboards around the register in Faggot's room. The room that used to belong to Jimmy.

A short time after his father's envelope came, Motherfucker stood on the entrance ramp to the Burrard Bridge and waited three hours for a lift downtown. Finally he walked the twenty-minute walk and stood in front of the Hudson's Bay Company for two hours more.

When he came home he announced he had decided to take matters into his own hands and get landed. He wanted to enjoy the Canadian scenery and the fruits of love. He wanted to be free of a political conscience and the watchful eyes of the FBI lurking on two borders and in every street sign and corner of his mind.

Mother said he was going to marry the Bride any day. If he married the Bride he would be landed and free to be divorced and then free to become himself again.

The Bride was a rather strange girl, pretty once but now a little dog-eared from too much courting and from too many drugs, or as some people might say, from living too much all at once.

But the Bride had one enviable plus besides her ability to cop dope and play a righteous piano. She was Canadian and marriage with a Canadian Bride guarantees instant immigration.

The Salvation Army is just like the regular army except it marries the girls it rapes.

PARTY-TIME

"What we need is a party," said Faggot. "We need to get a lot of people together and have a party. Who knows you might meet somebody you didn't know before. Why we might even meet some new brides."

"Sure," said Salamander, "it's a great idea but who do we know to invite?"

"You could invite some of the people you know at the church."

"Fuck off, Faggot."

"Didn't you know? The only reason Salamander goes to that church is to meet some nice girl and so far he hasn't met anybody but that dumb minister who came to the house looking for Salamander for some church committee and gave everybody heart failure because he rang the bell and nobody would answer it. Then he banged on the door and peered into the window and I had to go into the kitchen to hide. And if he came in I was going to have to go down to the cellar and get a hatchet and go around the front and..."

"Oh, go fuck yourself, will you, Mother."

"No. I'm just havin' a little fun," Mother said from

the kitchen doorway where he was scrunched up in a regular Mother position with his hands all stuck in his pockets and squirming down to his...

"I want a party," said Salamander.

"Whose havin' a party?" yelled Mushmouth as he reached over the banister and started grabbing at Faggot. "Whose havin' a party? I wanna go to a party, too. Doreen wants a party. Let's have a party."

"I'm having a party," said Faggot.

"Great, when's the party?" asked Mushmouth.

"Now."

Faggot was facing Mother who was still stuck in the doorway. At the same time Faggot put his hands over his head and grabbed for Mushmouth on the stairs behind him. As soon as he got a hold of something that felt like a Mushmouth he pulled it over the banister. Faggot turned around and patted Mushmouth's head. Mushmouth was hanging over the banister with the railing stuck in his stomach.

"I'm warning you, Faggot. I'm warning you. I'll throw up. So help me God. I'll puke."

"So puke. Somebody always pukes at a party, don't they, you little fucker," said Mother. He grabbed Salamander and Salamander went into his all-star bantam boxer routine. Mushmouth was turning red in the face and he was beginning to drool. Saliva dripped out of his mouth every time he said, "I'll puke. So help me God, I'll puke."

Salamander was dancing around trying to take on Mother who was holding him off at arm's length.

"Go get him, boy," Faggot yelled and Mother went after Salamander. "Don't let him get away."

Salamander's defense crumpled into sporadic arm and leg movements. Faggot flipped Mushmouth over the railing and held him by the waist until his feet found the floor on their own. Then he lay Mushmouth down on the floor, who was all the time gasping and trying to pull out his handkerchief and saying that he was going to throw up, that he'd never been surer of anything in his whole life than how sure he was about getting sick right there and then and throwing lunch all over the fake rug.

Faggot went for Salamander's feet and together he and Mother lifted him up and swung him back and forth like a rag doll in a hammock. Salamander closed his eyes and folded his hands across his chest with the perfect confidence of a corpse and let them take him wherever they were going to take him.

"Through the window. Through the window," Faggot shouted. But Mother made a face with his lower lip like "are you really crazy or something" and Faggot gave him a silly little-boy giggle.

They carried Salamander through the front door and went through a pantomime of tossing him over the porch railing. "So he can land on his fat ass," Faggot said.

Then Faggot changed places with Mother who said once, "Hey, be careful. Watch the bastard's head."

"Yeah, watch the bastard's head," said Salamander from his comatose-like state.

"YEAH, WATCH THE BASTARD'S HEAD," screamed Mushmouth from his prone position on the fake rug where he could see that with Faggot's grip Salamander's hair was scraping the wooden steps.

"We're watching it," assured Faggot.

"It's okay, Mush, he says he's watching it," Salamander repeated to Mushmouth who was cringing on the floor and peeping between his fingers.

With Faggot going first and Motherfucker bringing up the rear, they got Salamander's body to the front lawn and swung him back and forth a good three-four feet above the ground. "I'm gonna be sick," muttered Salamander. "Jesus, I'm gonna puke all over myself," he said to himself.

"We better put him down 'cuz he's gonna puke all over himself," Mother echoed.

"Sure, boy, put him down." And Faggot and Mother lowered him to six inches off the ground and unceremoniously dumped him.

While Salamander flopped over on the grass and clutched his stomach, Faggot and Mother went back into the house. Mushmouth came running out to the porch and watched Salamander moaning over his stomach. "Sweet Jesus," Mushmouth said. "I nearly puked. I nearly puked," he said to no one in particular.

Salamander came back into the house with Mushmouth and they all sat down in the front hall. They couldn't meet in the real living room because it was Mother's bedroom and a place that Salamander would never go near because he said in private that Mother gave him the creeps and anything connected to Mother was creepy.

Faggot leaned up against the stairway with his hands in his pockets, rocking back and forth.

Mother went back to his doorway and the two boys sat on the bottom steps of the stairs.

"I'm gonna have a party," Faggot said again. Mushmouth got up and did a little dance. It was a take-off version of a Peppermint Lounge Twist. He swung his ass and his hips rolled. "Oh boy, a party. We're gonna have a P-A-R-T-Y," he sang.

Faggot shook his head and laughed. He could barely control himself. Then he gave the old one-two-three appreciation with a quick twirl of his finger. "Heavy shit, man, like really heavy shit."

Mother smiled a good-humored Mother smile and Salamander tapped his feet against the floor like one of those frenzied four year-olds on a mid-afternoon TV show.

Doreen came in the front door with a brown bag from Leonard's that contained hers and her Martin's supper.

"Hey, what's going on?" said her smile because she wasn't yet up to asking a lot of questions. She was still behind the scenes figuring things out. The funny thing was it always stayed that way. There was never anything hanging out of Doreen. Maybe it was left over from her thinking there was so much of her and trying so hard all the time to hide part of herself.

"Faggot's having a party," said Mush who pretended she hadn't called him Martin.

Doreen's eyes traveled to Faggot who was standing in the middle of the fake living room on the fake rug smiling like he had just done something very good or very bad or very extraordinary in any case. "I'm having a party."

"Oh," said Doreen. "When?"

"Now," chuckled Salamander. "We're having a

party right now and you're in it."

Mushmouth got up to do his little dance again and Doreen looked at Mother smiling back at her from the doorway and she turned away. She moved into the kitchen to put away the things from the brown bag and get started on their supper. Hers and Martin's.

Faggot followed her through the doorway and into the kitchen. "Really, I'm having a party. It's gonna be this Saturday," he called over his shoulder to everybody hanging around the steps.

Salamander went into the kitchen to his special cupboard. He was having Red River Cereal with wheat germ and natural honey from non-insecticide bees on toasted hearts of oatmeal bread. Mushmouth and Mother sat down at the table. Mother started to roll himself a cigarette, then looked up in exasperation, amazed at what he was doing, and asked Faggot for a cigarette.

Faggot gave him one of those "you're-a-pain-in-the-ass" looks and tossed him a package of Sportsman.

"It's gonna be this Saturday night. I'm gonna invite all of the people from the Committee..."

"But we know all those people," Salamander broke in, "and they're all dumbshits."

"And I'm gonna invite a couple of people from work."

"You still working?" Mother asked in mock surprise.

"And I'm gonna invite the girl who works in the candy store next door who I have lunch with sometimes. And I'm gonna invite the landlady, if she'll come..."

"You do that, boy."

"And I'm gonna invite that minister, Peterson, who's really hip and all that. And I'm gonna have the candy store girl bring all the girls she knows. I'm gonna tell her this is the party of the year and she better not miss it. And I'm gonna tell the guy who plays the sax at work to come and for him to bring his wife and all the people she knows. I'm gonna tell everybody to bring everybody they know and we'll have fifty, maybe hundred people here and it will be the party of the century."

"How 'bout Breeze?" Mother asked.

"He can't come. I don't want any dumbshits at my party. No breezes."

"Good. I'll tell him to come." Mother flipped back the cigarettes and Faggot caught them and pulled one out for himself.

"What are they gonna eat?" Salamander asked.

"Yeah, what are they gonna eat?" repeated Mushmouth as he watched Doreen peel five or six potatoes at the sink and make two or three trips to the stove and back. "What are they gonna eat? You can't have a good party without food."

"They'll eat all that party shit. That's what they'll eat and they'll be dumb enough to like it," said Salamander.

"Yeah, chips and pretzels. A couple of cheeses. Crackers. Spreads. Party Shit," Faggot said.

"Onion dip," said Mother. "And not that Kraft Crap. The real thing. The kind you make yourself from fresh sour cream and real onions."

"Sure," said Faggot with another "heavy shit" sign. "Sure thing. And you bring all your church friends, Salamander," Faggot said. "They'll like the party. And if any of them don't drink, we'll give them grape juice."

"What are you making for supper, Doreen?" asked Mushmouth as he followed her motions around the kitchen.

"Don't rush me."

"Okay. Okay. I'm not rushing you. Really, I'm not. I just wanted to know what you were making for supper."

She threw the last potato in the pot and turned her back on the stove. Water splashed up from the pan and sizzled on the right hot-plate burner, the only one of two burners on the third stove that was working. Faggot's hand steadied the pot. The other two stoves were collecting dust in the back hall along with bags and bags of garbage that everybody was always going to put out.

"Yeah, Breeze'll bring us some good shit and we can all get properly stoned for once," Mother said.

"Breeze ain't coming," said Faggot.

"You think he can get enough for all of us?" asked Mushmouth. "It's been. Jesus, I think it's been about three weeks since we had any shit in this house."

"If he can get any," Mother said, "he'll get it for us."

Salamander sat down in front of his steaming Red River Cereal and reached for the wheat germ. Just when he had his hand around it, his chair collapsed. He got off the floor brushing the germ off himself.

"Shit," he screamed. He turned the chair upside-down and examined the leg that was shorter than the other three and kept falling out of its socket. "Fucking chair."

"Who's going to pay for this party?" Mother asked.

"You're not, that's for sure. You can't pay for the cigarettes you smoke," Faggot said.

"I can't give you any money," Mushmouth said. "I haven't got a job yet."

Faggot leaned against the burnt-out burner watching Doreen's potatoes. "It doesn't matter," he said. "This is my party."

"FUCK THIS CHAIR." Salamander yelled shaking Red River Cereal off his wrist. He jumped around for a while, knocking the chair over.Then he sucked the cereal off his wrist and picked up the chair by the back and smashed it down on the floor again.

"How much do you think the booze'll cost?" asked Mother.

"I don't know but it'll be expensive. We have to have good stuff--some scotch, some bourbon, maybe a little rye." Faggot looked at Doreen. "Wine for the ladies. Beer. We should have vodka. Some mixes. Then the soft drinks. You know, Coke and ginger ale. Grape juice for Salamander's friends."

"Tom Collins mix. We've got to have Tom Collins mix. Then I can have a real Tom Collins," said Mushmouth.

"Yeah, some Tom Collins," repeated Faggot, ticking the liquor list off on his fingers.

"GODDAMN THAT FUCKING CHAIR.

GODDAMN THIS FUCKING HOUSE WHERE YOU CAN'T SIT IN A CHAIR AND EAT LIKE A GODDAMN FUCKING HUMAN BEING."

Salamander picked up the chair and threw it out the window. It landed with a crash on the concrete near the cellar door.

Doreen froze at the sink. She watched Mushmouth go to the window and stare at the chair. He stuck his head and shoulders completely out the window. "You totaled it. Terrific."

"Do you think Tom Collins mix is really necessary?" asked Faggot.

"No. It's a waste," Mother said. "We need whiskey and onion dip. Sour cream and real onion onion dip."

"Yeah, I think so, too," Faggot agreed.

The day of the party, Faggot came home on his lunch hour to make sure that Mother, Salamander and Mushmouth had cleaned the house. He wanted a full report from Doreen about the Party Shit she was supposed to buy with the fifteen dollars he'd given her. He told her to spend ten and use the extra five only in case she ran short but she went with Mother and they spent all of it.

Faggot got on Salamander's back about shaking out the rug in the front fake living room. Salamander asked him why he didn't rent a woman to clean up for the party. Faggot, all pissed off and angry because he had to go back to his shitty job that he hated and that kept him busy all the time doing nothing even on Saturdays, told him he could just fuck off and if he wouldn't do it, then he didn't have to come to the party. Salamander said he didn't want to go to any party run by such a Faggot Fattass that Faggot was. At this, Faggot shouted out some more orders about ice and paper cups, waved his arm in the direction of the couch that was filthy and at the broom in the corner behind the refrigerator and stalked off to his car. As a parting gesture before he closed the door Faggot shouted out about the garbage in the back hall, "You better get off your ass, boy, and get that garbage out here before tonight." He flipped the ignition that didn't start and watched Salamander making Fatass Faggot take-offs through the sideview mirror. He laughed and tossed his Sportsman out the window when the car finally started.

"He oughta get a nigger maid like Tex suggested," said Salamander.

"Who's Tex?" asked Doreen.

"He's this guy who used to live here when we all first moved in but he took off to go someplace to get landed and nobody's seen him since," Mushmouth answered her.

"Hey, Salamander, who's this Tex?" Doreen persisted. "What did you say about this Tex person?"

"I didn't say nothing," Salamander said. "I forget." He left Doreen bewildered beside the rug that Mother had just dragged out of the hall and dumped on the porch.

Mother took charge in the afternoon. He really had a secret fetish for keeping things clean and it upset him to have to live in such relative disorder. He liked to be able to put his finger on everything just when he wanted it. "Hey, Doreen, you wipe down the table in the kitchen, huh. And you, Salamander, help me stretch out this rug so we can beat the shit out of it."

Salamander mumbled to himself but helped Mother stretch out the rug and get broomsticks and beat it and beat it and beat it until there was a thin layer of dust like smog settling around the front yard.

"Never looked that dirty in the house," Mushmouth said as he watched from the front porch holding a handkerchief over his mouth and nose and looking like he was going to die. His eyes were watering, too.

"Martin, you ought to get out of the dust," Doreen warned. "You should go in the house."

After some discussion about whether or not to wash the floors, they decided to do it anyway since they figured they would never get the opportunity to clean the house so thoroughly again.

Faggot managed to get himself out of work early. When he pulled up in front of the house, he got out of the car right away and hustled up the path. He flung the gate aside with one of his off-hand, backhand gestures. "You boys sure done a fine job." He looked around. "Really, it looks good."

Faggot tossed the car keys to Mother. "Go get some ice. I want to straighten out my room."

Mother followed by Mushmouth, followed by Doreen , headed for the parked car. Mother was a maniac behind the wheel. Salamander said he was like a caged animal released. He said Mother always drove too fast and although he thought he was a hot shit driver, he always seemed to shift too fast or too soon and the gears always grated. "You'd almost think he was Canadian, the way he drives," Salamander said.

"Get lots of ice," Faggot shouted from an upstairs window.

Mother, Mushmouth and Doreen were in the front seat. Doreen was in the middle.

"Where d'you want to go for ice?" asked Mushmouth.

"I don't know. I thought we could drive around for a while until we saw an "ICE" place in a gas station. Let's try Chevron Island first."

Doreen was squeezed between Mushmouth and Mother and whenever Mother stopped short or took U-turns that were forbidden or took the corners too sharply, she steadied herself with one hand against the dash. She was a little afraid to lean too heavily one way or the other. She was a little uptight about there not being enough room in the front seat in the first place but it annoyed the hell out of Mother.

"For Chrissake, can't you relax and sit back? Why do you have to hold onto the car for? Mushmouth, make her relax."

But Mushmouth couldn't make her relax and Mother drove faster and faster because Doreen wouldn't relax.

"Hey, slow down, will you," Mushmouth mumbled from behind his handkerchief. "You just missed an "ICE" place."

"Shit."

They did a quick u-ey, cut out a guy from the oncoming traffic and went back to the station. When they pulled in they saw that the "ICE" place used to be an "ICE" place but the "ICE" wasn't working anymore. It was leaning up against an old red Coca-Cola ice box that looked like it was left over from the Forties.

"Shit."

Chevron Island didn't have ice. They had leis, flags, gas and miniature hula-hip girls but no ice. The guy didn't remember them, either. That was funny, too, because there aren't many people who go to Chevron Island for fake palm trees, green leis and fifty cents worth of gas. But this guy was either wasted or extremely formal because he never once let on he knew any one of the people who kept coming back and bugging his ass for fifty cents worth. But then, like Salamander said, "He might just wear that stupid-ass look to fool people."

After Chevron Island they hit three or four more places but they didn't have any luck at any of them. They never expected it to be so tough to find "ICE" in a place the size of Vancouver. But it was. It was impossible to get ice from an "ICE" machine in Vancouver.

Away up the Kingsway on the road that leads to the Trans-Canada and east, they found a tumble-down station that had a beat-up "ICE" machine near the air hose.

Mother opened the ice chest--it looked like a second-hand freezer a man with a big family and a small income would keep in his living room. Inside were whole hunks of ice just like frozen bundles of hamburger.

"It doesn't come in cubes," said Doreen.

"What do you mean it doesn't come in cubes?'"asked Mushmouth, leaning over her shoulder and sticking his hands into the freezer.

"It's not broken up. Look at it. It's in big hunks. You can't put that stuff in drinks. It's crazy."

"You got any ice that's in cubes?" Mother asked the attendant who was standing beside the air machine smoking a cigarette.

"Why, what's the matter? Can't a big boy like you break up some ice?"

The three of them stared at him.

"You take a pick-axe and you hit it and hit it until you got cubes or don't you young people think at all? Or maybe it's because you never picked up a pick-axe in your life. A big boy, like you, too."

"How much is it?" asked Mother.

"Fifty cents."

"We'll take it."

"Suit yourselves," he said.

"We'lll take two," Mother said. He lit a cigarette and leaned up against the other side of the air machine.

Doreen went back to the car for her pocketbook. She handed a dollar bill to Mushmouth through the car window. Mushmouth carried the bill back to Mother and Mother dropped it into the man's out-stretched hand.

"Have a nice party," he said as Mother revved up the motor. Mother let the car slide backwards and then gassed it out of the filling station. He did a superb imitation of A. J. Foyt for somebody's benefit. He got his hands right on the wheel from seeing it on the backs of Wheaties, Breakfast of Champions.

Mother carried the two large blocks of ice up the steps to the front porch and disappeared into the cellar to get a pick-axe or the hatchet or something to crush up the ice with. Salamander came out to the porch to look at the ice. He was almost incoherent when he saw the glacial chunk that was supposed to pass for an ice cube. "Look at that. Look at that, will you? Will you take a look at that, Faggot? You send that dumbshit for ice and look at what he comes back with. A party? How can you have a party with ice that dumbshit brings back?"

"Shut up," said Mother coming through the doorway with both a pick-axe and a hatchet.

Salamander stepped aside, mumbling to himself. He crossed his arms over his chest and said, "I don't want any part of this." He went back into the house.

Faggot came out to see the ice and found Mother hacking at a block of ice while Doreen and Mushmouth scampered around scooping up ice chips and putting them in plastic baggies.

"It was the only ice we could find," Mother said.

Mushmouth and Doreen didn't say anything. They were too busy trying to grab the ice chips before they melted or got too dirty to use.

After a couple of hours the three of them managed to have half of both blocks crushed into chipped-up ice slivers suitable for mixing with drinks. The rest of the stuff was either pulverized beyond hope or dripping down the front steps or remaining, one huge mass of scar tissue, in ragged clumps scattered over the porch, the steps and the lawn.

Mushmouth put some ice chips down Doreen's blouse and she was angry. "Gee," said Mushmouth, "it was only a few ice cubes." She went to the side of the porch and pouted. Later when she'd decided it was okay, she came back and wanted to play. But by the time Doreen was into it, Mushmouth was out of it, wondering just what the fuck was going wrong.

Because when Doreen finally got into it, there was no stopping her. In a wild, crazy sort of way she threw ice cubes at everybody. Then she playfully put an ice cube down the back of Mother's shirt while he was bending over to straighten out the block of ice.

Mushmouth stood off to the side picking at his nose and wiping off his glasses and putting them back on again.

Mother turned around with the hatchet in his hand and caught Doreen. He put an ice cube on her neck. She giggled and tried to squirm away but Motherfucker wasn't angry. He grabbed her by the wrist and tried to put an ice cube in her blouse. She laughed and shook her arm up and down but Motherfucker wouldn't let her go until he managed to get an ice cube down her back. Then he threw an ice cube at Mushmouth and Mushmouth threw one at Mother and missed.

Faggot went to the Liquor Control Board himself. "You kids be good and clean up that mess," he said before he left.

By 5:00 o'clock the house was spic and span. The onion spread, personally prepared by Motherfucker, was cooling in the fridge. Doreen and Mushmouth left to go back to their apartment because Doreen said she wanted to change.

Faggot was shaving with Motherfucker's razor. Motherfucker made sure he'd used the razor first because he couldn't afford to let Faggot's dirty hair put him off on a day when he looked forward to an all-night drunk.

Salamander dug out his special Sergeant Pepper's Outfit from the hall closet for the occasion. Nobody knew he had extra clothes hidden all over the place but he had boxes and boxes of things he never wore or ate or used hidden under his bed and in the cellar and in the upstairs closet where he could keep a close eye on them. He was wearing his dude outfit, the outfit he could never wear to the Canadian Imperial Bank of Commerce because he looked like a half-brother to a skinny and undersized Doc Holliday. Big western pointed boots with skin-tight black pants tucked in, white shirt with Edwardian cuffs and collar, cuff links, black bow tie and mod jacket that looked like it was Salvation Army. His hair was growing in and he'd combed it down. His moustache was just beginning to crawl out of the messy stage and looked kind of appealing on him.

He knocked on the bathroom door. "You in there, Faggot? Hey, Faggot..." He leaned against the door. "Faggot."

Faggot opened the door. He stood in the doorway with no clothes on and one hand on the doorknob. He smiled. "Ye-es."

"Oh, for Chrissake."

"What do you want, Salamander?"

"I want to use the bathroom."

"Well, use it," Faggot said as he obligingly stepped aside. "I'm shaving."

Salamander waved his hand at him and tramped off downstairs. Halfway down the stairs he met Mother coming up to use the bathroom. "Don't bother," he said. "That Faggot's in there taking a bath."

"'Bout time," said Mother.

The guests were supposed to start coming around 7:30-8:00 o'clock. Nobody expected anybody to show before 9:30 but Salamander had doubts about anybody showing at all. At 6:00 o'clock sharp he brought out his rolled wheat hearts and started his supper. He said he couldn't eat Party Shit. He also said that watching Mother sample the onion dip was making him sick.

Salamander was vegetarian of sorts but he didn't stay away from alcohol. He just never bought any. He said it would never do to drink on an empty stomach because the liquor would be non-nutritive crap but mixed with rolled wheat hearts, liquor became protein-rich food.

Mother said Salamander was getting to be a regular pain in the ass with all of his doubts and ideas and comments. He wanted to know why Salamander couldn't keep his comments to himself like everybody else in that house.

At 7:30 Peterson came by and had a couple of drinks. He drank rye and ginger ale on some crushed-up ice. He held the glass up to the light and peered at the ice. He told Doreen how he thought the ice was kind of funny. Mother told him how they'd gotten it and what kind of a guy sold it to them. Peterson was very interested in that for a while. He said, "No kidding," twice. He told Mushmouth what a lovely girl Doreen was. Mushmouth looked into his glass and then into Peterson's face. He looked at Doreen across the room and back to Peterson's face and swallowed, "Yes." Somebody started talking about glaciers but Peterson was looking around for the other people at the party while he moved into his second drink.

"I guess I'm one of the first to arrive," he said.

"You're the first," Salamander said.

Fifteen minutes later two people from Faggot's Mighty Sound Center showed up with their wives. They looked at the house and seemed interested. The wives looked a little embarrassed. Mother leered at them and Peterson made small talk.

Then a dodger from New York City showed up. He said he'd known Faggot for about two months although he'd never come by the house. Salamander said he didn't believe the guy was a draft dodger. He thought he was a narc. He was a photographer and talked to Mush about lenses and frames but they didn't, either one of them, mention jobs. He wanted to talk to Faggot about renting the cellar and developing a dark room down there. Everybody, especially Mushmouth, thought it would be a good idea. Later,

Mushmouth said he didn't think New York was a draft dodger, either.

Mother was on his way to getting drunk with Peterson. When people started talking about the dark room, he brought up the FM radio station again. He said he knew how to run the thing and could organize it and show a profit but that he needed capital. Maybe five hundred dollars would do it but at the mention of money, Peterson started talking about how tough it was to get any money from anybody. Even the Canadians, he said, didn't want to give money. They especially didn't want to give money to people they thought the United States was shipping to Canada because they were freaks and unemployables and generally degenerated. Even the church groups that had collected money for war resistance relief didn't especially want any of their relief cases to show up on a Sunday morning in their churches.

Meanwhile the wives seemed a little bored and a little bewildered. They didn't know where to sit down and they were afraid to leave their purses lying around.

At 9:00 o'clock Peterson left because he said he had a busy schedule and he still had a few appointments to keep. Salamander waved "bye" to him from the front porch.

By 10:00 people were coming and going in twos and threes. A few people would come and rap for fifteen-twenty minutes. When they saw that nobody else was there, they'd leave and say "hello" to the people they met coming up the path. The couple next door started watering the roses at 10:00 in the evening to try to figure out what was going on but they could never see well enough to be sure of anything. They were happy thinking the worst.

Inside Doreen and Mushmouth were getting drunk on Brights President Canadian Sauterne. Salamander plunked himself in front of the fish tank in Mother's living room-bedroom and held his stomach. He was so drunk he forgot to remind himself not to go into Mother's bedroom.

Mother was standing in the doorway smiling and looking at things that seemed very far away, holding a glass full of chipped ice and bourbon neat. He was wearing a shiny black suit jacket that looked early Sixties-Beatleish.

"Where'd you get that coat?" Doreen asked who by now was on her way to getting smashed.

"When I was in high school I used to have a whole suit like this. This jacket cost seventy-five dollars and is the only part I've got left."

Mushmouth said he was very impressed. He didn't look impressed. He looked sore and was sitting by himself in the armchair-couch in the front fake living room. He said, "I didn't know you were such a playboy in your younger days."

Doreen glared at him.

"Any more people come yet?" yelled Salamander from his spot in front of the fish tank. He was watching the fish go round just like figures on a TV screen. As far as he was concerned it was all the same.

"Nope," yelled back Mother. "So far there's been fifteen people. Not counting the candy lady and her friends who haven't shown up yet."

"Where's Faggot?" Salamander shouted. "Where's the Faggot? Anybody seen a Faggot?"

"He's probably upstairs taking a piss," said Mother.

"Okay. He's upstairs taking a piss. I just don't want him to miss the party. I don't want him to miss all the guests that are still coming. I don't want him to miss all this great booze and his candy lady. When Miss Hershey Bar comes in call me, I want to be the first to lick her..."

A guy came that nobody knew. He said he was a friend of Faggot's and Doreen offered him some of her wine. She was slowly working her way through an entire bottle. He said his name was Goldstein.

"Goldwho?" asked Mother trying to be polite and suddenly playing host.

"Goldstein. I'm from Kelley's Sound Center."

"Oh," said Salamander and then in a voice that everybody could hear he whispered to Mushmouth who, looking troubled, had come to tell him something, "That's Faggot's friend, the Goldshit he's always talking about."

"Yeah," said Mushmouth as he tried again to tell Salamander something serious. "Goldshit."

Around 11:30, after Goldshit escaped with a few more of Faggot's other conventional friends from work, Mother opened another bottle of rye.

"Where's Faggot?" asked Mushmouth. "Get Faggot in here and give him some of this rye."

"Yeah, but he likes gin," said Salamander.

"He likes everything," said Mother. "That's part of his problem."

"Where is Faggot?" asked Doreen. "I haven't seen him the last hour or so."

"He's been around. You don't think he's going to up and disappear when there's more booze in this house than in the Liquor Control Board, do you?" yelled Salamander.

"Hey," said Mushmouth. "No kidding. I haven't seen him for the last couple of hours. Where is he?"

"He's having a piss," said Mother pouring himself another bourbon neat.

"Don't you ever get drunk?" asked Doreen.

Mother laughed.

"Oh, Faggot'll be back. He's not going anywhere. Where do you think he went? Washington D. C. or something?" And at that Salamander broke down. He kept saying "D.C." giggling to himself until it sounded like dizzy.

"We ought to look around for him," said Mushmouth. "In the condition that he's probably in, he could have fallen down somewheres or something might have happened to him or something..."

"He's always in this state and if nothing happens to him during the week what makes you think something's going to happen to him now? Now after all he's been through." Mother drained his glass and smacked it on the kitchen table.

"This stuff is all shit. Shit. All this stuff we're drinking is shit," Salamander said. "The only good drink is loganberry wine. But it's got to be homemade and I know the place in Oregon where you can get the best loganberry wine in the world. When I go back I'm going to bring back a whole gallon of the finest loganberry wine and then you can all see what good wine is and what shit this is."

"When are you going back?" asked Mother grabbing Salamander's arm and suddenly very sober. "How do you plan on getting back?"

"I'm just going to cross the border and then I'll be back but I'm not going to be dumb enough to stay, don't touch me. I'll visit a few friends and buy some things and get some loganberry wine and take your fucking hands off me. My parents won't even know I was there. Get off me. I don't like it."

That shut everybody up for a while. Salamander leaned back in a chair and thought about going back to Oregon and drinking loganberry wine. Everybody else was quiet thinking their own thoughts. On the table were three unopened bottles of booze and about five bottles of wine that hadn't been touched yet. Mother said there was a whole refrigerator of nothing but beer.

"When was the last time you saw Faggot?" Doreen asked.

"Come on. Who saw him last?" Mushmouth shouted.

Doreen said she couldn't remember seeing him all night. Mushmouth laughed and said Doreen hadn't been seeing anything all night. Doreen told Mushmouth to shut up. Mushmouth shut up and looked like someone had just hit him in the face.

Salamander said he saw Faggot in the bathroom and it took fifteen minutes for them to straighten out that when Salamander had seen Faggot in the bathroom it was 6:15 and the party hadn't begun.

Mother went outside and checked for Faggot's body in the grass in the front lawn that was now knee-high and around the sides of the house and in the back yard, all the way down to the Voice of China. He made a special double-check of the front lawn area by leaning over the porch railing and looking for Faggot along the sides of the house. All this took another half hour.

By now it was quarter to twelve and still no Faggot.

"Maybe he went for a walk," suggested Mushmouth.

"That's dumb," said Mother. "Have you ever known Faggot to go for a walk when there's five bottles of booze right here on the kitchen table?"

"Maybe he got tired and wanted some fresh air. I know that when I..."

"So Faggot's gone. So what? I could get used to this place without Faggot. It'd be great without Faggot running all over the place making everybody crazy. It might be normal here," said Salamander.

Mushmouth and Doreen drank off another half bottle of wine. Mushmouth said he thought he was getting drunk and Doreen tried to shush him up.

"But it's true," insisted Mushmouth. "I-am-getting-drunk."

Doreen walked away and Mushmouth guzzled the leftover wine. Mother opened another bottle and slid it across the table to him. Salamander, who'd been making trips back and forth from the kitchen to the fish tank all night, straightened himself out and decided to stay in the kitchen with the others.

"What do you suppose happened to Faggot?" asked Mushmouth with his mouth full of wine and having trouble swallowing. He'd switched to red wine because the white wine was for the cheese and crackers but nobody remembered to put the cheese out and now the sauterne was gone.

"Maybe he died," said Salamander.

"You know what this reminds me of?" said Mother. "This reminds me of the cocktail parties my parents used to give. There'd be a lot of booze and food and everybody would make small talk and drink too much. It was really far-out. My father used to be super host, 'And would you like that on ice and would you like ginger ale? Oh yes, we have Campari. I know it's hard to find but we have it, Miss So-and-So.' Like it was really the heaviest thing. It was just too much."

"What's Campari?" asked Mushmouth.

"It's this French drink you pour over ice cubes," said Mother.

"Oh. What's it taste like? Is it good? Most of this stuff makes me sick," Mushmouth said waving his hand at the table full of bourbon bottles and gin and rye.

"Yeah, it's okay. It's got a mild bite."

"Like a lobster," Salamander said collapsing into very silent laughs that shook his whole body.

Doreen stared at Mother. The drunker she got the more wooden she was. She had trouble moving from place to place and lost all sense of rhythm and movement. Now she was having trouble moving her eyes around.

"But when I was in high school," Mother said, "I used to drink quinine water. I found a botttle of the stuff in the bar and really got turned on to it. It was terrific."

"What did you drink that shit for?" asked Salamander. "Did you have malaria or something?"

"Naw, I just liked it. It has a good taste. Sometimes after I drank a lot of it, I used to think I was high. I think it does things to your system when you drink it in large doses." Mother looked around the room and blinked. "Breeze didn't come, did he? That means no more shit for a while. Somebody's got to get hold of him and shake some shit out of him. Soon."

"The last time I was drunk," said Mushmouth, "was the time when Doreen left me and a bunch of friends took me to a drive-in to cheer me up and I sat in the back seat and drank a whole bottle of Red Mountain wine and unless you've had that stuff you can't imagine what it can do to you and then it only got worse and worse and I cried and cried all through the movie. I thought I'd never stop crying it was that bad. The wine was awful and I felt so bad I drank all of it. Then I thought I was going to puke and I've never been as sick as I was that night. Afterwards I felt terrible and I felt doubly worse for making an ass out of myself but there was nothing I could do."

Everybody was silent for a while. Mushmouth shook his glass back and forth in his hand.

"Yeah, but Doreen came back. That was all that mattered," said Salamander.

"Yeah, she came back that time," Mushmouth said softly.

"You know where he is?" shouted Doreen from the stairs. "He's been upstairs in that crummy room, the one he always says he's going to move into and he's fast asleep."

"No shit. And you were worried about him," Mother said.

"Is he all right?" yelled Mushmouth.

"I don't know. He's lying on his back and he looks like he's dead."

"Fat chance," said Salamander. "Faggots don't die easy. He's probably drunk and passed out up there."

"Yeah, but all night?" asked Mushmouth.

"Sure, why not? He's been passed out his whole life."

"Shut up, Salamander," said Mushmouth. "Doreen, why don't you wake him up and get him down here."

Salamander snickered. "If you can get him."

Doreen went upstairs and came running back down again. "He only has his Fruit of the Looms on," she reported.

"Never mind. Get him. Bring us a Faggot," Salamander yelled back to her.

A few minutes later a very sleepy and confused Faggot came down the stairs squinting into the light and rubbing his eyes. He asked for a cigarette and he lit up the one Mother gave him. Mushmouth and Doreen and Salamander waited for him to say something.

"What time is it?" he asked.

"It's 12:30. Soon it's going to be 1:00 o'clock in the morning."

"No shit. I don't believe it," Faggot said. He rubbed his eyes again and leaned up against the kitchen door frame. "I don't believe it. Where is everybody?"

"That's what we'd like to know," said Salamander. "A few assed dipshits came and sat around for a few minutes."

"What do you mean?" asked Faggot in a voice that was as soft and slow as warm honey. "What do you mean?"

"Nobody came. Where you been, boy?" asked Mother.

"I had a little drink and then I lay down until the people came. I was tired."

"When was that?"

"I don't know. About 8:00? I think."

"Yeah, well, you've been asleep since then and it's almost 1:00 o'clock now."

"I don't believe it. I don't believe I could sleep that long. I was tired but..."

"Well, you did," said Mother. "You slept right through your own party."

"Party," Salamander snorted. "You got drunk and passed out."

"Fuck, shit, piss," said Faggot softly.

Mother shook his head back and forth. Doreen concentrated on listening and Salamander began to laugh. "He has a party and sleeps through it. Some party."

Faggot began to laugh. A soft, low laugh coming from the place inside where there are no words and no way of saying anything.

"Gee, I'm sorry," said Faggot. He threw his arms in the air. "I'm sorry."

"Naw, don't worry about it," said Mushmouth. "It could happen to anybody."

"Yeah, but it happened to me and I didn't mean it to happen. It just happened." He looked at everybody's face and wound up talking to Mushmouth.

"I know," said Mushmouth. "I know."

"Who came anyway?" asked Faggot.

"Peterson came," said Salamander.

"Did he stay long?"

"Naw. Nobody stayed long. They all came and looked around for a few other people and just when more people came they left because they were bored."

"Oh, no."

"And they were all looking for you and nobody knew where you were. And a narc was here."

"Shit. Is there anything left to drink?"

"And a RCMP in drag."

Mother waved at the kitchen table at two unopened bottles of hard liquor and at the fridge full of Country Style and Old Vienna.

"Well, at least there was plenty to drink," said Faggot in way of apology for something he was beginning to realize he would never forgive himself for.

"And Goldshit came."

Faggot opened a bottle of gin and drank from the bottle.

"But Miss Hershey Bar didn't come," Salamander said.

"Who?"

"The Candy Lady," Mother said.

"How am I going to face the people at work?"

"That's your problem," said Salamander as he swiped a bottle of something or other from the table.

"Goldshit came. Oh. No." Faggot fell into a kitchen chair and covered his face. "Oh, no," he moaned. He dropped his hands and looked at everybody in the kitchen. Salamander was cackling to himself. Mother was smiling at an empty bourbon bottle. Doreen was staring at the floor running her hand through her hair. Faggot looked at Mushmouth. Mushmouth came over to his chair and stood in front of him. He threw his hands in the air and let them collapse at his sides. He made a "sorry" face with his mouth and shut his eyes and drooped his head. "I know," he said. Faggot nodded.

"Well, I guess we can have a party now," Faggot said looking around the room at a stiff heap of onion dip and two dozen paper cups scattered everywhere.

"We had a party," said Salamander. "A few assed dipshits came and sat around for a few minutes."

"Yeah, well, let's have another one," said Faggot. He poured Doreen a full glass of Andres Medium Dry. "Drink up. We're having a party."

The wine overflowed the glass and Faggot lifted the bottle to his lips to lick up the wine running away. He took a drink from the bottle, tilting it back and guzzling it just like it was a sixteen ounce bottle of Coke.

Salamander laughed his private giggle. Mother lazily waltzed himself over to the kitchen table and mixed everybody drinks. Everybody kept drinking until 4:00 in the morning when they were all spread out in different armchairs and couches and beds all over the house, all quite wasted, except for Faggot who stone drunk was unable to put himself out completely.

THE WAR BRIDE

Motherfucker was busy chasing his Bride every night after supper and Salamander was busy trying to domesticate the cat he found in the vacant lot across the street. First he got the cat to sit on the porch for five minutes after supper and eat a few scraps from a glass pie plate he left near the stairs. Then he was trying to get her to hang around in the daytime although he admitted that would be hopeless because Motherfucker was on the porch every day and a cat, particularly Cat, couldn't stand to keep company with a crazed Motherfucker.

Mushmouth was coming over more often and staying around for supper. He and Salamander had secret talks in the vacant lot across the street while Salamander called for Cat and Mushmouth beat the grass in case she was hiding in the underbrush of dead wild flowers. Once in a while Salamander got Cat to sleep overnight in the house. It liked it in the pantry where it was dark and quiet and almost like a vacant lot. Faggot said he thought Cat had been around a lot and a few days later Mushmouth said he thought Cat was going to have kittens.

Every couple of days Mushmouth came over to the house terribly upset and Salamander let him stay upstairs with him in his bedroom. Faggot asked Mushmouth if Doreen minded staying all alone but Mushmouth couldn't answer. He stood in one place and twisted his handkerchief around in his hands and looked like he was about to break down and cry.

Faggot came home from work later or not at all. He always discovered Mushmouth on the front porch sitting with Cat and watching her belly get bigger and bigger. "She's going to have babies," Mushmouth said.

"Yeah, they all do," Faggot said. "They can't help it."

Then because Faggot was hungry and Mushmouth was always hungry, especially when he was upset, Faggot took him downtown with him. Faggot couldn't stand Wonder Bread sandwiches and he wouldn't cook himself anything decent to eat so every other day he went to the B.C. Royal restaurant in the heart of downtown Chinatown. He ordered sweet and sour pork and mushroom fried rice. The waiter smiled when he saw Faggot and brought him a large sixteen ounce Coke on a tray. Faggot thanked him and gave him his order which was always the same. In twenty minutes the Chinese man brought it back with another large sixteen ounce Coke and a bow and a very big smile. Faggot told Mushmouth they were the first civilized Caucasians who had ever eaten in the B.C. Royal.

Mushmouth had a quarter of the sweet and sour pork and picked at the mushroom fried rice. He talked with his mouth full while Faggot drank his Cokes and listened. Sometimes Faggot drove him to Doreen's and sometimes he dropped him off at the house before he disappeared to wherever he went to get drunk and be by himself.

Whenever Faggot saw Mother he asked him how his Bride was but Mother would barely talk about the Bride. He washed his flannel shirt and walked around for two days dressed only in his pants and drove the Rose Bush Lady out of her mind. He hardly spoke to anyone, Mushmouth least of all. Salamander swore that if he didn't mend his ways he would be responsible for upsetting Cat and causing things to go wrong with her pregnancy. But Salamander didn't know how Motherfucker held Cat in his lap all afternoon while he was off worrying about the business affairs of the Canadian Imperial Bank of Commerce.

Finally Salamander couldn't stand Motherfucker creeping around anymore and he asked him outright, "Are you getting married or what?"

Mother leaned back in his chair and said, "Well, it's like this..."

The Cat crept in from the pantry and Faggot paused on his way out.

"You know Alice, the girl who used to live in the church before it was a hostel and who stayed around afterwards?"

Faggot rolled his head in a semicircle and looked at the ceiling. "Lord."

"Yeah, well, she's Canadian."

"We know," Salamander said.

"Yeah, well. Sometimes it's on and sometimes it's off. It was on last week."

"Now it's off?" Faggot asked.

"Well, you know how you have to stay married a certain length of time and they come around to check on you? Yeah, well, I told her that after we were married she wouldn't have to live with me. She wouldn't have to see me, if she didn't want to. All she has to do is marry me. We could live together. It would be cheaper. I told her that after the number of years were up, we could get divorced if she wanted to. It doesn't matter to me and she doesn't care if she's married or not."

"That's exactly what it sounds like to me," Salamander said.

"When's the big day?" Faggot asked.

Mother skewered up his eyes. He exhaled and sagged in his chair. "That's the problem. Everything was cool until Tyler showed up. Now Tyler wants to marry her. He says he loves her. One day she sees me and the next day she sees Tyler."

"So it's touch and go you mean?" asked Salamander. It was the first non-hostile thing he had said to Motherfucker in over two months.

"Yeah," Motherfucker said in his direction. "It's touch and go." He put Cat in his lap. "I think I'm the one to go."

It was hard to figure out what was going on.

Motherfucker didn't know but Faggot enjoyed it. He tried to give Mother tongue-in-cheek advice about marriage and brides and the whole thing because he'd been married twice and was still married but Mother told him he didn't know what he was talking about. Faggot just laughed and got drunk and talked to himself. He really did know a lot about different kinds of women and different types of marriage but at the end of two bottles of wine, all he could say was that marriage was a mistake and ruined everybody and everything--and he ought to know.

Mother was still dressing up in his flannel shirt and going to church to meet his Bride. It was hard to say if he was making any progress. Maybe he should have brought his guitar with him and convinced Alice that he was a heavy blues man but Faggot reminded everybody how this Alice used to be a near concert pianist before she got fucked in the head and moved into the church--and Faggot knew that, too.

Mushmouth was hanging around all the time now. He didn't have any more money. It all belonged to Doreen. He never did get a job and he said that the landlady was going to throw him and Doreen out because she was beginning to suspect that he was no photographer, not even a third-rate amateur, and that Doreen was no wife but a very lonely and homesick girl who didn't know what the fuck she'd ever left San Francisco for and was too proud to admit that maybe her dumbshit father who voted for Alioto every time was right about some things.

Cat was doing fine. She decided to move into the house, too. She lived in the pantry and it wasn't long before she discovered that Faggot got confused and sometimes dropped things. Motherfucker was quiet and comfortable to sit on but she must never sit on him when anybody else was around. Salamander was just like Motherfucker only he made more noise and let her sit on him whenever she wanted to. She wasn't sure if she wanted to have her babies in the pantry or upstairs but she decided she would have them wherever Mushmouth wasn't. He made too much noise. She thought the garbage pile next to the stove was the best garbage pile she'd seen anywhere and as far as she was concerned, it was great to be in *Canadia.*

Soon Mushmouth was hanging around after lunch as well as in the afternoon and before supper and after supper and Doreen was showing up in the evening, sort of half-heartedly looking for him because it was better to be lonely with him than without him. Everybody was respectful of their differences, particularly Faggot who could smell an argument an hour before it happened. It was better than the TV they didn't have but that Faggot kept promising he would rip off from the Sound Center. He wanted to have it in time to see another Moon Walk. He said he couldn't bear to miss seeing the moon lose its cherry again.

When Motherfucker was courting his Bride, Mushmouth and Doreen argued in the living room. Doreen boiled over and popped out the living room door. Mushmouth followed her into the hall and ran around, helpless, following her from room to room trying to stroke her hair like Cat's or talk to her or apologize or anything. But Doreen wouldn't have any part of him when he was like that. She got angry like she was looking for a comb she'd lost. She wouldn't talk until she found it but she wouldn't tell anybody where she thought she'd lost it so nobody could help her look. It drove Mushmouth crazy.

Doreen liked to be strong when Mushmouth was weak and then she liked to be strong when Mushmouth was strong and all the time she wanted to be weak if Mushmouth could let her cry into his shoulder and if she could hear him tell her that it was going to be all right. But Mushmouth couldn't tell her anything like that so Doreen had to be strong all the time and hate herself and hate Mushmouth and hate so much the fact that all she wanted to do was be woman and loving, but all that was denied her.

Faggot sat on the living room couch, drunk beyond memory, watching them run after each other from room to room and he understood what they were doing even if they didn't understand. Only it was impossible to make people stand still and listen to him when he was slobbering drunk out of his mind and they thought he was a Faggot Fatass in the first place--and Faggot didn't want to be that way but he slipped into it and it happened to him before he could stop it.

It got to be impossible in that house with everybody waiting for a bride or a baby or a divorce. Salamander took all his remaining fish to Stanley Park and let them go. He said they couldn't survive in a place like that. He was also a full-fledged vegetarian now and he believed that it was wrong to keep live things cooped up against their will in a tiny fish tank full of algae when every living thing is a wild creature and deserves to run free.

But Faggot said, "Freedom means nothing left to lose, Janis Joplin period." Then he sang the song Janis Joplin sings and belched. He said he knew what he was talking about. But when he was drunk he wondered about the same things, only for him it wasn't a question of getting loose as much as it was disentangling so many knots that the thought alone was exhausting. And in the mornings Faggot's hands were so shaky he could barely light his cigarette. Besides, it was nothing he could tackle on a Sunday afternoon.

And there weren't any free Sunday afternoons in that house with Doreen and Mushmouth chasing after each other from room to room and Doreen denying that she believed in the Amerikan male myth of virility but wanting Mushmouth to hit her in the mouth and not knowing that herself and Mushmouth begging Faggot in tears if he could please come back to the house, even with Doreen, because he was sure they would work out their differences because they loved each other and she'd come all the way from S.F. to be with him. And Faggot surprising Mushmouth with his own tears and telling him to get off the floor and of course he could stay, forget about the money, stay as long as you like but for God's sake go in there and do something with that woman. And Mushmouth wanting with his wild wide eyes from behind his rimless glasses all the answers to the questions he didn't know how to ask but mostly wondering, without knowing it himself, if it was all right to hit her in the mouth and Faggot unable to answer that question because he was incoherent behind his tears: "Be a man, whatever that is..." And Motherfucker, unable to get a yes-no decision from his Bride, in there in the other room with Doreen, offering to beat the shit out of her if that's what she wanted but didn't know how to ask for.

Finally Doreen burst into real tears that everybody could see and hear and Mushmouth cried and cried to the Voice of China through a plastic shower curtain wondering what he was doing wrong in his life that he should see so many things crumble around him when all he had for everyone and everything was the best of intentions. He didn't know what Faggot knew and that was even the best of intentions can't save you. You go down all the same only he wasn't as advanced as Faggot who could say, "When I go down, it'll be my finger on the trigger." Mushmouth hadn't cried for enough useless causes to reach that level of comprehension.

So Faggot cried for him in the other room and on the wicker chair on the front porch that was beat to shreds by now and Salamander went away to Stanley Park and watched his fish every Saturday afternoon. He said he felt better knowing they were free in the lagoon. And Faggot asked how big the lagoon was and when Salamander told him, he laughed. He was drunker now than he had ever been before, even drunker than when MICKEY MOUSE came to stay.

In the midst of total no-food, no-money breakdown, Doreen and Mushmouth moved back to

239

the house and Cat decided to have her babies in the pantry. Salamander didn't mind having Doreen and Mushmouth back in the house, even if it meant he had to sleep in the hall until Faggot decided who was going to have to move where to make room for all the newlyweds and brides and kittens.

Salamander thrived on all the new company because he said that when there were more people around, he had to see Motherfucker less. He started to collect the odds on how many boy-kittens and how many girl-kittens Cat would have. Faggot said Cat wasn't going to have any kittens. She was going to have a baby rabbit because she was getting so big.

Salamander came home from a W. 4th health shop with a jar of natural bees' honey. He suspected that Cat was low on protein from lugging around all her unborn babies all day. He hoped she would cultivate a taste for honey and learn to lick all his honey spoons off.

"You know what I found out today?" Salamander waved around a twelve ounce jar of unpasteurized buckwheat honey.

Doreen and Mushmouth were too defeated and tired and sullen to be interested. But Mushmouth, from habit and a sense of duty now that he was living rent-free, perked up and asked, in an imitation of his former self, "No, what did you find out? Just what did you find out today?"

"I was walking along near Cypress and I met Breeze. He was spaced right out of his mind which isn't too difficult for a Breeze. He asked me for money to buy a popsicle and when I gave him twelve cents, he told me that there's going to be a big wedding the first of next month and everybody's invited."

"Mother and…"

"No." Salamander smacked the honey jar on the table. "Nope. TYLER and Alice. How do you like that? I think we all ought to go. And I think we ought to take all the fuck-ups with us. Mother and Faggot. It's at Lighthouse Park and there's supposed to be a lot of dope and booze and food. It's going to be a real party."

"Holy shit," Mushmouth said. It seemed like all the weariness and resignation came out of him in one big sigh and got stuck in the "Holy" of "H-O-L-Y" shit.

"Yep." Salamander unscrewed the cap to the honey and fetched a spoon from the sink. He spooned three tablespoonfulls into his mouth before he offered Doreen some. She took a tablespoonful and Mushmouth put his finger in and scooped up enough to run down his hand. He had to lick it off his wrist. Doreen was left making embarrassed motions about Mushmouth. The funny thing was she was the only one who was ever embarrassed about Mushmouth. But the strangest thing of all was how anything could embarrass her after living in that house. And maybe that was the root of all the embarrassment in the first place.

That night when Faggot wandered home Salamander told him about the wedding. Faggot asked if Motherfucker knew but Salamander couldn't say. Faggot was drunk enough to tell Mother and to everybody's surprise Mother said he wanted to go anyway because of the free dope. He said he wanted to go because he was tired of spending day after day with himself and he didn't give two shits about marrying Alice. Maybe he was relieved because he had enough instinctive sense to stay away from marriage and from Alice. And maybe the idea of a five-year divorce frightened him, too.

An hour ago Motherfucker waved good-bye to Faggot who was going to the beach to get drunk. Salamander said he was going for a walk but he was looking for a girl. Mother was sitting quietly by himself in the dark.

The evening was so still he could hear the echoes of his own sighs. He thought his sighs were tears but he was the only person who could hear them fall because the darkness blocked him off from the rest of the world.

He had been sitting on the porch for the whole day with nothing to do and nowhere to go. All day he repeated to himself, "There must be a place where life is less complicated." Mother looked at the lampost and told himself that there was a young girl in the country for him. She wore ribbons in her hair and lived in a house near a meadow. Upstairs there were four pairs of tiny panties neatly folded in a bureau drawer. He heard a harmonica.

"Breeze. Hey, Breeze, what are you doing here?"

A Breeze came out of the shadows and sat down on the porch steps. "Want to hear my new song?"

"Sure."

Breeze undid the knot at his waist. His belt and harmonica dropped into his lap. Motherfucker leaned back in his chair and listened. He felt sad.

"Did you like it? Huh? Did you like it?"

"You've learned how to play a new tune."

"Listen again. You can't hear it all the first time. You have to listen again and again and again."

Yeah, it was true. Breeze had a new note. Left on his own he played his new note for another five minutes.

"What did you come here for, Breeze?"

"I came to play a new tune for you."

"What did you come here for, Breeze?"

"Just wanted to come and pay a friendly visit. See how things are here at the house, you know."

"Sure. I know."

"How are things here at the house?"

"Fine."

"Everything working at the house?"

"Yes."

"That's good. I mean that's really far-out."

Breeze looked at the burnt-out house up the street and was quiet. Mother didn't want to talk and he didn't want to be quiet. He didn't want to hear Breeze play, either.

"Are you still living at the hostel, Breeze?"

"Can I have a cigarette?"

Mother got up and went to his bed in the living room. He came back with a package of papers and a small pouch of tobacco. "You can roll yourself one," he said.

Mother squeezed in the stray ends of tobacco with

the end of a match. Breeze forgot about his harmonica. Mother lit his cigarette for him. "Breeze, are you still living at the hostel?"

"Yeah," Breeze said. He shifted around on the stairs and seemed troubled. Then he brightened up. "Tex left, didn't he?"

"Oh, months ago."

"Any news from him?"

"Oh, no, Breeze. He'd never write." Mother's voice was gentle in the dark.

"George is gone, too. They took him away for drugs and nobody knows what happened to him."

There was a pause. Again Mother was the first to speak. "How are things at the hostel?"

"So-so. Sometimes it's good and sometimes it shits." He looked up at Motherfucker. "It's not like the old days when everybody was there." Breeze was quiet for a minute. He stroked his harmonica with his fingertips and looked at the ground. "There's a rumor that they're gonna shut the hostel down."

Breeze picked up his harmonica and played for a few minutes. For a while he was really into it but then it got away from him and he trailed off. He laid his harmonica down on the step next to him and looked across at a a street lamp. "I think I'm gonna go back to the States for a while. Like for a visit."

"What do you want to do a fool thing like that for?"

"I can't take it here no more."

Motherfucker didn't say anything. He had nothing to say. He couldn't tell him to be happy at the hostel. He couldn't tell him to get landed.

"Breeze, if I had some dope, I'd smoke it with you."

Breeze tied his harmonica back onto his belt. "That's a mighty fine sentiment. That's a very fine thing to say."

They were quiet for another little while. This time it was Breeze who asked Mother a question. "Can I take a bath in your house?"

"Sure. There's a towel up there you can use, too."

"Thanks," Breeze said.

He went upstairs and Mother didn't hear anything from him for the next forty-five minutes. Mother stayed on the porch and stared at the miniature expressway at the end of the block and smoked half a pouch of tobacco and remembered what it was like when he'd gone off to the woods north of San Francisco and how the meadow looked near the log cabin he was building for the U.B.C. professor and how the mornings smell in the mountains.

Later on Breeze came down and they sat on the porch together. The wind coming through the bathroom window dried up all the water Breeze left behind on the floor.

When it got chilly they went inside and listened to Salamander's records. Mother put on Arlo Guthrie and made Breeze a cup of coffee. They played "I Don't Want A Pickle I Just Want A Motorcycle" through three times.

Faggot came in with Doreen and Mushmouth when Breeze was drinking his second cup.

"What are you doing here?" Faggot asked. He stood by the door and stared at Motherfucker.

"Nothing," said Breeze. "I was just leaving."
Immediately he got up and went out the door. He left
it open and Faggot kicked it shut.

"What was he doing here?" Faggot repeated.

"Nothing. He took a bath. That's all."

LIGHTHOUSE PARK

On Sunday afternoon everybody piled into Faggot's car that Salamander called a cheap heap. The overflow went in Salamander's car that wasn't in any better condition.

Doreen wore one of her faded Indian shirts over a pair of bell bottom jeans. Mother and Faggot went as they were because they said they couldn't see getting dressed up for anybody's wedding. Mother insisted he was going for the dope. Doreen and Mushmouth hoped they would have a good time together at the wedding party and Salamander, who came to Lighthouse Park every other weekend to drop acid, wanted to see if the sea had changed.

It is a short ride to Lighthouse Park but anywhere outside of Kitsilano is an expedition. You go across the Lion's Gate and you follow the Squamish Road north. You make sure you turn off before you get to Horseshoe Bay and the ferry boat landing.

The road into the park is an extended shoulder on the opposite side of the parkway that keeps going and going until you are in the middle of a parking lot carved between the huge trees. Then you park the car on some tree root and everybody gets out. You take any one of a number of paths that are supposed to lead to the water or to the woods or to the lighthouse. It is very dark and quiet in the park and you look for cars that belong to people you know and you wonder which path leads to the water and which path leads to the people you know. You have trouble finding both.

"Isn't that McAllistair's car?"

"Which one?" asked Faggot.

"The Renault."

"Naw, he doesn't have all that shit in the back."

"Maybe he put all that stuff there since you saw him."

"No. He wouldn't have that kind of shit in the back."

"What about that one?"

"Which one?"

"The Pontiac. Maybe that belongs to? What's his name? You know who I mean."

"No, I don't. Who?"

"Let me out of here," Mother said. He scrambled for the door handle. "You fuck-ups are going to spend all the time trying to figure out who's here and not here. By the time you know the wedding will be over and the dope gone. I don't want to miss this party." He got out and against her will Doreen fell against Mushmouth in the back seat of Faggot's Buick.

"Okay, let's go, let's go," Mushmouth said slapping his hands against the back of the front seat. "All out before we miss the wedding."

Mother was already half-way up the nearest path.

"Where do you think the wedding is?" Mushmouth asked.

"Oh, Martin," Doreen said watching Mother disappear and wishing that her Martin didn't ask so many questions and did more on his own.

"They said the wedding was at Lighthouse Park so I think it's going to take place at the lighthouse," said Salamander.

"Yeah, but you heard from Breeze."

"I checked it at the Committee. It's true, they're really getting married here today," Faggot interrupted.

"Oh," said Mushmouth. "Well, let's go to the lighthouse." He reached for Doreen's hand but she had slipped behind Faggot. The trail was narrow and they had to walk single-file. Salamander went first followed by Mushmouth. Doreen was last behind Faggot. Salamander was walking quickly and he and Mushmouth went far ahead. Faggot held back and when they were well out of view he stopped and reached behind him for Doreen. He held her hand and pulled her down beside him on a log. They were off the path and out of sight.

Doreen was very docile. She talked very little. Faggot pulled her head into his lap and she lay still for a while. She whimpered and Faggot stroked her hair. She wanted to get up and begin talking and working through the explanation of everything but Faggot wouldn't let her get up. He lay his arm across her neck and she was unable to move. It was the full load on her and there in the woods alone with only a Faggot she could accept it.

"I know, I know," said Faggot. "I know," he repeated over and over in the way of explanation and consolation. But it wasn't enough, maybe too much,

249

because she started to cry her heart out. She cried in heaving sobs like she was tryinq to break herself apart and Faggot never stifled her or offered her support or even a dirty piece of kleenex. He was immobile with Doreen crying herself out and falling all over him. He looked away into the distance between the trees and seemed calm as Doreen beat herself to bits. When she was nearly finished, Faggot looked down at her and turned her face to his as if he was looking for something between her eyes or on her mouth but whatever he wanted wasn't there and she broke into tears again. Faggot accepted this, too, that she should cry and stop and begin all over again for as long as there was no place to go or be or do which is forever.

It was hard for them to judge how long they stayed there. Doreen said the wedding ought to be over. She was concerned that somebody might miss them but Faggot laughed. He knew better.

They wandered around on different paths, looking for the one that would lead them to the lighthouse. Occasionally they met other people. Husbands with wives and Boy Scout fathers with Cub Scout sons who turned around and looked at them. But Faggot never saw these people and Doreen was busy looking for the rocks on the path between her tears and her hair that was falling over her face. Faggot kept his feet moving but never looked down or back or in front of him. He was in motion and the gears hadn't changed yet.

They got to a hill of paths where it seemed that each path criss-crossed over each other path. The only differences between paths were in the form and number of the roots that were growing out of rocks and splitting them apart. Doreen tripped a couple of times and Faggot unconsciously slipped his arm under her and he held her up.

When they got to the top of the hill they could look out over the water and see the lighthouse a distance to the left. They stood still, not speaking of anything, and looking out over the water. Far below were clusters of speed boats and fishing boats that seemed tiny and directionless. The water was very still and calm and a very remarkable blue-green. It was easy to see how Salamander might want to come out here on a Saturday afternoon to ungag his mind. It was easy to see how a person might think he could find peace staring into the blue-green water. It was like looking into the flame of a sand candle when the wax has mostly been burnt away. It makes you dizzy. You look up and it goes away.

Doreen moved first. Faggot came back to himself as if from a long ways away. Doreen chose one of the paths and moving in the general direction they grew closer to the lighthouse. The lighthouse didn't make any noises, no fog horns or bells, just light and it was too early for light. So it seemed useless and small sitting on top of a hill waiting for dark so it could light itself up.

Doreen and Faggot stumbled around on different paths for a while. They met a group of fifteen-year-old boys who were trying to get drunk on Olympia beer. The boys started to say things to Doreen but they shut up when they saw Faggot. He flashed them one of his "I am Robby the Robot" smiles and they got scared as well as quiet. "You can never tell who you're going to meet in the woods when it's almost dark," Faggot said.

When they got to the lighthouse, Faggot was out of breath. He told Doreen how he was expecting his first coronary. He said he saw a TV feature on heart disease and as far as he could tell he was a prime victim. He lit a cigarette and offered Doreen one but she wasn't interested. It seemed she wasn't interested in anything since she and Mushmouth had moved back to the house. She started to climb down to the water's edge. The lighthouse was on top of a pile of rocks. All the rocks tilted downwards to the sea, to a channel really. It would be easy to climb down but tough to get back up again.

Doreen stood on top of a big boulder and looked out to sea. Faggot could see the bouy markers in the channel and he knew that soon it would be dark and the green, red, starboard, port markers would light up. Faggot sat still on his rock, thinking back to California, smoking his cigarette and thinking forward to his coronary.

It was growing darker all the time. Doreen sat down, cross-legged on her rock, and now she looked like some jive hip poster advertising Clearasil or Levi's jeans. "Come to Levi's Land and be happy." Only they were in Levi's Land and nobody was happy or with the wherewithall to get happiness. It was something that comes, like Salamander used to say about girlfriends, by chance or miracle. And they had just about exhausted all their luck and miracles are out of fashion.

There were crunching noises behind Faggot. He turned around and saw Salamander and Mushmouth creeping around like two Indians out of an old Davey Crockett show. He wondered what they'd had at the wedding.

"What have you kids been up to?" he asked.

Salamander smiled and Mushmouth took out his handkerchief and blew his nose.

"Oh, for Chrissake, put that thing away," snapped Faggot.

Mushmouth was stunned. "What's the matter with you?" he asked.

Faggot didn't answer.

"Where's Doreen?" Salamander asked.

Faggot waved in the direction of the water. Mushmouth looked alarmed but Faggot added, "She's down there in the rocks somewhere." Mushmouth took off in the direction of Faggot's arm, pulling out his handkerchief on the way and wiping it around his mouth.

"How was the wedding?" asked Salamander.

"I didn't go," Faggot answered. "I don't like weddings." He tossed his butt into a crevasse at his feet and drew his foot up suffocating it. He looked up. "Didn't you go?"

"Naw," Salamander said. "We couldn't find it. They must have finished before we got there or left or something. We walked all over this damn place and we couldn't find them."

"Well, where have you kids been all this time?" Faggot asked.

"Wandering around. We had a good time. We got into the trees. It's beautiful here." He started to walk towards the water.

Faggot opened his mouth to say something but stopped in mid-sentence. That was the way it was. They left you in mid-dialogue and they walked away. Faggot laughed and scratched the side of his face and said, "Sheet," like Motherfucker and laughed again when he heard what came out of his mouth. "Your thoughts are your own, that's all that matters," he thought.

Faggot stayed on his rock smoking cigarette after cigarette. Salamander climbed over the rocks and was with Mushmouth and Doreen wherever they were. Faggot was happy in his own way to sit still and watch the night coming over the harbor and check if there were any lights on the boats below or on the markers in the channel.

It was very quiet by himself. The fifteen-year-old boys had taken their beer and gone someplace else to get drunk. Faggot leaned against a rock and was watching the sky for the first star. He felt hands on his neck and he stiffened.

"What the fuck...Are you trying to give me a coronary or something? Jesus." The vein in the side of his neck was bouncing. He shook himself and crumpled up.

"Where's everybody?" Mother asked.

"Why do you always creep around?" Faggot demanded.

Mother laughed and repeated himself, "Where is everybody?"

"In the water," Faggot said.

Mother started for the rocks. He stood on top of the same rock Doreen stood on an hour before and looked out to sea.

"Do you see them?" Faggot asked.

"Yeah, they're down there," Mother answered. "Did you find them? I went to where the wedding was but nobody was there. I asked some people, too, but they didn't know anything about it."

Faggot was laughing. He was becoming hysterical.

"What's the matter with you?" Mother turned around.

"Nothing," Faggot managed to say. "We missed the wedding, that's all."

"Yeah," Mother said glumly.

"Maybe we'll make it to divorce court," Faggot said to himself.

Mother was looking over the water and jumping from rock to rock. His legs were long in the shadows. He seemed spider-like and unreal springing from rock to rock.

"I don't see Salamander," Mother shouted. He stood on a rock with his back to Faggot and his form against the sky.

"Maybe he went back to the water," Faggot said.

Faggot couldn't be bothered to get up and look over the rocks. He preferred to sit still in one spot and watch for the moon and for the stars. He wanted to be the first one to see the first star and point it out. He looked around. Mother disappeared over the edge to join the others.

Doreen was sitting on top of a rock very close to the water with her shoes off. Mushmouth was sitting to the side with his knees drawn up to his chin and his head resting on his arms. Doreen was watching

255

Salamander.

They were at the water's edge. There were four or five big rocks that were sitting in the water. If the sea were rougher, the water would spill over the rocks they were on. They could see water marks on all the rocks where the waves had come over before in storms. Also, the rocks were worn smooth. "They are polished," Doreen said.

Salamander was crouched over the corner of two rocks, leaning in the water. There was a small channel worn away by the sea between his two rocks. Every wave slapped into the hole and made a smacking, sucking sound. Salamander leaned over the hole and held his hand out to the water rushing back to the sea. Now and then the onrush was exceptionally strong and water splashed on the rock that Doreen was on and came over Salamander's knees. He leaned over and ran away from each oncoming wave. He was fascinated.

"Don't you think you ought to watch out?" Doreen suggested.

"Yeah, don't you think you ought to be careful?" said Mushmouth.

But Salamander brushed them aside. "Nope, I'm not going to fall in." He looked up at Mushmouth. "Do you remember the time we were all at Kitsilano Beach and Tex was throwing rocks in the water and he hit me?"

"Yeah," Mushmouth said soberly. "He hit me, too. I wonder what happened to him."

"I don't care," said Salamander. Just then a big wave came that almost caught him. But he scampered safely aside and laughed. He was like a rat playing beside the water. In another life he could have been an otter or a raccoon that lives by the water and washes everything it eats before it eats it.

"Do you know who's up there watching us?" Salamander asked.

"God," Doreen said.

Mushmouth snickered.

"Nope. Better than God."

"Big Brother," Mushmouth volunteered.

"Nope. More destructive than either God or Big Brother."

"Who? I give up," said Mushmouth.

"Motherfucker."

"Oh," said Mushmouth as Doreen turned around to catch a glimpse of Motherfucker nearly impaling himself on a spindly tree sticking out of the side of the rock cliff.

"Jesus, he's so clumsy for a big Motherfucker," Salamander said.

"I nearly killed myself getting down here, too," Doreen said.

"How are we going to get back up again?" Mushmouth asked looking at the place where Mother was and the place beyond where he couldn't see, but where Faggot was sitting by himself waiting for the first star.

THE CAT

Motherfucker didn't believe what was happening. At 9:00 o'clock in the morning an explosion shook him out of bed. He stood on the front porch without a shirt and scared two secretaries late for work on Broadway.

Across the street they were ripping the lot to shreds. They had a Caterpillar and three men on the job. One guy went ahead and cleared off all the moveable brush and one guy ran the Cat and one guy, Boss man, told the guy in the Cat where to go.

"Sheet," said Motherfucker. He tried to fall asleep but it was impossible. The noise wasn't steady--it rose and fell like the breathing of some somnambulant beast. "Sheet."

At 11 o'clock Boss man waved to the guy in the Cat and he cut the motor. They went to Leonard's and had a pint of milk each. It was the first quiet spell in two hours. Mother was getting a headache.

At 11:30 they were back on the job. It was brutally hot and Motherfucker could see the sweat running down their shirts. They knocked off again at 1:00 o'clock for lunch. After lunch they got smart and took their shirts off.

Motherfucker couldn't think. He couldn't hear himself play guitar and he couldn't listen to the radio unless he sat on top of it. He thought about going away for the day but there was no place for him to go. The more he thought about going away, the angrier he got. First he was angry because they were going to build a warehouse to match the mini expressway at the end of the street. Then he was angry because he couldn't sleep with the racket they made building the warehouse. He was angry because he lived in that house and there was no reason why he had to go away from it to be able to hear himself think.

All day he watched the three guys work. He couldn't make up his mind if they would break again at 3:00 or 4:00 and was disappointed when they stopped at 3:00. That meant the afternoon stretch would be longer

The Cat was bulldozing the whole plot. Motherfucker figured they'd knock everything out and then level the ground. At 5:30 he couldn't stand it anymore and went in the house. He shut and sealed the downstairs windows with masking tape but it didn't make any difference. He still couldn't hear himself think. He was so upset he didn't sit on the porch and freak out the rush hour from Broadway coming to pick up their parked cars--and that had always been one of the chief highlights of his day.

Abruptly at 6:00 o'clock the noise stopped. Motherfucker stood on the threshold of the front door and blew smoke at the three guys and their Cat. They picked their shirts off the ground and brushed them off. Then they picked up their milk cartons and waved good-bye to each other. They tucked their shirts in and got in their cars and drove off.

Mother threw a kitchen chair against the front wall of the porch. Parts of rotten shingles fell away. He scooped them up in his hands, slammed his feet against the railing and threw them piece by piece across the street at the construction site.

He was staring at the Cat when Mushmouth and Doreen came up the street. Doreen was carrying a bag of groceries and Mushmouth was trying to open a bag of potato chips with his teeth. They came up to the porch and Doreen made a beeline for the kitchen. She didn't want Mother to see what she'd bought.

"You look like you're waiting for something," Mushmouth said after Mother hadn't said anything to him since he'd come up on the porch. "The way you keep staring at the thing over there," he flipped his hand in the direction of the Cat.

Motherfucker didn't move.

Mushmouth stuck the potato chip bag between his teeth and placed his hands on his knees. He leaned over and squinted at the Cat with the same angle as Mother's. "Okay," he slapped his hands to his sides and straightened up. "I give up. What are you waiting for?"

"Godot."

"Is he landed?"

"Oh, Martin," Doreen sighed, moaning and rolling her eyes. "He's in a book."

"Lucky fucker," Mushmouth said crumpling up the potato chip bag and throwing it over the railing. "Whoopie." He looked from Doreen to Mother.

"Whoopie," he repeated. "I'm so goddamn tired of this," he said, his voice catching. "You know, I looked for work every day this week. Every day. I didn't take any days off. I had my ass out there 9:00 o'clock Monday, Tuesday and Wednesday morning." He ticked the days off on his fingers. "And you know I didn't get anything. Not a single thing." His voice was rising and Doreen called his name in warning, "Martin." Mushmouth turned to look at her. "It's true. It's goddamn true. I'm never gonna get landed. I can't get a job. I can't stand hanging around. I can't get landed. I can't go home. I can't do anything," he said looking straight at her.

Doreen watched his face and bit her finger. Mother stared straight ahead at the Cat.

"Jesus," Mushmouth said to himself.

"They came this morning at 9:00 o'clock and they worked until 11:00. They had lunch at 1:00 o'clock. They stopped again at 3:00. They went home fifteen minutes ago. That makes two hours of quiet in nine hours," Mother spoke without ever taking his eyes off the Cat.

"Great," said Mushmouth. "Just wait'll Salamander finds out about this."

"They're going to come every day for the next six months. There's going to be more of them."

The three of them looked at the vacant lot. The Cat had upended a tree and it hung over the embankment. When the wind blew, soil loosened and fell on the sidewalk. Dandelions and purple and white flowers were stuck on the big Cat's wheels. They were drying up and dying in the heat.

"All that good earth going to waste," said Motherfucker.

"Yeah," said Mushmouth. "Wait'll Salamander sees that. Do you think that Cat can survive in there?"

"Nothing can survive what man is doing to this universe," Mother said steadily staring at the Cat. "Nothing. Look at that, will you," he gestured to the ramp at the end of the street. "You think that's necessary? They keep on ripping up and building their fucking concrete warehouses and office buildings and apartment houses everywhere. Where are PEOPLE supposed to live?"

"I don't know," said Mushmouth shaking his head and looking somber. "Don't ask me. I'm not landed."

"I can't live here with that going on every day. Starting at 9:00 and going on day after day to 6:00. I can't breathe it's so loud." Mother turned to Mushmouth. His lips were twitching. "A fucking expressway and a warehouse on the same street. Sheet." He slammed his feet down.

He moved to the door and Doreen got out of his way to let him by. Mother turned around at the doorway. "You know," he said, "I could run that thing better than those guys who were here today." He jabbed his head in the direction of the Cat. "Yeah, I could."

That weekend Salamander went down to Oregon. He drove his own car with his Oregon plates and his brand-new fan belt. He said he didn't expect any trouble. He said they'd never get him.

"Don't you think it's too risky?" I asked.

Faggot opened a beer bottle. "Jones, he's old enough to know what he wants."

"They won't get me," Salamander said grimly. "You're the one they ought to get."

"How's that?"

"You're a Jew. They always get the Jews."

The weekend Salamander was away nobody missed him. That is everybody pretended nothing unusual was happening but everybody was worried. Motherfucker didn't play his guitar all day Saturday or Sunday and when he thought nobody was looking, he locked himself in the bathroom and looked up "Punishments and Penalties" in the footnotes of the *Manual For Draft-Age Immigrants to Canada.*

Salamander was supposed to be back on Sunday night. He said to start looking for him sometime after dark. Around 7:00 o'clock Faggot took Mother to the Liquor Control Board because Mother said he hadn't been out of the house in the last three weeks. He said he was waiting for some job to come through but Salamander always said nobody would be dumb enough to give him another job. Motherfucker, who couldn't be bothered to give Salamander any more backtalk, now wanted to get drunk waiting for him to come back.

By 9:00 o'clock everybody was getting drunk waiting for Salamander to come home. Mother wanted to know where Doreen was. "She's not feeling too good," Mushmouth said testily and Mother let it go at that.

Every few minutes Mushmouth went to the porch and looked up and down the street for the car. Mushmouth said he couldn't recognize Salamander's car anymore because Salamander had the fan belt replaced and put in a new muffler.

"Shit, he's not here yet," Mushmouth said.

"We know that," Faggot said. "Sit down. You make me nervous."

"Yeah, but I..." Mushmouth was fingering his handkerchief. "I just thought maybe..."

"He's not here yet," Faggot said again. "Now sit down."

"What do you think they would do to him if they caught him?" I asked. "You know, his mother or somebody might turn him in."

"Jones, they don't want Salamander," Faggot said.

"Yeah, but they wanted you, didn't they?"

Faggot laughed and took another beer bottle out of the refrigerator.

"They want everybody they can lay their hands on," Mother said. "Even Faggots."

Mushmouth made spot checks every fifteen minutes. He was nearly picking his nose apart with his handkerchief when Motherfucker jumped on him and told him to sit down. Mushmouth got so scared he collapsed in a corner. Faggot had to go over to him and put his hand on his shoulder and tell him Mother didn't mean it. Mother said he did too mean it but Faggot shushed him up.

Faggot started talking about some new loans he wanted organized. Mother took the cue and started an independent conversation about pushing dope and recruiting runners from the Committee. Faggot told him it was impossible. He told him mixing dope with politics always spells disaster. How fucking commercialized hippies wouldn't know if it was revolution or the movie. At the same time I was bugging Faggot about getting his tape recorder back. Next Mushmouth was whining for a TV and Motherfucker was calling everybody plebian, bourgeois wipe-outs because "the real culture," he said, "was with FM radio." He wanted Faggot to rip-off the best FM equipment he could "requisition" from the Mighty Sound Center. Faggot laughed and said maybe something was coming his way.

Around 10:00 o'clock Mushmouth, who'd been waiting on the porch for the last thirty-five minutes, came screeching through the house. "He's back. He's back," he shouted. He shook Faggot by the shoulders and made him miss his mouth. Beer poured down the front of Faggot's shirt and Mushmouth screamed, "JE-SUS FUCK."

And I smiled to myself thinking that I thought he was the Quiet One that crazy day when Faggot called me "Jones" and we went to the Aluminum Crab and Faggot threw all his money away, hitting the Crab with nickels and dimes. But I never got to say any of those things because Old Vienna and wine bottles were going round and round and now Salamander was bursting through the door carrying brown shopping bags shouting, "I made it. I made it," and Mushmouth picking it up and calling back and forth in the living room, "He made it, did you hear that? He made it."

Motherfucker grabbed Mushmouth on one of his return trips through the kitchen. He shook him up and down like a daiquiri mix. But Mushmouth was so excited he was embracing Motherfucker until Motherfucker had to drop him on the kitchen floor.

Salamander came into the kitchen and Mushmouth was screeching, "Gifts. Gifts. He brought GIFTS."

Salamander opened up the first big shopping bag and brought out about fifteen albums that he spread out on the kitchen table while everybody hung over them like vultures. Then he pulled apart a second shopping bag and a gallon of loganberry wine sat on the table. Salamander ran for glasses and poured everybody a cupful. "You gotta drink this. This is the heaviest shit there is," he kept saying. "This is the best, the ultimate." Everybody was drinking loganberry.

Faggot made a face. He liked dry. Super dry. He said, "Jones, the only reason you don't like Super Dry is because of all that Mogan David shit you've had."

Salamander balanced the gallon on his shoulder and drank from the jug. Everybody watched him running around like a madman. Everybody was out of their minds because he'd come back just like he promised. Tomorrow everybody could start picking on each other again but it was great for the time being.

I was leaning up against the stove with a beer bottle in my hand. Already that week I'd told Faggot a half dozen times that the stove wasn't working anymore. But I knew that would only register when

Faggot wanted to light a cigarette off one of the coils and neither one of the burners would work. Then there'd be some action and a collection. A little extortion, no tape recorder and in a few days there would be a new stove.

"What's the matter with you, don't you like it?" Salamander asked.

"Yeah, I think it's great. It's got a great taste," I said.

"That's too bad," Salamander said, "because you wouldn't know what a great taste is after all the shit you drink in this house." He pointed to all the bottles on the table and in the general direction of the pantry where there were at least two hundred beer bottles. I know because I counted the first two hundred and fifty. Faggot dumped the second set of two hundred and fifty with an old man who just about fainted when he saw so many bottles come out of one car.

"How come you're not drinking?" Salamander asked again.

"I am drinking." I held up my glass to show Salamander. "I drank this much," I said pointing with my finger to a make-believe line on the side of the glass.

"Jews don't know how to appreciate anything," Salamander laughed. Then he disappeared again and this time he came back with underground literature and Zap Comix for everybody. He said he'd spent two days in Oregon, in the heart of downtown Portland, and nobody except for a few trusted friends knew he was there. Salamander said even his own parents didn't know he was in the same town, only two miles away from them. And, of course, the police and the FBI let him slip through their fingers.

NINE FALL LETTERS

September 3rd
Dear Jones,

Salamander is leaving us. He was transferred about 1000 miles away to Prince Rupert. All that's there are loggers, miners, and whores. Today is his last day of work and he'll be leaving by ferry. They pay the transportation on the ferry.

And did you know that Motherfucker is gone? Some surprise actually. Yesterday (Labor Day) Faggot drove him to the border at Blaine and he was going to hitch home. His father has been seeing a lawyer about getting Mother a deferment and it seems as though he has a pretty good chance.

Martin got a job offer (phony, but nonetheless official-looking from an architect who is "sympathetic"). He drove down with Salamander to the border at Sumas last week and went through the legal shit and was denied.

So today he is seeing a lawyer and is going to try to find out about alternative measures that can be taken. It's frustrating to think that there is nothing you can do about getting a job, etc.

And then there's Faggot who's been going through some heavy shit with Evangeline, his girlfriend from California, and is really upset. No one really knows what's going on. He has a girlfriend at Oakridge who works in the candy store there and he brought her over. She's really beautiful--19 years-old--and really nice. It's hard to tell just what's happening ever. We're all here going around in circles trying to figure out what-the-fuck.

Peace and love,
Doreen

September 10
Dear Jones,

Mushmouth tried to get landed at Sumas and got turned down. He got a letter of refusal and they wouldn't even let him back into the country. Faggot says he is leaving on October 1st. Motherfucker went back to Berkeley last Monday for good, I hope.

A new guy just moved in. Tyler is
okay. He has been laying grass on us
for a week. He got landed marrying a
Canadian named Alice who is okay, too.
She is going to come live with him next
week. She says she likes cats.

It had been kind of a bad scene
around the house the week before I
left. Two girls from Eugene, Oregon
moved in and one of them had two
children, a boy 8 and a girl 10. They
are supposed to be making a movie about
draft dodgers for TV. I don't know how
the movie is coming but those two kids
are the shittiest kids I've ever seen.
They are driving everyone crazy.
Mushmouth has blown his top several
times and Faggot the great psychologist
who always said he would never touch a
kid once picked up the boy by the shirt
and held him off the ground until he
screamed and cried. It is really awful.

I came up on the ferry. I saw a lot
of killer whales.

Your friend,
Salamander

September 12th
Dear Jones,

Two girls and two kids (7 and 10

years old, boy and girl) are making a
film on draft dodgers and deserters.
They're from Oregon. These kids were
obnoxious. Like Martin almost lost his
mind and then their mother made him
really sad because she said he was
terrible with children, cruel, vicious,
and should be in Viet Nam, etc.
 We are finishing painting the room.
It should be finished in three days.
 Salamander left and we're all sad
about that.
 Faggot got a stereo. No rip-off and
he installed it today. (What class!)
 We washed the floor in the living
room and we are painting it (the living
room, not the floor) purple and white.
Sounds garish but it's pretty.

Keep the faith,
Doreen

September 16
Dear Jones,

 Then Faggot turned on the TV with
the sound off. These two Bible armies
were having a big battle and I saw
clubs, hearts, spades, and diamonds
flying all over the place. Then the TV
scene changed and this leader was
rapping and he was pissed off. I saw

his facial features accentuated by red
lines to make him look like the devil--
complete with horns and fire coming
from his mouth. Without Faggot I don't
know what would have happened.

   Hear you have a turtle. Well, if it
isn't starved to death by now maybe you
could try hand-feeding a bit of meat
every couple of days. Most turtles
don't dig that flaky fish food. Mine
never touched the stuff. Also, he is
probably having a hard time handling
that plastic dish—if it's possible you
might arrange something a little more
natural--the best thing would be if he
had someplace to hide. The biggest
reason that turtles don't last long is
that people don't realize what they
need for a solid trip. What they don't
need is mammal style affection--
holding, petting, etc.--the only
affection they need is food and
shelter.

   What turtles die of is cultural
depravity--the same thing you would die
of if a turtle owned you and had you
sitting on a subterranean glob of mud.

Yours truly,
Salamander

September 22nd
Dear Jones,

   Things around here are much better
than they were before. Actually they're
pretty groovy. Our room is finished and
looks great. Tyler and Alice
(Motherfucker's "ex-fiancee" and her
new husband, a deserter) are living in
the other room and are also fixing it
up. We're actually getting Faggot's
room fixed up ok. I wouldn't be
surprised if it turned out to be the
nicest in the house. Of course, Faggot
has his problems with tidiness, but
that's minor.
   Leonard is gone and there's a new
owner at the HANDY STORE. His name is
Dennis. He's like Leonard only fatter
and not as quick-witted.
   We got a new stove with four burners
and with an oven that works, even. Far-
out.

Vinceremos,
Doreen

   P.S . Everybody says "hello," but
they're too fucked in the head to
write. Martin says "Hi."

October 6
Dear Jones,

   School is still where my head is at
even if my body is in Prince Rupert. I
have been on a real exploration-
discovery trip for the last 2 years and
this trip was most cruelly interrupted
by Uncle Sam. That is the main reason
that my being stuck in this place is so
disgusting--and is why my stay in
Canada so far has been unhappy--never
mind all that bullshit about making the
best of things because I definitely
don't belong here.
   This town is crawling with ravens
which the Indians considered holy.
   Doreen got landed so I guess
Mushmouth is saved. He is very lucky.
   I discovered Dylan's "It's All Over
Now, Baby Blue"--the title tells the
story. The words are beautiful:
   All your seasick sailors they are
rowing home
   Your empty-handed soldiers they are
going home
   Your lover who just walked out the
door
   Has taken all the blankets from the
floor
   The carpet too is moving under you

And it's all over Baby Blue.

Your friend,
Salamander

November 3
Dear Jones,

Bad news. Mushmouth went back to the
USA. He is going to turn himself in. He
left a couple of weeks ago. He must
have had terrible problems in his mind
to make him do something like that.
Doreen just got landed and they were
going to get married. Everything seemed
perfect.

Mushmouth never learned to handle
his problems. Instead of reconciling
himself he carried on by force of brute
strength. Ironically he always
considered himself very weak and Doreen
very strong. Actually, it only seemed
that way because Doreen could handle
her problems and do anything she
wanted. Now he thinks going to jail is
the answer and I'm afraid it's a
terrible mistake.

I am going back to Vancouver. I
can't stand it any longer. Before I
take another job I might travel around
a little bit, maybe down into the
States. I can't see sitting around that

house with only Faggot there.

Your friend,
Salamander

December 8
Dear Jones,

    I got a letter from Mushmouth last
week. He is now on an aircraft carrier
named "The Coral Sea." He was not
punished for desertlng for eight
months. He was put on active duty the
day after he turned himself in. I guess
all they care about any more is just
getting you in the service. Martin,
fucked up as he is, is only worried
that we might not like him anymore.
    The FBI knows that I am in Prince
Rupert and that I work at this place.
They sent the RCMP over to my place to
ask me if there was any chance that I
would go back and if I knowingly and
willingly broke the draft law.
    I just called Faggot a month ago and
his line is disconnected. I don't know
what the deal is.

Your friend,
Salamander

You discover that there are two seasons in Canada: Time to move and time to sit still. Either you want to spend the winter someplace else and and get it together to go out on the highway or you decide you'd better find a few more friends and make up with your girlfriend. You need a reasonable place to live with a rent you can afford in a house that is warm and dry.

You discover that Canada in the wintertime is Siberia. When the cold first hits you between the eyes like a sledge hammer, you begin to understand the nature of your exile. In Montreal it's impossible to walk down the street, it's that snowy and that cold, and I guess it's the same in Winnipeg and Calgary and Kitchener and Halifax, too.

And in Vancouver the sun never shines. Then it starts raining day after day and you wonder how the sea gulls manage to survive. A month later you wonder why the birds don't die altogether when you and your friends and all the clothes you own and all the clothes you've lent to friends who you'll never see again are dying from mildew. And when everything is mildewy, you are soggy and sad all the time.

But you didn't know those things when you watched your friends burn their draft cards on the steps of the Arlington Street Church but now in Toronto inside the Brunswick House you remember and stoned out of your mind you go up to the stage to burn your draft card again when the Fat Lady gets up to sing, "I'm an Okie from Muskogee." The only thing happening now is the fat bouncer who tells you not to do those things because you may start a fire.

Nobody sees the tears in your eyes. You're too far from home and nobody cares here.

You walk down Yonge Street looking for Back Bay and you know it doesn't exist but you keep walking, maybe down Bloor or up to Bedford Avenue because the name sounds familiar. You stand on the corner, patiently waiting for the lights to change, knowing that your wait will always be obligatory, somewhat smug and disdainful, knowing and remembering other cities and other places where you can run across curved and twisting and forked roads and no one looks or cares.

You look for the long-haired people in the crowd. The slim boys with their arms circled around willowy waists, elusive in knit sweaters and mock cowboy belts. You love them because they remind you of who you are or who you used to be at any rate. You, the person who looks out at you every morning from the bathroom mirror but who isn't you anymore. You love them, too, because they remind you of the Americans you knew once, of the American who used to be you, long ago, long past remembering or caring, past the time when you loved images of yourself because they acted as barriers to guard you from the things that surround you now but that are not you.

You love the girls in their ugly shag haircuts, even though you'd never want a girlfriend with a haircut like that. You love them because they remind you of the girls you used to know in high school or in three years of college who are all grown-up and far away from you. You love them because they blot out the possibility of any real girl past or future.

The lights change. Stop-Go-Yes-No. Just like the girls you used to pick up in your father's Chevrolet Impala. You've grown your hair long and cut it off and let it grow in again and you've changed, too. You walk all over Canada looking for Amerika in a Bobby Orr Pizza Shop.

You hate Amerika. You love Amerika. You hate Amerika with every fiber of your being and you know that all your hate is a measure of your love.

You hate everything about Amerika that makes it unliveable and you hate Canada more for having those things in manageable amounts and not being Amerika. You hate billboards and garbage. You hate North Philadelphia and Chicago and the whole state of New Jersey. You hate the Berkeley Bay Bridge and Daly City. You hate the Hudson River and Miami Beach. And yet, behind the backlog of hate, you love Brigham's ice cream and Baskin and Robbins and Wannamaker's and Macey's, the Boston Common, the mall in Millwaukee, Hamm's beer and the Gold Coast. You love the Blacks, civil rights, segregation, Chicanos. You love tacos and Orange Julius and jimmies and places like Texarkana and Mountain Home, Idaho, because there it is home.

You hate everything you know. You hate Amerika and you hate this substitute country that is not a country and that is not a home. You hate that you remember everything except your anger. You hate that you still love Amerika. You hate that you are still Amerikan without Amerika because, Baby, YOU MISS AMERIKA AND THERE'S NO GOING BACK.

December 12
Dear Jones,

I am still working at the Mighty
Sound. Mushmouth went away and then
Doreen went away. Salamander went to a
bank in Prince Rupert you already know
that. I am living alone here and it is
all right maybe Evangeline will come
next month I don't know. I have been
playing music by myself.

I don't know what the fuck with
Salamander. Did you know that Breeze
went home to N.J.? His brother turned
him in and he is in jail. Are you
coming for Christmas?

COALDUST

One day in the summertime (Salamander said it was the end of June when everybody was hopeful about a home and before Doreen came) a man came to every house on the street. He rang the bell and asked if anybody was interested in "good shingles. Cheap. Perfect for the winter."

Motherfucker had just gotten up and was the only one home. He stood in the doorway scratching his belly button saying, "Gee, I don't know."

"Best get them now while the price is right. Later on you'll pay double for stuff like this and it gets pretty damp around these parts once it starts raining."

Mother was dubious. He went out to the porch where he could see a dump truck full of shingles. "Okay," he said. "I'll take them."

Mother went back inside for his moccasins while the guy in the truck drove around the block and into the backyard. Meanwhile Mother forced open the door to the back hall and made his way around two broken stoves and five plastic bags of garbage. The place was full of flies and he was glad to open the hall door and go down the rickety back steps to the yard.

"Where should I put 'em, mister?"

"Oh," Motherfucker said staring at the empty yard and making futile motions with his arm. "Oh, I guess you'd better put them there." He pointed to the bare patch of cement that was flush to the house.

Motherfucker moved to the side and the man in the battered-up dump truck pulled a lever and the back of the truck dropped off. A pile of off-yellow shingles fell to the ground, covering up two broken chairs and a half dozen cracked dirty dishes that Salamander kept throwing out the windows. Motherfucker stared at the pile while dust drizzled over everything.

"That's twenty dollars, mister."

Motherfucker didn't move. He stood at the edge of the pile, pushing some of the chips around with his toe.

"That will be twenty dollars mister," the man repeated, impatient and wishing he had gotten the money from Motherfucker before he pulled the lever.

"Yeah," Mother said in a kind of a sigh. He went back up the porch stairs and into the shaving kit bag by the side of the bed where he pulled out two ten dollar bills and gave them to the man who was waiting on the back porch, peering into the back hall counting flies.

"You should get Raid. Kill those bastards," the shingle man said reaching for the money.

"Guess I can stack it in the cellar," Mother said but the man was already going down the stairs and getting into his heap of a truck.

Mother watched the truck pull out in a daze.

286

Then he stared at the pile of shingles in the backyard that hadn't been there ten minutes ago, seeming for all the world to have dropped down from heaven while the wind made noises with the weeds in the yard and a couple of birds sang from telephone wires. He looked at the Rose Bush Lady's white sheets drying in the wind next door and he felt a strange surge of emotion. He couldn't put his finger on it right away so he stared at the shingles for a while longer until he found it. He was exhilirated.

Mother had breakfast and worked the rest of the day carrying shingles into the cellar. He cleared out a corner down there that smelled like moldering dead leaves. He kept expecting to come across a dead sparrow but he didn't find a single thing. He stuffed shingles into that same spot near the furnace until Faggot came home.

"What d'you do, boy?" Faggot asked bewildered, looking out the kitchen window at a pile that was still a good eight feet tall.

Mother stood in the doorway rocking back and forth, smiling. "I bought us some shingles. In the winter they'll be fuel for the furnace down there." He pointed to the cellar door. "Keep warm on. You know, like fire, Faggot." He was crazy happy. "Later on, Faggot you'll have to pay double for stuff like that. It only cost you twenty bucks today."

Faggot whistled through his teeth and put his finger in the air. "Bloop."

But that was in June and in December a whole truckload of shingles for twenty dollars lasts one week in the furnace. When Mother had first bought the load, Faggot thought it was a pretty good idea, too. He said it was almost a good thing because it kept Mother happy for a few days and out of mischief while he pretended he lived on a farm. He said it did for him what tadpoles did for Salamander. Salamander said it was a dumb thing in June and he said it was a dumb thing again in December when there wasn't any heat and nobody around to hear him bitch.

Salamander quit The Bank and came back from Prince Rupert. He couldn't stand the crows and the whores in that city anymore and he was convinced if he stayed there a month more The Bank would succeed in kidnapping his mind. He didn't think he was weak or anything but he said they caught up with you once they managed to separate you from your friends and your mental environment. He didn't think Faggot was any kind of mental environment but at least he wasn't a crow or a whore.

The first thing Salamander said when he came back was, "How come this place stinks?" He started in the living room and sniffed all over the house. By the time Faggot came home from work, nearly having his coronary when he discovered Salamander eating rolled wheat hearts in the kitchen, Salamander had his list of grievances drawn up. "The house is freezing. The place stinks. There's smoke everywhere. You can't breathe. There's hardly enough coal in the cellar to toast a marshamallow. My nose is running and my eyes are watering. This isn't any kind of environment even for fuck-ups."

"Are you a guest or a resident?"

"I'm a resident." Salamander threw his bowl into the sink. "What do you think?"

"Well, in that case you'll have to get used to it." Faggot went into the living room and turned on his TV. "If you don't like it, I'll get you a room in the Hotel Vancouver."

"A human being can't breathe in this atmosphere," Salamander yelled out the kitchen door.

"They do in New York," Faggot called back in a sing-song.

"Well, no wonder they're retarded there. Why didn't that fuck-up of a Motherfucker sell that wicker chair to the junk dealer instead of wasting all that money on rip-off cardboard fuel?"

Faggot didn't answer him. He had his own problems to worry about. He was still working at the Sound Center waiting to hear from his old girlfriend Evangeline from California or to get fired. Mornings he got up wondering whether it was the day Goldshit would finally tell him to go to hell or whether there would be a postcard from Evangeline saying she was on her way to see him. He had no way of knowing which thing was going to happen first.

"I bet you can't stand the suspense, Faggot," Salamander said to him one night when Faggot was watching TV in the living room. Salamander dragged a kitchen chair into the room and sat down directly in front of the TV.

Faggot took his eyes away from the screen without moving his head.

"Faggot you gonna get fired first or is your ex-girlfriend gonna come up here first?"

Faggot moved his eyes back to the TV. "I don't know." The wine bottle came to his lips and went back to its position in his arms. He held it like a baby.

"You're gonna get fired first, Faggot. Because you've been late every day this week and yesterday you never went back after lunch hour."

"How do you know?" Faggot asked surprised.

"Because I went in there to buy a record and you weren't there and nobody knew where you were."

"Where do you think I was?"

"I bet you don't know either, you fuck-up faggot." Then Salamander jumped out of his chair and began prancing around in front of the TV. "It's the middle of the winter and I have to be stuck in a house with a fatass faggot and nothing to do and no place to go and no people around who aren't assholes."

"You're beginning to sound like Mother," Faggot said in an even radio voice. He dug a piece of tobacco out of a tooth and began chewing on it. "Get your ass out of the picture."

Salamander shut up and threw himself into his chair relocated next to Faggot's. "Faggot, how can you stand to watch this shit?" he asked. "Night after night."

"But it's good," Faggot said like Salamander was crazy. They were quiet during the commercials. "I'll buy coal at the end of the week when I get paid."

"What are you going to do when they fire you, Faggot?"

"Tell Goldshit to suck my dick."

Salamander cackled and folded his arms tighter around his chest. "Fuck," he said. He was going to hug himself to death.

"Fuck yourself, Salamander. Did you make supper?" Faggot looked at him for the first time all evening.

"Yeah, and I ate it, too, Faggot."

"Why d'you do that?" Faggot showed Salamander a hurting face. He looked at Salamander. "Tch. Tch. Why do you do things like that?" All Faggot's questions were in the same soft voice, as if all the liquor he had ever drunk finally caught up with him and was coating his vocal cords.

"Because, Faggot, I was hungry and I don't want to share with no assholes, faggots or fuck-ups. As soon as Mister Rogers came on, I came in here and ate my supper right in front of him. He's no asshole."

"Want some wine?"

"Yeah, Faggot." Salamander's hand snatched the bottle out of Faggot's arm. He drank as much as he could get away with before Faggot grabbed it out of his hands. "I'm the breadwinner around here," Faggot said pounding his heart with a closed fist. "I want steak and cannelloni. I want..."

"Wait one minute, you faggot." Salamander attacked Faggot's legs. "I've paid my rent two months in advance and this place isn't worth any rent because there's no heat. You ought to pay me for living here and by breathing warm up the air."

"There's heat. But it's like fucking, Salamander. You have to know what you're doing to the furnace."

Salamander got rabid. He nearly started to drool

like Mushmouth used to when he was excited about something. "You. You, faggot, you. You know, you always choose the wrong time to be a prick."

"Thanks." Faggot flashed a robot smile at Salamander who got up and stomped upstairs. Then he went back to his TV and his wine bottle.

"Where are you going?" Faggot yelled up the stairs.

"None of your goddamn business, Faggot."

"Peace."

"Fuck yourself," Salamander screarmed down the bathroom radiator.

Faggot shuddered in the living room.

A half hour later in the middle of Walter Cronkite Salamander came downstairs in his dude suit. He had on his cowboy boots and Doc Holliday tie. Since he wasn't working anymore his hair was almost down to his neck again. He stood in front of the TV fingering his beard because he wanted to make Faggot jealous. Because Faggot worked at the Mighty Sound Center he had to wear a suit and a tie and pay six dollars to have his hair styled once a month by a lady hairdresser.

"Boy, I bet you wish you could grow your hair, don't you, Faggot?" Salamander asked him one night when he was feeling particularly bitchy. "Can you roll a cigarette while you're fucking?" Faggot tossed back. He exaggerated the "ing" and Salamander shook a fist and stalked out of the room.

"Where are you going dressed like John Wayne?"

"I'm going to the Daisy," Salamander said. "Not like some fuck-up asshole faggots who sit around all the time feeling sorry for themselves."

Faggot was about to say something when Walter Cronkite read the day's Vietnam death count. He leaned over in his chair and turned up the volume. After the war news and the casualties were over they started talking again.

"You're going to grab ass? Well, I hope you get some chick," Faggot said.

A commercial flashed on showing a muscular man in a bathtub talking about problem perspiration. "You have to look like him if you want to get one of those girls at the Daisy." Faggot was lecturing Salamander who was smirking at the man taking his bath. "Because even if he has smelly armpits, he's the kind of guy they want."

"Yeah," Salamander agreed. "That's because they think he's all cock."

"But he is, isn't he?" asked Faggot in his new silky wintertime voice.

"Shut up, fuck-up," Salamander answered in his new wintertime voice.

Faggot raised one arm in a fist and shook it at Salamander. "Give my love to the daisies. Don't pick any colored ones."

Salamander slammed the door and Faggot was left alone. He was spending more time alone than he had ever spent with himself in his life before. Most of the time he felt like he did when his first wife told him she was leaving him. He'd gotten into his car and drove up and down the highways for two weeks, never knowing where he was, pulling over to the side of the road and sleeping when he was too tired to drive anymore. The memory of that time was a slow deadening mist where it took centuries for the screams to leave his mouth and come real-to-life-true in his ears. That was what this time was like now.

He waited for the last commercial before the first new show before he went downstairs to the cellar. He sniffed the air. Yep, it still smelled like something died down there. He stopped in the middle of the basement. He remembered that a guy came to see him about setting up a darkroom here. He walked over to the coal corner and looked at how much was left in the bin. This was the end of the second batch of coal he had bought since the weather turned lousy. That guy had set up a makeshift darkroom where he developed pictures. He had the basic equipment, not too much besides. He paid fifteen dollars a month for darkroom privileges. Then Salamander discovered he'd started to live in his darkroom. Faggot looked at the coal marks on the floor. It was weird stuff, he thought. It left traces of itself everywhere. Whatever happened to that guy in the darkroom? The funny thing was he couldn't remember. He hadn't even remembered that there was such a guy until just then. That was what was so weird about the whole thing, he decided. People disappeared and you didn't have the slightest idea of what had become of them.

It was funny, he thought, how Salamander really couldn't get the hang of the furnace. He opened the grate with a stick and looked inside. It was out. Dead cold out. Shit. No wonder Salamander said he was cold all day. Four or five weeks back there were some people from around Toronto who had come and stayed in the house. They paid $8.25 a week but they couldn't make the furnace work, either. "It is because nobody has any idea how this thing works," Faggot said as he collected some big chunks of coal and a few old newspapers from a pile across the room. He twisted the newspapers into tight rolls and laid them down on top of the dead ashes inside the furnace. "These are called 'Scotch Knots,'" he said in an imaginary lecture to Salamander. Then he got some coal chips and scattered them over the newspapers. He took out his matches and lit the ends of the newspapers and the edge of a single sheet of newspaper that he held in his free hand above the furnace door. When that paper was completely aflame, he threw it into the furnace and watched the other papers ignite.

Some of the coal chips started to smoke and then glow. He arranged them side by side with his stick and when a sizeable number were red-hot, he banked the whole business by alternating layers of fresh coal with the coals already hot. "Now the secret is to never let it go out," he said in a kind of farewell statement, banging the grate shut and rubbing his hands on his knees. His hands left long black streaks on his pants. "That's because we have bought cheap coal, children. Your daddy can't afford a new furnace this year."

He went upstairs and sat down in front of the TV again. He didn't want to think and all he did all day was think. As soon as he got up in the morning he thought whether or not he should go to work and he thought all day about what was becoming of him and where his life was leading him, so in the evening to think less, he drank wine and watched TV because he didn't want to say out loud that his life was wasted and he had done all that before his twenty-fourth birthday. Applause.

The smoke was beginning to seep through the walls. Faggot got up again and reluctantly dragged himself into the kitchen and checked that the cellar door was shut. Then he sealed off the kitchen and took off his first shirt. He opened another bottle of wine and collapsed into his chair in front of the TV. "The problem is simple," he said. "There is no out." He lit a cigarette and watched himself exhale. For the fun of it he made smoke rings until he started coughing. It occurred to him that if he couldn't see his smoke, he would stop smoking. Then he understood why he didn't smoke in the dark. "Because if you can't see your breath, then you are dead." He thought that last one was quite profound. He reminded himself to save it for Salamander. Then it occurred to him that maybe Salamander who never smoked was dead. He was sure he was thinking a lot of things lately that were profound but that were useless. Yes, he was learning a lot about himself sitting with his television night after night while Salamander went to the Daisy hoping for a girlfriend. As if you really picked them.

He knew he should get up and check the furnace again. "Now is the critical time, my children. It is necessary to add a heavy layer of fresh coal." Faggot raised a finger in warning. "Otherwise no heat. No. No. No." He opened the kitchen door and pulled the front of his shirt over his mouth and nose. He shut his eyes and stumbled to the cellar door. He ran his hand along the edge of the wall and took the steps one at a time. When Faggot got to the bottom of the stairs he opened his eyes. "Fuck, shit, piss," he said softly.

He pried the grate open with his stick and flung the door aside. Inside the furnace was red-hot. Flames were licking and tearing at the walls. Tentatively he held his hand to the fire. "Hot." Faggot drew his hand back but stayed in front of the flames. The open furnace threw jagged light into the corners of the cellar, lighting up his face, burning it redder than any wine. He squinted at the flames. It was funny but he couldn't remember the face of the guy who had lived in the darkroom in the cellar for a couple of months. He let him live rent-free after a while but he couldn't remember when he left. It must have been sometime in the summer. He wished there was somebody he could ask because suddenly his knowing was crucial to something, but like his acid trips, he wasn't sure what.

He slid the tab from the cellophane to his mouth and nothing happened. Then he went for a walk and a kleenex box flew by. In the hiatus of flight he found something, some cyclical eternal moment of truth, but then he lost it. It left him with the footprint and not the person. Then he went inside and Jones was there. Or was she? He was never sure where she was. Yes. She was eating bread and butter. She took the butter out of the refrigerator and slipped a butcher knife into it. "Stop. Stop," he yelled and stepped farther away from the furnace. "It burns. You're slicing away layers of my stomach with that knife." He clutches his stomach and she stops but she eats. Next he goes out again and a bus runs him over. Then he lies down and dies and wakes up and can't tell if he is dead or not. He cries, he thinks, but he can't remember what his tears are for. Then he lies down on somebody's lawn and he becomes a blade of grass. It is his fulfillment. It is what he has always wanted to be. Then he goes back to the house but is afraid to go in. He has to wait a year before he can go in. But why is he afraid of the house? Then this time he knows he is alive and he sleeps. In the morning it is creation again and he eats pancakes in the Sportsman's Cafe and feels he has been purged of everything he has ever done. Then he must change and go to the Mighty Sound Center the morning after he has been with God. Yet he walks around for two weeks glad to be alive but cannot remember who lived in the cellar of his house in a darkroom. Jones might know but he wasn't sure where she was now, either.

He gathered more coal for the furnace and tenderly almost lovingly fed the fire. It was eerie in the basement with the flames on the walls and on his clothes. He spit against the steel and watched his spit sizzle and evaporate. Faggot spit again and again, each time waiting for parts of himself to dissolve. The fire was burning a hole through him. He laughed and wondered why it bothered to burn a new one. He was surprised to find he was crying. His tears humbled him. They were searing furrows down his face. He wanted to know why they didn't land on the furnace and sizzle away into nothing. He would have enjoyed hearing them melt into the roar of the furnace.

He must have fell asleep because Salamander was standing over him coughing. "Can't breathe. Can't fucking breathe. Do something or somebody will call the Fire Department."

The room was full of blue smoke that settled like a cloud over everything. It engulfed you and sucked you in until you were part of it and indistinguishable in smell. It made you drowsy and you felt drugged all the time. Dick Cavett, however, stayed clean and bright-eyed and razor-sharp.

"Yeah, but it's warm," Faggot said. "If you didn't let it go out during the day I wouldn't have to start it up every night. It's only like this when it first gets going."

"The fuck it is."

"Open a window. Suck my dick. Move out. Do anything you like but don't let it go out again," Faggot said in a firm voice.

"Fuck off, Faggot."

"What's your trouble?" Faggot rummaged around the floor in front of the TV. "Weren't the daisies cooperative?"

"Why don't you go fuck yourself, Faggot?" Salamander pulled up the kitchen chair and sat down staring at the set with his hands tucked into the top of his pants. "Faggot, what are you watching?"

"Same old shit."

"Don't you get tired of it?"

"It's always different. They fix it every time so it's different."

"It looks like the same shit to me, Faggot."

"It *is* the same shit. Some of the commercials are new."

They ran out of things to talk about. Salamander

was the first to speak. "You know, Faggot, I'm not wasting my money there anymore." Faggot looked at him. "They're all a bunch of half-assed dipshits. I'm not going there anymore."

"Good. You can buy the TV Guide now. You're rich."

"Faggot, you're fucked."

Faggot looked at Salamander, leaning his head back and squinting out of his left eye, the one that barely could see anything at all. "I like you, Salamander," he said reaching over and patting Salamander's knee. "I like you a whole lot."

"Hey, Faggot, fuck off." Salamander slapped Faggot's hand hard and retreated. "I don't need any half-assed faggots to like me. I don't need any fuck-ups to like me."

"That's why you're so fucked-up, Salamander."

They held on until the TV shut off and the American flag crept into their living room with the Star Spangled Banner compliments of cable TV. Salamander always had some choice remark about Old Glory until they developed a contest to see who could make up the best one-line obscenity about the U. S. of A. and its conglomerates. If Faggot won two days running Salamander became unbearable. He couldn't stand losing to a Faggot.

Every day it was getting colder and wetter. The house was always damp and stuffy at the same time because the furnace was failing. At first Salamander enjoyed being back in Vancouver with Faggot off to work every day and no bank to steal his mind. He didn't work and despite all the literature he'd read to the contrary, it didn't harm him or disturb him or weaken his resolve. Never was there anybody so happy to do nothing. He lived off of money he earned in the bank in the summer and he tried to meet new people and have intelligent conversations but when that fell through, he was glad staying home all day and feeling happy because he didn't have to go to a bank unless he wanted to withdraw money. Salamander acclimated himself so well that after a while he didn't mind the coal or the smell or the dust that settled on everything and made your eyes water. He wore two shirts in the house and long underwear under his corduroy pants that he never washed. He asked what the point was when everything around there was always black from coal dust. And he had this irritating new habit of calling Faggot "faggot" all the time.

In the evenings Salamander ate rolled wheat hearts or Red River Cereal with Mister Rogers. When Faggot came home, starved because he wasn't eating anything all day, Salamander told him how good it was for his digestion to eat with kids rather than with people or with faggots. Then Salamander threw his bowl into the sink where it stayed until it was time for breakfast and waited for Faggot to come back with the wine. On some nights when Faggot was feeling generous he bought Salamander a bottle of wine for himself. Unconsciously he felt that the faster he spent all his money, the quicker things would be over for him. On those nights they insulted each other through the obscenity contest and into forty-five minutes of dead TV snow. Sometimes Faggot never went to bed but fell asleep in his chair in front of the TV.

In the morning a weather report promising more rain or a college credit electrical wiring class woke him. Two hours after Faggot had somehow put himself together and limped off to another day at the Sound Center, Salamander went downstairs and rinsed out his bowl. He ate Red River Cereal or rolled wheat hearts with Captain Kangaroo.

Late one Monday afternoon Faggot came home in time for the beginning of Mister Rogers.

"Faggot, what are you doing home?" Salamander shut off his Bob Dylan record. He was getting ready for supper.

"They sent me home."

"Who sent you home, Faggot?"

"Goldshit." Faggot was standing in the living room pouting. He looked beat-up. He looked like he did the day Salamander brought Mickey Mouse to the house.

"Are you fired, Faggot? Did they fire you?"

"No. Not yet. But he said my clothes are dirty and I smell like smoke and my general appearance is 'disheveled and disordered.'" Faggot collapsed into a chair and rested his head in his hands. "I have a headache. I'm tired," he said to himself.

"Who does this Goldshit think he is, Faggot? The President of the United States or some other Big Ass? 'Disheveled and disordered.'" Salamander's voice was full of contempt. "I didn't know Goldshit had such a big vocabulary."

"He went out with a Playmate of the Month. June, I think. Maybe July."

"*Play-Mate.* Shit. He can fire you, yes, but he

can't tell people that they're smelly. HE CAN'T TELL PEOPLE THINGS LIKE THAT."

"He told me." There was a pause. "Salamander, you want to do me a favor? Sit down. You're making my headache worse."

"It's. It's..." Salamander was clenching his fists. "It's..."

"Humiliating," said Faggot. "I know. You don't have to tell me."

Salamander didn't look at Faggot wiped-out in front of his TV in his kitchen chair in his next-to-best suit. Instead he went into the kitchen where he swore at Faggot and threw pots around because his Red River Cereals were sticking to the burned-out bottom of the pot.

Salamander stood in the doorway to the kitchen and stabbed a spoon in the air at Faggot. "Just try to see Goldshit live under these conditions," he shouted.

Faggot waved a peace sign at him. He took off his glasses and wiped the lenses on the front of his shirt that he pulled out for that purpose. He rubbed his eyes.

Salamander came back and sat down again. Faggot put his glasses on. "Faggot, you ought to quit," Salamander said.

Faggot didn't say anything. He turned around and stared out the living room window. Most of the bottles Motherfucker had put there had been thrown out months ago. They'd put a plastic bag against the cracked part of the pane and it held for two weeks. Now it was beginning to rattle in the wind. It was annoying.

"I read *The San Francisco Chronicle* today," Faggot said. "There was a copy somebody left lying around the store and I picked it up and read it on my lunch hour. There was an article about some hitchhikers freezing to death. They were in a snow storm and nobody would pick them up. Then there was this other article about cannibalism among this group of hippies on Highway 101. The newspaper called Route 101, dig this, Salamander, 'The Hippie Highway.'"

Salamander laughed to himself.

"I thought you'd appreciate that," Faggot said.

"Yeah, Faggot, it makes me glad I'm in a civilized country where people are allowed to freeze to death in the privacy of their own homes."

"Why, was it cold here again today?" Faggot was suddenly concerned.

"Faggot, is the pope Catholic?" Salamander snapped.

"I've heard that one before."

"Yeah, well, Faggot, it was freezing in here. I didn't let it go out today but we're low in coal so I tried not to use much. I wasn't exactly roasting, you know."

"It's not too bad now." Faggot sniffed the room.

"No. I have the upstairs windows open so when I go to bed after another wonderful evening at home with you, Faggot, I'll be able to breathe."

"You should take up cigarettes," Faggot suggested. "Then you wouldn't mind the smoke."

"Bullshit, Faggot."

Faggot went into the kitchen and came out with a cold hot dog and three pieces of white bread. "There's nothing to eat here," he whined. "We need a cook and a housekeeper and a nigger maid."

"We need a furnace that works," Salamander yelled from his chair in front of the TV. And some women."

"Why don't you go out and get yourself laid?" Faggot asked stuffing half a hot dog in his mouth. He held his hand over his mouth until he swallowed.

"Why don't you mind your own business, Faggot? That's how faggots get in trouble. They snoop into other people's business. All faggots are half-assed fuck-ups. They should be sent to Vietnam and shot."

"Who's buying the ticket?" Faggot managed as he giggled and spit out a soggy crust. He went through the motions of drooling over Salamander. Salamander squirmed away and made horror faces. Finally Faggot sat down in front of the TV. "Supper," he said. "Feh." He brushed crumbs off his shirt like he was playing guitar. He belched.

The picture blurred and Salamander tried to fix it.

"Leave that alone." Faggot slapped Salamander's hands away from the controls. He moved the dials himself until the picture came back.

"Faggot, where were you yesterday? I came into the store and you weren't there."

"I went to the zoo."

"Oh, come on, Faggot. The zoo?"

"Sure. Why not? Nice polar bears. Gimme those cigarettes." Faggot grabbed them out of Salamander's hand. "And there's this far-out French couple that are always there. They don't speak any English. She wears this short white fur down to here," he showed

Salamander with his hand. "And he's got a real expensive black one down to there." He hit Salamander in the calf. "They take their pet mouse with them. She talks to it in French and he talks to her in French and then they bring this mouse to the bats. She squeezes it around the neck and holds it against the glass. It screams and they laugh in French."

"Faggot, you're full of shit."

Faggot shrugged his shoulders. "I can't help it."

The more Salamander thought about Faggot's French couple and their mouse, the more he thought Faggot was crazy. But a few days later he drove out to the zoo to see for himself. The polar bears were in their island preserve behind an iron fence. The aquarium was empty. He went to the covered-over walkway that houses the snakes, birds and bats. In the middle of winter the zoo is deserted but on the other side of a fake tree he discovered the couple. The lady was rubbing her thumb and forefinger together around the mouse's neck. Her boyfriend-husband was shelling peanuts and slipping them between his wife's lips. Salamander was watching the bats sleeping upside-down when the lady turned and smiled at him. She had bright red lipstick and pale skin. That night Salamander told Faggot he thought she was a lady vampire. Faggot wanted to know why he hadn't asked her for a date.

Salamander got tired of Faggot and Faggot got tired of Salamander and they were both tired of TV and a lousy furnace they had to babysit for and the relative red light their lives had come to. Salamander said he thought things would pick up in the spring, but Faggot doubted it. The one thing Faggot said he was sure of was getting fired. Then there would be another round with Evangeline who had written to say she was on her way. After that he would be just where he was now except he would be without a job but with another chapter completed in his relationship with Evangeline that already spanned two countries, a thousand miles and three years and was as far away as ever from resolution. They merely took turns trying out new things on each other and this time it was Evangeline's turn. Sometimes Faggot wondered how he would feel if the time came when he and Evangeline would get tired and give up trying to make a final statement. He thought he would miss her terribly. There was a great psychic ache in him that living with her could never resolve and living apart would never satisfy.

As the winter wore on Salamander worried more about his money. He started to write down everything he spent in a pocket notebook he carried with him everywhere. He reached for that instead of his wallet. Faggot started looking for food bargains everywhere. He made Salamander go to all the different Econo-Marts and Save-On-Meats whenever there was a sale. They ate canned pears and day-old bread and cheap cold cuts. Faggot refused to eat peanut butter. Salamander said he had nothing to worry about because he wouldn't let him have any even if he really liked it. He also said he wouldn't feed a faggot but when there was food, they shared.

Like the time Salamander bought an eighty-four-cent chicken thinking it had to be the bargain of the century. He told Faggot the Great Chicken lost his address. Salamander cooked it for two hours smothered in carrots. When Faggot came home they discovered it was a stewing chicken that was about ten years-old and needed two months of cooking in order to get soft enough for a human being to get his front tooth through the skin. Faggot pushed it around in his plate with his fingers. He ate three slices of carrots, holding them between his fingertips as if they were gourmet snails. "Fowl," he said. "Feh." Salamander said,"Shit," and tried for half an hour to eat it. Finally he threw the old bird leg against the wall and cooked a batch of Red River Cereal. Faggot started his old refrain, "I want steak and cannelloni."

They were falling into a routine. The furnace was no better and no worse than it ever was. Faggot still went to work smelling like a Cub Scout weenie roast and Salamander kept on eating Red River Cereals and rolled wheat hearts for breakfast and supper. They lived as if they were secretly hoping something would happen to them. A new variety of disaster would be a welcome change. Anything that promised termination to the way they were living.

Near the bottom of his second newest box of Red River Cereal Salamander's financial situation became acute and he started to think seriously about selling *Georgia Straights*. Faggot told him to go sell his body to the highest bidder and Salamander told him a variation of the usual. They were getting on fine. Faggot said that when he lost his job he would begin to pawn everything he owned, starting and ending with his body. Salamander told him that if he ever pawned anything that belonged to him, especially his record player, he would cut off his balls and make him into a real faggot. Faggot said he would never do a thing like that. "You'd better not, Faggot," warned Salamander, "because if you do you'll never be a gigolo."

Three days out of five Faggot didn't go back to work after lunch hour. Some days he drove to the Spanish Banks and watched the winter waves come in. He felt better when he watched the sea although he always felt lonely there. He didn't exactly enjoy skipping work. He hated the feeling of doing something bad and then making himself available for the punishment. He knew for a long time that he was going to lose his job--but he was unable to do anything about it one way or the other. He could have quit or made an effort to stay or had himself fired but he couldn't do anything. That was probably the reason Goldshit wanted to get rid of him. Goldshit with his Playmate. He let it happen to him because he was unable to say that there were alternatives and that one thing was better than another. He was waiting to get fired and secretly he hoped it would be soon so that it would be out of the way.

Faggot parked the car alongside the beach front and looked at the empty beaches and thought about Goldshit and his Playmate. Sometimes when it wasn't raining and sometimes when it was because he didn't give a shit about the weather, Faggot left the car and walked the length and breadth of the beaches, watching the sand fall backwards into his footsteps. Often he got the urge to take his shoes and socks off altogether and walk barefoot. The feel of the cold damp sand against his body was exhilirating. It seemed real somehow.

Other days when he couldn't bear to be alone he went to the zoo. He stood by the polar bears and watched them swim and dive and play with each other even on the coldest days. The zoo is empty on winter afternoons but he liked it there. He thought the bears were company because they are social creatures and almost human in their pleasures.

Sometimes he pretended about bringing his daughter to the zoo to see the polar bears and sometimes when he felt hopeful, he pretended he was bringing Evangeline. But in his heart he knew neither fantasy was possible. Christine would never come to see him in Vancouver and he could never go to see her. At worst, she would come and be homesick for her mother and her friends and her new daddy. Evangeline would come to him in bed and then she would want to talk and then she would want to go to a restaurant. They would promise each other not to find the same faults and surprise one another with finding new ones. In a few weeks she would say, "Nothing has changed," and he would have to agree with her and then she would have to leave. He would bring her to the airport and they would cry and kiss, saying the words of love that are real enough, although the words themselves were lies, tricking themselves into believing they could try one more time while the airline ticket in her hand waved forewarned insurance against any more madness.

Faggot watched the bears behind their bars and

tried to believe that timing was responsible. He wanted to be a good father to his daughter in California but here he was in Canada, losing his job in the zoo, knowing that postcards from Christine were abbreviated messages of somebody else's guilt. He wanted to be in more than one place at one time and in some places he could never go back to or look ahead to. Now he felt he was going into places he might never get back from and the going was effortless, like falling forward into snow.

"Hey, Faggot. I want to ask you a question."

"Oh, Jesus," Faggot said. He slumped into a kitchen chair and put his head in his hands. "Don't ask yet. I'm not ready." He lit a citgarette and covered his eyes with his hands. "Okay. I'm ready."

"Faggot, how come we're the only two left?"

Faggot dropped his hands. "Jesus, Salamander, don't scare me like that. I thought you were going to ask me a question."

"I am asking you a question, dumbass. How come we're the only two left, Faggot?"

Faggot opened the refrigerator door. "There's nothing in here to eat," he said.

"Faggot Fatass, I'm asking you a question. How come we're the only two left?"

Faggot slammed the door. "Well, it's simple. We're the oldest."

"What do you mean we're the oldest? How about

Motherfucker? Faggot, what's this got to do with it anyway? Mushmouth was the only teenie-bopper."

"He was not."

"What do you mean, Faggot?"

"Oh, Jesus, Salamander. I'm twenty-four. So are you."

"I'm twenty-three, Faggot. My birthday is in two months."

"Okay, so you're nearly twenty-four. Mushmouth was eighteen, maybe nineteen."

"He just turned nineteen, Faggot. Wherever he is."

"Okay. And Motherfucker was nineteen, too."

"Oh, come off it, Faggot. Motherfucker couldn't be nineteen."

"He is. And that's why they fucked up. I mean, could you come up here and do all this shit when you were nineteen? Especially Mushmouth he..."

"Especially Mushmouth, Faggot... MOTHERFUCKER. It's Motherfucker," Salamander shook his head. "You coddled him all the time and gave him car keys and ran a regular kindergarten for him."

"They were only nineteen, Salamander."

Salamander looked at the floor. "Shit. I didn't know that. I didn't know Motherfucker was nineteen years-old. Shit." He looked at Faggot.

Faggot was pushing all the bread crumbs on the table into a pile with his fingertips. "I know," Faggot said. "He didn't look nineteen."

DOREEN

I heard a long time later, on the QT from Faggot
who had somehow squirmed it away from
Salamander, although I think Salamander told Faggot
for free when they became friends of sorts and out of
hatred for Mother, that sometime that summer while
Mushmouth was trying to get a job and pretending he
was a freelance photographer and before Doreen and
Mushmouth had the final split-up that left
Mushmouth in tears and Doreen determined to do
something, probably go back to S.F., that Mother had
something in common with Mushmouth. It was more
than just sourdough bread.

There was very little that could keep Mushmouth
down. That is there was very little until the business
with Doreen. It would have been fine if you could have
called that episode tragedy, if you could label all the
bad things that happen to you under the grand name
of tragedy, but although you may tell it to friends like
high-class stuff, you know it's only third-class
melodrama, soap opera, and it aches more than it
sears...

Well, it seems that Mother was plain bored. Or
mischievous. Maybe both. From the first time he'd

seen Doreen, he'd given himself ideas and maybe as soon as Doreen saw Mother she knew that she was going to do something that maybe she shouldn't do but couldn't help. I don't know if it came from having too much time on their hands or no commitment to anything or if it always comes to it by itself but...

Mother hustled and hustled until Doreen thought maybe it was a good idea to go to bed with Mother. Mother wanted somebody in that big brass bed of his so bad he didn't care where he got it. The funny thing, too, is that it never happened in that big brass bed. Nothing happened in that bed except old cigarette papers and some lousy dope.

It wasn't that Doreen loved Mushmouth less or Mother more. She didn't know what she wanted and anybody can do anything to find out what it is that you've got and what it is that you used to have and what it is you don't have anymore and maybe don't miss, either.

Doreen and Marty were playing house. But there wasn't any money and there wasn't any scene to shine in so it all got to be kind of a drag. Doreen would never admit it but it was a pain in the ass to take care of Martin and get fuck-all for it, so she wondered just what the fuck she'd gotten herself into by coming to *Canadia* and thought maybe she would have to go back to S.F. after all. It pained her, I think, to know that she'd given up her cushy job in the S.F. Post Office where you get to wear granny glasses to work every day and meet a groovy group of gays and chicks and guys with long hair and all of them American. So in the end she didn't so much chuck Mushmouth as she started to take care of herself. She started to look to her experiences in *Canadia* and she wanted to broaden her horizons.

I don't know if Mother was the one to do, but she did him and that's that.

Only the way I got the story, Salamander asked Mother point-blank why he had chosen Doreen and pestered and pestered and pestered her until she made up her mind when Doreen was the girlfriend of a person who lived in that house and was a good friend of Mother's. He wanted to know why, when there were all those other girls on 4th who were just dying to jump into bed with a Motherfucker, he had to choose Doreen. Salamander told him that if he wanted to, he could go down there and get a girl for Monday and on Tuesday trade her in for Tuesday and use Thursday on Wednesday and give Wednesday Saturday off for Sunday. Just why the fuck, Salamander wanted to know, did he have to go after Doreen when it nearly broke Mushmouth's heart and he nearly killed himself four times in the week that his life crumbled and Doreen said she was going back to the States because it was over and she didn't love anybody, not even herself.

And Mother said she was free to choose and that he hadn't raped her and if Mushmouth couldn't keep her that was Mushmouth's problem, not his.

And Salamander said, "You fucker. Why you fucker, you," and nearly punched Mother in the mouth for real. But Mother stood by his justice and said no wrong was done that wouldn't be done anyway.

"Why Doreen'd take him back and then throw him out again in two weeks," he said. And that's exactly what happened, too. Not once but three, four times. Why it goes on all the time.

Salamander didn't have anything to say to that but from that time on he never said anything to Mother again. Not ever as much as a grunt in the morning.

Afterwards Mother walked around more and more dejected and he stayed that way, even though Mushmouth and Doreen patched things up between them and got back together again.

But Salamander never spoke to Mother again and when there were only the two of them there in the daytime, it was tough on both of them, but especially Mother because he began to think that maybe he'd done wrong.

January 15

And a letter came today for Mr. John A. Huser and I don't know who he is and nobody I know knows who he is. It came from the Vancouver General Hospital delivered by Her Royal Majesty Post to this crazy house where all the shadows of the dead still lurk. Jimmy lived upstairs locked into his little room and I never remembered who he was until I saw the lock hanging open on Faggot's door.

January now. Fewer people. More people who have come and passed away and added to the shadows of this house--that no one knows entirely but the ever-continuous, never-the-same stereo that speaks to them all--and all in a different language.

The same cup of coffee I left in August is ready for me now. Five months snap of the fingers and I have turned around and come back again and my coffee is still here and still ready.

Salamander is upstairs asleep in his bed and I wonder about him. I wonder about the coal-burning furnace in the cellar and about myself and about...But Salamander is something else again. He is twenty-four years-old and I read the letter he sent to Doreen where he wrote, "I think I am adapting to my environment. Maybe someday by chance or miracle, I will have a girlfriend."

And Doreen is out of her mind with boredom and loneliness and being horny in the great and wonderful city of San Francisco. She is waiting for Mushmouth who voluntarily went back and turned himself in and whose only ambition in life was to grow his hair down to the crack in his ass. Now he is on an aircraft carrier in the Gulf of Tonkin and worries about his self-respect.

He was too young and too confused and without any alternatives--he needed to be a motherfucker or a faggot or a salamander to squirm by. He was just a high school kid who tried to do the right thing and did everything wrong...What do you do? You shut your eyes. *You fall from the eternal hammock but you never get the relief of the final crash.*

The sun comes in the parlor now and catches the bottles on the sill, casting reflections on the floor. Mother used to sleep there and now nobody knows where he is. Mother who made the best eggs and I suppose like the rest of us follows his stereo around, never really knowing or understanding but still vaguely dissatisfied.

Are they happy here? *I don't know. I really don't know. I really don't know anything at all.*

Perhaps when Salamander gets up we will go to the beach.

FOUR MORE LETTERS

February 27
Dear Jones,

Faggot is totally without hope, his last leg of sanity is crippled for life. He got fired. His car broke down. The chimney is plugged. The stove won't work.

He says he is going to sell *Georgia Straights*.

I'm trying to get a job. I have been selling *Georgia Straights* for 6 weeks. If I get a job, I might straighten this place out and run a hostel for draft dodgers.

I only have 2 kittens left. I gave the other 3 away.

Motherfucker sent a friend up here. He is on his way to Alaska. He says Motherfucker is coming up pretty soon. Apparently he doesn't like the USA anymore.

Faggot went to Stanley Park one day. He met a girl. She is 25 years old and makes $25,000 a year as a veterinarian. That night they flew to Victoria and stayed in a motel. She paid for the whole thing.

I tried selling LSD but it didn't work very well. I bought 50 blotter papers for 90 cents each and tried selling them for $2.00 but I wound up just selling them to friends for $1.00 each and keeping a lot for myself. I was searched by the police once when I had 2 blotters on me but they didn't find them.

I gave one to Faggot and really blew his mind. He thought it was pretty good. You can either peddle your ass or your brain. Faggot is an ass so he doesn't have to peddle his brain. I have to think up new ways of making money.

Bob Dylan and the Beatles and the Rolling Stones all have different meanings under acid. The words of their songs have meanings that can only be understood when you're stoned. The same goes for most other groups like The Band and The Byrds.

Faggot is out of his mind.

Yours truly,
Salamander

March 12
Dear Jones,

Faggot doesn't work. He doesn't eat.
He doesn't watch TV. Every night he
goes out with some new girlfriend and
sometimes he doesn't sleep here and
sometimes he sleeps with them and
sometimes he brings them back here.
When he is away the house is nearly
liveable. I am alone here and sometimes
I am able to think and sometimes I am
too messed in the head to think,
particularly if Faggot Fatass has been
here two nights running.
Faggot Fatass has slept with 22
girls. He says he doesn't know what
that means but it must mean something.
It means that there are 22 girls who
are more fucked in the head than Faggot
Fatass. I sold my aquarium for $5.
That's $6 less than I bought it for.
Faggot Fatass has slept with 22
different women in less than 2 months.
He always has 3 girlfriends. One is new
and one is old and one needs an
abortion. Faggot Fatass says he likes
women. He says he'll stop when he gets
to 50. I gave away the rest of my
kittens.
It is criminal to have to live in
Canada in the same house with a Faggot
Fatass who has slept with 22 different

women.

Your friend,
Salamander

May 4
Dear Jones,

The house is now a hostel for
American refugees. Faggot turned it
that way at the beginning of April. I
moved into a fine house in West
Vancouver last month. But we all got
kicked out because the landlady doesn't
like hippies.

It's really shitty because me and
these other people really dug that
house. It had 5 acres with fruit trees
and everything. Then the absentee
landlady found out we were hippies and
kicked us all out. There is a full page
story in *The Georgia Straight*.

Now I'm back in Faggot's place. I
sleep in the little pantry in the
kitchen. There are about 25 people
here. My cat is going to have kittens
again.

I still don't have a job. I have
been making money selling *Georgia
Straights* and going to the Casual Labor
Office.

Your friend,
Salamander

June 10
Dear Jones,

   I got a job for 4 days at a pulp
mill. We worked 12 hour shifts at $3.20
per hour. I made $156 so I went to the
USA for the month of May.
   I spent 2 1/2 weeks in Portland and
1 1/2 weeks in San Francisco. Now I'm
back in Faggot's place.
   Motherfucker is trying to get up
here. He was turned down at the border
7 times. I might mail him some Canadian
ID.
   Faggot enjoys running the hostel. He
says he's getting married on June 15. I
am going to be his best man. I don't
know if Faggot's getting married or
not. He keeps fucking up with this
chick. He also pawned his TV.

Yours truly,
Salamander

JULY 27

July 27 is a cold bleak day in Vancouver. It is one of those cold foggy days that only comes after two or three days of rain and showers and drizzle. The City needs the following day or two to dry its tears and welcome the sun.

It is about 4:00 o'clock in the afternoon and I feel wet and cold and damp now that it is late summer in Vancouver and a day to be inside and thinking of other things. I have a hole in my shoe and the water seeps in and spreads sponge-like into my sock. I know that wherever I go I will be able to take my shoe off and squeeze a puddle of water from my sock. Because it is raining and I know it is a perfect day to be at home or in bed, if you have one or in somebody's arms if you know somebody's arms, I know that Larry Faggot will be home and I know that although I go for a walk my wet sock leads me directly to the house.

I notice that the gate is missing and I wonder why. But I also notice that the yard is cleaner and although everything is older and seems more faded and worn-out there is an attempt at cleanliness and order and a wild fling at some kind of demented respectability and I wonder why. There are only a few scattered cigarette butts in the garden. The flowers don't look well, but there is very little litter. There are hardly any beer tops at all. Hardly any candy bar wrappers or matches or cigarette papers and I wonder why. The door is shut but as always never locked. There is a single footprint left behind me from my wet sock sopping through the soleless shoe. Crippled, I step up to the porch and I push against the door.

Inside all is dark. I see the large room before the kitchen and everywhere there are faces peering out from the half-light. I fasten my eyes on a bearded face that appears more coherent somehow than the others. I have a wild fear that I have stumbled into a den inhabited by all of Breeze's cousins and younger and older brothers and uncles and grand-uncles stretching all the way back to the French and Indian War. But I remember that Breeze went back to New Jersey and his brother turned him into the police.

"Yeah," the beard says. And I remember who I am and what I want and I ask, "Is Larry here?"

"Yeah," he says. "Go upstairs and he should be in his room on the top of the stairs to the left of the bathroom." I know that room well because that's the room where Jimmy lived and then that's the room where Marty and Doreen peeled off all the paint and re-painted the walls. They were supposed to live in that room so I knew the room but I wondered what color paint Doreen had chosen. I had seen that room just last January and it had been yellow. So now I knew that Faggot was still in the same room and I remembered that room must be yellow.

At the top of the stairs I stepped aside and a tall Afro guy with a fox on a leash went by. I turned to look at him and then I realized that his girlfriend was with him. She was following him down the stairs behind the fox. Both she and the spade wore vests and jackets of fur hide. I wondered who else lived here but I couldn't remember anymore or maybe I'd forgotten but most likely I never knew anyway.

I stood by the stairway and I traced the outline of the wall beneath my fingers. It felt firm and solid. I approached the door and I paused. I didn't hear anything but I saw the padlock on the door. I wondered what I would see inside the door and then I remembered that Jimmy had stuck a padlock on his door once upon a time, too, and that I had been in that room in this house just this past January. I was relieved to see that I was remembering things again. Of that I could not be certain but it was the rain and the cold and the wetness in my shoe that made me realize I was tired of coming back to this house to watch the workings of the people involved, like some sickness that could not stop my hand from knocking on the door anymore than my fascination for it all could stop the breath in my lungs or...

"Who's there?"

"It's me. IT'S ONLY ME."

And the door swung open just like it used to and just like I remembered it doing and just like it does at least thirty-four times every day while all the other people in the world are busy in their washrooms or in their kitchens or in the supermarket and he said, "My God"and "Come in."

BUT THAT'S NOT WHAT HAPPENED AT ALL. THAT'S WHAT HAPPENED IN MY IMAGINATION WHILE I WAS LOOKING AT THE GARDEN

OUTSIDE AND WONDERING WHY THERE WERE SO FEW CIGARETTES EVERYWHERE AND WHY THE HOUSE SEEMED SO QUIET AND DESERTED IF NOT FOR THE RAIN.

I went up to the door and it fell open before me when I entered the hall opposite the kitchen and to the left of the stairs where a bearded face comes at once and asks me with his eyes what I want and I tell him with my voice that I want Larry but my eyes want to know why the bottles are not there and who he is and what exactly has been going on before I appeared at the door like so much milk delivered unasked for and by mistake.

"Just a minute," he said. "I'll get Larry."

I stood in the hallway and peered around. I saw the house was much more beat-up and worn-out inside. I marveled at what it means when so much care should be taken to preserve the outside of a house that molders in the rain while the inside of a house that is to be protection and warmth and home crumbles and fails and falls away altogether.

There was a sound of footsteps on the stairway and *I was leaning over the banister on the next to bottom step and it was already 2:30 in the morning. "Faggot, Faggot," I called. Faggot was in Mother's bedroom and when he came over to the stairs I realized he was a little more drunk than he had been just a half-hour ago when I had gone upstairs.*

"Yes? Yes," he repeated and his face looked up into mine, a little drunk and a little tired but very soft and quiet. It was almost contrite. "What is it?" I unfolded the money in my hand and I said softly so

that nobody else would hear and nobody else would
come out of Mother's bedroom where the bottle was
still going round and round. "I want you to have this,
Faggot, because I have not paid you any rent and I
have not given you any money and I have not..."
"You don't have to pay rent or give money or
anything. You just have to be here," he said. I said, "I
can't be here but you must take this money to help
pay some of the things." He held my arm for a minute
and looked at me and I knew that he would take the
money and I also knew that he would get his tape
recorder out of the pawn shop but I did not know
that he would understand. I gave him the money over
the banister and he kissed me and I wondered if I had
done the wrong thing to give him twenty dollars that
I didn't need and that I didn't want but that are
useless anyway.

I looked up into Faggot's face. When you first
looked into his face there was something there that
you recognized but were unable to place. Later, after
you'd known him and watched him and seen the
bottles creep around the window sills of the house,
you knew what it was. His face was the color of yellow
and red mixed together which was always the color of
Faggot's face. The yellow is his hair and the fairness of
his features and the red is his skin with the flush of
blood and sunburn and most likely a half bottle of
Andres Rose. My own face smiled but my features
contorted so that inside of me the smile felt like huge
rifts and cracks breaking loose from the secret place
inside of me where the heart is supposed to be hidden.

"What are you doing here?"

329

I stayed still and smiled at him.

"When did you get here? Well, look, come upstairs and we'll be able to talk." He seemed a little embarassed but I was sweating under my arms and down my back.

I followed him upstairs and we each of us said nothing until he stopped in front of his door. Then I realized that he had been talking to me but he wasn't making sense out of anything. The door opened and we went into the room.

The room is the same. The bed was still on the floor but the mattresses were arranged to make it look like it was off the floor. In front of the window and to the right was the little sink where Jimmy used to wash his face and rinse out his pots and his pans and urinate for all anybody knew. The room was still painted yellow. I was surprised because the house didn't smell like coal dust anymore yet it seemed to me that July 27 is the same day with the same weather as some day in the winter, January, I think, when I had last been in this room and had spoken to Faggot. *"What do you want to do, Faggot?"*

"I'm so tired," he said. "Let's go upstairs and lie down for a while. I've been getting up at about 6:00 o'clock every day this week and I've only averaged three or four hours sleep the whole week. I'm so tired."

"I can't breathe," I said. "I can't breathe this coal dust and everything smells."

"I know," he said. "I'll go fix the fire and then

we'll go upstairs and lie down. I'll open the window and then we'll be able to breathe."

When Faggot opened the door and we went in, the girl was lying on her side propped up on one elbow. The closet door was open and there was a chair beside the bed. Next to the chair was a huge cardboard box. Faggot sat in the chair. I sat with my back to the window and the girl squirmed around in the bed but when you are caught in bed there is never any place to go, even if you get up, because you must eventually sit down again. In the end there is only the temporary squirm in bed and then the submission and the rearranging of the limbs to find a more comfortable and appropriate position.

"This is Tara."

"Sarah?" I look into her face for the first time and try to find her name there.

There is a noise at the door and then the door opens and a fat girl in a plaid woolen cape stands in the doorway and looks into the bedroom. "Hello, I'm Ting."

"Hello, what did you say?"

"Ting. My name is Ting. I didn't mean to wake you up. I just wanted to speak to Faggot for a minute."

"What's your name again? I didn't hear it the first time.""

"Ting."

"You know. Ting. Ting, like do your own Ting," said Faggot.

"I see. Ting. Ting."

"Yes, Ting. Can I speak to you, Faggot, for a minute or should I come back later?"

"No, stay, Ting. What Ting is on your mind, Ting?" Faggot asked.

"Oh, cut it out," I said. "Who are you, Ting? Who is she, Faggot?"

"She's Ting. She used to live in the pantry downstairs."

"Oh, I see. Hello, Ting. Why don't you come in and close the door?"

"I came about the money, Faggot. You owe me five dollars."

"I know. I know. Can you come back later for it? I don't have it right now."

"Okay. I'll come back about 11:00 tomorrow."

"Ting, would you shut the door on the way out, please."

"Sure, I didn't mean to wake you up but I need the money and you said to come today."

"I know."

"What does she do for her five dollars?"

"I don't know. But she does some stuff that wouldn't get done at all if she didn't do it. You don't think that Salamander would do it, do you?"

"I know that you wouldn't do it. You'd rather pay five dollars for a crummy job than do it yourself. Where does she come from?"

"Hawaii."

I look into Faggot's face but he looks away and

twirls his fingers. He is not with me or with Sarah for that time. He sits in the chair next to the bed and his eyes go from the girl's face back again to my own.

"Tara," he repeats.

"Sarah," I say. "I see."

Faggot introduces me. "She is one of the people from last fall when there were dodgers and this was a house and not a hostel."

We say nothing. Again Faggot looks from one to the other of us and back again to his box on the floor. He gets up and turns on the stereo behind my back. It used to be against the stairs in the small room outside the kitchen. When he turns away he pats my leg and turns to that girl on the bed and pats her leg, and then he pats his arm and sits down. Tara or Sarah has stopped moving around on the bed so that now we will have a chance to begin.

"What are you doing, Faggot?"

"I'm cleaning up my room."

WHAT ARE *YOU DOING NOW, FAGGOT?*

"What's all this junk?"

"It's my whole life."

Oh Jesus. Oh fucking Jesus Christ.

He hands me one of my own blue airmail letters dated September.

I gaze at it in my hands.

He laughs. "I'm cleaning up my life again and putting it back in the box." He is laughing and his hands shake. "Would you like to see my recommendations..."

"No, you've showed them to me before."

He hands me a photograph. Instinctively I expect

to see the picture of his daughter Christine in the backyard in San Diego. I was disappointed. It was a picture of himself taken a month ago with this girl.

"My hair was long then. It looks pretty good there, doesn't it?"

I agree. *Oh Jesus. Oh fucking Jesus Christ.* I tried to pretend to believe in this and to forget that I was sweating so that he would tell me what really was going on and so that I might understand about the people downstairs and the fox on the stairway and the lock on the door and then maybe through intuition I might understand the reality and validity of the girl propped up on her elbow sideways on the bed.

"She's Jewish, too," Faggot said.

I looked at Sarah and she turned away. She was acting nice and trying to facilitate things.

"Do you ever hear anything from Motherfucker?" I asked.

Faggot handed me a confidential report from a psychiatrist about James K. Winston dated one year ago. I read it and kept my eyes focused on the paper while Faggot, I knew, looked at the girl with eyes that suddenly appeared hopeless and caught and the girl looked at Faggot with her soft eyes that said, "I understand."

The report said that James K. Winston was psychologically upset and emotionally disturbed. He had problems relating with people and was subject to severe fits of unexplained depressions. Occasionally he spoke of suicide and his inability to become part of society. Of course, this was written for the Berkeley Draft Board.

He was psychologically unfit for military service. He had been seeing a psychiatrist in his last year of high school. He was introspective and suffered from feelings of inadequacy and incompetence. He had a long history of running away from home and had trouble relating to his father. He had been a problem child.

I handed the report back. "Do you think this is true?"

"I don't know," Faggot said. "I've never read it. What does it say?"

Then Faggot told me what I had come to hear. Ten minutes ago coming up the stairs with him he had explained as much of it as he would ever be able to explain. But I missed it because I expected it to be much more complicated or wordy or sensible.

"I work for the Committee now. Tara and I got busted and we might get deported."

Sarah came alive because this was part of the present, alive and functioning with this man Faggot. She had been brought to the police station and questioned and arraigned. Now she was talking about deportation to Sweden with Faggot and with no money. I thought, "This is too fantastic and this running off to Sweden will never occur because whatever the trouble is I know that the police are not interested in one Faggot Fatass and this nondescript Jewish girl from Montreal."

"We might have to go to Sweden."

"Why? Tell me the whole thing," I demanded. I demanded that they tell me what they were doing. A total stranger in somebody's bedroom demanding to know the cause and plans and substance of midnight dreams and flight and hope of escape. I began to sweat again for fear that they would see me--an intruder in the mystery.

"A week ago we were at Kitsilano Beach. There was some kind of hippie riot or something and the police were trying to clear the park. I was drunk I think. A policeman grabbed me and Tara and they took us to the police station in a paddy wagon. The Committee was angry because the cops found out I am a draft dodger. The publicity is bad."

Faggot handed me a newspaper clipping. There was a picture of him and Sarah. I was impressed.

I looked at him questioningly and he told me, "I knew Tara before but after this we got closer together and she moved in here with me."

"Do you have a match?" Sarah asked. She was going to have a cigarette and Faggot lit it for her. There was a yellow blanket on the bed.

"So tell me, Faggot, how's Salamander?"

"You'll want to see him, won't you?"

"Sure, of course."

"Well, he's selling *Georgia Straights* and living down the street."

"What's he doing that for? What's he doing with his cartoons?"

Faggot shook his head. "I know. I know." Faggot looked like he knew something about Salamander I would never understand. "He's not doing anything with his cartoons."

"Couldn't he get them published with *The Georgia Straight*? One of his cartoons is better than all the rest of the garbage they print every day in that paper."

Faggot looked at me with that little boy face and I know he is going to tell me something. I have to sit quietly and hope that it is on the level and for once in a long time from his heart.

But I remembered that the girl Sarah is still on the bed and an audience of one, a very special one, because she sleeps here and holds Faggot's head against her breast in the nighttime. I wonder if anything I have heard is true or if what I am going to hear next will be true. I think everything passes for truth and I believe all the approximations of the truth. I wonder how much Faggot is that the girl still believes.

Faggot speaks in a soft and convincing voice. It is the voice of a man who has had to speak to two wives and longtime girlfriends and girls by him in need of abortion and the girl on the bed and the girl under the bed and all this in the same voice as when he first had to rehearse the speech, "I lost my job today."

I know that he will lie and that he can't help it. I know I won't always catch the lies he tells me.

"Salamander needs a good relationship with a woman. He can't get anything going without somebody behind him. I think he wants more than the whole world for someone to be his girlfriend."

All he has to do is go down West 4th Avenue. Hasn't anybody told him that yet?

Faggot was talking to the female audience that stretched twenty-four years behind him and maybe thirty years ahead of him. It is impossible to sort out all the lies connected with that audience.

337

"Salamander is the only one who really can't get away from this house. He's tried three times and each time he comes back here. There was the first time he left for Prince Rupert and then there was the time he came after he took a cottage with Tyler and Alice, do you know them? And there was the time he went back to the States. Now he says he's moving back here next month." He looked at Sarah, finishing her cigarette, propped up on her side. "I don't know where I'll be next month." His foot kicked his box. "If I'm not here, then Salamander will be running the hostel. You'll never guess who's back?"

"Who?"

"Tex."

"You must be kidding. I thought he was gone a long time ago."

"He was but he's back. I was glad to get him out of here the first time."

"I still remember the day we drove him to the 401 and it was raining. He shook everybody's hand as if he expected to meet them all again in a day or two instead of disappearing into wherever he thought he could go and disappear into."

"Well, he's back. He showed up one day and he had no intention of leaving until I kicked him out. I can't stand him creeping around here."

"Oh, come on, Faggot. He's not as bad as all that. He can cook, too. Were you here the day he went to Leonard's and bought eggs and made scrambled eggs and toast for everybody? It was before you went to see someone at the employment agency. The guy who got you the job at Kelley's Sound Center."

"That guy was Jewish and knew Goldshit."

"I know. Also I think it was the day you drove Tex to the highway and everybody shook hands."

Now Faggot began to squirm around in his chair. I knew he wanted to put his life back into the box and prodded by the secret looks and faces of the girl on the bed next to him get up and go out to supper and order one or two bottles of Heineken.

My sock was luke-warm now. I put on my shoe again. It was cold and soggy. When I looked up, Faggot was standing up and ready to walk me to the door. I stood by the door for a second or two and said good-bye to Sarah or Tara or whatever her name was.

Outside in the hall Faggot told me again that he and Sarah had become really close.

"Is it any good, though?"

"I don't know," he said.

WILL YOU EVER KNOW WHAT YOU'RE DOING, FAGGOT?

But I didn't know either. Faggot didn't know. He didn't know anything about these things--the things he hadn't known anything about his whole life but the funny thing was, he looked at you and you felt you understood those things even though you hadn't any more knowledge about them than Faggot did himself.

"Look, you want to see Salamander? Do you want to go see Salamander?" he asked.

SALVAGE

Faggot goes first. Everything's dark.

"Hey, wake up. Guess who's here? No, don't open your eyes. Wait. I said wait, you dumbass. Wait, why can't you?"

Faggot pushes me out in the open. I stand numbly in front of him. Maybe I even shut my eyes.

The light goes on.

"Oh, no. Oh, no. It's you again. Oh, no." He squirms on the floor, writhing in his sleeping bag. He wishes he has his pants on.

Oh, no. Fucking Jesus Christ. It's Tex in the corner, too.

"You Faggot. You, faggot, what are you doing here? What are you doing bringing a JEW into my berdroom? Just what are you doing?" Salamander asked sitting half-way up in his sleeping bag and swearing.

Faggot wasn't listening. He was laughing and folding up on himself as if he was drunk instead of excited. "Look who's here. Look who's here, will you? Jones walked up to the house and I came downstairs and let her in."

"A Jew and a Faggot together in one room. No, two Jews in the same room." Salamander waved his arm in spastic semicircles to include a girl sitting cross-legged in the half-light opposite Tex's corner. "I can't breathe," he said pulling the covers up to his neck and clutching at them with his wire fingers. "I can't breathe. How do you expect me to breathe with no clothes on and two Jews and a Faggot all in the same room together? You can't lie down anymore for a decent bit of sleep. You can't fall asleep in the privacy of your own bedroom, that isn't even your own room," he said looking in Tex's direction, "without creeps and faggots and stray Jews wandering in off the streets and making pests of themselves and ruining the rest of an honest hard-working man."

He sat up and turned on me. "When did you get here? How long are you staying?"

Tex was sitting in the corner hunched up over himself. Salamander was pulling himself out of his surprise and I could see the slow smile spread around his mouth that would warm his eyes and soften his whole face.

But I was stunned to see Tex so I turned to him first. "WHAT ARE YOU DOING HERE? I thought you were in Saskatchewan or someplace trying to get landed."

"Yep, I got landed all right and then I came right back here."

"Salamander, how long has he been here?" I nodded at Tex who wasn't moving except for chewing on his bottom lip opposite the cross-legged girl.

"I don't know. He came by one day and said he'd

been staying at Faggot's and got kicked out of there. Then he showed up here with his sleeping bag and I said he could stay for a few days. That was about two-and-a-half weeks ago." Salamander was speaking as if Tex wasn't there.

"I remember the day you left. It was raining, wasn't it? How did that day go after all?" I was talking as if Salamander wasn't there.

"Well, it started off pretty poorly but all in all it wasn't such a bad day. I just sort of walked up the road a ways and when it began to rain I stopped and rolled up a cigarette and leaned up against a tree and waited for it to pass by and it passes by and I got a lift after a while and I got on into Alberta and eventually I got landed."

"All that money's used up now, isn't it?"

"Yep, all that money's used up now." Tex laughed in that special mindless way that made him attractive to very young girls. At the same time he flashed one of his Southern country smiles and you could swear he'd just stepped out of Parchman if you didn't know better and realize that those things don't happen today. Besides, this is Vancouver, Beautiful British Columbia, *Canadia*, nineteen hundred seventy...

I sat down on the floor and caught sight of Salamander sitting up in his sleeping bag and I began to wonder if he'd squirm around or if he'd really do something. I thought, "If he really has something in him, he'll do something decisive." I was sitting there growing cold at the edge of the bed asking him how come he was living there in that house on a pallet on the floor above a whole house of creeps and with Tex for a roommate. Meanwhile the girl with granny glasses teetering over the edge of her nose sat there silently knitting away. She only looked up when she didn't believe we were there but had imagined us, as if we were some number of stitches that she'd forgotten about or had to count every now and then.

And Salamander sat there and locked his arms around his knees and said nothing. Then he glanced at Tex who merely sat looking out on the whole scene before him like some stupid bullfrog that was about to puke.

"Well, I guess I'd better put my pants on," Salamander sighed.

It didn't bother the girl and Tex kept staring straight in front of him looking more and more like he was going to throw up. Tex cleared his throat once and looked nervously to the right and then to the left. Then he started talking some involved nonsense about how the United States of America and especially the State of Texas was the most repressive institution ever created by the hand of God. I looked at Salamander hoping for some sign of explanation but he looked away, furtive-like, as if he wasn't used to putting his pants on in front of such a big crowd.

Salamander slid into his pants, the same old faded ones with the bags at both knees. I remembered the big glasses of milk he'd drunk the summer before with the three heaping spoonfuls of nutriment that was supposed to build him up and I suppose make him irresistible to girls. Instead he'd gotten skinnier and the corduroy pants stretched out bigger to accommodate his body that would have filled out with or without the help of nutriment whether here in this filthy room or at home in the loganberry fields of his father's place in Oregon.

"Well," he said.

The girl kept on knitting, every now and then holding the thing up to the light and counting the stitches. All the time Tex sat cross-legged on his little pallet and I wondered for the thirty-third time in the last ten minutes how they all got to be in this little room down the street from Faggot's house.

I wondered who the girl was and who she belonged to. To Salamander? I didn't believe it. To Tex? It was possible but I didn't think Tex was in a state to believe it. The girl looked like she wasn't in a state to believe anything except the last two stitches she'd just dropped and was busy looking for all over the floor and down the front of her blouse and on her knee socket where her fingers wandered from time to time to pick up lint or scratch before turning her eyes back to the task of her stitches and her own impossible riddles.

"Boy, I'm glad that Faggot's gone," Salamander said zipping up his fly and sitting down again.

"What's he doing here?" I asked again pointing at Tex.

Salamander laughed and said, "I don't know what he's doing here. I don't think he knows what he's doing here. He was politicized in Saskatchewan and now he's the great radical. He's going to lead the revolution."

"Oh."

"You see, I was living here by myself trying to

avoid Faggot up the street and the dipshits downstairs who watch television all day and come around to borrow money for cigarettes or dope or potato chips. One day last week, either Monday or Tuesday, I can't remember the days too well, they seem so much alike, Tex showed up with his sleeping bag. He asked me if he could stay and I said all right. He put his stuff down in the corner and he's been living here rent-free ever since."

Salamander was sitting cross-legged on his sleeping bag watching everybody and everything in the room. He could have found the girl's stitches if he wanted to.

"This is Carol," he said. "She lives downstairs and comes up here to knit."

I said "hello" and looked back to Salamander who was watching Tex with a mixture of disgust and dismissal and acceptance.

"I came here," Salamander said, "after March or maybe it was April. You know Tyler, don't you? Well, anyway Tyler's married to Alice and just after December or January, I can't seem to remember, Tyler and Alice rented a cottage out in the woods off of Vancouver Island. They asked me if I wanted to live with them so I moved out of Faggot's house—that's where I was living when I saw you in December or January."

"It was January."

"Then it was at the end of March that I moved out to Vancouver Island with Tyler and Alice. Faggot," Salamander shook his head. "Faggot's crazy now. He's gone completely crazy. In the winter he met this girl in

346

Stanley Park and he went with her all over the place. They rented a plane and flew to Vancouver Island where they stayed in the best hotel and had room service and spent all the chick's money. Then Faggot got the chick back here on time for work Monday morning so she could earn some more money so that she and Faggot could go off on other weekends."

Salamander was licking his lips and talking whether I was listening or not.

"So you see Faggot was doing very well with the women around this time which was great for Faggot's ego which is always in need of something and I was glad to move out of Faggot's house because I never could stand Faggot anyway. In the middle of all these women Evangeline writes and says she's going to fly up again and Faggot really didn't know what to do because he's one of those dumbasses who needs a woman to tell him what to do all the time and he just keeps making messes for himself that he can't get out of until he introduces all the women to each other and they eventually decide among themselves what to do anyway. And I couldn't stand living in the same house with Faggot anymore--except for the week he went to Vancouver Island with that girl and the house was quiet and I was okay with Faggot gone. In fact, you could imagine that Faggot never lived there at all. Right after that I moved out with Tyler and Alice into a fine little cottage. They're the nicest people I've met since I've been here. You can talk to them. They're not juvenile dipshits like the people downstairs who sit up all night in front of their rented television set and spend all their money and mine, too, when they trick me into giving them a nickel or a dime for shit food that doesn't have an ounce of nutrition in it. And they're not fuck-ups like some of the people who lived with Faggot in that house in the summertime. Then Ting, this Hawaiian girl who was living in Faggot's pantry, came to stay with us for a few weeks and I decided to go back to the States.

"No, I didn't have any trouble crossing the border. I took all the precautions I could but I just had to go. I headed straight for Portland. I stayed in the same town where my parents live and visited all my old friends and went places and had a wonderful time. My parents didn't know I was there until about a month ago. Then I went down the coast to San Francisco and met Doreen who put me up in the city. I spent seven weeks down there and had the time of my life. I stayed with some more friends of Doreen's and they were really nice to me. They took me most any place I wanted to go." Salamander closed his eyes and nodded briefly. It was the first time he'd stopped talking in over fifteen minutes. He licked his lips. "By the way, Mushmouth's still in the Gulf of Tonkin with another year to go.

"When I got back I found out that the landlord who'd rented the cottage to Tyler and Alice and me had discovered she'd rented to a group of hippies and evicted us while I was gone. Tyler and Alice packed up all the stuff that was there and put it in brown boxes they'd gotten from Econo-Mart and lugged it all back to Faggot's house. So when I got back I found out I was living in Faggot's house again. Then I discovered I'd lost eight hundred dollars in Canadian Savings

Bonds that had been in the cottage along with my cats and cartoons and records and books. We looked all over but we never found them."

I looked away from Salamander's face and saw Tex leaning over his knees listening to Salamander's recital. Carol, the knitting lady, was someplace else, looking for things on the floor while her knitting unraveled in her lap. I wondered how much speed a person can shoot and still keep knitting...

"We looked all over but we never found them."

I looked back to Salamander's face. He was licking his lips and still talking. "Tyler or Alice lost them while they were moving. I'd saved up all that money when I was breaking my ass working for the Canadian Imperial Bank of Commerce and living in an apartment on top of the bank and working all hours of the night and day and weekend with nothing else in that godforsaken city except black crows and whores. The government said it would take eight months to a year to locate them and check everything and replace the money. That was the money I was saving to go back to school for the fall term to get my head back in shape after it'd fallen out of use with all the asses and stupid people I've met and lived with and after being so long with Faggot who is so fucked-up he doesn't even know it anymore and doesn't realize he is probably the most fucked-up person he is ever likely to meet in his whole life.

"Right after that I started to sell *Georgia Straights*. Actually before that I bought some lids and tried to sell them. It cost me ninety dollars and I wound up just giving them to friends. Tyler and Alice used up most of it. After that I got it together and moved out of Faggot's house again and I've been living here and selling *Georgia Straights* three or four days a week.

"The only other time I was back at Faggot's was the night I ate twenty-one peyote buttons and freaked out..."

Tex's face came alive when Salamander said peyote. His eyes jumped out of the spot on the floor he was staring into. He looked smaller than I remembered. He was wearing a pair of cheap, cream-color perma-press pants.The pants the Ivy League boys used to wear in the early Sixties when they advertised the casual look of easy-to-take-care-of-clothes for the first batch of helpless middle class males that went away to the big university and never came home again. He was different without his tight jeans and his plaid shirt and his leopard hat. Now his legs seemed shorter and he seemed slack somehow. Like his hips couldn't take his weight anymore and collapsed while the rest of him around the ass and stomach turned to jelly. He was little and wizened up as if he'd been sick and a long time getting over it.

Tex opened his mouth and drooled. I expected another prophetic political statement to come gushing out with the new strange hiss the words made when they tripped over the false tooth instead of falling backward into a hole. His blue eyes were the same but foreign, wandering helter-skelter over the floor and the ceiling, giving a clear picture of the inner workings of his mind. And the weak flick of his tongue running up and down on his lips and moistening the mouth that kept him going. Salamander would have continued but he saw me staring at Tex who was beginning to tilt forward and speak into the floor.

"I've tried a lot of drugs," Tex said. "Now you take peyote and mescaline. The first thing to know is that mescaline is a synthetic, man-made type of peyote. The first time I ate peyote I retched up for an hour and lost my whole supper." He looked at me from across the room with a funny wild-eyed face. He was a convert now.

"But you just gotta keep trying," he advised, "until it agrees with you and your system can take it. Then you will see the power that the drug has just like the Indians have seen the power in that drug for the last hundreds of thousands of years. And I know because I've tried a lot of drugs this winter. I wanted to experience as much of the drugs that I could and I got a hold of mescaline which is the most wonderful drug there is." He raised his hand and looked at me sideways. "It's not a drug, really. It's an experience."

Salamander was giving Tex a few more minutes. I thought he'd tell him to shut up but he didn't. He let him have his say. All this time Tex was talking faster and faster until he was staring glassy-eyed into Salamander's face and was out of breath.

"Mescaline is the one drug that I would recommend for everybody. There should be a law that says every person should have the privilege of experiencing the effect of that drug at least once in his or her lifetime. When I took mescaline I could see the whole conspiracy in the United States of America that is preventing me from going down to the State of

Texas where my aunt left five hundred acres for me to plant and sow as I like. But the government of these supposedly free United States is preventing me from ever laying eyes on the property left to me. I got the deed to it right here in my pocket..." Tex slapped his leg and his hand fell to the floor. "And I'll be damned. I'll be damned if they'll ever get it back from me. I'll let that land rot before I ever sell it back to the State of Texas so they can go ahead and put another superhighway on good bottom land they prevent me from claiming and farming. I've never set a plow to any one of those five hundred acres and I'll probably never live to see the day when I can but I'll be damned if they're gonna put up another superhighway or an Econo-Mart..."

Salamander was fidgeting. Tex's watery eyes drooped over the floor. His soft Southern drawl filtered around us and lay like a shawl over the thin shoulders of the girl sitting cross-legged on the floor. She never understood a sentence and never heard a word.

Finally Salamander said something sharp but Tex ignored him. Tex kept talking until Salamander made a half-turn toward me and continued his story where he'd left off. Salamander raised his voice the slightest degree. He made a mental note to screen off Tex and concentrate on what he'd been saying before Tex opened up his mouth about drugs. Calmly Salamander said, "I ate twenty-one peyote buttons one after another. Then I rolled on the floor and I thought I was going mad."

But Tex kept on talking, becoming more dogmatic

and insistent and loud. His eyes darted furiously over the faces and bodies of the people in the room until he dribbled away into silence when he realized he'd lost his audience. He looked at Carol but she was holding her knitting thing up to the light to count the stitches.

"I knew then how you can go mad," Salamander said, "and how some people, the less strong ones, let go their hold for a single second and never come back again. I thought I was going mad, truly losing my mind. All the horrors came alive in my mind and I saw things that I didn't imagine but knew for sure existed in me and outside of me, in this room and in all the rooms of the world. There were things I couldn't handle by myself so I set right out for Faggot's house and I didn't stop running up that street until I turned in at the gate which is broken now because of all the assholes he has living there with him and I ran right up the stairs to his room which used to be Jimmy's room and Marty and Doreen's room and I fell right on top of Faggot as he he was lying in bed and grabbed his hand. It was 10:30 at night and I told Faggot I couldn't leave him because I'd just swallowed twenty-one peyote buttons and if Faggot left me I'd walk out of my head directly and become mad. Did you know Faggot has fooled around with a lot of drugs, although he doesn't do very much now? Well, he held my hand that whole night and we walked all over the place. I was like a little boy again. I wouldn't let Faggot out of my sight. If he went into the bathroom I'd go in right after him because I couldn't afford to let him get away and leave me to go insane by myself."

Salamander looked to me for belief and when he

was satisfied went on. "Anyway, Faggot stayed up with me that whole night and although I personally dislike Faggot he's all right for doing that. I guess he's one of the people I know best in this city." Salamander looked pensive but it lasted for a second so it could have been the light.

"It's criminal that he's as fucked as he is and still able to go through all the motions and able to wander around loose to fuck even more people up." He swallowed. "After that experience I gave up a bit on drugs and sold *Georgia Straights*."

"So then you were still living here, weren't you? That must have been sometime in the spring or the early summer."

"Yes, I was living here because after Faggot started going out with all these girls and was afraid to go to the door because he couldn't keep straight which one was supposed to be at the door and which one was supposed to be in bed with him upstairs and which one he was supposed to be in bed with in some apartment somewhere and which one of his ex-wives was supposed to be at the door or on the phone or in bed with somebody else, he started to run the house as a hostel. He lost his job with the Mighty Sound Center sometime in the winter and then he'd just go out with one of his girlfriends or spend his time trying to figure out his life or parts of his different lives that he's spent with different women in different places. He let his hair grow long and he got a new pair of glasses so he didn't look like Clark Kent anymore and it seemed that every week he had a new girlfriend. Although how someone like Faggot can get so many girlfriends is unexplainable to me but must be further proof as to how dumb girls are. I don't know."

He paused for a moment. He looked at the girl knitting and at Tex who was crunched forward, leaning on his knees, listening, ready to jump into his own conversation. Salamander jerked his head and his whole body gave a convulsive shake. He stared at them for a minute or two and eventually he turned to look me full in the face again.

"Now the house is a hostel again but there aren't any more dodgers coming. Most of the people are deserters and they may stay in that house forever because they can't, anyone of them I guess, get landed. They have eighth grade educations and they stole hub caps in high school and have petty police records. Somehow Faggot runs the place and gets enough money out of them every month to pay the rent and keep it going. He gets them to keep the place up and kicks them out if they don't pay or work and somehow he keeps order that way.

"Then the Committee started to pay him a little, too, for running the place. Mostly he pretends he's indispensable and as a big ass he makes himself obnoxious like only a Faggot can. Now he's got this trouble with the police for being stone drunk at that small riot on Kitsilano Beach last week and he got into trouble with that girl, whatever her name is, who was in the riot with him and got picked up, too, and now lives with him there in the room that used to be Marty and Doreen's. His case comes up in court soon, Thursday or Friday, I don't know which. But what I'd like to do is run the hostel this winter and go to school in October." Salamander squinted at Tex and the skin got tight around his mouth. "I know I could do a better job than Faggot does running that place. I know I could."

Tex looked up with his little mouth working as fast as it could, already priming his tongue to oil his lips and throat and his one false tooth in front so he could open his mouth and assert his suffering Southern male vanity to say, "Faggot does a damn good job of managing the place over there. Faggot does one helluva good job. You probably couldn't do much better considering what the conditions are over there. Now..."

"How often do you go over there?" I asked but Salamander wasn't listening. He shot Tex a piercing look and Tex stopped in mid-sentence. Tex petered out and contracted over his folded-up legs that I remembered once as being so long. Tex's eyes darted around in full paranoia while he stretched out his cream-colored legs and just as quickly withdrew them under him again. Stuck away in the corner he looked like some wet muskrat that might bite you on the hand.

Salamander looked him in the face for a few seconds more and Tex crumpled away into something harmless and pitiful. Then the girl knitting looked up aimlessly for a second and let her eyes graze the length of Tex's body until he looked up and briefly met her gaze but turned away rat-like after just a second.

Salamander turned back to me for the third time that night and said with some surprise and some determination and some small bitterness, too, "I don't go there at all now."

On the corner of Granville and Dunsmuir there is Woolworth's with the cheery young girl selling glazed doughnuts, fifty-four cents a dozen, behind the bakery counter. In front of the Hudson's Bay there is an Indian youth with hair down to his shoulders, a crippled man and an old lady in an Easter hat. You look for people you might know but you know that they do not shop here and that if you want to see them you must go to Save-On-Meat.

You look at the newspaper vendors and they are not who you are looking for. You think he might be behind the bakery counter with the cheery young girl at Woolworth's but you keep looking at the faces, nonetheless. At the corner of Granville and Robson you cross on a yellow light. There is no one on that corner, either, and you feel dejected. No, wait. There is someone leaning over a green laundry bag in a doorway.

"Shit. Who sent you down here?" he asked straightening up and bringing five papers back with him.

"I came all by myself."

"Hmph."

"I see they took that barrier down. The one that kept everybody on the sidewalk until the light changed."

"Yeah, now all the dumbshits run out on the street

while the traffic's going and every other week somebody's falling off the curb and getting his big toe run over. That's because people are like sheep. They get so used to having barriers set up for them their whole lives they can't think for themselves when they're out of the rabbit patch."

"I see you haven't changed any."

"Why should I? You haven't. You still ask dumb questions. Ha-Ha." Salamander looked at me and laughed. "How do you know I haven't changed? Can you look inside of me and see what's going on?"

"You've changed."

He stopped laughing and we looked at each other seriously.

"I know," he said softly.

"I know, too."

"Yeah," Salamander said bristling. "Jews don't know anything. Especially paranoid Jews and all Jews are paranoid."

"You only say that shit because you wish you were Jewish instead of Anglo-Saxon."

"Jews are more fucked-up. Faggot's so fucked-up he's nearly Jewish." Salamander pulled a handful of coins out of his pocket. "Fuck," he said.

"What's the matter with you?"

"Nothing's the matter with me." His fist closed over the money. "But if I could have been born anything other than myself I would have chosen to be an American Indian because they have grace, humility and a sense of the spiritual--all the things that Western Civilization in general and North American culture in particular lacks."

358

"Oh."

He looked at me impatiently. "Being Jewish you wouldn't understand those things. You have to be Anglo-Saxon."

"Oh..."

We watched the traffic for a while. Salamander told me that business was awful, that there were too many vendors and not enough customers. How it was impossible to sell any papers except for Monday and Tuesday.

"I don't know how you made it through the winter."

"I don't know, either. After you left the furnace broke down completely and there wasn't any heat. But there wasn't any smoke."

"What are you doing, Salamander?" I asked. "What are you doing living with Tex and eating off the floor and selling *Georgia Straights*?"

He laughed shaking his shoulders and cracking the papers back into position. "I don't know." It was a funny laugh. The kind that hangs in the air like a question mark stopping conversation. "You know I was in the States this spring? You know that, don't you? Yeah, well I went down to Portland again and to San Francisco. I was in Berkeley but I didn't like it at all. I wandered all over Berkeley getting sunstroke and I saw Allen Ginsberg in every garbage pail and a guy in a black leather jumpsuit who thought he was Mick Jagger and people with no clothes on and people getting their asses screwed off behind fountains. I didn't see Motherfucker, though. He was supposed to be selling pretzels on Telegraph but I didn't see him.

Nobody knows where he is. "

"Were you glad to get home here?"

"This isn't my home," Salamander snapped. "Neither is America." He watched somebody waiting for the light to change who seemed to be reading the *Straight* headline. He didn't buy.

"The first thing you notice when you get back here is the affluence that exists in the States. There's so much waste and bigness that Canada still hasn't got yet." Salamander waved his arm at the people passing but because of his build, his thinness, he looked like a scarecrow trying to be graceful. "Not that these people aren't trying their best to catch up with the States and have as many shopping plazas and car washes and used car lots and hamburger places and junkyards as they have down there."

"Yeah, that's the one thing that impressed me when I was in San Francisco. That you could go from coast to coast and wind up in the shopping mall at Daly City and think you'd never left wherever it was you started from."

"Just hope it doesn't get here all that fast because I have to be here for a long time and I hope it's still good while I'm here." Then he laughed at the papers in his hand. "At least I'm not doing anything to improve things around here."

"You know, Salamander, you keep losing weight. Do you eat?"

He laughed once or twice nervously. "Yeah, I eat," he said wetting his lips with his tongue. "I eat but the people downstairs are always trying to bum money off me. They get almost fifty dollars a month from welfare and the second week of the month they're broke. Can you believe that?"

"Faggot..."

"Faggot is eating worse now than he ever did." Salamander's vehemence surprised me. "I think he's not drinking as much as he used to because he doesn't have the money. Whatever he drinks now he drinks by himself because the people in that house could drink up everything he brought in there in less than five minutes."

"That's why he keeps the padlock on his door?"

"Yeah. Also because those people would steal anything. It's a different group of people who come up here now from the States. Most are deserters who are just now getting to the idea that they don't want to be in the Marines for their whole lives. It's an altogether different thing."

I remembered the spade on the stairs with his fox and the people in the kitchen and the fat boy who was standing in the doorway of the living room where Motherfucker used to hang out.

"Does Tex give you any money for living with you?"

"No. And I haven't t asked him for any. He doesn't have any. I think he's looking for a job. He has experience as a short- order cook but he quits a lot and then finds another job. You can't work at that kind of a job too long before it gets to you. What he really wants to do is become a chef because he says there's big money in that. He told me he was going to look for a job as a cook in one of these restaurants in town. He'll probably get one, too, because he's experienced. Do you know there's 6.9 percent unemployment in B.C. right now?"

"Yeah, and you're one of them."

"Yep, I 'm one of them," Salamander said smacking his lips together and looking around his corner. Salamander was crazy proud but this was a new dimension to his sarcasm. "But it could be worse." The smile disappeared. "I could be stuck in the Atlantic Region where unemployment is 10. 5 percent or in Quebec where it is the worst with 7.9 percent and the most people people out of work. The only safe place to be is in the Prairies where it's only 4.3 percent so it's gonna get you no matter where you are. It's enough to make a person give up looking for a job."

"I see you're still studying."

"Of course." Salamander whipped the handful of change out of his pocket and put it back. "I'm not like some of the dumbasses around here who don't have any brains or like Faggot who's lost all of his."

"Why doesn't Tex stay at Faggot's instead of coming over to your place?"

"That's simple. Because Faggot can't stand having him around. When Tex was there he was always hustling Faggot because he'd gotten it into his mind that Faggot is really a faggot. He got that into his mind last summer when everybody kidded Faggot for being a faggot. Only Tex really believed it and now he wants to make Faggot. But the other thing is that Tex, like Faggot, is really good with the women. He's really screwed up. Some nights he'll be with a girl and then some nights he'll follow Faggot all over the house and drive Faggot out of his mind. He came over to my place when Faggot kicked him out because Faggot said he couldn't stand it anymore. Then Tex brought over this girl. First he met her on the street and she came home because she had nothing to do and wanted to stay and talk. Next thing you know it's suppertime and she stays and eats up my food. Then it's nighttime and she thinks she'll stay over and sleep on the floor because it's too late to go home. Next thing she's taking off her clothes and before you know it, she's in Tex's sleeping bag. She stayed three days. She was really nice, too," Salamander said shaking his head. "I don't know. But Tex can't keep any of his girls. The girls really fall for him. I don't know why. You see, he's bisexual."

"So what's he supposed to do? He doesn't bother you. He only bothers Faggot. It's not his fault."

"He's supposed to control himself like the rest of the world." Salamander shook the papers in his hand. He pressed his lips together and was quiet for a few seconds. "Really, I don't know. I don't know but if Faggot catches him in the house one more time, I think he'll probably kill him. He nearly drove Faggot out of his mind and Faggot's got enough problems with his girlfriends and his own mind without that."

I laughed. "I guess Faggot didn't get married after all, did he? Did the girl get rid of him or what?"

"I don't know. Nobody knows. I don't care, either. If any girl is dumb enough to get mixed up with Faggot he deserves her."

"What are you going to do? You know, you've been selling these papers for four months now. And you haven't sold a single one since I've been here."

"I KNOW." His voice was balancing on the edge of something. "I don't know." Salamander threw his arms up in the air. "I don't know. I don't know. I wanted to go to school but now I don't know if I can do it for October. For one thing I don't have money and for another I don't have a place to live. I want to get my head together and you can't do that when you live with creeps and they're always bugging the hell out of you for a cigarette. He got tough for a second. Then the toughness became something else. "Faggot won't sell papers, though, and instead he gets to run the hostel and he doesn't even do a good job of that."

We were quiet for a while. I looked for Easter hats and he looked for customers.

"You know, why don't you come over again this evening? It was impossible to talk with that girl in there and Faggot running all over the place. Of course, Tex will be there but you pretend he isn't there and you can usually talk with him in the same room and not know he's there. There'll be a bottle of wine because I've got some money from last week's papers. It won't be loganberry but it will be as good. When are you leaving anyway? I thought you'd already left."

P.S.

August 23
Dear Jones,

Faggot Fatass goes scot-free--the
charges were dropped. He had an
excellent defense and a shitty
prosecution so all is forgotten and
forgiven.

I moved into the house on August 1
for the fourth time in my life. I have
been taking care of the place since
Faggot works at the Committee all day
and is generally too fucked in the head
to take care of it anyway. Faggot still
retains last word and all that bullshit
but I keep track of everybody and all
the beds, etc. and help him think up
new rules and take rent. We have a guy
named Jean to take care of cooking and
kitchen duties which is pretty lucky
for us because Faggot and I would be at
a loss without him.

We charge $6 a week here at the
hostel and if they haven't got it we

loan them $5 and make them sell *Georgia Straights*. Faggot gets a lot more money in that way but we still went $250 in the hole for August. We're getting a lot of donations, though, so we're still hanging around.

There are always 20-30 people here and few are not dumbshits. Some are crazy and many are aggravating but I don't mind too much, since there is some sense of purpose here.

Your friend,
Salamander

SALVATION

When I had last seen him he was coming home at exactly five past five and eating rolled wheat hearts for supper. That was two Junes ago before the winter rains fell and washed out my memory and confused the patter of events. The rains first fell in September of that year when I was no longer living there and dripped into the bathroom and for the first time created a puddle unrelated to bath or shower or piss on the floor .

The house is still there and the Voice of China is still in the backyard, although the plastic curtain in the kitchen window is gone. Jimmy is gone, too. He may have gone away with the man who lived next door with his rose bush and his wife. Leonard sold out and the man after him, too, and nobody knows the new man who is Leonard but not Leonard.

There are no more frogs or cats in the house. That would please Motherfucker but not Mushmouth who always knew what the right things were but found them so hard to do. The building in the empty lot is not a warehouse. It is a clinic and there is another one farther up the street.

Faggot drinks beer only. He says he will give up

women when he reaches fifty. That doesn't count repeats. He says he should be celibate and live in an ashram and play the flute. His salvation is in music "only it's so hard to come down, to come back to this life when you've been there." And he's been everywhere, in drink and in sex and in love and in the make-believe of no-love and in his mind and out of it, and Mother is lost. Maybe he's in the woods north of San Francisco sitting on top of the San Andreas Fault waiting for the world to blow sky-high and maybe he's still in Berkeley because he never left there in the first place.

"Can you roll a cigarette while you're fucking?" Mother used to ask, leering into the bathroom where Faggot stood by the bathroom sink shaving with Mother's razor. "Can you, boy, huh? Can you fuck and roll..."

And the only answer Faggot has now is wound up in the handwoven brown tie he uses as a tie strap for his flute case. Evangeline bought that tie as a final going away gift when Faggot waved good-bye to the FBI in the San Diego airport. And now he has two flutes, a Mummy flute and a Baby flute that he bought with the final pawning of his TV and tape recorder and stereo.

Salamander is with his Sweetheart who is perhaps not his sweetheart, but better than cats and fish, in a log cabin two-and-a-half miles outside of Yellowknife where he mines gold and thinks God-knows-what in his mind.

Faggot is vegetarian. His hair is down to his shoulders and he doesn't shave with a razor, not his or

368

Mother's or anybody's. He doesn't work for anymore Goldshits in anymore Mighty Sound Centers. He doesn't drink Coca-Cola and eat sweet and sour pork in the B.C. Royal or hot cakes in Stanley Park. He likes health foods and is very skinny and dreams about making his fiftieth girl so he can quit.

Salamander eats meat. He eats anything he can get his hands on in Yellowknife. He doesn't tell anybody if he has money enough to buy ice creams at the Dairy Queen. He is with his Sweetheart and he is saving money to come back to Vancouver but they must take a taxi to and from the mine because there is no public transportation in Yellowknife. The Salamanders no longer have a car.

A long time ago Faggot told me he threw a quarter at the Crab that very first time. Now he has no more quarters to throw at anybody so he borrows them and throws them at whoever he likes. If Salamander were in Faggot's house instead of his letters, he would scurry after Faggot's money and become rich enough to move out of the house again.

Tex is in chef school and Faggot won't eat anything he might learn to cook. He won't even talk about Tex unless somebody brings up the topic. Then Faggot says he has to go to the bathroom or take a walk or write Genevieve Bujold for a date. So it seems it's only possible to talk to Salamander on street corners when he can't sell papers and it's not possible to talk to Faggot at all.

I asked Faggot why he threw a quarter at the Crab and he shrugged his shoulders. He said he felt like it then. Now he feels like playing flute and going out to the country and reading and he does some of these things.

Salvation? Salvation. In a cup of coffee and in a log cabin and in a flute. But with no resolution.

What do you do? You lower your voice and you keep to yourself.

NOTES

The following excerpts are taken from *The Manual For Draft-Age Immigrants to Canada*, sixth edition, completely revised and edited by The Toronto Anti-Draft Programme. (This book may be ordered from The Toronto Anti-Draft Programme, P.O. Box 41, Station K, Toronto 315, Ontario, Canada).

CANADA CAN STILL BE THOUGHT OF AS A REFUGE for those leaving the U.S. to avoid military service. However, things have changed here since the first wave of mid '60s draft dodgers arrived. Businesses in Canada by and large are either owned or dominated by U.S. based corporations. Estimates run as high as 60-80 percent U.S. control over the Canadian labor market. Increasingly, these businesses are refusing to hire American immigrants of draft age. The excuses vary, but the end result is a lack of job possibilities for you. At the same time, Canadians are reacting to this American takeover, both in business and in the universities. A backlash has been created, showing itself most strongly through the increasing reluctance of Canadians to hire immigrants while so many Canadians are out of work. In the cultural and educational fields, a sense of national pride has led to decisions to increase the percentage of Canadians by hiring only people of Canadian origin.

What does all this mean to you? It means that finding a job becomes more difficult, and finding one in your field becomes an even harder task. This automatically makes immigrant status harder to obtain.

Counseling services in both Canada and the United States do not encourage people to leave the States or to desert the military. The aim of resistance is not to create an American community in Canada but to end the war. Canadian counselors do their best to find legal means to help resisters return to the States or, in the case of deserters, to obtain discharges from the military. But if these measures are impossible, then acquiring permanent residence is the final alternative.

IMMIGRANT STATUS IS YOUR GOAL

Americans who want to live in Canada must apply for landed immigrant status. A landed immigrant is anyone who has been lawfully admitted to Canada for permanent residence.

A landed immigrant can work, attend school and in general carry on as any Canadian, except that he cannot vote in Canadian elections, cannot obtain a Canadian passport, and can be deported for a variety of well-defined reasons.

A landed immigrant who has lived in Canada for any five out of any eight years is said to have acquired "domicile" and is eligible to apply for Canadian citizenship. Applying for citizenship is not a requirement but Canadian domicile is lost by a person "voluntarily residing out of Canada with the intention of making his permanent home out of Canada and not for a mere special or temporary purpose."

A landed immigrant is able to travel to other countries or attend school or work elsewhere—temporarily--without losing his immigrant status. Time that an immigrant spends in residence outside Canada will not count towards domicile but will not jeopardize his immigrant status. No time will be counted towards domicile that the immigrant spends in jail or in a mental hospital. Of course it is best to lead a productive life as a landed immigrant and going on welfare may be grounds for deportation.

A landed immigrant is not expected to make periodic reports to the Canadian authorities; there is no "alien registration" as in the U.S. However, if you intend to leave the country for an extended period you might file a letter with immigration assuring that you intend to return to Canada to reside permanently.

An immigrant's taxes should go to the government of the country in which the taxable income was earned.

American citizenship is not affected by landed immigrant status and the immigrant can return at any time. Even if a warrant has been issued for his arrest, Executive Order 11325 (1/30/67) will permit some disillusioned draft resisters to choose between jail and army service, at the discretion of the Director of Selective Service and the Attorney General.

An American who obtains landed immigrant

status as a dependent of his parents will not lose his status if his parents return to the U.S.

There is one application form: You can apply at the border... by mail from the U.S...at a Canadian consulate...or by nomination--But always seek counseling in the United States first.

There are nine crucial factors for assessment: (An applicant must have a total of 50 units but the final decision rests with the immigration officer).

(a) Education and training, 20 units maximum.
(b) Personal assessment, 15 units maximum.
(c) Occupational demand, 15 units maximum.
(d). Occupational skill, 10 units maximum.
(e) Age, 10 units maximum.
(f) Arranged employment, 10 units maximum.
(g) Knowledge of English and French, 10 units maximum.
(h) Relative, 5 units maximum.
(i) Employment opportunities in the area of destination, 5 units maximum.

The work of counseling, advising and housing resisters continues. Although President Nixon has quieted the opposition and taken the issue off the front pages, the Indochina War is still a very real war. Many young men are still refusing to participate or support the government action in S.E. Asia. The Canadian Aid Centers need financial support to continue their work of immigration, job, draft and military counseling. Post-dated checks for contributions or small monthly or bi-monthly allowances will aid in helping young men to make the wisest choices in decisions that will affect the rest of their lives. Please help.

ALBERTA
Alexander Ross Society
4703-105 A Street
Edmonton
(403) 439-7311

BRITISH COLUMBIA
Vancouver Committee to Aid American War Objectors
Box 4231, Vancouver 9
Office: 628 East Georgia Street
(604) 255-1918

MANITOBA
Winnipeg Committee to Assist War Objectors
175 Colony Street
Winnipeg
(204) 774-9232 or 533-8793

NEW BRUNSWICK
St. John Anti-Draft Programme
11 Prince William Street, Apt. 2
Saint John
(506) 657-1149 or 639-4651

NOVA SCOTIA
Nova Scotia Committee to Aid American War Objectors

P.O. Box 19 Armdale
Halifax
(902) 429-6390

ONTARIO
Kitchener-Waterloo Aid to War Resisters
Dr. Ron Lambert, Department of Sociology
University of Waterloo, Waterloo
 (519) 742-2510 or
Mr. Chris Laing
19A Mooregate Crescent
Kitchener
(519) 742-2510

Toronto Anti-Draft Programme
P.O. Box 41 Station K
 Toronto 12
Office: 11 ½ Spadina Road
(416) 920-0241 or 920-0247

QUEBEC
American Refugee Service
Case Postale 5, Succ., Wsmt.
Montreal
(514) 843-3132

SASKATCHEWAN
Regina Committee to Aid American Refugees
 3058 18th Avenue
Regina
(306) 527-9545

ABOUT THE AUTHOR

Nancy Naglin graduated McGill University. She wrote for *The Toronto Star*, CBC Radio and numerous Canadian publications. Author, film critic and freelance writer Nancy Naglin has been the Art-House columnist for *The Phantom of The Movies' VideoScope* since 1993. Her work has appeared in numerous publications, including *The New York Daily News*, *New York Magazine*, *The Village Voice* and *Crawdaddy*.

Made in the USA
Middletown, DE
14 August 2017